ZERO TOLERANCE

ABOUT THE AUTHOR

The Old Grey Owl has worked as an English teacher in Greater London since 1982 and has been Head of Department, Assistant Head Teacher, and Deputy Head Teacher in a variety of schools. The Owl also worked for over twenty-five years as a senior GCSE English moderator for one of the major examination boards.

The writer of three novels and several short stories, the Owl has adopted a secret identity to guarantee their freedom, in the face of a Non-Disclosure Agreement, to expose some of the most dubious developments in national school policy and leadership practices: free schools, forced academization, zero tolerance behaviour regimes, the narrowing of the curriculum and the widespread promotion of rote teaching. These developments represent a serious threat to democratic accountability and educational standards. They are done in the name of rigour, but threaten real learning by focusing on exam performance and compliance.

The Owl regularly blogs and tweets on education, politics and culture.

You can follow The Old Grey Owl on Twitter at @OldGreyOwl1 or via the blog https://growl.blog.

You can contact The Old Grey Owl at oldgreyowl.57@gmail.com

ZERO
TOLERANCE

THE OLD GREY OWL

Matador
9 Priory Business Park,
Wistow Road, Kibworth Beauchamp,
Leicestershire. LE8 0RX
Tel: 0116 279 2299
Email: books@troubador.co.uk
Web: www.troubador.co.uk/matador
Twitter: @matadorbooks

ISBN 978 1838592 868

British Library Cataloguing in Publication Data.
A catalogue record for this book is available from the British Library.

Printed and bound in Great Britain by 4edge Limited
Typeset in 10pt Minion Pro by Troubador Publishing Ltd, Leicester, UK

Matador is an imprint of Troubador Publishing Ltd

This book is dedicated to two groups: the first, all of the teachers, support staff and students who have been bullied and mistreated in schools across the country and those who continue to suffer. The second, refugees across the world and those who struggle on their behalf against blinkered and intolerant governments. It does not have to be this way. Let's campaign for ethical leadership.

BOOK ONE

1

THE BOY POKED HIS HEAD AROUND THE FLAP OF THE
tent. Amidst the jumble of carrier bags, bin liners and sleeping bags,
in the shady gloom, another figure could be seen, lying propped up
against a rucksack.

"Hey, you wanna play football? We're all playing."

The figure on the ground said nothing and stared ahead of him.

The question was repeated, this time in Arabic. The boy looked
up at him and slowly shook his head. From outside the tent other
voices could be heard.

"Leave him. Come on, let's play."

He withdrew his head and closed the flap. Outside a group of
boys had gathered.

"But what about him?"

"You tried. He don't speak. He don't do nothing."

The speaker, a scrawny thirteen-year-old in a stained Ronaldo
T-shirt that was too big for him, made a gesture with his finger,
tapping his temple with it and turning it around.

"Come on."

They ran off towards the scrubby patch of land they had found behind the latrines. The first boy looked back at the tent, shrugged his shoulders, and then ran to join the others.

Inside the tent, the boy lay back down on his sleeping bag, and closed his eyes.

*

That afternoon, after he had eaten some rice and vegetables doled out to those that had stood in the midday sun to queue, he did his regular walk around the camp. He had nearly covered every inch of it and soon he would start again at the beginning. He walked slowly and methodically, not making eye contact with anyone, listening out for the sound of young girls' voices. He passed the remains of burnt-out fires, passed terrifying groups of older men, sitting around whittling wood with knives and smoking, shouting out blood-curdling curses about what they would do to anyone they got hold of.

Some days he caught a glimpse of a girl and his heart would begin to pound and his breath would come in shallow gasps. He would follow them until he could get a better view and then, always, when they turned, his face would fall and he would walk the other way to try a different trail. Once, he had been so convinced that he ran up to the girl in a crowd, shouting "Evana! Evana!" He grabbed her by the shoulder and the girl turned around, her face a picture of fear. It wasn't her, of course.

He had put his hands up in apology but had to flee from the snarling of a suspicious mob. It had been the only time he had spoken since arriving. He ran straight back to his tent, and waited, his heart racing, listening to the sounds outside. When he thought the danger had passed, he carefully pulled out the photograph from the pocket of his rucksack, and lay back on the ground, studying it. He would find her, wherever she was.

*

4

The next day he found himself in a queue at the main administrative tent in the Jungle. When he got to the front, a tired-looking man asked, "Name?" without looking up.

He was silent.

The man stopped writing on his form and looked up at him.

"What's your name?"

Again, there was silence. The man repeated the question, but this time as if he were talking to a simpleton.

He gave up and moved on to his next standard question.

"Your passport, please."

It was handed over in silence. The official pored over it, filling in details on his form.

Later, in a smaller, more private room, the Syrian translator went through the whole story. Several times he left the room to talk to other officials. The final time, he came back, a broad smile on his face.

"I have good news for you, my friend. You are eligible for asylum in the United Kingdom. You are very lucky. A change of policy, you see. You will be transferred to a holding centre and then over the channel."

"When? When will this be?"

"Oh, probably in about three days' time. It's all over for you, my friend, you've made it."

The boy stared at him.

"No, I can't go."

The official stared back, his face quizzical.

"What do you mean, you can't go? That is why you are here, surely? Everyone out there," he jabbed a finger in the direction of the wall of the tent, "would give anything to be in your position. They risk their lives every night trying to get across illegally."

He shook his head again.

"I can't go. I can't leave my sister."

His mouth began to tremble and he crumbled. The months of fear and exhaustion and grief, that he had suppressed to enable him to survive, could not be held back any longer. He wept uncontrollably, his wiry body shaking and heaving.

Outside, the queue got longer and longer.

2

BARRY PUGH PEERED AT HIS REFLECTION IN THE MIRROR. A firm square jaw, clean-shaven, with ice blue eyes staring determinedly from a face that retained a healthy tan from the expensive holiday he and Alison had enjoyed last month. Yes, he thought, with some satisfaction, that is the face of a man to be reckoned with.

He glanced at the clipboard hanging beside the mirror and then applied two squirts of Creed eau de cologne, one to either side of his neck. Then two squirts of Listerine into his mouth. Finally, after a preliminary rummage in his boxer shorts, two squirts of his stud delay spray, to help with his unfortunate problem. Had to be careful not to get those aerosols mixed up, he thought to himself with a smile. And people thought he was humourless! He reached over for the clipboard and with the attached Montblanc roller ball, he systematically ticked off all targets achieved.

He turned to go, then stopped and reached across to the other side of the mirror. Unhooking the blue cord, he ducked his head through the loop of the lanyard and arranged his Ofsted ID card so that it hung symmetrically between the lapels of a lush, deep pile white dressing gown. "Nearly forgot," he muttered under his breath. He picked up a set of pink fur handcuffs and amended his checklist on the clipboard, ticking the boxes marked "Ofsted ID" and "Fur handcuffs (pink)".

"Alison," he called, as he marched into the corridor, "ready or not, here I come. Get the prayer book ready."

3

RICK WAS RUNNING A LITTLE LATE SO THERE WAS ALREADY a sizeable crowd milling around the foyer when he arrived. Most people had already signed in and were heading towards the conveyor belt croissants and coffee that were always laid on at these events. He joined the queue and scanned the room, looking simultaneously for a friendly face and for those he really should avoid getting stuck with. The latter list was a lot longer than the former. It seemed more crowded than usual, and at first sight it seemed to have drawn out some heavyweights, rather than mere deputies and assistant heads. Hard to believe that the Education Secretary, one of the most ridiculous men on the planet, could be such a draw, but Rick often underestimated the magnetic attraction of power and often overestimated the intelligence of some of his fellow professionals, who would lay down with their legs in the air for their tummies to be tickled if someone important suggested that might be helpful to them and their career.

8

He signed in at the desk and picked up the sheaf of conference papers and his laminated badge and wandered towards the coffee, his eyes flicking left and right, scanning the horizon for predators. He was an old hand at these events and navigated the crowds skilfully, finding a gap in front of one of the coffee machines where he got something that purported to be a cappuccino and a plateful of mini pastries. He hesitated before turning away and went back for a second raid on the pastry platter, adding a pain au raisin and a pain au chocolat to the heap. Now he had to negotiate the crowds, balancing coffee and an over-laden plate on his conference papers, with his shoulder bag precariously swinging from his right shoulder. This was not a skill that had been delivered to him on his teacher training course fifteen or so years earlier, but it probably should have been, if the last ten years was anything to go by.

He looked up, slowing down for the sake of stability, and peered over the heads of his fellow delegates, looking for a seat or someone he knew and could bear to talk to. On the far side of the room, by the entrance to the conference hall, he saw the top table, casually milling round as if they owned the place. Which they did, to all intents and purposes. These people were conference royalty, the movers and the shakers of this august organisation that was hosting today's jolly. There they were, the usual suspects: Alastair Goodall, chair of the organisation, revered by the foot soldiers for his dynamism, his sharp suits, his relentless pursuit of better grades. He had convinced all of the delegates that anything was possible, with belief and leadership, with charm and charisma, with practical solutions, with certainty and imagination. He was a very smooth and convincing speaker, but lying just underneath the surface of this seemingly warm and clubbable individual, who could sway an audience with language that was very similar to ordinary English, was a cold, calculating chancer.

Then came Camilla Everson, flashing her brilliant smile at all and sundry, a headteacher beloved of this organisation and of the government for her steely, uncompromising leadership and her mission to generate outstanding examination results for all students regardless of background. Or at least, that was her stated ambition,

9

which, in a world of spin and smoke and mirrors, was more important. Rick glanced down at the agenda, which he could just about make out in between his coffee cup and the pain au chocolat that had slumped to a precarious angle on the edge of his papers. Yes, he thought so. She was due to give one of the key talks in the morning, taking the audience through the steps of her magnificent leadership of the Coldewater Academy, taking it from Special Measures and an examination results profile of 14% to its current status of Outstanding, results of 85% and an innovative programme of social entrepreneurship for Young Offenders. Rick sighed. Oh God, he thought, having endured more than enough biblical tales of renewal by blessed headteachers, all intoned in front of an identikit PowerPoint presentation.

Just when he thought it couldn't get any worse, it did. He caught sight of Barry Pugh at the end of the line, beaming, pressing the flesh and pointing his suit at anyone above him in the food chain. There was an air of desperation surrounding Pugh, that broke through his corporate intensity. When at the end of a line of important people, he strained every sinew of his mind and body to move closer to the centre. Rick watched him operate, fascinated, but this took his mind off the balancing act he had been performing and, inevitably, the pain au chocolat made a bid for freedom, sliding inexorably off the edge of his papers. He saw it, too late, and tried to correct the fall but this only made him jerk the papers the other way, spilling his coffee in the process.

"Shit," he exclaimed, fumbling around with papers, cup and plate to try and minimise the damage.

"Does your mother know you're out on your own?" came a voice behind him, a hand on his elbow.

He spun round, feeling horribly exposed.

"What? I—" he began to explain and then stopped. "Avril, don't sneak up on me like that."

"Sneak up! Don't get paranoid, Rick, just because you've made a complete fool of yourself by piling too much onto your plate."

She saw he was struggling and decided to put him out of his misery. She smiled a broad beaming smile and reached for his cup and plate.

"Here, you silly bugger, let me help before you throw the rest of all of that stuff over someone important."

"All the important people are up at the front, it's just floor meat here. That's why I spilled it all, it was looking at Bazzer the Wazzer that did it."

"Oh no, is that wanker here again? Why doesn't someone tell them? It's embarrassing, it really is."

"Yeah, he's up there trying to be best friends with the cool kids." He nodded his head towards where they had all been holding court but the space was empty. "Oh look, they've gone in. We must be kicking off in a minute or two."

"Quick," said Avril, "you get a seat and I'll grab a coffee. At the back on the side. We want to be able to slip out if we have to."

"It'll be on your file, you know. They see everything. You'll never be asked to present at one of these things, you'll be marked as a loser, or 'not one of us.'"

Avril sniggered. "Good, it's working then. Go on, grab a table quick. I'm buggered if I'm going to sit up the front with all the arse-lickers. Oh, and here, take these." She gave him a gentle push to send him on his way, handing back his stuff, while she joined the other latecomers who were desperate to hoover up the last of the coffee and croissants before entering the arena.

When she slipped through the double doors at the back of the auditorium, she quickly scanned the back rows before spotting Rick on the right, about two rows from the back. He was looking out for her and beckoned her to come and sit down. It was such a relief to Avril to come to these things with Rick. He was a little more enthusiastic than she was, but then he was nearly twenty years younger and at a critical point in his career. Avril was in her late fifties and knew she had climbed the greasy pole as far as she was ever going to get. There had been a time when she thought she might go all the way and get a headship, back when she had worked with inspiring people and there seemed to be plenty of schools in London, and just outside, that had clung on to a liberal management culture, but those days seemed long gone now. These days to be a head you had to take the academy shilling and power dress and talk a lot of bollocks, while simultaneously lying and cheating. Or was it just that she had got a lot more cynical? Either way, she felt liberated from the pressure of having to toe the line just so that you could be seen as a credible professional. She left that to others these days. People like Rick.

He swung his legs out of the way to let her get past and sit on the inside seat to him.

"Why can't I sit on the end?" Avril protested. "Why do I have to put up with your manspreading? It's bad enough putting up with the mansplaining."

"Oh, shut your face, you feminazi. You're emasculating me, you know that, don't you?"

"You poor love," she cooed. "I thought Jo had already done that to you at home."

Rick raised an eyebrow and opened his mouth to reply but was interrupted.

"Look, we're about to start. It's Alastair."

He looked at the stage where Alastair was dead centre, standing at a podium opening his PowerPoint and beaming beatifically at the crowd, knowing that his silent, expectant smiling would very soon be met by that of the audience. A hush settled and Alastair went into his familiar welcomes, greetings and group self-congratulation. Particularly deserving acolytes were named from the stage and forced to stand and bask in the warm approbation of the group for the outstanding improvement in results achieved in the summer under their leadership, nurtured by the supportive, spreading tentacles of the Partnership, a rapidly growing powerhouse of school improvement.

Its official title was Partners in Challenge for School Excellence, but, in fact, it was the organisation of a thousand names. It was called 'the Partnership' by the elect, a name carrying echoes of John Lewis-type respectability and quality. Rank and file disciples called it PICSE, a name that evoked naivety and innocence. The unbelievers called it POCSE, a name eagerly taken up by hard-pressed teachers who were forced to endure whatever nonsensical initiative it came up with next.

Avril turned back to him and mimed putting two fingers down her throat. Rick whispered back, "Kum By Yah, my Lord – we should have brought a tambourine."

"Hey, that's my church you're talking about, you know." She looked at him, eyes narrowed. "Are you being racist, Richard? I've told you about that before."

A horrified look flashed across Rick's face and his eyes darted left and right in case anyone had heard.

He whispered, "Avril, for God's sake, not here. Not everyone's got your sense of humour."

"Oh, stop wetting yourself, no-one's interested in you here. Now hush up and listen to Alastair."

Thankfully, after his opening salvo of self-congratulation, Alastair turned to the future and POCSE's plans for the coming academic year. Rick found his cynicism gradually being eroded as George outlined some new initiatives. As usual at these meetings, Rick found himself making notes and thinking periodically, *Yeah, that would work.* Occasionally he would look over to Avril, only to find her looking over at him, both smiling and nodding as if to say, "That would be really good to do with our Year 11s."

There was always a handful of imaginative schemes and in the past, ideas they had adopted at Fairfield had worked. It was just the certainty he objected to, the idea that it would be heretical to voice any criticism of any of their strategies, and frankly, some of them were either bonkers or required staff to work even harder than they were already doing. He also harboured a suspicion, one he knew Avril shared, that some of the POCSE strategies, and some of the POCSE strategists, crossed a line into the area that was ethically questionable. Such a thing could never be said, of course, and he had no hard evidence, just a nagging doubt that gnawed away at the back of his mind.

Finally, Alastair wrapped up the opening session and handed over to the next speaker. "So, without further ado, I'm delighted to welcome an outstanding headteacher, and one of the Partnership's own, to take us through the journey her school has been on, from Special Measures to Outstanding. Please welcome Camilla Everson."

There was a thunderous burst of applause as Camilla jumped up from her seat in the front row and bounced onto the stage, oozing energy and brio. She seemed to have been on the same training session that American presidents and David Cameron obviously attended, the one that placed great store on physical exercise. People of power had to be seen routinely engaging in vigorous exercise: jogging in America or cycling around the streets of London. It suggested dynamism and discipline. Camilla had obviously attended the advanced course because she was also clutching a reusable bottle of still water in a fetching shade of green, another signifier of virtue and moral rectitude.

Camilla walked up to the rostrum. She was tall and slim, with an off-the-shoulder bob of pale blonde hair. She wore a pencil skirt, high heels and a crisp white blouse showing the smallest glimpse of smoothly-tanned décolletage. Once behind the rostrum she put down her bottle and flashed a dazzling smile at the audience, her startling blue eyes seemingly back-lit. Rick swallowed. There was no doubt about it, she was a devastatingly good-looking woman, the poster girl of POCSE. She was also fearsomely efficient. Without any of the usual self-deprecating protestations of IT illiteracy or the bumbling, amateurish, uncertain fiddling with the mouse, she launched her PowerPoint, which sprang into life behind her.

All eyes switched away from Camilla and onto the screen, which proclaimed with stark simplicity, 'Zero Tolerance'. Zero Tolerance in mile-high letters next to Camilla's left shoulder. Avril shook her head and whispered to Rick, "Zero tolerance my backside. The world's gone mad. This is a bloody conference full of teachers, for God's sake. If we haven't got any tolerance, who the hell will have? It sounds more like a mission statement for the National Front rather than for schools."

Rick hesitated. "Well, I can see what she means. You know, what's that expression, er, 'sweat the small stuff'?"

Avril's withering response to what she saw as Rick's naivety would have to wait. Several delegates around them had turned to stare and, clearly, conversation during Camilla's star turn was totally out of order. They were duly chastened and turned their full attention to the speech.

Camilla was terrifying. Brisk, abrasive, fluent, strident and ever so slightly deranged. There was a hypnotic quality to her speech that, for long periods of the talk, made what she was saying sound perfectly reasonable, but then, every now and again, the content would inexorably break through and the spell was broken. Her message essentially was that Coldewater Academy's meteoric transformation was brought about by shaking things up and challenging the liberal consensus.

She went through her recipe for success and each example of 'Zero Tolerance' was warmly received, generating a hum of approbation, head nodding, and meaningful looks between colleagues. Of course! It was obvious when put like this. Why had they all been so wet and liberal for so long? If only they had had the courage of their convictions and imposed their authority on these feral kids years earlier. The figures were incontrovertible. Exam results rising year on year, from 14% to 85% this year. Who could possibly argue with that?

And so, the prescription from these National College of School Leadership quacks was more of everything, except of course art or drama or music or anything that might ignite a flame of creativity or provide solace for a lifetime. What poverty of imagination that required teachers to work harder and longer, students to be drilled endlessly in a repetitive series of mock examinations, parents to be fined, demonised and castigated as problem families, all policed by the all-seeing, all-knowing Ofsted, who toured the country lambasting staff and failing schools in the name of child protection because someone delayed putting their ID lanyard around their neck.

Education, education, education.

This was the soundtrack in Avril's mind as she watched one platitudinous slide follow another. At last Camilla finally arrived at her peroration. She paused, both hands gripping the lectern, eyed the audience with a steely glint in her ice blue eyes, took a morally bracing swig from her water bottle and gathered herself for the final assault.

15

"So, colleagues, our mission is to tread a lonely path. We do not court popularity, we do not want the easy acclaim from the staffroom cynics or the high-fives from being down with the kids in the playground. If you want to make a difference and you decide to join me on this rocky road you must prepare yourself for isolation, unpopularity, even, yes, hatred. But this mission is nothing if not a moral crusade."

"The journey I've outlined to you this morning has not been easy. We have been opposed at every step of the way by the unions, by old staff stuck in the ways of the past, more concerned about workload issues than about going the extra mile for the children in our care. To succeed you will need to get rid of staff who don't want to commit to making the lives of children better. We have the powers so let's not be afraid to use them. This is a job not for time servers or clock watchers but for staff with a burning sense of moral purpose to make things better for all children. And if I hear the phrase, work-life balance, one more time, trotted out as an excuse not to work harder for kids, I'll scream."

Here Camilla, judging the growing approval from the audience, paused, leaving a gap for some spontaneous rumblings of approval to grow. She picked it up again and surfed on the rising volume of the 'hear hear's and ripples of applause, gradually raising the volume of her voice as she did so.

"My school's journey from 14% to 85% has been achieved by zero tolerance. Yes, zero tolerance of lazy teachers, moaning about Ofsted and mock inspections, zero tolerance of low standards, no uniform, leaving at 3.30, mobile phones, poor behaviour, zero tolerance of idle chatter, low-level disruption, holidays in school time, trendy haircuts, the list is endless." Each item on the list accompanied by a clenched fist thump of the lectern and a cheer from the audience, like the announcement of every player on the team list at a football match.

Please, thought Rick, rolling his eyes, beaten into submission by this relentless force of nature in front of him, *not endless. I think we've got the message now.*

The atmosphere in the auditorium had reached fever pitch now and the PowerPoint behind Camilla had reverted to the mile-high slogan, 'Zero Tolerance'. Avril had her head in her hands by this stage, appalled by the mindless frenzy that had been created by this latter-day Nuremburg rally. She turned to Rick, who was transfixed by the performance, staring at Camilla open-mouthed, half admiring, half aghast.

She laid a hand on his arm and leaned over. "I really don't think I can take any more of this. How much worse can it get?"

Rick didn't get a chance to answer. Avril's phone pinged loudly and she scrambled to check her messages. Her brow was marked by concentration before it creased with a furrow of concern.

"Shit," she said, "that's all we need."

"What? What is it?" demanded Rick.

"It's Jane." She passed the phone over to him and he read the message, stark in its simplicity: "Ofsted inspection starts Wednesday. Emergency SLT this afternoon."

Without a word, they both gathered their stuff, scraped their way to the end of the row and slipped out of the back of the hall, the thunderous applause that greeted the ending of Camilla's speech ringing in their ears.

On the other side of the hall at the back, where he had been sitting since the start, unnoticed, Barry Pugh watched them leave, a half smile of steely determination on his face. He bent to his clipboard, ticked two boxes, and wrote a brief note against the names.

4

JANE CHECKED HER WATCH. JUST ENOUGH TIME TO MAKE sure she was presentable before stepping out onto the stage. Despite the fact that her break-time tour of the school grounds was a daily feature of life at Fairfield High and had been for the last ten years, she still got a touch of stage fright before she left her office to brave the corridors. When she was at school and out on public display she was playing a part. One last glance in the mirror, a flick of a piece of fluff from her lapel, a deep breath and she was off, striding through the doorway into the foyer, her corridor smile firmly fixed in place.

"All well?" she asked Steph on reception, before she made her entrance into the bowels of the school. This foyer area could be deceptively calm, a tranquil oasis of pot plants, large posters of Fairfield students past and present caught in poses of dutiful academic endeavour, or spontaneous communal warmth, beaming smiles and racial harmony, interspersed with motivational sayings. She remembered her first visit to the school in advance of her interview ten years ago, when the foyer was a more transparent reflection of what the school was really like. Back then there was no sealed door separating the student corridors from the entrance, and students would regularly spill into the area in a flurry of shouting and occasionally fisticuffs, pursued by a chasing pack of other kids, followed by a harassed selection of senior staff, desperately trying to keep the peace.

It had taken her about thirty seconds to realise that the foyer summed up everything that had gone wrong with Fairfield High, that it would be easy to fix and provide a quick win for whoever it was that took over. It was her, of course, the Governors being impressed both with her clear practical solutions and her easy, warm manner when talking, whether it was to a hall full of parents, a Year 10 student with a knife, or an Ofsted inspector. She knew straight away, back then, that changing the foyer wasn't going to transform the school overnight, and that she was committing the rest of her professional career to the long hard path that taking on Fairfield High was undoubtedly going to be.

"It's been pretty quiet so far actually, Jane," said Steph, looking up from her computer screen. "There've been no callouts during the first two periods. We had a bit of a kerfuffle with George Mason over his earrings, but what's new?"

"No callouts? Really? Excellent. They've started really well this year, haven't they?"

"Yes, I think you're right you know, Jane, really well." She watched as Jane disappeared through the doors into the main corridor just as the bell rang for the end of period two and the start of break.

"They always bloody start well, Jane," she continued, talking to herself. "It's how they bloody finish that counts. And now is round about the time the honeymoon period is usually over. Don't kid yourself, girl." She shook her head and bent back down to her computer screen as the rumble of newly-released children increased in volume as they dashed out of classrooms towards the queue for food in the dining hall.

Jane continued her smiling progress down the corridor. Soon the corridors were a sea of jostling children, shouting and pushing, energised by their liberation from restraint. Whenever the kids spotted Jane they instinctively moderated their behaviour, gave her space to pass and indulged in cheery greetings. "Hello Miss." "Morning Miss Garner." "Oops, sorry Miss."

"Morning everyone," beamed Jane. "Let's be calm, please, don't run, we walk in corridors, don't we?"

The crush gradually thinned out and conversations began as individuals emerged from the mob.

"Hello, Jason, have you had a good morning? I've heard great things about you from Mr Foster."

"Don't forget, Courtney, I'm expecting you to come and see me at the beginning of lunch, with your report, please."

"That uniform is much better, Deon, well done."

By this time, she had made it to the end of the main corridor and was about to go out into the playground. She made a mental note of which members of staff were in place on duty and which were not and worked her way around the upper school playground, navigating a route in between the games of football that had already broken out, towards her usual spot, a raised corner by the end of the tennis courts. She always placed herself there until the member of staff, whose duty position it was, arrived. It allowed her to see the smokers, and more importantly at the beginning of break, it allowed them to see her. The usual suspects turned the corner, clocked Jane atop her vantage point, and, shoulders drooping, sullenly turned back, knowing that they weren't going to have a fag break that day. Jane smiled as she watched them go. Every little victory counted. If there was time before the SLT meeting she'd call some of the prime movers in her office and have a little rant at them and maybe even do a few "random" bag searches. It was important to lay down a marker.

As usual, the first part of her patrol had made her feel better. The students were calm and polite and good-humoured. Uniform was still pretty good. The Indian summer continued, and bright sunny warm September days seemed to fuel the feelgood factor, both amongst the pupils and the staff. Two weeks since the start of term and nearly everyone was out on duty where they were supposed to be. As the term progressed and people got tired she knew that that would not last. Gaps would appear and as a result of that incidents would proliferate.

But for now, things seemed quite tight, the honeymoon period was lasting longer than usual. Maybe this Ofsted was perfect timing. Books still looking pristine with a little bit of work in them but not too much so that teachers had stopped marking them as frequently as they should. She hadn't told anyone about the Ofsted call, apart from messaging Avril and Rick. She knew they would just come straight back to school for the SLT meeting without being told to do so. She wanted time to think before the hysteria that the announcement would inevitably generate. She needed to think calmly and clearly before the meeting this afternoon.

She knew this could be the end of her career. If it all went wrong and they came out with a Satisfactory or heaven forbid, an Inadequate, the Governors would be under huge pressure to get rid of her, even though they had always been supportive. Her age counted against her. Waverers could be persuaded to throw her to the wolves because she was close to retirement anyway. But she herself wasn't ready to go just yet, even though she found herself crippled by exhaustion by the end of most days. Not with Jim as he was. She hadn't told anyone at school about Jim. She couldn't bear the concerned looks, the constant well-meaning enquiries, the whispered conversations as she left a room.

She checked her watch. Five minutes to go until the end of break. Time to make a move. On the way back to her office Jane broke up a fight and sent both boys, with a walkie-talkie call to the Head of Year, to stand outside the student welfare office, enquired after the alcoholic mother of a Year 8 girl, fielded a request from Erica Smith, the Head of Modern Foreign Languages, for a 'quick chat' at lunchtime, straightened the ties of six separate boys and tucked in the flapping shirts of another eight, removed the trainers of a Year 9 boy , who thought about starting to argue but then stopped when he remembered what happened last time he tried that with Ms Garner, praised a Year 11 girl for her improved work in maths, ate a sweet proffered by an excited group of Year 7s, popped in to

21

the sixth form common room and reminded the slouching group of seventeen-year-olds about the university visits that had been launched in assembly. Her last port of call, as usual, was to pop in to the canteen to shoo away to lessons the last few stragglers before collecting her daily bacon roll from the counter.

"Ooh, we thought you weren't coming, Miss," exclaimed Maureen, the lead dinner lady. "You been busy today?"

"Not as busy as you lovely ladies by the look of it," Jane replied cheerily.

"Very busy, but no problems. Children been as good as gold. The little Year 7s, bless 'em, they all look so smart in their new uniforms. Even the older ones have scrubbed up better this year for some reason. I do need to talk to you though, Jane, about the stealing. We really need to tighten up on that. I need more staff, Jane, I really do."

"Talk to Lisa and make an appointment, Maureen, whenever you're ready, all right?"

"All right Jane, thanks. And here's your roll, love." She hesitated. "Are you sure you're looking after yourself? You look a bit peaky."

Jane took the roll and turned to go. "There's nothing wrong with me that your bacon roll won't sort out, Maureen. Thanks."

She made it back to the sanctuary of her office without having to field any more questions or interruptions and popped her head round the door of the adjoining office. "Lisa, I'm having half an hour of thinking time. Is there anything in the calendar?

Lisa looked at her screen. "You had a couple of people booked in. John Rogers about that parental complaint and Theresa Johnson about her appraisal."

"Get hold of them and cancel. They'll understand when we have the staff meeting this afternoon."

"Staff meeting? No, there isn't a staff meeting, Jane, that's next week."

"There is now."

"But—"

"You'll be the first to know, Lisa, as always. Half an hour thinking time. No calls, no meetings, no interruptions. Got that?"

She didn't wait for the answer, turning into her office instead and closing the door.

She sat at her computer and put her head down to rest on the tips of her fingers, eyes closed, gathering the thoughts she had had during the break patrol. Thirty seconds later she sat up, opened her eyes and opened a document labelled 'Ofsted visit checklist'. After scanning it she printed it out and for the next half an hour made handwritten amendments to it, ticking some items, crossing off others and adding yet more. At intervals she opened other relevant documents or scrambled in her cupboard looking for paper documents and whole box files. She picked up the phone and rang a number. "Lisa? I need a dozen copies of the full Ofsted reports, please." There was a pause. "Yes, now please. Thank you." Eventually, she had accumulated a neat pile of documents, had printed a dozen copies of the amended document and had drafted the email to go to all staff. She looked at her watch. 2 pm. The cursor hovered over the send button, her finger resting on the mouse.

"Okay, here we go." She clicked.

"Showtime."

5

Alastair raised his hands to quell the gathering applause. "Thank you, colleagues, thank you."

The tumult subsided, and a quiet descended on the audience, as they gathered their attention for the main event. There was a rustling of papers and an organising of coffee cups and bags and a general settling after their break for coffee that had been abuzz with enthusiastic chatter about Camilla's presentation. The dissenters either gathered together to grumble quietly, or joined knots of true believers and simply listened, nodding occasionally, to the eulogies of praise and the shared plans for following in Camilla's footsteps with plans for their own schools.

Love it or loathe it, Camilla's performance had energised the whole hall. And now with the Secretary of State for Education himself due to give the keynote address, the POCSE delegates felt as if they were at the cutting edge of major social and educational change. It took every last ounce of professional self-restraint to stop them hugging themselves and squealing quietly with pleasure.

"Colleagues, I'm sure many of you, like me, feel that when we leave today we'll have had a momentous day, armed with the ideas and energy needed for our important work. It's a mark of how far this organisation has come, an organisation that is built entirely on the energy and enthusiasm, the skill and dedication of you, its members, that our next guest has chosen this venue and this occasion to deliver a major policy announcement. I'm delighted to be able to welcome to the stage to give our keynote speech today, the Secretary of State for Education, the Right Honourable Marcus Grovelle."

There was thunderous applause, as a slight, bespectacled man got to his feet from the front row and was ushered to the lectern. Marcus Grovelle gripped the sides of the lectern and blinked at the audience.

"Well, good afternoon. It's a pleasure to be able to deliver this long-planned speech to this particular group of teachers, a group, I must confess, I've had my eyes on for some time."

He paused for effect and surveyed the crowd. There was a ripple that filled the space he left, a ripple that mixed those that appreciated the joke they thought they had divined and those that nervously interpreted his words as some kind of threat.

"But before I get on to saying more about that, I must first pay tribute to the extraordinary speech given this morning by Camilla Everson, a remarkable lady who has achieved remarkable things. I feel privileged to have witnessed it, as I am sure all of you do, and I am hopeful that sitting in this audience are many, many more potential Camillas who want to bravely tackle the educational establishment that has held back young people for far too long in this country and who are going to make no excuses in their pursuit of academic excellence for all of our young people."

*

"So, have we missed anything?" Jane surveyed her Senior Leadership Team around the elongated central table that was littered with the debris of a long and occasionally fraught meeting: piles of papers covered in scrawled notes, stained coffee cups, depleted plates of biscuits, and a token and largely undisturbed platter of fruit. "Well? This your last call before we meet the staff. We need at least to look as if we know what we're doing when we walk into that hall."

"We're staying open until nine every day, is that definite?" asked Julia. "Are you sure that sends the right message? We don't want people to feel under pressure unnecessarily."

Gordon nodded. "Yeah, the last thing we need is for the staff to be exhausted before Ofsted arrive. And have you cleared it with the site team?"

The others around the table managed to hide their knowing smiles. Everyone knew that what Gordon actually meant was, I can't be bothered to stay late three nights in a row. There's Champions League football on the telly on Tuesday night and it's my turn to cook for Sheila on Wednesday.

Avril chipped in, partly out of irritation with Gordon, whose driving motivation was to cover his own arse and to minimise his workload, and partly to publicly back up Jane.

"Look, that's down to us and how we communicate it. Some people will definitely want to spend some time getting themselves ready. They'll want to plan and prepare materials and to have all their books marked. It's actually a way for them to control their stress. But we'll be absolutely clear that no-one is expected to be here until nine every night, that we trust people to make their own decisions."

Rick backed her up. "Yeah, we'll give them that checklist of minimum expectations around marking, targets and lesson planning and then just be available to check and support anyone who needs it."

Gordon held up his hands in mock surrender. "Okay, okay, I was just checking." He was used to being 'corrected'.

Jane had heard enough. "All right, that'll do for now. The last thing we want is to start to go round in circles. Are you all clear about your priorities and list of tasks? You've got your individual times to come and see me to go through your progress? Yes?"

There was a general nodding of agreement.

"Good. Now the most important thing, when you leave this office for the next three days and for the duration of the inspection, is that you are overwhelmingly positive, encouraging and supportive of the staff. All the staff. Everyone will be looking to us to lead. We have to set the tone. Okay? Thanks everyone. Can you sweep the classrooms at the end of the day to get everyone down in the hall, just in case some people haven't got the message? I'll see you down there in about fifteen minutes."

They all gathered up their papers and trooped out.

"Avril, Rick, not you. I need a word before you go."

The two of them turned back and took their seats again. It was not unusual for there to be an extended meeting with Jane and her two deputies, so there was no comment when they were called back.

The door closed and, in the corridor, Gordon turned to the others. "Bloody typical," he said in a low voice. "The talking shop continues with the bloody intellectuals, while the poor sodding workers have to go out and do the real work."

There was half-hearted agreement as they all grumbled their way down the corridor and out into the school.

*

Grovelle's speech was reaching its zenith and the crowd, seduced by the charisma of power, were lapping it up, with its strange mixture of flattery, eccentricity and outright madness.

"And there are so many points of agreement between this government's challenging of the status quo and the Partnership's challenging of sloppy teaching and low standards in exams. We have broken the dead hand of local authorities and their monopoly control of education, we've provided real choice with the creation of academies that have transformed educational standards in this country, and took that step further with a whole new category of free schools, giving parents the right to set up schools that will give greater priority to standards and old-fashioned values. We've finally dealt with the runaway grade inflation and cheating that flourished under the last socialist government, introducing exams that are rigorous and which don't patronise working-class children and instead expect the same high standards for students whether they come from a council estate or a country estate.

"So, ladies and gentlemen, we are clearly cut from the same cloth. We want the same things, we have the same passion, we refuse to accept the same old excuses. Now, I ask you to join me in our new venture, the next step in transforming Britain's education system and moving from being the laughing stock of the free world to being the best in the world. I can announce today, that after consultation, from next September we will be introducing the following major reforms.

"All students will have an entitlement to follow a five-year course, leading to GCSE, of Latin and Greek. These courses will be double weighted in the performance tables, to incentivise more timid institutions to embrace the reform. Let's bring back the standards from historically our finest institutions and spread them to Bash Street Kids Comprehensive.

"We are going to tackle the problem of teacher recruitment with a series of bold and innovative initiatives. Every university, college and higher education institute will be affiliated to a network of local schools, and undergraduates will be able to supplement their maintenance loans by taking up the places that will be on offer as affiliated teachers. This will, at a stroke, get the brightest and the best of our young people working in the secondary school system without the need for costly and time-consuming training, most of which frankly, could have come out of Jeremy Corbyn's Marxist handbook."

Here he paused and beamed at his audience, evidently delighted with his clever joke, one he had personally inserted in the text of the speech, against the wishes of his Central Office writers. The audience nervously blinked back, not sure of what their response should be to these extraordinary proposals. Grovelle steamed forward.

"We will tackle once and for all the divide between vocational education and academic. For too long we have been in thrall to

28

the crazy notion that everyone should go to university. We have denigrated practical subjects and sneered at those who have chosen to follow their aptitude for hands-on work. Our new apprenticeships were a start in tackling the ludicrous, over-complicated schemes of the last Labour Government, but now we are going to go one step further. I am delighted to be able to announce today that, from September, from the age of fourteen all students will be able to choose to sign up to do National Service, either in any of the armed forces, or, and this idea is truly inspired and revolutionary, in our National Health Service, with particular emphasis on social care. The sneering naysayers in the Remoaners camp, who constantly talk this great country of ours down, have carped and moaned continually about how our great institutions would collapse without foreign workers to staff them. Why on earth should we condemn the bottom forty percent of our young people to failure in the academic exam system, just for the sake of political correctness? We anticipate that, in the first instance, there will be a traditional gender split, with boys opting for the armed forces and girls for the caring professions, but the choice will be available for anyone to express a preference for either. The only obstacle they would have to face would be the comments of their friends." Again, Grovelle paused to allow the audience to show their appreciation of his daring joke. He was rewarded with a few nervous titters.

"Imagine, the problems of social care, the NHS, the Armed Forces in the face of the conventional threat posed by Russia and by terrorism and the academic standards of the bottom 40% of our young people, all solved at a stroke."

The expressions on the sea of faces in front of him told their own story of people picturing the reality of what had just been described to them. There were expressions of bafflement, incomprehension, with a few furrowed brows of those who were turning to anger. Grovelle, oblivious to his audience, ploughed on. The unthinkable had to be thought, and he was the man to think it.

*

29

"You know this is going to be touch and go, don't you?"

Avril and Rick looked at each other quizzically.

"What do you mean, Jane?" asked Avril.

"They'll focus on our data, which is not really good enough. I absolutely need you, Rick, to nail that, otherwise we're dead in the water. I need that paper putting a positive spin on the results by tomorrow so we can brief the whole staff. You know, value added, no underperforming groups, the usual malarkey."

"Yeah, that's no problem, I've just about got that finished already. I don't think it's briefing staff you need to worry about, though," replied Rick.

"Go on then, tell me."

"It's the rest of the Senior Team and the Governors. Honestly, Jane, they are bloody embarrassing. Did you hear Gordon tonight?"

Avril agreed. "It's going to take more than a briefing to bring Gordon up to speed. And Julia and Deepak are just as bad. We need to make sure that they are not interviewed by any of the Ofsted team on their own, otherwise we're snookered."

Jane sighed. "See what I mean? We're doomed, doomed I tell you. No, I've already doubled up on the likely interviews. A lot is resting on our shoulders, you do realise that, don't you? I'm depending on you to do the business."

Rick smiled. "Don't worry, Jane, we know what we're doing. We'll be fine if the lessons and behaviour are good and because it's early, we've got a fighting chance with the kids."

"Are you on top of Safeguarding, Avril? I don't want to fail seconds after they've walked in the door and they discover our procedures and registers are not up to scratch."

"They're all good, Jane, trust me." She paused and then tentatively began again. "You seem a little negative though, Jane. It's not like you. Is everything all right?"

She hesitated, got up out of her seat and walked over to her window, watching the students stream down the main path to the gate. There was chatting and screaming and laughing and balls being kicked and arguments being settled. "Look at them. Off they go.

They have no idea how much all the staff put in to their wellbeing. All the hours, all the worry, all the discussion, all the care. Some of them will never be cared for as much as this again in the whole of their lives."

Avril and Rick exchanged a quick glance, eyebrows raised.

"Jane, now you're worrying me." Rick said this half as a joke, but he had his fingers crossed that her reply would put his mind at rest.

She turned back to them.

"Why do you think we're having this inspection now?"

"What do you mean? I know it's earlier than we anticipated, but that often happens, doesn't it?"

"Not as often as you might think. And not a whole year early."

Avril interjected, "What have you heard, Jane? Come on, this must have come from somewhere."

"You know the authority are expecting us to fail, don't you?"

"What? What do you mean, 'expecting us to fail'? How do you make that out?" Rick was indignant at the suggestion.

"They think we're shit. They think we don't know what we're doing because Avril and I are women of a certain age and we don't talk the talk and we don't do some of the dafter, trendier things that BetMore777 academies do. They think we're old school, more like social workers than senior leaders."

"What?" exploded Rick. "That's outrageous."

"Oh, they like you, Rick. They like the fact that you're young and you know the latest trends. You've made a great impression at the Managed Admissions Forum you go to. And they love the fact that you're so involved with the Partnership. They think you're the only reason we haven't sunk already."

Rick was amazed. He had no idea that this was what was being said within the local authority. He was flustered and tried to splutter a demurral. Jane waved away his attempted objections.

"You're very good, Rick, you'll go far. But so are we. And we've already gone far."

"And we're not ready to bloody stop going far just yet," rumbled Avril, outraged at being written off as a dinosaur.

"No," agreed Jane. "Not quite yet anyway. So, the point of all this is that the odds are well and truly stacked against us. We will have to be even better than usual to survive this because they are gunning for us. And there's no better weapon when you're trying to get rid of a leadership team than a shit Ofsted outcome, no matter how rigged it is. Especially with our results."

"Hold on a minute," said Rick, comprehension dawning on his face. "Do you mean that you think there's been some kind of collusion between the authority and Ofsted?"

"Well," said Jane enigmatically, "you might say that but I—"

"Couldn't possibly comment," chorused the other two. "Yes, we know."

"But surely, Ofsted are supposed to be independent. There can't be that kind of set-up, can there?"

He looked from one to the other of them.

The two women of a certain age looked at each other.

"Bless," said Avril, "they're so sweet when they're young, aren't they?"

Rick's face hardened. "Well, sod that for a game of old soldiers. I'm buggered if I'm going to be stitched up like that. We've worked too hard to be written off before they even start the bloody inspection. If it's a fight they want, well let's give it to 'em."

Jane collected together her papers from the desk. "Good. I was hoping you'd say something like that. And now, let's go and rouse the troops. Oh, and I hope I don't need to say that this last conversation was strictly between ourselves. From the second we walk out of this door, it's our job to project supreme confidence." She swung open the door of her office and marched down the corridor towards the Hall, head held high, a spring in her step. Avril and Rick trailed in her wake, scurrying to keep up.

*

Grovelle seemed frozen in the spotlight, still gripping the sides of his lectern. The stunned silence that had flooded the arena after his speech, settled on the venue like a softly billowing sheet. Delegates looked nervously at each other, uncertain. The silence grew and spread and Grovelle's easy smile had begun to ossify into a rictus grin. He saw his whole project, including a smooth flight path to Number 10, teetering on the edge of the abyss. And then, just as the silence was beginning to be painful, Alastair sprang to his feet and clapped. His applause grew in strength and he smiled appreciatively at Grovelle and took it in turns to half face the audience and whip them up into joining in. Barry Pugh cast down his clipboard, which clattered to the ground as he, desperate to be the third person to join in a standing ovation, jumped up and belaboured his palms in a frenzied show of approval. Those that were instinctively against the proposals in the speech, hunkered down in their seats, uncomfortable and unsure. In the great tradition of brutal dictatorships down the ages, the fever spread like wildfire as everyone scrambled to be on their feet applauding, to avoid being that person who was taken out and shot for lacking revolutionary fervour. The doubters, their objections diluted by the great tide of enthusiasm that had surged up from the floor, began to question their instincts. Maybe they should be bold enough to think the unthinkable.

Sometimes, the unthinkable was unthinkable for a very good reason.

6

Alastair Goodall smiled as the television news rounded off its headline report on Marcus Grovelle's speech to POCSE earlier that day. The cameras panned around the room, taking in the euphoric applause, the beaming smiles, the prominent 'the Partnership' backdrop. He was gratified to catch the shot of himself in the background, dark suit and sky-blue shirt, soberly applauding, every inch the modern, dynamic leader.

You couldn't buy publicity as good as this. A mass audience on the national news. It had been a major coup when he pulled it off and there had been many who had counselled against it, uncomfortable with some of Grovelle's wilder ideas, but the gamble had paid off handsomely. It was a bonus that the media appeared to have been swayed by the enthusiastic applause that the crowd at POCSE had provided on camera, and that the spin placed on this major policy announcement had been entirely positive.

It had been an entirely successful day so far, but there was one last piece of the jigsaw needed to cap it off. He poured himself

34

a sliver of very expensive malt whisky, picked up the phone and punched in a series of numbers. He sipped his tumbler of single malt, savouring its smokiness, while he waited for the tone to change.

A voice crackled through on the other end of the line. "Hello? Alastair?"

"Hi. Did you see the news?"

"Yes, it's on now. That suit looks good on TV, Alastair. Who's your stylist?"

"Never mind that now. I understand that you've had some success. The inspection is Thursday, I believe?"

"How the hell do you know that already?"

"Already? I've known it for a while actually, I was just waiting for confirmation. You know what has to happen, don't you?"

"Yes, Alastair, I'm fully aware of what's at stake."

"Good. Make sure you don't forget it."

"There's no need to be so George Smiley about it. The school is crap and the leadership is an embarrassment, something from the dark ages. It's bound to go our way, without the need for any leverage at all."

"Let's hope so. We'll talk again at the weekend." Alastair put the phone down without waiting for an answer. He took another sip of whisky and began once again to turn over in his mind all the moves made so far and all those yet to come. It would be a sweet moment when everything finally fell into place.

*

"Rick! Rick! Come on, it's on the telly, that thing you were at today. Headline news," Jo shouted back towards the kitchen.

"What? Now? Are you sure?"

"Of course, I'm sure. I'm not a moron. Come on or you'll miss it."

Rick bounded into the front room and bounced down onto the sofa. Jo bounced up in response and only dexterous control of her wine glass prevented serious red wine spillage.

"Careful, careful. This stuff will never come out if it spills."

"Sorry, darling," soothed Rick. "Best drink it quick to avoid the possibility of spillage."

He reached for his glass of red as if in solidarity.

"God, look at him. What a wanker!"

"I know," replied Jo, "I can never look at him without thinking of some appalling character from a Billy Bunter story. You know, 'Marcus Grovelle, the sneak of the Remove.'"

Rick guffawed. "Exactly." He paused. "What exactly is 'the Remove' anyway?"

Jo was suddenly exercised by the substance of the report. A detail that had made its way through the external noise suddenly hit home.

"Shh. Listen to this. This is unbelievable."

The reports went on with the usual mixture of video footage from the conference, commentary from the reporter who was there and then live studio interview with the chief political correspondent. It was clearly a major news story. Both Jo and Rick fell into silent disbelief as the substance of Grovelle's speech accumulated.

The item finished and the news presenter segued into the next item. "The group of unaccompanied Syrian child refugees that had been stranded in Calais while negotiations continued over the numbers the British Government would accept, arrived in the United Kingdom this morning. The *Daily Mail*…"

Rick reached for the remote and switched off.

"Sorry," said Rick sheepishly. "I can't deal with any other news at the moment after that Grovelle thing."

"Have I got this right?" she said. "Did he really say all that stuff about grammar schools and National Service and the Health Service? Is it just me, or did he really say that thick kids can leave school at fourteen and work for a pittance in the Army or wiping old people's arses?"

"You're being a little unfair, darling. They're also being given the opportunity to study Greek and Latin between the ages of eleven and fourteen. You know, he is bringing back proper academic standards."

"Oh yeah, of course. That's why he's letting headteachers sack anyone they want so they can employ undergraduates from universities to teach the smelly kids. And all of this was going on at the conference you were at today, except you weren't there for the only important bit."

"No, Grovelle was due to speak later and we got that text from Jane so we had to go."

"Are you all set for the inspection then? Presumably you're not going to be much use round here for a few days."

"Sorry love, I can't take the kids to school on Thursday. I'll have to be there before seven. And I'm not going to be back before half nine every day this week. What's your work situation for the rest of the week?"

"What about swimming club?"

Rick looked sheepish. "I'm really sorry, I'll be working all hours. I really can't get out of it."

"I'm supposed to be going out with the girls on Thursday. Bloody Ofsted." Jo gave him a look of tight-lipped disapproval and disappointment.

"Look, next week, when it's all over, I'll do all of that stuff to pay you back."

"The school run as well. Every day next week?"

"Yes, darling. Every day."

Jo's poker face broke into a smile and she leaned over and kissed him.

"Okay. I'll make this sacrifice for your career. But promise me one thing."

"Anything sweetie, anything."

"Promise me that when you're a headteacher you'll never introduce Latin, send thick fourteen-year-olds to wipe someone's bottom and you'll never, ever replace a qualified teacher with a spotty undergraduate with an overdraft or a social conscience."

"I thought you married me because I was a thrusting go-getter. Full of drive and ruthless ambition."

"I certainly didn't marry you for the money. You're a PE teacher, for God's sake. I'm the lawyer, I'm the one that's going to bring home the bacon. When the partnership comes along, that'll be job done. I want us both to be able to sleep at night with a clear conscience."

"If only Lady Macbeth had said that to her husband, everything would have turned out fine."

"I'm serious, Rick. You love your job, you don't need to take any rash decisions because of money or ambition or pride or anything like that. Just enjoy doing a proper job." She leaned over and kissed him again. "Look, I'm going up now."

"I've got more to do. I'll be another hour at least, probably."

"Don't do too much. You need to pace yourself until it's over. And if I'm asleep, try not to wake me."

She left the room and Rick reached for his laptop. The screen flickered into life as he went through the password combinations. He opened the last document and started to type, pausing every now and again to think. He was finding it hard to pick up the thread of his argument. He couldn't get that last conversation with Jo out of his mind.

What was it she had said? "When the partnership comes through, that'll be job done." But what if it didn't come through? Jo had committed the cardinal sin of ambitious professional women. She'd had children and they had derailed her career. Or at least delayed it. If she'd been a man he knew that she would already be a partner. And this was in a left-wing set of chambers, one that prided itself on its progressive workplace practices.

They couldn't stay in this house much longer, they really needed to trade up for more space and a bigger garden. He checked himself even as he thought this. The house was worth a small fortune compared to the properties that all of his friends who were still back home lived in. He knew that whingeing about not having enough money was ridiculous when so many of the kids he taught could only dream of the disposable income and house that he and Jo enjoyed.

And it really didn't feel right to him that he should be dependent on Jo's career. His parents and some of his old friends ribbed him about being a kept man. He always laughed along and made the feminist argument in justification, but that just wound them up even more. And somewhere, deep down inside, part of him agreed with them. He didn't like it, but he couldn't completely suppress thousands of years of gender conditioning. He had his pride. He wanted to provide for his family. And if an opportunity came up, maybe as a result of this Ofsted inspection, he didn't think he would pussyfoot around and walk a politically correct tightrope. He'd grab it and do whatever had to be done.

Jane had had a bad feeling about the inspection. She had made it clear that she thought that they were expected to fail. Well, maybe so, but if they did, he'd make damn sure that everyone knew that he'd been the star. Just to be in pole position when the dust had settled. He turned back to the screen and began typing again.

7

"Yeah. Yeah, we're all very pleased here, Jane. Well done, well done to the whole team. It's nothing more than we expected." He paused, apparently listening to the voice at the other end of the phone, his face set in a thin-lipped weak smile. "Pass on my personal congratulations to all the staff. Okay? I'll see you next week."

He set the phone back down on its base and reached for a packet of paracetamol. He swallowed three pills with a swig of water. Maybe that would shift the pounding headache he'd had all day. The phone rang again. Christ, that was all he needed. Why couldn't they all just leave him alone, just for five minutes. Wearily, he picked up.

"Harrison."

"Andrew, I've got Alastair Goodall on the line for you. He says it's important."

His heart sank. This was all he needed.

"Shit, already?"

"I can put him off if you like. Ask him to call back later."

"No thanks, Jenny, best get it over with. Put him through."

Andrew steeled himself for the conversation that would inevitably follow. The line crackled back into life and Goodall's familiar steely voice cut through.

"Andrew?"

"Yes, hello Alastair."

"'Good', Andrew? Fucking 'Good'? Are they having a laugh?"

"'Good with outstanding features', actually, Alastair."

"Outstanding fucking features? Jesus wept. What outstanding fucking features?"

"Umm, Safeguarding, SEN and EAL, Student Well-being, actually."

"This was not how it was supposed to go, Andrew, as well you know. What the fuck went wrong?"

"Well, Alastair, I think we may all have underestimated them. Maybe they're not quite as useless as we thought. And your lad, Rick Westfield, played a blinder, apparently."

"Yes, I heard that. I've got plans for Rick. I think he could be useful in the short term. But doesn't completely explain the result. Maybe they lucked out and got some old-school Ofsted lead inspector who's off-message. Someone who's gone native. Jesus, Andrew, you've been there, it's one of your schools. No, correction, it's your only school now, and it's a basket case. Full of feral kids and knives and drugs and teenage pregnancies."

"Alastair, the school didn't make them feral. These kids exist. Someone's got to educate them."

"And that, Andrew, is exactly why all of your schools have become academies and your empire has shrunk. That's a recipe for losers, Andrew, and I do not intend to be a loser. They may have to be educated somewhere but I don't give a toss about that. As long as they're not educated in one of my schools, bringing my figures down."

"Alastair, what exactly is the point of this phone call?"

"Plan B, Andrew, as discussed. I can't wait for the next set of crap exam results. This has got to be done now. It's time to play the BetMore777 card. Within the month."

"A month! Christ, Alastair, on what grounds? They've just risen from the dead, for God's sake."

"I'll leave that to you. Ring me when you've started the ball rolling. Oh, and Andrew?"

"Yes, what now?"

"Don't make me ring you. That would not be very wise."

The phone went dead, leaving him holding the redundant receiver, staring into space.

"Fuck, fuck, fuck, fuck, fuck." He paused for a moment, and then concluded his analysis, slamming the receiver back down onto the cradle.

"Shitting, fucking fuck."

His headache pounded on.

8

RICK STOPPED JUST OUTSIDE THE DOOR TO THE MANAGED Admissions Forum. He adjusted his tie and made a huge effort to control the spreading grin on his face. He had been looking forward to this since the outcome of the inspection, but he needed to filter his euphoria through a coolly professional lens. Punching the air and high-fiving all and sundry, which is what he wanted to do, would be a little gauche.

He pushed open the door and strode through, poker face determinedly assembled. Harsh neon strip lighting bleached the bland corporate furnishings of this brutally functional space. Tables arranged into a rectangle, computer, white board and flip chart at the front, no windows and arctic air conditioning, it was an arrangement repeated in thousands of hotels, municipal buildings and converted schools around the country. There were several people milling around with coffee and a few others who had already claimed their seat, anxious to avoid unfortunate couplings with latecomers.

They looked up at the sound of the door. "Well look who it is," came the first voice, "Rick Westfield, the hero of the hour." A few others joined in and there was the beginning of a ripple of applause. Those nearest the door came up to him and shook hands and offered their congratulations. As he made his way to a seat, there were more slaps on the back and 'well dones' and he broke into a broad beaming smile. His icy demeanour had lasted all of three seconds and he basked in the warm approval of his colleagues.

He squeezed himself into the seat between Anwar Hussein and Lydia Charles, two of his natural allies on the group. Anwar leaned over and shook his hand warmly.

"So, you old dog, how the hell did you pull that off?"

"Oh, you were expecting us to fail as well?" Rick replied. "You of all people should know that you don't have to run a school like a prison to succeed."

"Obviously, I know that theory, I just didn't expect Ofsted to know it."

"No," chipped in Lydia, "particularly with your results. You know very well that you can do what the hell you like if your results are good, but if they're not, you have to conform."

"Well, clearly," replied Rick, "Ofsted still has people working for it with brain and judgement, despite all the rumours to the contrary."

"Speaking of brain and judgement, I didn't see you guys at the last POCSE thing the other week. You know, the one where Grovelle dropped his bombshells," said Anwar.

"Yeah, I was there with Avril. We had to leave after Camilla Everson's presentation. We got the call about Ofsted that morning and had to get back to Fairfield. Three-line whip from Jane."

"What did you think of Camilla?" asked Lydia.

"Terrifying. Cross between Nanny, a Nazi camp commander, and that replicant from *Blade Runner*. She must be a nightmare to work for."

"We appointed someone from Coldewater Academy in the summer. Used to be Head of Science there, and he's come to us as a classroom science teacher. Bruised and battered from his experience under Everson. Constant bullying, perpetual observations and surveillance. He couldn't wait to leave."

"Well, it works, doesn't it? Their results have been outstanding since she took over. She's the future, I'm telling you. POCSE love her and Grovelle was wetting himself. We'll all have to be like that eventually," said Rick.

"Bugger that for a game of old soldiers," retorted Lydia, "I'd rather stack shelves in Tesco."

"And obviously it doesn't work. According to the lad from Coldewater, it's all smoke and mirrors. Fiddling figures, cheating, getting rid of Year 11s early, the works."

"Christ. How do they get away with it?"

The question was left hanging in the air as the conversation was cut short by Shirley Latimer's arrival, the chair of the forum. As soon as she entered the room, those people still milling around chatting swiftly made their way to the remaining spare seats at the rectangle of tables and settled themselves for a prompt start. Shirley was known to be a stickler for timekeeping and protocols. Lateness was anathema to her and it was not unusual for tardy delegates to feel the sharp edge of her tongue.

"Well, good morning colleagues, if we can make a start please. As you can see from the paperwork in front of you, we have a packed agenda this morning. First things first, though. Before we move on to the morning's main business, I think it's appropriate for this committee to show its appreciation and deliver its congratulations to Fairfield High School for their success in the recent Ofsted inspection. I know it's not in the public domain yet and rest assured, this won't be minuted, but I think we'd all like to congratulate you, Rick. Please pass that on to Jane and Avril and all the team."

The applause died down. "And I'm sure," continued Shirley, "that when it has been made official, you will be receiving lots of requests from Longdon, what's left of it, and from individual schools to come and present and tell the rest of us exactly how the hell you managed it."

Shirley left just enough time to allow a smattering of laughter before moving on. "So, if we could turn our attention to the first student on the list, please."

Everyone round the table turned to the details in their booklet, as Shirley went through them. After a couple of hours, they had reached the last student to be considered.

"Ah yes," said Shirley, "an interesting one, this last case. This is one for Fairfield, Rick, I think."

Rick looked doubtful. "Come on, Shirley, I think we've taken our fair share already, don't you?"

"Well, don't be too quick to close the door, Rick. Let's have a look at the details."

They all looked at the booklet with more interest this time.

"Yes, let's see," continued Shirley. "This one is Karim Atbal, aged fifteen. Syrian refugee, just arrived from the Jungle at Calais."

Everyone's ears pricked up.

"So, is this part of the Dubs Amendment then? That recent agreement to take more unaccompanied children to stop the government being embarrassed?" asked Anwar.

"Yes, that's more or less correct, without the political point scoring." Shirley peered at him over the top of her glasses, her mouth pursed in disapproval. "The boy is originally from Aleppo. Father, mother and brother all killed in the bombing. He and his younger sister were sent out at the beginning of the year and have spent the last few months in Calais. He is currently a Child Looked After, about to be fostered. He is also awaiting news of his sister. They were separated on the journey through Europe. Hmm, let's see." She paused to examine the detail on a separate sheet.

"Yes, that's right. Very little English, apart from that picked up in the Jungle. He is, apparently, an elective mute, some form of post-traumatic stress disorder."

"An elective mute? Come on, Shirley, we're not miracle workers, you know. He obviously needs specialist help and we can't give him that." Rick looked around the table for some measure of support.

"Well, yes, you'd think so, wouldn't you," Shirley agreed, "but apparently not. He has his own specialist therapist who would be with him throughout the day. It's thought that what the boy needs more than anything is safety, normality, routine. And a chance to learn English quickly. And that's where Fairfield comes in."

"Our language provision, you mean?" asked Rick.

"Yes, of course, that's what it's for. That's why you receive the money."

"It's hardly a goldmine, Shirley. I think what you're trying to say is 'Thanks for helping us out of that very expensive and politically embarrassing hole.'"

"No, Rick, what I'm saying is that we have a responsibility to this young person and your school is best placed to handle it. It has the facilities, it has the capacity and it has the resources, no matter how paltry you think they are."

Rick thought for a moment. "I suppose that this is quite a high-profile case. National media interest and the like?"

Shirley smiled. "Oh, yes. There's a lot of kudos to be had here. Could make someone's career, being involved in this selfless act of public service. Not that anyone here would be swayed by such base considerations, of course."

"Hmm. Well, let's say we have an agreement in principle. Presumably it's not all set up yet, start dates and the like?"

"No, but it's not far away."

"Leave it with me. Let me talk to Jane. Come back to me the minute you're ready to roll."

9

Barry Pugh swung round into the drive and parked his BMW precisely equidistant between the two terracotta pots on either side of the garage doors. He turned off the ignition and savoured the dying cadence of the throaty hum of the engine. He sat for a moment in the gathering silence to collect his thoughts, allowing the smell of the leather seats and the bunch of freesias to wash over him. Sometimes he needed to take a moment to wallow in the trappings of his success. He deserved it, there was no doubt about that. He'd heard the jealous whispers and carping, of course he had. Occasionally, he succumbed to wondering whether he could keep all of this going. It was expensive. Too expensive for what he earned, but he wouldn't be earning this for much longer. It was a relief, frankly, and he was looking forward to the evening, telling her his news and basking in the glow of Alison's approval. Adoration even.

He reached over for the flowers and champagne, collected his attaché case, and climbed out. As he opened the front door he called out, "Alison? I'm home."

"I'm through here." Her voice came from the front room, flat and lifeless.

He went through. She was sprawled on the sofa watching *Come Dine with Me*.

"Hello, darling," he began.

She looked over and saw the champagne and flowers.

"Oh Barry, for God's sake, you know we can't afford all of that stuff. It's a Tuesday, we can't just keep celebrating. We've got nothing to celebrate."

His beaming smile widened. "Well, we have actually, darling. I've got a new job."

"A new job? What do you mean? You didn't say you were going to an interview. What is it?"

"Well, it wasn't exactly an interview. It's with Alastair."

"Alastair? Alastair Goodall?"

"Yeah, that's right. He's headhunted me to be the new Director of Learning in his MAT."

"His what? Speak English, Barry, you're not at a conference now."

"His MAT, his Multi-Academy Trust."

"But I thought he was headteacher at Bellingford."

"He is, dear, but they've formed this trust and taken over about five other schools. And he's got amazing plans for expansion, at least another seven or eight schools to make it viable. It's the way the government want us to go, just to get rid of local education authorities altogether. And he's asked me to work with him. It's an incredibly exciting role. An extra £20k a year."

Alison was amazed. She had always had a nagging doubt at the back of her mind about Barry. Maybe she'd judged him too harshly in the past. After all, Alastair was an astute chap, there was no doubt about that. She'd met him once. He had been very impressive, the sort of man not to suffer fools gladly. Then why, she began to wonder, and immediately, with a guilty conscience, put that thought to the back of her mind.

"So, does that mean your school will drop the disciplinary proceedings, then?"

Barry looked pained. "They're not disciplinary proceedings as such, Alison darling, I've told you that before."

"No, but they'll be dropped, won't they?"

"Well, yes, I suppose so."

"That's a stroke of luck then, isn't it? You should have told me about all of this, Barry, really you should have done."

"I didn't want to get your hopes up. It might have come to nothing. And besides, it's all happened so quickly. Anyway, it's done now. Let's celebrate and have some champagne. You get some glasses."

Alison went out to the kitchen to find a couple of champagne flutes while Barry grappled with the cork. He twisted the bottle, then pushed the cork, which suddenly fired off like a gun, leaving a vapour trail and a spume of bubbles spilling over the side. He filled the two glasses and raised his own, clinking it against his wife's.

"Cheers. Here's to the future."

"Do you think we could decorate the dining room now, Barry? We were going to have it done, weren't we?"

Barry sipped his champagne. "Why not?" he concluded. He put down his glass and reached for his briefcase. Opening it, he pulled out his clipboard. He scanned it and with his Montblanc, added another line to the items on the list. He checked the list again, a faint smile spreading across his features.

"And maybe we could tick off another item on the list tonight. After all, darling, it is Tuesday." He reached over and squeezed her thigh with his hand.

She gulped her next mouthful of bubbly, squeezing a weak smile out of her hesitant face.

"Why not, darling? Why not?"

10

"No, you've lost me, Andrew. Run that by me again." Jane could not believe what she had just heard. Naïvely, she had anticipated this sudden summons to the Director of Education's office was in recognition of their dramatic escape from the clutches of Ofsted, a pat on the back, a cup of coffee and a cream cake on some bone china, with maybe some tentative discussion about additional resources by way of a reward. How wrong she had been! She was getting soft in her old age. She wouldn't normally let her guard down like this. Expect the worst was her motto, and it had served her well over the years, inoculating her against disappointment and buying time to deal with whatever shit was going to come her way.

And there would be shit coming her way. That was the stark reality of working at the sharp end of state education with damaged families clinging on in poverty. Extra money from New Labour had made the job manageable after the millennium, but that was now a distant memory as hard-line ideology and gleeful austerity had eroded all of those gains. It was wearying and dispiriting. There'd be a time soon when she wouldn't be able to shake herself down from the latest setback, regather her inner strength and go again. She was starting to feel a little old. This unexpected conversation, with an Andrew Harrison who exuded guilt and shiftiness, was not helping.

Harrison took a sip of coffee and hesitated before speaking. Finally, with the air of a man closing his eyes and jumping off a cliff, he plunged in.

"Look, Jane, don't get me wrong. You've done a brilliant job at Fairfield over the years, capped off by your amazing performance in the inspection."

Jane interrupted. No matter how old she felt, she could not be, would not be, soft soaped.

"'Capped off by'? Ah, I see. You're getting rid of me. Who's to say there isn't better to come? Capped off by indeed," she demanded.

"Jane, this is out of my hands. You're the last secondary school run by the borough of Longdon. Local authorities are finished, those days are gone for ever. Fairfield is going to be an academy, come what may. You can do it the hard way or the easy way."

"Which is which?"

"The hard way is that you dig your heels in, refuse to co-operate and you'll be swallowed up by a predatory academy chain, probably one with expertise in gambling, or some other such educational commodity. And you, and probably the rest of the Senior Team, will be out on your ear, regardless of your previous glittering achievements."

"Jesus wept," Jane muttered. "And the easy way?"

Harrison leaned forward and lowered his voice. "We know of a group of trusts that are looking to expand. They are quite choosy about who they go in with. They want, umm…" He hesitated, searching for the right phrase. "They want like-minded partners. People who share their values."

"And what values would those be, I wonder?"

"Well, that's for you to find out. We'll set up a series of meetings with any of the lead schools who you don't rule out straight away. And then it's down to you and the Governors."

"So, either we jump, or we're pushed?"

Harrison smiled. "Succinct as always, Jane. Succinct as always."

"So how long will it take you to compile a list? What's the timescale here?"

Again, Harrison hesitated. He really would have to change his technique. Hesitation immediately gave the game away and put the other person on their guard. He would have made a terrible poker player.

"Andrew, stop being such a girl, for God's sake. Come on now, this will soon be over and you can go back to playing Candy Crush on your computer. Be brave. Embrace your inner bastard. I'm a big girl now, I can take it."

Harrison squirmed. God, this was bad enough without Jane helping him get rid of her. Talk about humiliation. He really should have stayed dealing with budgets and spreadsheets. Then he could have avoided all this nasty, messy difficult conversation stuff with other people. He gritted his teeth and ploughed on, reaching into his case for a folder. He removed a slim document from the folder and slid it across the table to Jane. She took it, handling the corner between thumb and forefinger as if it were contaminated.

There were three names on the list, schools she had heard of. For each name there were details of their finances, other schools in their trust and, crucially, a statement laying out their principles. She flicked through it and then put it back down on the table. There was silence.

"Well, Jane, what do you think?"

*

Marcus Grovelle beamed a glowing smile at Camilla as he oozed into the space next to her on the deeply-buttoned leather sofa.

"I'm so pleased you could make it, Camilla, at such short notice. I hope you'll find it's worth your while."

"Well, Mr Grovelle, it was a bit of surprise, I don't mind telling you that. I was waiting for someone to start laughing at the end of the line and was amazed when it turned out to be a genuine call."

"Oh, call me Marcus, please. I really have no time for stuffy ceremony, you know. I have a reputation in the party as being something of a moderniser." He reprised his nuclear smile.

Camilla glanced around his office and took in the oak panelling, the massive twin-pedestal mahogany desk and the muddy oil paintings on the wall. She saw the photos: one of Margaret Thatcher and one of Winston Churchill. Then the books casually lying around to give the impression that Grovelle was in the habit of reading them: Bagehot's *English Constitution*; Hayek's *The Road to Serfdom* and for light relief, Ayn Rand's *The Fountainhead*.

Moderniser, she thought to herself, *you're as tweedy and traditional as Prince Charles.*

She smiled sweetly at him.

"So, er, Marcus, why exactly have you asked to see me?"

"Well, apart from the fact that it's always a pleasure to see a woman as attractive as you are, Camilla, I, er," he faltered, to give him enough time to steal a glance at her face to measure her reaction.

Camilla maintained her serene smile, successfully masking the growing feeling of queasiness she had.

Grovelle, emboldened, ploughed on.

"I was very impressed with you and your speech at the Partnership conference. I'd heard a lot about you and your work and I was not disappointed, I can assure you of that. You're exactly the kind of modern young woman who we need to get involved in government. I think you could make a great contribution in establishing my reforms."

Camilla sparkled at him.

"Well, that's very flattering, Marcus. What exactly did you have in mind?"

Grovelle's eyes glittered.

"I'm minded to put your name forward for an honour in the New Year's list. A CBE. Services to Education."

He licked his lips and laid his hand on her knee.

"It's no more than you deserve. For your work."

His smile doubled in size.

54

Later, as Camilla waited outside the Tube, she googled on her phone, '#metoo', and spent a few minutes scrolling through everything she found. Then she googled 'Marcus Grovelle'. With a wry smile, she closed it down, put her phone away and descended the stairs to the platforms.

*

"Andrew. I trust this is good news?" Alastair Goodall's reptilian voice crackled at the end of the line.

"Yes, I think so," replied Harrison.

"You think so? I'll need a little more certainty than that, Andrew."

Andrew looked around his office. There was a time when it had matched his lofty position. He remembered when he had first walked into it as the incumbent, had strolled over to the plate glass expanse of one wall, with its panorama of towers, and flyovers and chrome and sheen. When working late he would indulge himself, before leaving the office, with five minutes of drinking it all in and imagining he was in a Hollywood film, a captain of industry, a mover and shaker. It was surprisingly easy to do for a spreadsheet man. In those days his empire had foundations. On the floors below him, an army of advisors and deputies and inspectors and executives had toiled away, trying to make things better, and sometimes succeeding. Now there was just a handful of people left, rattling around in a few tiny rooms, shuffling pieces of paper back and forth, because they were too expensive to get rid of. Someone had to carry out the last remaining statutory responsibilities of an education authority, all of them fearful of falling foul of the Great God, Safeguarding, called to account by cynically judgemental tabloid newspapers and chief executives passing the buck.

Occasionally, he doubted that any of this had ever happened and that it had always been this way, with him an unimportant, ineffectual man in a cavernous office on top of a ridiculous skyscraper, but then he caught sight of the array of photographs he hadn't been able to bring himself to take down from the walls. Him shaking hands with Tony Blair. Prince Charles visiting one of their flagship projects. A delegation of dignitaries from America as part of that twinning arrangement. He smiled faintly at the memory. What was the name of that woman in New York?

"Andrew? Andrew, are you still there?" Goodall's rasping insistence dragged him out of his reverie.

"Yes, Alastair, I'm still here," he sighed.

"So?"

"Well, she didn't go completely mad, although she treated me to one of her standard Marxist rants. I gave her the list and she's thinking about it. We're going to talk again next week. It's more or less done. You just need to be patient."

"Patient? Jesus, Andrew, this is painfully slow."

"Alastair, you can have this done so that you get what you want, or you can have it done badly but quickly. You can't have both. And if you've written up your bit properly, she'll go for you. You know she's a sucker for inclusion and community and partnership and all of that malarkey."

"Yes, all of that's in there. I'm not stupid, you know. Oh, and speaking of stupid, we appointed little Bazzer Pugh today."

"Barry Pugh? Dear God, were you short of a cleaner or something?"

"Very funny, Andrew. No, Barry has his uses. He has the imagination of a house brick, he's a dedicated sycophant and he will doggedly do absolutely everything I tell him. His main strength is that he has not had, to my knowledge, one original idea in his life. And he's absolutely loyal and obedient."

Andrew thought for a moment. "Couldn't you have just got a Labrador? Might have been easier."

"The thing about Labradors, Andrew, is that they lack a killer instinct. So does Barry, obviously, but his brain isn't big enough to question orders from his superiors. He will do whatever I tell him to do. He thinks it must be right because I am more important than him. He has the moral compass of a middle-ranking Nazi in Berlin in 1942."

"They used to have a Labrador in one of my schools, you know. They used it for students who were suffering from anxiety and depression. Apparently, it's very therapeutic for the kids to spend time stroking the dog. There were so many of them with mental health issues they were considering getting another one. It was getting a bit stressed itself, being stroked so much. Was a very imaginative solution."

On the other end of the phone, Alastair was baffled as to why Andrew was wittering on about educational issues. He cut across him.

"Yes, that's all very interesting, Andrew, but let me remind you that that used to be one of your schools but it's run by Betmore 777 now and they've actually got rid of the dog. They had it put down."

"Oh no, that's terrible. Why on earth did that happen?"

"I dunno. Failed its lesson observation, I think. It wasn't adding value, Andrew, and these academy chains are ruthless when it comes to carrying passengers."

There was a pause as Andrew took in what had been said. He looked around his office, blinking nervously. The dog had been killed because it had failed its lesson observation. He swallowed and falteringly began, "That's, um, that's a little, um, harsh."

"Hahahaha! Joking, Andrew, joking." The crackling voice down the line cackled harshly, enjoying Andrew's evident discomfort.

Andrew smiled ruefully. "Ah yes, Alastair, you got me there. A joke. Very good. Yes, very amusing."

He tried his own stab at humour. "Well, at least Barry is safe. No plans to put him down, eh?" And to signal the joke he laughed weakly.

"No, not yet anyway," Alastair replied.

"Presumably, now he thinks he's a cross between Nelson Mandela and Donald Trump. Christ, he'll be insufferable."

"A small price to pay, Andrew, for the services of a useful idiot. Oh, and by the way, there might be a job for you in the empire in the future. You've done very well so far."

Andrew looked across again at the photos on the wall. Past glories, never to be recaptured.

"And let's face it, Andrew, soon you'll be in sole command of Longdon's paper clips. Frankly, I think you can do better than that. Think about it. I'll be in touch."

11

A CHILL, BLUSTERY WIND SCATTERED PILES OF GOLDEN LEAVES
and crisp packets into dancing eddies in every corner of the
playground. Jane did up another button on her coat and turned
up her collar against the sharp blasts. Summer seemed a long
time ago now. Ofsted, and the euphoria of the unexpected
outcome, even further away. Books, uniforms, behaviour and
tempers, particularly of staff, were all more than a little frayed.
Numbers were rising in the inclusion room week on week,
external exclusions were also on the up and the last round of
lesson observations had been more than a little disappointing.
How had Avril described them? Shit. Yes, that was it. Shit. The
honeymoon period, as Steph had rather prematurely declared,
was well and truly over. She wondered whether they had
all just taken their eye off the ball. It was a well-documented
phenomenon that schools after an Ofsted inspection dipped
sharply in performance. Results always went down in the year
of the inspection, as if the adrenaline-fuelled spike in maniacal

over-work had an equal and opposite reaction, like some manifestation of a law of physics.

Whatever the reason, things had been a bit sticky for a couple of weeks. She was not looking forward to the staff meeting after school. The news, she knew, would not go down well. It hadn't gone down well with Avril and Rick when she'd told them, and it certainly wasn't going to go better with a staff group that were feeling the impact of the daily battle with an increasingly recalcitrant student body. She was lucky with her classroom teachers. In the main they were committed and talented, with a fierce loyalty to the school and the students. There were a few no-hopers, as in all staff rooms, but the school had made steady progress in either weeding out people who weren't up to it, or in helping them get better. There were still one or two to go, but then again, there always were. As a head she had learned long ago not to make the mistake of thinking that there was an army of talented teachers out there just waiting to be employed. It wasn't perceived to be dynamic or muscular leadership, but sometimes what you had was better than what was available. Sacking people was not the silver bullet it was often held up to be. But the very qualities she discerned in the staff were exactly those qualities that would make the meeting difficult.

A sudden gust of wind howled through the playground and elicited a corresponding howl of excitement from the kids in the playground, their fervour whipped up by the madly-swirling leaves. This wind was all they needed. It was guaranteed to turn the most placid, well-ordered school into a madhouse. Experienced teachers who had lessons period five, straight after lunch, inwardly groaned. They knew instinctively that no matter what carefully planned lesson they had up their sleeve, they would have to gird their loins and get ready to do battle with classrooms full of kids shaken into a wind-induced frenzy of low-level disruption. And worse.

She surveyed the playground. Packs of Year 9 boys had begun to chase corresponding groups of Year 8 boys, past the tennis courts, into the downstairs corridor and back out again, skittling quieter knots of young people chatting in the few nooks and crannies they could find inside. The Year 10 boys, having lost their football over the back fence to the sour-faced woman who was always complaining to the local rag, had pulled rank and stolen the ball from a Year 9 game in progress on the adjoining pitch. A couple of the braver Year 9s, outraged by this obvious injustice, were shaping up to demand their rights and were accordingly about to be taught a sharp lesson in the realities of power relationships in society. A shrill group of hard-faced Year 11 girls, having been denied their recreational cigarette break, were facing up to a rival posse, and were in the name-calling phase of the ruck, the calm before the storm of pushing and hair-pulling began.

She'd clocked, as she made her way around the grounds, that just about everyone was on duty, but it wasn't enough for circumstances such as these. They needed more adults out here, just to nip it in the bud. She reached for her walkie-talkie, pressed the button, and said into the hissing airwaves, "It's Jane here. We need a lot of staff outside, please, and in the corridors. The kids are on the verge."

"Okay, Jane. Will do."

There were several other replies from the staff already on duty, each of them tooled up with a walkie-talkie, and Jane relaxed, knowing that it was in hand. Sure enough, in the next few minutes the playgrounds and corridors were heavy with staff presence. Voices were raised calmly. A hand stretched out to stop groups running. Students were pulled apart and escorted to wait for their punishment outside various offices. In some cases, a raised eyebrow was all that it took. Justice was administered in the great football dispute and the guilty Year 10 boys slunk away, saving their revenge for another day.

As she watched this from a distance, satisfaction rising at the skills and dedication of her staff, Rick strolled up behind her, two Year 8 girls in tow.

"Afternoon, Miss. All quiet?"

She turned. "Ah, Mr Westfield. Yes, all quiet. The cavalry turned up. And who are these two young ladies?"

The girls had downcast eyes and managed to look, at the same time, guilty, apologetic, defiant and fearful. Their faces were unnaturally pale and they both had eyebrows that resembled fat, hairy slugs sliding in single file across their forehead.

"Oh, just a little problem over some unpleasant Snapchat messages. We'll have a little talk about it during period five before I contact home."

"Oh sir, don't tell my mum. She'll kill me," wailed the smaller of the two.

"You should have thought about that, young lady, before you were so stupid," Jane intervened in her most severe tones. "Now, take yourself off to wait outside my office. I need to talk to Mr Westfield for a minute."

They turned to go.

"And hey," Jane called after them, "I hope I don't need to remind you that you'll be in even more trouble if you don't get there sharpish. Be there when I get there and behave on the way. Remember, you're on camera all the way there."

"Good response to your SOS call?" asked Rick.

"Of course," she replied, "they know it makes sense. Five minutes now will save a lot of hassle later. And the kids get the message as soon as they see more staff out and about."

"So, how are you feeling about the meeting this afternoon?"

"Oh, you know," she began. She looked around again. There were several Heads of Year and members of SLT in evidence now. "Come and walk with me back to the office. Everything's under control here now. We were going to meet with Avril to talk before the meeting, so we may as well start now."

They picked a path through the hordes of children still playing, determined to wring every last minute of pleasure from their lunchtime freedom. They did not continue the conversation, preferring instead to acknowledge the other staff that had given up part of their lunchtime to be out and about and to chat to the kids they encountered en route to the peace of Jane's office. Rick had picked up the signals from Jane straight away. It usually meant that what she wanted to talk about was not for the corridors, where eager ears, both staff's and students', were alert to indiscretions, which would be recycled immediately.

Finally, they arrived at the inner sanctum. The two Year 8 girls were sitting on chairs outside the office, on their phones. "No-one told you to sit down," barked Jane. "And I haven't sent you here so you can have a nice time playing on your phones, no doubt causing more trouble. Hand them over." She extended her hand and both girls automatically placed the phone in her outstretched palm. "And make sure you're standing up when I come out for you. I'll be five minutes." She and Rick went into her office and the door closed behind them, sealing calm and quiet in a protective bubble around them.

"What's up?" began Rick, cutting to the chase as usual. "Not like you to worry about a staff meeting."

"No, I know. It's just that I've got a bad feeling about all of this. I don't trust Goodall as far as I can throw him. Nor Andrew Harrison. And I'm really pissed off at being forced into a position where I have no real choices."

"Well, look, I know it's not perfect, but anything must be better than being swallowed up by the BetMore 777 academy chain. We all know what they're like. At least we've all still got jobs this way."

Jane snorted. "For now, at any rate."

"Well, everything Goodall has said fits the bill, doesn't it? Commitment to inclusivity, no trust-wide operating systems, autonomy over our own decisions. You couldn't ask for much more than that, could you? And, from what I've seen, he's got real commitment to disadvantaged kids. That's what POCSE is all about, whatever you think of their methods."

"Too perfect, don't you think? It's easy to promise what he knows we want. That's to make sure we choose them. Once we sign on the dotted line, we've got no more leverage. And I don't trust Harrison an inch. You know they must have been planning this together, don't you? That dossier they gave me must have taken weeks of preparation. They were obviously expecting us to fail Ofsted, which would have made this process much easier for them. This is plan B."

"Why are you telling me all of this, Jane? You are going to go ahead, aren't you?"

"Of course, it's gone too far to pull out now. I just want you to be careful, Rick. Avril and I have only got a few years left. It's different for you. And, to be frank, I don't see the two of us lasting much longer than the time it takes for them to finish the takeover."

Rick stared at her in disbelief. "No, they wouldn't be that stupid, surely? They would completely lose the staff if anything like that happened. And anyway, I know Alastair is a bit slick, but his heart's in the right place. No, I really don't think you have to worry on that score."

Jane's face clouded over with a sceptical frown before she pushed it to one side.

"Well, whatever. Que sera, sera. The important thing is, that in the next few days, starting straight after the staff meeting this afternoon, you get out there amongst the staff and reassure them. You need to touch base with as many of them as possible, starting with the big beasts. Big up the Partnership and Goodall, underline the commitment to inclusivity, and repeat the stuff about contractual continuity and no changes to conditions of service and pensions and all of that. I'm going to have to leave straight after the meeting, so I'm going to say that you and Avril are available to talk to anyone who wants to, okay?"

He shrugged, "Yeah, fine by me. Where are you going? Everything all right?" It was unheard of for Jane to miss any after school meeting for any reason at all.

"What? Oh yes, I've just got something I can't get out of. It's nothing, but I've cancelled it a few times already. Anyway, are you going to give those two outside a bollocking? And can you be out and about this afternoon and when the kids leave, just in case? I just need to get on with preparing for the meeting."

He was being dismissed. He didn't mind that in the slightest. He actually welcomed the clarity. Jane was polite, but always to the point, so you always knew where you stood with her, which was a bonus in Rick's eyes. And he had some things to think about as well, just as soon as he'd dealt with the two naughty girls outside.

"Okay," he said, opening the office door, "I'll see you later." He strode into the corridor and the two little girls, still standing forlornly, jumped to attention. "Come on you two, my office. Let's try and turn you into responsible members of the community." He marched off down the corridor, the girls scrambling in his wake. One girl whispered to the other, "What's he mean, responsible members of the community?"

"Fuck knows. He probably just wants us to be good. Wanker."

*

"So why do we have to get into bed with this, what did you call it? This MAT? Why can't we just stay with Longdon? We all know they're as much use as a chocolate teapot but at least we know who they are."

Kwame looked around the hall for confirmation and there was a smattering of agreement, with a few comments shouted out in support.

"Yeah," called Charlotte Green, "how do we know they're not going to change all of our contracts the minute we sign on the dotted line, or make us submit lesson plans every week? We've all heard those horror stories about BetMore777."

This contribution stirred the pot even further. The disquiet in the room was palpable. Rick shuffled in his seat. Jane knew she had to close this down as quickly as possible, while at the same time appearing to listen and be sympathetic. She raised both hands in the air, smiling and patting down the disruption.

"Yes, thanks for that, Kwame, it's a good question. But as I explained, the choice is not between Longdon and the Trust. It's between BetMore777, and all of the things we know about that particular Empire of Evil, and the Trust. And I'm sure I don't need to remind you that there are people sitting here, people with the respect of all of us, who can tell a tale or two about life in BetMore 777 Academy. When you accept that, there isn't really a choice."

Charlotte put her hand up again. "But how can we be sure that the Trust won't be just as bad? Or even worse? We only have their word for it."

"Well, the short answer is, we can't be sure of anything. But I have to say I've been impressed with the initial discussions we've had with Alastair Goodall. And we've worked with him for some time through the Partnership."

At the mention of POCSE a groan involuntarily slipped from the mouths of the assembled staff. Although the approaches POCSE had championed had brought great success in terms of improving their results over the past few years, that success came at a price. Every new POCSE initiative required yet further effort and time for staff members. Lessons for 'marginal students' at 7.30 am, 7 pm, at weekends and in the holidays. Compulsory last-minute walk-throughs of exams for all students on the morning of each exam, regardless of any evidence that that approach worked. Failure was your fault individually. Any attempt to put some responsibility onto the students was labelled as 'blaming the kids'. Goodall and the POCSE posse banged on about moral purpose and anyone who didn't buy into that philosophy might as well have been a war criminal. 'Zero Tolerance for failure' was the endlessly-repeated mantra. It was a brave person who would dare to put their head above the parapet and question this fanatical devotion.

Jane looked across at Rick and raised her eyebrows. He got up.

"All right everyone, I know we're all burned out with Partnership initiatives, but that's the reality of the world we live in at the moment. And there's no doubt about it, with the emphasis on data and tracking, they've made every single one of us a better teacher."

From the back of the hall came a stage-whispered comment from Kevin Nolan, the staffroom barrack room lawyer. His timing was consummate, developed over twenty years of a career dedicated to making life awkward for senior management. "They've made every single one of us a results slave, more like it. And completely shagged out. Whatever happened to work-life balance?"

As usual, his intervention was greeted with a peal of laughter from his acolytes and the general rumble of discontent stirred again.

Jane looked down at her watch. "Kevin, constructive as always. I'm sorry, I'd love to be able to continue this discussion, but I'm afraid I've got another appointment. Rick and Avril will take more questions from the floor and we are all available to talk to anyone about their concerns in the next couple of weeks. I've already arranged to meet with the union reps at the end of next week and I believe there will be meetings next week for the purpose of consultation. Before I go I'd just like to reiterate, we genuinely believe that this move is in the best interests of the school, the staff and the students. We understand that change is worrying and that you have many legitimate questions. I'm very confident that we can all make progress on this together as a school community."

She collected her papers together and left the stage. Rick assumed command.

"Now, Kevin, what was that excellent question again?"

*

The big beasts gathered in Kevin's classroom on the top floor. It was the go-to place in the school to foment revolution, and it was natural that after the staff meeting they'd just had, an impromptu discussion group would coalesce there, without any formal arrangement. There were five of them sitting around a nest of tables at the front of the room, the tables laden with coffee and an array of cakes and biscuits to keep them going. The walls of the classroom appeared to have been decorated in homage to the great revolutionaries and agitators of history: Karl Marx, Martin Luther King, Nelson Mandela. There were further posters eulogising the contributions of Emmeline Pankhurst, the Paris Commune, Nye Bevan, the Levellers, Oliver Cromwell. It was a shrine to struggle and was kept immaculately.

A keen observer would have detected a second, minor chord in this symphony of interests: Meteorology. There was a series of charts and posters celebrating warm and cold fronts, great extreme weather events in history, with explanations of isobars, pressure and humidity. He did occasionally teach a little lower school geography, where his knowledge of weather systems came in handy, but the posters were more evidence of a personal obsession, an obsession confirmed by a glance at his computer screen, displaying, as always, the Norwegian Meteorological Service and its current snow forecast for Europe.

"So, what did you make of all that, Kev?" asked Kwame, reaching for a cream horn.

"Well, we're fucked, aren't we? Caught between a rock and a hard place."

"We don't know that for certain, though, Kevin. It could be that Bellingford is as liberal as they claim. They've said all the right things about contracts and non-interference and inclusivity." Even as she was saying it, Charlotte wasn't convincing herself.

"Give over, Charlotte. Do you think for a minute that if your results go down in English next year that they'll be inclusive and non-interfering and liberal? Will they bollocks, they'll be intervening for England, and you'll be coming in every Saturday morning to squeeze the kids through, regardless of the cost. They won't give a toss that you and your team have sweated blood for the kids here and that your results over the last six years have been nothing short of a miracle. And if that doesn't look as if it's going to work they'll expect you to cheat."

"Cheat?" Kwame spluttered on his cream horn. "How can they get away with that?"

"You should talk to Martin in science, you know, the new lad who started in September. He's got all kinds of horror stories about what they had to do at the BetMore 777 in Chelsford."

"In suppose we've been pretty lucky here with Jane and the SLT," said Charlotte. "They do roughly approximate to human beings. You are allowed to make an honest mistake."

"Well, that's not surprising, is it? They make enough of 'em."

There was general agreement and laughter at this resumption of normal service. It was all very unsettling, this uncertainty, and familiar territory was like a comfort blanket.

"So," resumed Kwame, "what do you think we should do?"

"Do? There's nothing we can do except wait and ask a lot of questions. But if I were twenty years younger, like you guys, I'd be looking for a new job and sharpish before it gets sticky here. I've got a bad feeling about what's in store for those of us who are stuck here."

"Trouble is," mused Charlotte, "everywhere is exactly the same now. It's harder and harder to find a school that's not run by a graduate of the Adolf Hitler College of School Leadership."

"This is too depressing," wailed Kwame. "Come on, Kev, cheer us up." He nodded towards the computer screen. "Any sign of snow yet?"

Kevin suddenly gave the impression of a man who had been talking about an interesting hobby for the past twenty minutes and was now turning his attention to the really serious business. "Well, Kwame, it's funny you should ask that, because there is some unsettled weather in the Arctic coming this way. But really, it's a little early, it's only November. I'm pretty sure though, that we're on for a few snow closures this year, either side of Christmas. But hey," he broke off and wagged an admonishing finger at them, "don't say a word in the staffroom. I don't want people getting their hopes up and then come blaming me when it doesn't happen. I still remember 2011."

"Don't worry, Kev," said Charlotte "Our lips are sealed."

"Listen," said Kwame, "I've got to make a move. I've got a stack of marking to get through tonight."

"Yeah, I'll come with you, I've got stuff to do as well," Charlotte added.

The others took this as their cue and they all trooped out of the classroom. Kwame turned at the door and said, "See you tomorrow then, Kevin, all right?"

Kevin was already glued to the computer screen, using the app that modelled the likely weather over the next forty-eight hours. "Yeah," he mumbled, "see you tomorrow." He turned back to the screen. "Now, if only that wind would pick up from Tromso."

Out in the corridor, Charlotte walked ahead with Kwame. "Well, a good bit of news to end on at least."

Kwame looked at her, puzzled. "Good news? How do you work that out? It all sounds disastrous to me."

"A snow day before Christmas. He's never been wrong since he found that Norwegian site. What a result that would be."

12

JANE STARED AT THE PICTURES ON JOHNSON'S DESK. There were three of them, framed, of him, his wife and his three children, all in blazing sunshine and beach wear, smiling. Some on the beach, some by a pool, all of them screaming, 'Look at us, we're a happy family'. Pictures can lie, though, she thought. Everyone smiles for the camera, no matter how much pain they're in. That's just what you did. There were pictures like that in their house, all over the place, but they didn't really mean much. Or rather, they meant everything, but it was impossible to tell what, exactly. If someone were to take a picture of them now, they would probably still smile for the camera and no-one would know. No-one could tell.

What she could tell, from the moment she and Jim walked into his office, was that things were never going to be the same after they had walked out again. There was something in his eyes, a certain forced airiness in his voice that sent a tremor down her spine and made her legs quake. She heard him speak as if from a great distance.

"Ok Jim, Jane. Thanks for coming in, both of you. As you know, we were monitoring your progress and reviewing some of the tests we'd carried out and having a closer look at some of the scans we had done." He paused. Jane felt mounting, irrational anger. Why have you left a gap? What do you want us to say? Do you want us to make this easier for you? She pursed her lips into the thinnest line she could imagine.

Jim, as usual, filled the gap in the appropriate way. "Yes, that's right, doctor. It's been quite a tense time waiting."

Jane's knuckles gripped the side of the chair. For God's sake, Jim, don't make a joke of this, for once in your life don't be a pushover.

Johnson continued. "Yes. Well, I'm afraid it's bad news, Jim. There's no easy way to break this news so I'll just tell you straight. I'm afraid the cancer has spread. Quite considerably. It's an unusually aggressive set of tumours."

Jane gasped. She felt her eyes sting and her heart pound. She shook herself and gripped the chair with even more vigour. She would not cry. She must be her normal self for Jim's sake. She must endure, for both of them. Johnson's voice had faded out by this stage. She had no idea what he'd been saying. She'd have to ask again.

Jim reached over and took her hand and squeezed it. He turned to Johnson again. "So, what sort of timescale are we talking about here?"

"I'm afraid it's a matter of a few months, six at the most."

"Six months! But…" Jane found herself speaking and then made herself stop.

Jim filled the gap with an easy calmness and responded to the consultant's half of the conversation. He even had the presence of mind to ask a couple of questions when invited to, like a well-prepared candidate at an important interview. He hurried through the rest of the consultation, eager to get to the end without appearing rude. Jane got through to the end in a daze, the discussion filtering through to her from a great distance, down a long tunnel. And then they were shaking hands and were back out in the corridor, neon strip lights freezing tasteful architectural pot plants in a death-ray sheen.

Later that night, when they went to bed, Jim clung to her and wept, his whole body shaking with fear and rage. She stroked his head and waited for him to fall asleep. They didn't talk. By that stage they were all talked out, at least for that day. In the middle of the night, quietly unable to sleep, she turned to look at him in the faint glow from the clock radio by his side of the bed. His body rose and fell rhythmically, and he occasionally made little snorts and grumbles. He looked so peaceful.

She was gripped with a ratcheting fear. What was she going to do when he died? Because he was going to die, she knew that. She despised the endless round of featured cancer sufferers in the weekend supplements who talked about fighting and positivity and opportunity. Good luck to them, but she didn't buy any of that and she knew that Jim didn't either. She looked down at him again. He could be so annoying, so infuriating, so disappointing at times but he was hers, for all his faults. They had been together for a lifetime. What on earth was she going to do?

13

Every evening after school Kevin could be found in his classroom. Here he divided his time between three activities. He supervised the group of Year 11 history students who would regularly turn up for extra tuition and exam preparation. He scoured the Norwegian weather forecast site. He periodically marched over to the bank of windows down one side of the classroom and stared at the horizon. There was a low moon which silvered the banks of cloud piling in on the stiff wind. The situation of the classroom on the top floor of the building and the topography of the site gave him a panoramic view to the west. Ninety percent of the time, that was where the weather came from. From this vantage point he would note cloud formations in the distance and check the strength of the wind. He'd invested in a barometer and a cheap amateur weather station, which nestled in the corner of the room by his desk. He also had an A4 Moleskine pad, with creamy, smooth, squared paper that served as a journal and record book of all the data he took. He loved that notebook, regularly picking it up, sniffing it and smoothing down the faux leather binding and the texture of the pages, enjoying the contrast between the blank sheets and those covered in closely-written notes.

He looked at his watch. Five o'clock. Time to call it a day. The fifteen students in front of him were still silently scrawling their answers to the exam practice question he'd set. If he'd let them they'd go on regardless for another half an hour.

"Okay everyone, let's finish there for tonight. If you can just finish the sentence you're writing and I'll quickly come round and take in your answers."

Jason, an enormous white boy with hands like massive bunches of bananas, said immediately, "When are we gonna get these back, sir?"

"They'll be ready tomorrow, Jase, if you turn up after school."

"You gonna mark 'em?"

"No Jason, my little fluffy pussycat, I'm just going to give them straight back to you. I couldn't possibly be bothered to mark them."

Jason looked at first puzzled and then a little disappointed. The faces of his peers all around him were already smiling broadly.

"Of course, I'm going to mark them Jason, you muppet. I wouldn't let you down like that, Jase, have a little faith."

"Oh, sorry sir," Jason replied.

"And do you know why I'm going to mark them by tomorrow, everyone?"

They all chorused, "Because you love us and don't want us to go to prison."

"That's right, you lovely people, that's right. Okay then," he continued, a bundle of papers in his hands, "great work tonight, everyone, well done. I'll see you all tomorrow."

The students bundled out of the room, a growing buzz of chatter developing, released from the exam quiet of Kevin's classroom. One or two of them called as they left, "Thanks, sir. See you tomorrow."

He went back to his computer, sheaf of papers in hand. "I'll just have another little look before I start," he said to himself, settling down in front of the screen. He scrolled over charts and clicked links to project into the future, but it was the same as before – nothing.

"I don't believe it," he muttered, "nothing. Nothing at all. It's the second week of December and still no sign of snow. I was sure we'd have some before the end of term."

He shook his head. "Oh well," he said, "might as well get started on these."

He turned to the pile of exam papers just completed, took the first from the top of the pile, and began to flick through the scrawl, ticking and commenting as he went.

*

Rick settled himself comfortably into one of Avril's squashy armchairs in her office and reached for a piece of glistening chocolate cake. The walls of Avril's office were covered in children's art work and messages from grateful students and parents from down the years. There were a couple of canvases done by her daughter, some family photographs on her desk and an array of glossy pot plants that exuded good health. At one end of the office, where Rick was demolishing the chocolate cake, was an arrangement of black leather sofas and an armchair around a Persian rug and a low table. To the side was a coffee machine that was permanently, it seemed, half full of fragrant coffee.

The other end of her office told a different story. A row of battered gunmetal filing cabinets. A couple of classroom desks, surrounded by four classroom chairs, bore piles of exercise books, folders and papers, with class sets of *An Inspector Calls*, *Macbeth* and *A Christmas Carol* teetering on the edge. There were piles of papers, her planner and a few DVDs scattered around.

Avril came over to join him, cake and coffee in hand. "So, you've noticed it too, then?" she asked, sitting on the adjacent sofa.

"She's been acting a bit strange for a few weeks now. I thought maybe it was to do with the takeover. After all, it's all gone through incredibly quickly. The new regime starts in January. No-one expected that at the start."

"Well, that's partly because she hasn't made a fuss, isn't it? The unions are less than useless these days and she is raising no objections to any of it. And as far as the authority goes, they can't get shot of us fast enough. I dunno, she seems to have lost a bit of her fight somehow and I never thought I'd ever say that."

"Do you think maybe that she knows they are going to get rid of her? Maybe that's a done deal and she's keeping quiet about it because she wants to protect the rest of us. That's the sort of thing she'd do."

"Yeah, that's true, but if she was going they'd have already had the conversation with me, and up till now they've been all sweetness and light. They couldn't have been any more complimentary or friendly. No. I don't think it can be that, it's too early."

"Do you think maybe she's ill?"

"Well, I'd though that too. I don't know whether you've noticed, but she leaves school pretty early these days."

"Yeah, I had noticed that. If she were ill, would she tell you? I'm never quite sure how close you two are."

"We're good professional colleagues, but I wouldn't say we were friends. She's a very private person, I've always thought."

Rick put his plate down, having made short work of Avril's *Bake Off*-inspired treat.

"That was delicious, by the way. You're getting very good at cakes, Avril."

Avril gave him a look. "I'm working on a side-line that will keep the wolf from the door when they do sack me next year. A cake shop. And even if they don't sack me, selling cakes would be more congenial, not to say more ethically sustainable, than dealing with all of the bollocks that's coming our way next year."

"You mean the Grovelle bollocks?"

"The very same. I can't believe that there hasn't been a mass outcry at all of this nonsense. National Service, leaving school at fourteen, apprenticeships, Latin and Greek, grammar schools, sackings at will. It's all madness. I'm telling you, Rick, back in the day, any one of those things would have brought the profession out onto the streets."

"It seems like you can slip out anything and get it through in the middle of all of this Brexit chaos."

"Honestly Rick, I really don't envy you. You're on the cusp of the most exciting period of your career, or you should be, and now you'll have to spend it bringing in a load of old nonsense and trying to make it work. I'm glad I'm on the way out, I really am."

They both paused and stared into their coffee.

Rick broke the silence. "Do you think we should say anything to her? Ask her what's up? There's only a week and a half before the end of term."

"I dunno. It's the worst time to raise anything. It's been a long, hard term and everyone's exhausted and at the end of their tether. It might do more harm than good. Let's just leave it for now."

He nodded and they both turned their attention to a plate of delicate almond thins.

14

IT HAD BEEN THE KIND OF DECEMBER DAY THAT NEVER REALLY gets light, a smudgy, damp greyness having hung over the day for hours. It was completely at odds with the manic, unhinged hysteria that had reigned at Fairfield from the moment the first students had arrived at about 7.30 am. A non-uniform day, strictly in aid of charity of course, the last day before the Christmas holidays was traditionally a day to be endured. Damage limitation was the name of the game. Students were arrayed in tinsel, hats and flashing festive jumpers and nearly all of them were toting huge bags full of cards and sweets and presents. The whole day was a battle between staff and students to keep them all off the corridors and in classrooms. This had always been a struggle, but since the advent of mobile phones and messaging in all its forms, it was now nigh on impossible as students were alerted to the best party (Miss has got pizza for everyone!), the best DVD showing or when and where the assembly entertainers were rehearsing.

Just after the lunch the final students were escorted off the premises, the last bus duty had been completed and the last angry phone call from a local shopkeeper or resident about behaviour on the buses had been taken. Senior Team and the long-suffering Heads of Year had answered the calls and patrolled the local area, trying to keep a lid on high spirits. Now, at about two o'clock, with early darkness closing in, everyone congregated in the staff room for the farewells and drinks. The first couple of drinks took the edge of the empty-eyed, numbed exhaustion that pervaded the room. This first half an hour at the end of the autumn term was almost painful, so exquisite and acute was the sense of release from torment. So much time stretching out in front of them, with no early starts, no marking, no planning, no late meetings.

There were just a couple of staff leaving, so the event would be mercifully short, allowing the younger staff to pile down the pub before going out on the lash for the rest of the evening and the older staff time to get home early and have a nap on the sofa before a quiet night in in front of the telly. The real victims were those in between with young children, who would have already calculated the amount of Christmas shopping they could get in before getting home to play with the children and make the dinner.

As they were waiting for everyone to arrive and for the speeches to begin, staff congregated in their friendship groups, staking out territory in comfy chairs around low tables, hoovering up twiglets and warm white wine. Charlotte, found herself in between Kevin and Kwame.

"So, you going away in the holidays either of you?" she asked.

"No such luck," grumbled Kevin. "We're hosting this year. We've got a house full for about five days. It's costing me an arm and a leg."

"What about you, Kwame?"

"Yeah, we're taking the kids to my sister's in Leeds. We're not setting off until Christmas Eve. So I'm looking forward to a few days of sleep before then. She's a great cook, my sister, and the kids really get on well with her kids so it should be good. Then it's our turn next year."

"Lucky you," said Kevin. "Enjoy this one while you can. What about you, Charlotte?"

"We've got John's mother staying with us for the week, so that's a week of back-breaking hard work, with no thanks and constant moaning from the Queen."

"Difficult, is she?"

"Nightmare. She thinks I don't look after him properly and that I'm a mad career-obsessed harpy who couldn't wait to farm the kids off to childcare."

"Knows you well then, by the sound of it."

She shot him a look. "Hmm, very funny. Honestly though, it's just a week of torment. I'll be glad to get back to school, I'm telling you."

"See, I told you, she's got your number perfectly," retorted Kevin, warming to his second glass of wine.

"Oh, I'm not talking to you anyway, Kevin, after you let us all down so badly with the snow. What was it you said? Definitely snow before and after Christmas. I can't tell you how that promise has got me through some tricky days in the last few weeks. And for what? Absolutely nothing. Not even a bit of frost. I thought you said that Norwegian site was infallible."

"Sorry guys, believe me no-one's sorrier than me. I don't know what went wrong."

Kwame changed the subject. "So, who's leaving today then? How many speeches do we have to sit through?"

"Just a couple," said Charlotte. "That young technician, Matt, I think his name is, you know the one that looks about twelve years old and that woman who was on long-term supply in science."

"Plankton, then," said Kevin. "Good, we'll be out of here in twenty minutes."

"Ey up, here she comes," said Charlotte, as a quietening of the crowd indicated that something was afoot.

Jane stepped up to the front of the room, waited a second for quiet to descend and then encouraged it on its way.

"Okay, colleagues, the sooner we begin the sooner we can finish. I know we're all desperate to draw a line under this term and to have some quality time with our nearest and dearest."

The hum of chatter subsided and all eyes were on the front. Jane, normally so easy and generous with her end of term addresses, that had become something of a local legend for their humanity and good humour, was strangely clipped. The two speeches and exchange of gifts for the two admittedly minor departures were rattled through and almost before people had settled in, they were at the end.

Almost before the departing IT technician had mumbled his thank-yous and farewells Jane was back out front, resuming her role as Mistress of Ceremonies.

"So, not long to go now," she started with a smile. Encouraged by the ripple of laughter this created she pressed on. "I don't want to keep you much longer. I just wanted to take this opportunity to thank you all, particularly those of you who have been with me on this journey for the past ten years, but all of the rest of you as well, for all of the hard work and dedication you show to the children in our care every day you come to work. We don't get much thanks these days for the work we do with our client group, our students, as they used to be known. And since no-one ever went into teaching for the money, thanks are an important currency in terms of morale. Our kids are frequently described in the outside word as problems, burdens, difficulties to overcome. I'm quite used to that lack of understanding from the media, who frankly get just about everything wrong that they report, but it gets harder and harder to take when the people who should know better, our glorious leaders, seem to revel in their own ignorance and parade their prejudices as if they were great new insights to be proud of."

Jane's voice had dropped and the audience, raucous and irreverent minutes before, were enveloped in an air of intense concentration. What was happening here? This was not the speech they had been expecting. She continued.

"I want to thank all of you for your outstanding work during Ofsted, but more than that, the outstanding work you do day after day, not to get a pat on the back from Big Brother, but because it makes a difference to our kids, many of whom arrive at our doors looking for respite from damaged and difficult family circumstances.

The kid who has spent the night in emergency accommodation. The kid who has not eaten since free school meals the day before. The kid who lives in fear of a family member coming into their room at night. The kid who watches their mother battered and brutalised. For those kids, we are the nearest thing they have to love and security. And on their behalf, I want to thank all of you for that."

Rick, standing to the side, felt a lump rise in his throat. He battled his stinging eyes and wondered where this was going next. If he hadn't known better, he would have sworn this was a resignation speech.

"Many of you will have worked out that this will be the last ever farewell speech I will give…"

What? Rick's heart skipped a beat and his mouth fell open. Avril, standing next to him, held her breath.

"…in a Fairfield High that is a local authority-controlled school."

They both began breathing a little easier. Rick remembered to close his mouth.

"Now, I'm sure you will all agree that Longdon have been a signally useless local authority for much of that time, but at the very least, they have been our useless local authority, with human beings we know and can talk to and have some kind of productive relationship with. With some sense of accountability and transparency. From January, we move over to the control of the Bellingford Multi-Academy Trust, and things will change, inevitably. So far, I am reassured by what Alastair Goodall and the Trust have been saying about their plans for the future, and I hope that this marks the beginning of a prosperous and harmonious new relationship."

She paused and looked around the crowd. The gap she had left grew, and in it everyone in the audience mentally inserted the next part of her speech for her: "But I don't think it will."

She left that unsaid, of course and pressed on. "So, I am sure that the Trust has lots of additional work lined up for all of us in January. That makes it even more important that we all have a relaxing and enjoyable holiday. Spend quality time with those you love, family and friends. Just in case, in January, work takes over, and it becomes harder to give those people the time they deserve. Merry Christmas to you all." She raised her glass to the audience, who did the same and chorused, "Merry Christmas."

While conversations carried on, mostly about the weirdly affecting tone of Jane's speech and everyone's holiday plans, and people decided to have one last drink or another sausage roll, Jane slipped out of the staffroom before Avril or Rick could buttonhole her. Avril was about to follow her, when she was collared by someone who was rather exercised by a mistake in her December payslip that had just materialised in her pigeonhole. She watched her go, over the shoulder of Joyce, who was worried about how she was going to pay for Christmas without the correct salary. Just in time, Avril averted her eyes from Jane's departure, and gave Joyce her full, smiling, yet concerned, attention.

By about four in the afternoon the school site was just about deserted, with a mere handful of cars left in the car park. Rick and Avril both found themselves outside the closed door of Jane's office.

"You as well?" said Avril, as Rick rounded the end of the corridor.

"I just wanted to check she was all right. I've never heard her give a speech like that before."

"Me neither. But she's gone. I knocked and tried the door. It's locked."

"Gone? But she's always the last to leave. Without fail."

"Listen, it's probably nothing. I'll ring her later, just to check. Don't worry about it. Go home and start the holiday."

"Yeah. Yeah, you're probably right. I will. Have a good Christmas."

"You too. See you in January."

By four-thirty there was only one car left in the playground. Tony, the site manager, was stomping around jangling a huge bunch of keys. He was desperate to lock up and put his feet up. The school was a much pleasanter place to work when there were no students in it and a positively delightful place to work when there no teachers either.

"Bloody Kevin. What the hell is he still doing here?"

Up in the top floor observatory that was his classroom, Kevin was putting the finishing touches to his leaving preparations. He had spent the previous twenty minutes doing last-minute checks of the Norwegian weather site. This was partly because Kwame and Charlotte had spent the twenty minutes before that mercilessly taking the piss out of him for his snow closure obsession and the failure of his predictions.

He stared at the screen, an expression of triumph on his face. "Ha! I knew it! It was right all along."

Then triumph turned to disappointment. "What a bloody waste of a fall of snow. What a criminal waste," he lamented.

Five minutes later he passed Tony jangling his keys as he went through the main entrance to the car park.

"Sorry mate, didn't mean to keep you. Have a good Christmas."

"Same to you," he grunted, rattling the doors as he locked up behind him.

Kevin loaded up his boot with marking and a bag full of cartons of Celebrations and bottles of wine his grateful students had given him for Christmas and opened the driver's door to get in. At that moment, the first fat snowflake floated down from the lowering darkened skies and landed on the bonnet of his car. By the time he drove through the car park entrance onto the road, the air was thick with flakes.

Kevin peered out of his window at the sky full of silent white feathers. He shook his head as he drove off. "What a terrible waste," he muttered.

15

THE SNOW CONTINUED TO FALL FOR THE NEXT COUPLE OF days, giving the beginning of the Christmas holiday a Dickensian air. Snow in London was rare and snow in London at Christmas was unheard of, so there was a frenzy of seasonal activity in the first few days of the holiday, as if people were afraid that if they didn't cram it all in, they might never get another chance.

Rick was on more or less permanent sledging and snowballing duty, while Jo, as usual, took the opportunity afforded by the school holidays and Rick's free childcare, to build up some brownie points at work by getting in early and leaving late for the next few days. It was just as well he took advantage of the snow because on the third day it had stopped, on the fourth day only a sad brown sludge was left on the streets, only cruelly clear ice in the back garden and by the time Christmas Day dawned, normal service had resumed. It was mild and grey with an intermittent, half-hearted thin drizzle, the weather that, for as long as he could remember, had been seemingly compulsory on December 25th. Perhaps in the future, he mused, Christmas cards and wrapping paper would be adorned not with snowmen and Breughel-like scenes, but with umbrellas and milky edge-to-edge mist.

They had finally got to bed just after midnight on Christmas Eve, having spent the previous hour manically wrapping presents and hauling them into two named piles in front of the fireplace. There was much agonising, counting to make sure that the piles were equal ("Is that equal value or equal numbers?"), finalising the elaborate pretence of those presents that Santa brought and those that Mum and Dad and relatives had bought. This fraught process was not made any easier by the amount of alcohol he had got through without really realising and the beginnings of a throbbing headache was gathering behind his temples. The final chore was the construction of stockings using two of his football socks, which were placed just outside the children's bedrooms. Exhausted, flopping into bed, they both vowed never to do this again. They were asleep before the complaint had been fully articulated.

And then, apparently minutes later, they were rudely awakened, by the scramble of footsteps up the stairs, the bursting open of their door, and squeals of delight and excitement from the kids. Rick looked across at the alarm. "Jesus, five o'clock."

"Jesus, Daddy? It's his birthday," announced his daughter Sophie earnestly.

*

"Now, who's for goose?" asked Marcus Grovelle, carving knife poised over the steaming golden bird that was the centrepiece of a table that appeared to have come from central casting, Christmas Department. He beamed contentedly around at his guests, his chef's hat at a rakish angle, and started to carve expertly before anyone had time to answer. The company had already polished off half a dozen bottles of Bollinger, most of it taken care of by Grovelle himself, and his usually jovial and gregarious self was supercharged by this influx of top-quality bubbles.

He was feeling even more smug than usual. After they had got through the Christmas dinner and charmed Victoria's parents and brother and family, there were presents and charades to look forward to. He loved charades. He always thought that in another life he would have made a fine actor. Or a historian. He had an excellent turn of phrase as a writer and a real grasp of the big ideas in the sweep of history. Perhaps he could get that into the charades somehow? No, that was it. He could have been a great historian, but one that presented heavyweight programmes on BBC4. Like that, what was he called again? Simon Schama, that was it. He giggled to himself. No not Schama, he was a bit too much of a pinko, the other one, what was he called? Starkey, that was it.

"Marcus, darling, are you all right?" Victoria asked, a look of concern on her face.

"Hmm? Okay? Yes, I'm fine, darling. Never been better. Here, have some of this fabulous Chateau Lafitte."

He made to fill her glass with the red, but she shook her head and covered the glass with the palm of her hand. He proceeded to fill his own glass and circulated the table, the master of ceremonies, filling everyone else's. He spilled a few drops.

"Woops! Not to worry, eh?"

And then tomorrow, when they'd packed off all of these ghastly people, it was the highlight of the festive season, Boxing Day lunch round at the PM's. Handy that her cottage was only in the next village. That was the great thing about the Cotswolds. Everyone who mattered was just around the corner. She hadn't got back to him yet to confirm, but heaven knows, she had a lot on her plate at the moment. Still, he'd better check later, just to make sure.

"Marcus? Marcus darling, are you all right?"

*

Karim sat at the dining table, a paper hat perched on his head, and a plate of turkey with all the trimmings piled up in front of him. Joan and Eric had agonised for days over the dinner and had spoken at length to Karim's key worker, Ahmed, and the people from the council. They had eventually agreed that having traditional food from both cultures was the only safe option, particularly as Karim would not be drawn on his preference.

"Are you sure you don't want any of the lamb and pomegranate? Or what about these, what are they called again, spinach fatayers? They are fantastic, they really are."

"No thank you, Joan. I must be English now. I will have this delicious turkey. Very good. Thank you."

"Well, if you're sure, love," said Joan uncertainly. "I know," she continued, brightening up, "we can all have the lamb and pomegranate tomorrow, how about that?"

"Yes, Joan, thank you. That will be very good. Thank you."

Later that night in his room, he lay on his bed and searched in the bedside drawer. He pulled out a photograph, the only one he had managed to keep hold of. It showed his father and mother, him and his brother and sister at the university where his father had worked. Last Christmas, they had all sat round the table in their house and eaten lamb with pomegranate stuffing and spinach fatayehs, amongst other things. Given what had been going on in Aleppo then, it was little short of a miracle that his mother had been able to get hold of such delicacies, but money and influence still helped. Not anymore. He thought again of Saleh and Evana. If only he had gone to play football with the boys rather than Saleh. And Evana, where was she? She was only twelve...

His face crumpled, like the photograph in his hand, and he buried his head into the pillow to muffle the gasping sobs that came with the hot, salty tears. The only way this could get worse for him was if Joan or Eric heard him crying and came up to talk to him. It was exhausting being nice to them. Exhausting, but he knew his parents would have wanted him to be polite.

*

Avril took another sip of her Guinness West Indian porter, a recent discovery of hers in Tesco. She had finished the turkey crown with all the trimmings, also from Tesco, had cleared away and stacked the dishwasher, and could now settle down to shout at the Queen's Speech with some enjoyment.

This was her fourth Christmas since Joseph had passed away, but the first since then when neither of her children could make it home for Christmas. They had both produced rational and logical reasons for this and she had been careful not to make a fuss. She couldn't bear to be thought of as difficult or needy in any way. They both had long-term partners of their own, and she was fairly certain that it wouldn't be long before weddings were being arranged, and heaven help us, children being produced. The balance of power had inexorably shifted and somehow the baton of adulthood had passed to the next generation. She was no longer at the centre of things. She was someone who was on the periphery. Someone who, though loved, she was sure of that, was beginning to inhabit that space labelled 'problem'.

She had no real inclination to be a grandmother, having found the whole business of being a mother largely underwhelming, a strangely feted role, that seemed to consist of nothing more than a series of extraordinarily dull activities and pursuits, many of which involved heavy duty cleaning and self-infantilisation. No, it was self-interest alone that made her look forward to the arrival of grandchildren, because it would be the point when she might have some genuine purpose again.

She looked at her watch. It was two-thirty. The children were going to Skype after the Queen's Speech. She was going to have to put some clothes on after all.

*

Jane's children were both there, in their usual places in the front room. Lucy was four months pregnant, but she was there on her own, Ben having been given strict instructions to spend Christmas with his parents. Owen, the younger child by a couple of years, was currently single, but knowing him, that was a blessing at the moment and would be a temporary state of affairs, thought Jane.

They had finally told the children a couple of weeks before and had said that they both wanted a last Christmas together, without 'significant others', as Jim had put it. *Without 'significant others',* thought Jane with a wry smile, *what an irony. This will be my last Christmas with a 'significant other'.*

Both Lucy and Owen were positively fascist about maintaining the Christmas traditions of their childhood. Any suggestion of minor tinkering was met with outrage. Every change of the previous ten years or so was fought over tooth and nail, like every ten metres of ground between the trenches in the First World War. No new pyjamas on Christmas Eve. What? No stockings inside their bedrooms. How could you? No fairy lights and greenery from the garden garlanded up the staircase. That's so unfair. It was the ultimate war of attrition. Until now. And Jim's war was not a proper war because it could never be won.

The children were also equally uncompromising in their steadfast refusal to do anything to contribute to the production of this fairy tale Christmas. Part of the magic, apparently, was the return to childhood in the form of the creation of the fairy tale without any seeming effort from anyone. Magic in its truest sense. Jane thought that the thing that most upset the children about Jim's terminal condition was the impact it would have on the longevity of their Christmas fantasy world. On some level, she thought, they felt let down by their father, who was being selfish. How could he possibly go and die and ruin what was left of Christmas for them?

And because of this, she was not looking forward to this Christmas. She couldn't be certain that she would be able to keep it all in and not blurt out accusations and recriminations that would be very hurtful. She wanted someone to blame, and the children were the most convenient target. She knew it wasn't fair, but she wasn't feeling any inclination to be fair. She wanted to lash out.

After they left, the day after Boxing Day, a quiet descended on the front room, a quiet such that the ticking of the clock on the bookshelf could be heard. Eventually Jane could stand it no longer.

"That went quite well, don't you think? They did their best, both of them."

Jim smiled. "It was wonderful to see them. It was a beautiful thing. I wish… I wish…" He faltered and his voice broke.

"Oh Jim. What love? Tell me," implored Jane.

"I won't ever see Lucy's child. Our grandchild. I…" He broke down and Jane rushed over to him, holding his hand and drawing his head to her breast.

"I'm sorry, I'm sorry, it's just that…" The sobs came thick and fast.

"Ssh. Ssh. It's all right, Jim. It's okay."

Later that night, when Jim was upstairs asleep, held securely in the arms of morphine, she stared into the dying embers of the log fire. The lights were off and the flames reflected in the glitter and baubles on the Christmas tree in the corner. The familiar smell of woodsmoke and pine needles was an agonising comfort to her. She knew what she would have to do in January when school started again and she would do it, whatever the cost.

16

THE FIRST DAY BACK AFTER CHRISTMAS WAS BRIGHT AND crisp, and thankfully, pupil-free. As usual, a training day had been organised, ostensibly to launch the first day of the new academy, but in reality, its main purpose was to give staff time to shake off the cobwebs from their holiday heads and get psychologically prepared for the new year.

When Jane, arriving early, walked through the foyer to her office, she passed the relics of Christmas still clinging to the fabric of the building. A stray ribbon of tinsel hung from the doorway to the main entrance. In reception, the twelve-inch fibre-optic Christmas tree caught the eye, next to an unopened packet of mince pies. She let herself into her office, and the chill of a building unused for the previous two weeks sent a shiver down her spine. It was compounded by the array of Christmas cards, still up and on display, and the small pile of cards received at the end of the very last day of term, still unopened. There was nothing more poignant than last year's Christmas trappings that served as reminders of the passage of time, of jolly times gone for ever. This January, more than ever, it was the very last thing she needed.

She swept the cards down and dumped them, and the unopened ones, straight into the bin. First things first. She fired up her computer, got the coffee machine going, and looked at her diary for the day. She had the opening staff meeting first thing, after the free breakfast that was the only thing that passed for a perk on these days. Then a meeting with Avril and Rick before the full Senior Team meeting. Later in the afternoon, Alastair Goodall was coming in, partly to address the staff, like the opening of Parliament, on this historic day and partly, at her request, for a meeting with her. He'd messaged her in the holidays after she had made the request, to let her know that Barry Pugh, the new Director of Learning, would be there. He hadn't taken up his post yet but was familiarising himself with the school and the staff. It wasn't perfect by any means, and it certainly wasn't what she had been planning, but it would have to do. She didn't have time to reschedule. It had to be done today.

She was deep in thought, going over what she would say to Alastair later, when a knock on the office door brought her sharply back to the present. She looked up.

"Hi there, Happy New Year and all of that."

Rick's broadly-smiling face greeted her.

"Hi Rick," she replied, "Happy New Year to you as well. How was your Christmas? Jo and the kids all well?"

"Yeah, yeah, great thanks. Yeah, we had a lovely time. Hey what about that news? Amazing, wasn't it?"

This was met with a blank look from Jane.

"News? What news? What are you talking about?"

There was a pause and Rick's smile broadened as he waited for her to announce the joke. Instead she looked both puzzled and pained.

"God, you're serious, aren't you? Where the hell have you been all holiday? Did you deliberately go off grid to get away from it all? I can't believe you don't know."

"Well, yeah, it was that kind of holiday actually. We just spent time on our own away from the world. We, er… needed a rest. So, come on, put me out of my misery. What's the big news?"

"The New Year's honours list. Camilla Everson, of all people, got a CBE. For services to education."

*

"And so, I'll finish this speech as I started it, by saying that I personally, along with the whole Trust, am incredibly excited that Fairfield has joined our family of schools. For us, today marks an exciting new chapter in our development. From the very first discussions with Jane it was obvious to me that the Trust and the school share the same values of inclusivity and the same belief in trusting the staff, putting children first, and playing an active role in the community. I'd like to pay tribute at this point to Jane, her Senior Team and the whole school staff for all of the work you have done, in sometimes difficult circumstances, over the last few years. We hope to provide the support you need to continue to do that work and improve it. We certainly have no intention of interfering with the way the school runs. We think that it's in very safe hands and see our role as one of support, not interference."

He paused to take a sip of water from the glass on the lectern.

On the back row Kevin turned to Charlotte and whispered, "Bloody hell, he's learned the script off by heart. In the movie, he'll be played by Tom Hanks."

"I'm impressed actually," said Charlotte. "He's been very convincing."

"Come on, Charlotte, Christmas is over. You'll be telling me you believe in Santa Claus next."

He didn't get a chance to find out the answer as the end of Goodall's speech was signalled by thunderous applause. Evidently, everyone in the audience was willing to believe in Santa Claus, at least for the time being.

As with all training days, the building emptied at 3 pm with the speed of a well-practised fire drill. Having gently broken the psychological barrier of going back to work without any children to deal with, everyone was exhausted. An early finish, a lie down on the sofa, a cup of tea and the paper were all required to repair the damage done by the shock of work.

Jane had gently but firmly suggested to the rest of the Senior Team that they all left early as well, on the grounds of looking after her staff and actively implementing work-life balance. Most of them didn't need telling twice. Gordon did a double take, as if the thought of staying beyond 3 pm had never occurred to him. He had the presence of mind to catch on in time to frown and look terribly disappointed that he wouldn't be able to stay working until six.

Jane, of course, had an entirely different motive for dispatching her senior colleagues. She needed to make sure that she could have her meeting with Alastair with no-one else around. She had been building herself up to this all day, rehearsing lines, going through different scenarios. Once or twice she had wobbled in the course of the day, but each time she thought of Jim and their Christmas holiday and her resolve strengthened.

There was a knock at the open office door.

"Hello, Jane. Are you ready for us?" Alastair filled the doorway, with a second figure half-hidden behind him.

"Alastair, yes of course. Come in, please. Let me get us some coffee." She shouted beyond them to the corridor. "Lisa. Can you get those coffee things, please?"

She gestured for Alastair to come in. As he did so, the figure behind him followed.

"I'm not sure if you've met Barry before, Jane. This is Barry Pugh, our new Director of Learning. Barry, this is Jane Garner."

Barry came forward with hand outstretched.

"Hello, Jane. Nice to meet you at last."

"Hello, Barry," she replied, shaking his hand. She glanced at Alastair. "No, we've not met before, but I've heard a lot about you."

A momentary look of panic flashed across Barry's face before he gathered himself into an oily smile.

"All good, I hope."

"Oh yes, of course," said Jane. She noticed his cuffs came about halfway down his hands and that he was holding tight to a clipboard in his left hand. Jane was on the verge of saying, "I've heard a lot about your clipboard," but checked herself just in time.

"Come in, come in. Come and have a seat and let's get started." She gestured to the meeting table at one end of the office.

"Well, the speech went very well I think, Alastair." She thought it wise to open with a compliment.

"Do you think so?" asked Alastair. "I'm pleased. The staff seemed to appreciate it, at any rate."

"Yes, they have been rather worried. Academy take-overs have a bad reputation amongst teachers. It was important to get off to a good start and I think they were pleased to hear your commitment to inclusion and to letting us run the school as we've always done."

"Well," interjected Barry, "perhaps not exactly as you've always done. After all, you want to improve, don't you?"

He mentally ticked off a box on the spreadsheet on the clipboard. He wanted to signal to both Alastair and to Jane that he was someone to be reckoned with. The trouble was, in this schmoozing phase that Alastair was engaged in, it was so difficult to second guess exactly what Alastair actually wanted.

There was a knock on the door, and Lisa entered with a tray of coffee and biscuits.

"Thanks, Lisa. Can you just put them down here, please? And then you can go. I'll see you tomorrow."

The ritual of dishing out coffee allowed her to ignore what she considered the rather crass intervention of Barry Pugh, who clearly was just as much of a puffed-up idiot as Rick and Avril had said. She decided that she should plunge straight in.

"Alastair, before we go any further, I need to talk to you about something. It's something you need to know about. It's awkward, as this is day one of a new regime, but I've got no control over the timing."

Both Alastair and Barry sat forward in their seats.

"Go on Jane, what is it?"

She took a sip of her coffee, her stomach churning. She wished that Pugh wasn't there. It just seemed to make things harder somehow. The pause continued as she struggled with her emotions.

Alastair softened his voice. "What is it, Jane? There's obviously something the matter."

"It's my husband, Jim." She paused again.

"Yes? What about him, Jane?" His softened tone was accompanied by a look of Mother Theresa-scale compassion.

"It's hard to talk about. I haven't discussed this with anyone else. Jim was diagnosed with cancer before Christmas. Quite a while before Christmas actually. But before the end of term they confirmed the treatment hadn't worked and that the cancer was terminal."

"I'm very sorry to hear that news, Jane," said Alastair. "That's a terrible thing to cope with."

Barry was silent and petrified. He was a long way out of his comfort zone. His spreadsheet had no box to tick for responding to personal tragedy or terminal illness.

"The thing is," Jane continued, "the illness has progressed very rapidly. It was not a good Christmas. He does not have long left. I've decided that I need to take some time off to care for him at home."

"Time off?" repeated Alastair, only just holding on to his compassionate persona. "What do you mean, time off? How much time off?"

"Two months." She gulped and her eyes started to sting. She had never said it out loud before. It somehow seemed to make it more real to her. "Perhaps three. Rick is more than ready to act up as headteacher temporarily. It'll be very good for him. And he knows the school inside out. I know it's not perfect timing, in terms of the run-up to the exams, and I know our results this year are even more important than ever, but I don't feel that I have a choice. Jim deserves this from me."

"Does Rick know anything about this? Or Avril?" Alastair's reptilian brain, behind the mask of concern, had at last clicked into gear.

"No. No-one knows about it. I've kept it to myself. It's a relief to talk about it, actually."

"Jane, you have my deepest sympathy, you really have, and that of the Academy Trust as a whole, but this puts us in a very awkward position."

"What do you mean? I think I've proposed a simple solution."

"I'm sorry, this is not a request we can just grant. We can't set a precedent and we can't treat you any differently to any of our other staff. Right at the beginning of this new relationship, it's vital that we have a smooth undisturbed start, to create confidence."

"So you're refusing my request? What's your solution, then? How can I fulfil my responsibilities to the children with the worry of a dying husband at home who will shortly need full-time personal care?" Her voice had started to rise and harden.

"Well, Jane, that's really not the responsibility of Bellingford Trust, now is it? There are lots of options. Macmillan nurses can provide palliative home care. Many people are in this position without having to have time off."

Jane looked from Alastair to Barry and back to Alastair again. Barry squirmed uncomfortably in his chair. She shook her head.

"I see. And this is the caring compassionate, people-centred inclusive fucking Academy Trust you've just been talking about to the staff? You bloody hypocrite. This whole thing is one big con."

"Jane, calm down. Really, you can't use that kind of language in a meeting. We have a code of conduct for that sort of thing."

Jane exploded. "Code of conduct! You can take your code of conduct and shove it up your arse. I don't believe you people."

Barry was roused into action. He'd heard enough to know from Alastair's approach that he could go with his instincts and be punitive rather than fluffy and caring.

"Jane, really. Don't be so selfish. Where is your sense of moral purpose to the children?"

There was a terrible silence in the room. She stared at him. All of the years of her professional life she had dedicated to these children and families in the most difficult of circumstances, all of the time she had instinctively acted as a compassionate employer when her staff came to her with genuine news of tragic situations, all of the occasions her own family had missed out because she was compelled, ethically, to go the extra mile for those in her care, did these count for nothing?

"My sense of what?"

"Your sense of moral purpose. These children have been let down for too long."

She couldn't take any more. The years of sacrifice and lack of support and late nights and constant criticism had hollowed her out. Finally, spectacularly, the building collapsed around her.

She screamed, "My sense of moral bloody purpose? Here's my sense of moral bloody purpose, you useless wanker." Reaching for the vase of flowers in the middle of the table, she grabbed it and threw the contents all over Barry Pugh. He recoiled, blinking, tulips and freesias in his hair and on his lap, foul-smelling water dripping down his face into his mouth. He spat it out and wiped a hand across his face as he sprang out of his chair.

"Now get out of my bloody office." She grabbed him by both arms and pushed him, with reservoirs of unknown strength, out of the office into the corridor, where he stood dripping, mouth open.

Alastair, having observed all of this with an icy calm, managing to suppress a smirk of satisfaction, was already on his feet, walking out of the office to join a hyperventilating Barry.

"Jane, that was an unfortunate mistake. I'll see you here first thing in the morning. I think you know what you've done."

"Yes, I do and you can fuck off as well," she screamed and she moved threateningly towards him.

Alastair, taking Barry firmly by the arm, ushered him out of the corridor, through the foyer and into the car park to their cars, leaving a trail of freesias and tulips behind them. They both stood between the cars, Barry still in a state of shock.

He finally managed to gasp, "What the hell is wrong with her? Has she gone mad?"

Alastair smiled, "Mad enough, at any rate. Well done though, Barry, you played a blinder in there."

Barry was thoroughly confused. He hadn't really done anything but nonetheless, it was very gratifying to have the praise of his new boss.

"What will happen now?" he asked.

"Leave that to me. Barry, you've done your bit. Now it's my turn. I'll be in touch."

Alastair got into his Mercedes and reached for his mobile. While he waited for a connection he was soothed by the leather seats and the luxury of it. He watched through the window as Barry climbed into his car and drove off. His call was answered.

"Alastair, how did it go?"

"Perfect, Andrew, just perfect. Barry really is an idiot, isn't he? He's got the sensitivity and people skills of a rugby scrum. Which was just what was needed. Not that he knows anything about it, mind you. She went crazy and attacked him."

There was an explosion of laughter at the other end.

"She attacked him? Good God, sounds like *EastEnders*."

"It was. Anyway, she doesn't know this yet but she'll be suspended tomorrow first thing. And then we'll move with Rick. I'll let you know what happens." He ended the call, enjoyed the throaty roar of the engine and pulled away and out of the car park.

Barry, in his car, was elated with the way things had turned out, though he was still a little confused. He stopped at a traffic light and looked down at the passenger seat. His clipboard and spreadsheet, covered in water from the vase, was ruined. Why could nothing ever end perfectly?

Jane, alone in her office, surveyed the wreckage. A cup of coffee had overturned and there was a spreading stain on the carpet in front of her desk. The floor was strewn with flowers. She sat at the table and picked up a chocolate biscuit from the plate. It was sodden, the plate awash.

She put the biscuit back and, watching it disintegrate in the puddle, wept. She sobbed until she had no tears left to cry.

17

AVRIL'S CAR PULLED IN TO THE CAR PARK THE NEXT morning just as Rick was getting out of his. He waited for her to come over.

"Did she call you last night as well?" Rick asked.

"Yeah, I can't believe what's been going on. Why didn't she tell us about Jim? Must have been hell for her keeping all of that to herself."

"Did you hear what she did to little Bazzer Pugh?"

"I know. If it wasn't so serious, it'd be hilarious."

"Yeah, it is serious, isn't it? Otherwise, why would she ask us to come in and meet her at this ungodly hour?"

"It's all right for you, you've got young kids, this is normal for you. I haven't been out of the house by this hour for years. I'm not conscious until nine in the morning, even if I'm booted and suited."

"Well come on, now we're here, we might as well go and find out what's going on."

They walked towards the entrance, their shoes crunching against the thick hoar frost that had been laid down in the night. It was still dark and the street lights and school sign lit the path to the entrance with diamonds of glitter on the frosty surface. Jane was in the foyer to meet them. She was wearing an outfit that neither of them had seen her in before and she looked strangely polished, like a stock photograph of a female executive from the internet.

"Morning. Thanks for coming in so early."

"No problem, Jane, you know that. Is that a new outfit you're wearing? I haven't seen you in that before."

"Well spotted, Avril. It's my equivalent of wearing my best frock before facing Madame Guillotine. Anyway, come through and have some coffee, you must be freezing."

When they were all sitting down, around the same table that she, Pugh and Goodall had occupied just the evening before, Jane began.

"Look, I'll cut to the chase because we haven't much time. I'm expecting the execution party to arrive soon."

"The execution party? Jane, what exactly is going on?"

"It's pretty obvious that I'm going to be suspended for what happened at the meeting I had with them last night. Thinking about it, I wouldn't be at all surprised if Goodall had engineered the whole thing. I was upset and I lashed out and I've given them the perfect excuse to get rid of me. Anyway, all that's beside the point. I've thought about it a lot and given the circumstances, it's not such a bad result. I need to be at home to look after Jim, and I don't think I want to work for Goodall and his Trust. I don't trust him an inch. And I can screw as much money out of them as I can."

"But can't you fight it? You can't just go like that. It's just not fair. And the thing with Jim, Jane. Why didn't you tell us about that? You needed support to see you through this."

"No Avril, really. I appreciate what you're saying, but I didn't want to give you both that burden as well as everything else. I'm fine with this, honestly. It's time to go. And you can't fight things like this, they go on all the time. The unions are useless. The academies have all the cards. So listen, this is important. They will arrive before too long, with their HR officer in tow. They'll take me through a formal procedure, and you can bet your life they will do it by the book. I don't think Alastair Goodall will make the schoolboy error of getting caught out procedurally. I will be asked to empty my desk, hand over my keys and leave. They will almost certainly say that a condition of this is that I cannot compromise any investigation by being in touch with anyone. Anyone at all. And they'll say the same thing to all of the staff. That's why this meeting is important. It's going to be the last time for a while that I will be able to talk to you about all of this."

"What?" exclaimed Rick. "How are they allowed to do that? That can't be right, it's treating you as if you were guilty."

"Employment and contract law, that's how. But shush and let me talk. Goodall will want you, Rick, to take over on an acting basis. I know that you, Avril, are the more senior, but he'll want someone younger and someone who he has worked with through the Partnership."

"I wouldn't want it anyway," protested Avril. "We need someone with more energy than me."

"But how can I take it? It would be like stabbing you in the back." Rick shook his head, aghast.

"That's exactly what you've not got to do, to think you're letting me down. It's the other way around. It's essential that you take the job and blow them away with how good you are. It's vital for the school, for the kids and the staff, that you get the job permanently. If it goes to one of their faceless automatons, someone like little Barry Pugh, the school is finished. They have no idea how hard it is to keep this school going and they are so arrogant, they think that we've been getting it all wrong for all of these years and they are just going to breeze in, kick ass and everything will be fine. There will be some satisfaction in watching that go horribly wrong from afar. But not enough."

"I'm sorry, it just seems all wrong, that's all," said Rick.

"It is all wrong," agreed Jane, "but there's nothing we can do about that. This is a big opportunity for you, Rick, and I'm glad that at least some good might come out of it. Avril, you need to know that they'll be gunning for you next and probably most of the Senior

Team and the heads of english, maths and science, eventually. These people are brutal."

"Why will they want me out?" asked Avril, puzzled. "I haven't been that bad, have I?"

"Avril, you've been brilliant, but you don't fit the template for what senior managers should be like, in their eyes. You're old school, and they haven't the imagination to see that that might be better. But what I need you to promise me, both of you, is that you won't do anything foolish. Don't, whatever you do, argue with them, or slag them off about the way they've treated me, or gossip to the staff. They'll chop you off at the legs if you do that. Keep your head down, do what they want and play along. You need to play a longer game. And you, Avril, need to string this out for a couple more years for your pension. Change the habits of a lifetime, and for once put yourself first."

Suddenly, there was the sound of several cars pulling up outside Jane's office. She got up and looked out of the window.

"They're here. They must want it all done before there are staff and students around. Remember what I said. And thanks for everything in the last few years. When this is all done, we'll meet up for a drink and debrief. Now, you go and meet them in the foyer and be polite."

They both came over to her and gave her a kiss and a hug and then left to meet the Horsemen of the Apocalypse in the foyer. And there were four of them. They swooped into the entrance, Alastair at the front, followed by Barry and two others they did not know.

He extended his hand and shook hands firmly with Rick. As an afterthought he did the same with Avril. "Morning Rick, Avril. I need you to both be available in your office in half an hour. You'll need to call a staff meeting for after school today. Don't release any details yet."

Rick nodded, and the four visitors breezed through the foyer to Jane's office. Twenty minutes later the two unidentified Horsemen accompanied Jane to her car and saw her off the premises. She never stepped foot in the school again.

18

Karim looked again at the crumpled letter that he kept in his bedside drawer alongside the treasured photograph of his family. He traced the words with his finger and read aloud, stumbling occasionally.

"We are pleased to inform you that you have been allocated a place at the Language Unit based at Fairfield High School. Your first day in this placement is Monday January 17th and the placement will last for two terms, finishing on July 21st. You should report to the unit at 10 am with your support worker, Mr Ahmed Hussain. It is not necessary to wear school uniform, as the unit is officially not part of Fairfield High School. You should ensure you have the necessary equipment for learning."

He was nervous. Ahmed had tried to reassure him that there were many other young people there who were refugees and whose English was at an early stage, but still he found it difficult to believe, after all he had been through, that there were people who were going to try to help him. On his long journey from Syria he had experienced many acts of random kindness from strangers, but more often hostility, and anger. If there was one thing he had learned, it was that hatred for foreigners in general and Muslims in particular was the norm in Europe. The everyday kindness of Joan and Eric was beyond mere gratitude. He wept when he thought for too long about it, struggling to grasp the boundless compassion of two people who had no idea who he was, and had no connection to him beyond their common humanity.

His finger went back to the page, tracing the same line over and over again. "You should ensure you have the necessary equipment for learning." The sentence thrilled him. The necessary equipment for learning. A world where survival did not fill up all of the available space of his waking hours seemed a kind of paradise to him, and he was determined to make the most of it.

"Karim," Eric shouted from downstairs, "Ahmed is here. Time to go."

An hour and two buses later Ahmed and Karim arrived at the locked gates of Fairfield High School and pressed the security buzzer. As they were waiting for an answer Karim caught sight of a huge, shaven-headed boy who was skulking on the corner, half hidden by a tree. He furtively poked his head around the tree, keeping a weather eye on the gates where Karim and Ahmed were waiting. As he did so he sucked intently on the spliff that he was trying to conceal in his hand. In his other hand he had a can of lager. He drained the dregs from the can and crushed it on the tree trunk, took a final drag on the spliff which he then pinched between finger and thumb and secreted in the pocket of his hoodie, presumably for later. Satisfied with his preparations for school, he wandered from behind the tree towards the gate. At that moment a car parked on the opposite side of the road started up, its engine revved for all it was worth. The protesting noise of the engine could not compete, however, with the thumping bass of the in-car sound system that cranked up at the same time. As the car pulled level with the school entrance, the front window wound down and a hooded head poked out, shouting, "Laters, yeah fam? Go and kill them exams, man."

Delighted with his own wit, the driver snickered. Spliff boy shouted back, "Got bear revision to do man. It's so dead. See you later, yeah?" The car roared away, the bass insistent but fading into the dust cloud.

Ahmed and Karim watched all of this unfold as they waited for an answer from the intercom. Spliff boy strolled up, and as he stopped next to them, he let fly a theatrical belch. His face was round and very red, with golden stubble all over his head. His eyes, red and bloodshot, added to the porcine appearance. He wore a grubby white shirt under his blazer and a school tie with an enormous knot that hung loose a couple of inches below the open neck of his shirt. His neck was of such a prodigious girth that any attempt to do up the top button was doomed to failure and even the most persistent and hawkish teachers had long since given up trying. His bulging neck was covered in tattoos.

"You trying to get in?" he asked, to neither of them in particular.

"Yes," replied Ahmed. "I rang the buzzer and spoke to the receptionist but then nothing happened."

Spliff boy looked both of them up and down. "What do you want?"

"Karim is starting here today," said Ahmed.

"Don't he speak?" demanded Spliff boy. "What's wrong with 'im?"

Ahmed was feeling increasingly uncomfortable. He had seen situations like this develop before and knew he had to be calm and polite.

"He is coming here to learn English. He doesn't speak much English at the moment."

Comprehension dawned on Spliff boy's face. "Oh, is he going unit then, the Language Unit?"

Ahmed smiled. "Yes, the Language Unit, that's right."

"Full of fucking foreigners that unit. Refugees, asylum seekers, terrorists, the lot. What the fuck are they doing here? They should fucking go back to their own country. Where's he from anyway?" he said, nodding his head at Karim, who stood eyes down and silent.

"Syria. We are both from Syria."

Spliff boy spat on the floor, an inch away from Karim's foot. He shook his head. "Fucking Syria? They are the worst of the lot. Is he in ISIS? Is he a terrorist pretending to be a refugee? Or is he just a cunt?"

"Please," said Ahmed, "We would just like to go into the school."

Spliff boy jabbed his finger on the intercom button. From a far universe a voice crackled. "Fairfield High School, how can I help you?"

"It's George. I'm outside with two terrorists. We wanna come in, can you open the gate?"

The voice crackled again. "You're with what?"

"Can you just let me in, please, you're interrupting my education."

"Er… just wait a minute, George. Mr Westfield is on his way out."

"No, no, no, no, no, just open the gate." There was a note of panic in George's voice and when the gate did not buzz to open, he began rattling the bars furiously.

"Open the fucking gate, man, come on."

After another thirty seconds the buzzer sounded and George pressed against the gate. It swung open. Ahmed and Karim followed him in. George looked down the path towards the main entrance. Already striding down the path towards them was Rick. He did not have the walk of a man at peace with the world.

"Oh, fuck," muttered George. He turned back to Ahmed and Karim, who were a few paces behind him. Ahmed was doing his best to reassure Karim that all would be well, but he did not look convinced.

"Oi," he said, in their general direction. They both looked up.

"This is your fucking fault, you Paki cunt. You don't say a fucking word, otherwise you're dead, understand. You'll fucking wish you were back in Syria with a bomb up your arse."

Karim couldn't understand him. He spoke too quickly and Karim didn't understand the slang. He picked up the general thrust of it though. In the last year he had learned to recognise hostility in several different languages. Ahmed, however, understood him only too well. There was a point where, when meekness had failed, it had to be abandoned. He stood tall and took a step towards George, his mouth set in a straight line.

"Don't threaten us, please. We have done nothing to you."

George was completely taken aback. Within the school premises, no-one had ever answered him back, including for the past two years, many of the teachers. His mouth fell agape as he tried to process what had just happened.

"George! What on earth are you playing at? Get yourself down here immediately." Rick's booming voice cut through George's confusion. He turned, head bowed, and walked down to meet Rick half way.

"Well? What the hell is going on? What time do you call this for a start? You're an hour and a half late for school."

"Sorry sir, I missed the bus," he mumbled.

"And I hope you have welcomed our guests to the school," Rick continued, ignoring George's excuse as not even being worthy of comment. He nodded behind him towards Ahmed and Karim. As George turned to look in that direction, Rick sniffed the air and exploded. "Have you been smoking weed, George? Well?"

"No, sir, I…"

"Don't bother to deny it, lad, you stink of it. When will you ever learn? Get yourself down to my office and wait for me outside."

George trudged off towards the school entrance.

"And George?"

He turned. "Sir?"

"Don't go anywhere else. Not to the canteen, not to the toilet, nowhere. Understand?"

"Sir."

George continued down the path, like a condemned man walking to the scaffold.

"Shit," he thought, "why did it have to be fucking Westfield? He's gonna search me, I know he is." He fumbled in his pocket for the remains of his breakfast spliff. When he quickly looked behind him, he saw Rick in conversation with the two visitors, shaking both of their hands, and he took the opportunity to jettison the spliff in the bushes by the side of the path.

When Rick got to his office, Ahmed and Karim in tow, George was sitting meekly in a chair outside. As he showed them into his office he turned to George and wagged a finger at him.

"You, don't move. I'll deal with you in about fifteen minutes. Understand?"

"Sir, I haven't done anything. It's not fair, sir."

Rick sighed. "George, you are not an unintelligent boy. Use your brain power in the next fifteen minutes to think about what might be the best way to make this better for yourself."

Rick popped his head into Lisa's office.

"Lisa, get hold of Avril and the senior person on duty. I need a bag search of our friend George here. And he needs to be sitting where he is now in about fifteen minutes, when I'll be ready for him, okay?"

He went back into his office, closed the door and walked over to Ahmed and Karim, who were sitting at the round table.

"So, where were we? Yes, I'm very sorry about George, he is one of our more challenging students. What exactly happened?"

"I'm sorry to have to tell you, Mr Westfield, that he was extremely aggressive and racist towards us while we were waiting outside. And he was standing outside the school drinking beer and smoking marijuana. It was not a good advert for the school."

Rick was horror-struck. "Once again, Mr Hussain, I can only apologise."

Ahmed looked doubtful. "Mr Westfield, I am not sure that it's a good idea for us to proceed with the placement. Karim has been through an awful lot. He is only just beginning to recover and make progress. He was worried about coming in the first place today and he was rather shaken up by the incident outside the school."

"Mr Hussain, let me reassure you. The unit is completely separate from the school. They have different hours, different break times and lunchtimes. There's no need for Karim to come across George or anyone else for that matter. Towards the end of the placement students can be integrated temporarily into mainstream classes, but that would only be if Karim was comfortable with that."

Karim interrupted. "And who is in the unit, please?"

Rick was amazed and his face gave him away.

"Karim has a good understanding of English, though obviously he has a lot to learn," explained Ahmed.

"Yes, of course, it's just that I thought he wasn't able to speak at all," explained Rick.

"That was the case when he first arrived but he has made a lot of progress. He is a highly intelligent boy."

Rick turned his attention back to Karim. "There are six or seven students currently in the unit at present. An Afghani, a Libyan, and several from Eastern Europe. The other thing you need to understand is that the vast majority of our students are not like George. We are a very harmonious community with students from all kinds of backgrounds, races and religions. We don't tolerate any kind of racism or bullying or discrimination of any kind."

Karim looked across to Ahmed, who translated for him. Karim added a further question to Ahmed.

"What will happen to George?" Ahmed enquired.

"We'll investigate and there will be an appropriate sanction if we find he has broken our code of conduct."

"I do not want to cause any trouble," said Karim.

"Karim, there won't be any trouble, that I can promise you. This is a school that looks after people."

Karim thought for a moment, then looked across to Ahmed and nodded.

Rick personally delivered Ahmed and Karim to the unit. Before he left to go back to his office to deal with George, he looked through the window. Karim was sitting at a table next to Naseefa with a pen in his hand, shy smiles beginning on their faces. He nodded with satisfaction before striding off. "Now for George," he muttered.

19

EVERYTHING RICK TOUCHED FROM JANUARY ONWARDS turned to gold. Having excluded George Mason for five days following the incident with Karim and Ahmed, he followed it up with a series of high-profile exclusions of students that had been the bane of all but the most formidable of teachers for the previous few years.

By the time they reached the last half term of summer, at the beginning of June, there was a tangible air of optimism and confidence in the air. One evening early in June, Rick was working late in his office. There was a tentative knock on the open door. Rick looked up.

"Hi Avril. You still here?"

"Yeah, I've just been going through the stuff for new staff induction. Have you got a minute?"

"Yeah, of course. Come in and shut the door."

He got up from his computer and joined her at the table.

"So, what's up?"

She looked around the room. "You've changed the way Jane used to have it in here, haven't you? Different pictures or something."

"Well, yeah. I suppose I wanted to make a point about it being mine, certainly after they announced her early retirement." He suddenly looked worried. "That's all right, isn't it?"

Avril was surprised. "All right? Yeah, of course it's all right. You can do what you want."

"Yeah, I know, but I just meant, it's not presumptuous is it? I still feel bad about what happened to Jane. Have you heard from her at all?"

"I contacted her when Jim died. She has good days and bad days. You know they made her sign a confidentiality agreement? Her lump sum, that was part of the settlement, is dependent on her not talking about the agreement or even saying it exists."

"Bloody hell! Can they do that? Doesn't sound right somehow."

"Yeah, it's all above board legally. They do it all the time apparently. Just stinks morally. She was saying she'd like us all to meet up after they've confirmed your appointment, right at the end of term maybe."

"Yeah, that would be nice. We've got a lot to talk about."

"Speaking of which, a little bird told me that Camilla Everson has left Coldewater."

"What? You're joking. When did that happen?"

"Just before half-term. And you hadn't heard?"

"No, not a whisper."

"Yeah, I thought so. They're really trying hard to keep it under wraps."

"Well, do you know why? What's going on?"

"There are rumours about a government role. She's caught the eye of Grovelle, apparently. He needs a pretty face to give his Great Education Reform Bill some headwind."

Rick shook his head. "My God. Well, they just about deserve each other those two. If she keeps going at this rate she'll be Holy Roman Emperor by Christmas."

Avril smiled. "Unless you get there first, of course."

Rick frowned. "Sorry, I don't get you."

"Rick, you must know that since January you've done an outstanding job."

He looked a little embarrassed. "Really? Well, I thought I'd done all right. It's hard to tell sometimes when you're so close to it."

"You're a natural. It comes so easily to you, you don't even know how good you are. All the consultation and involving people and listening to them that you just take for granted as the proper way to do the job, well most Heads just pay lip service to all of that. You just do it instinctively."

"Thanks Avril, I really appreciate you saying all of that, it means a lot."

"Nobody on the staff will ever tell you you're good, it's just not done. And you know with me, because I'm getting close to the end, that I don't need to butter you up."

"You're going to stay on for a while then?"

"Yeah, I think we can do great things together in the next couple of years. I really feel that the school's on the verge of going places. I'd like to finish my career that way. It's amazing really. Back in January when Jane was stabbed in the back, I never thought I'd be looking forward to the next few years. I thought it was the end. I feel kind of revitalised, you know. And I'm so proud of the work we've done with that young Syrian boy, Karim. It reminds me why I came into the job."

"He's done really well, hasn't he? His support worker is amazed, but he is a very clever boy. Just the kind of kid we want to keep permanently. I think he's going to be integrated into a few lessons from next week, just to give him a taste of it."

"After all he's been through it's the least he deserves. That's why it's important that you're in charge. There's a lot of Heads who wouldn't have touched him with a barge pole."

"Don't count your chickens, Avril, I haven't got the job yet. This might all be for nothing."

"You'll be fine, believe me, they're not that stupid. Have you heard when the interviews are going to be?"

"Yeah, I just found out that they're scheduled for second week before the summer holidays."

"Well, there you go then. It's obviously got your name on it. Jobs advertised that late always get a second division field. All the good candidates have already been snapped up. It's a classic trick if you want to appoint a favoured internal candidate but you still have to advertise nationally. If I were you, I'd book that expensive summer holiday of a lifetime and start spending your massive new salary."

"Yeah, maybe, but actually my current priority is to finish all of this paperwork for the Governors' meeting tomorrow."

"Okay, I get the message." Avril stood up to leave. "Don't stay too long, though, you need to pace yourself."

"That's what Jo said to me only last night. I won't be long. See you tomorrow. And thanks for the chat. It helps to talk about it."

"No problem. Good night." Avril closed the door as she left.

Rick went back to his computer and called up the document he had been working on. He stared at it blankly for a minute or so, rubbing his eyes with both hands. He was tired and his mind was empty. Finally, he switched to the internet and called up his Google homepage, typing in 'Villa holidays in Barbados'.

20

KARIM STOOD IN THE ENGLISH CORRIDOR OF THE MAIN
building, his eyes flicking left and right, just outside a classroom
marked 'E10'. There were a few stragglers left in the corridor, serial
dawdlers who always rolled into lessons at least ten minutes late,
pursued by the senior member of staff on duty, who patrolled the
corridors ushering the flotsam and jetsam into classes like border
collies herding sheep. The majority of students, however, were in
lessons and a strange quiet had descended.

Ahmed tried to reassure him. "Karim, they are expecting us, it
has all been arranged. There will be a seat for the two of us. This is
the top set, so there will be no bad behaviour. I will be with you for
the first few lessons."

"What if I don't understand it all? I don't want to look
stupid."

"Karim, of course you won't understand it all. Don't be too hard
on yourself. Do your best and we'll see how it goes. All right? Come
on, we have to go in now."

He put his hand on Karim's shoulder and steered him towards the door, pushing it open so that Karim could go first. As they entered, the buzz of a classroom full of students discussing work suddenly quietened and everyone stared at the two newcomers. Karim and Ahmed scanned the room, searching in vain for the teacher to introduce themselves. From the far corner of the room, a diminutive figure stood up from where she had been steering the discussion of a group, and came forward, smiling broadly.

"Ah, hello, we were wondering where you had got to. Welcome to 10Y1. You must be Karim, and Mr Hussain, is it?"

"Yes, that's right," said Ahmed.

"I'm Miss Hartley," the tiny figure announced. "If you'd like to join the group over there, I've left two spaces for you. The group will explain what's going on. I'll come over and check in a minute once you've got settled. We're just starting *Macbeth* and the group are discussing what they think are the characteristics of brutal dictators."

Ahmed and Karim exchanged a look. This was an area they both had some expertise in. They went over to the table and sat down.

*

Alastair took a sip of his double espresso and checked his Rolex. He still had fifteen minutes before his meeting was due to begin. Good, just enough time to check emails and firm up the meeting with the Surrey headteachers next week. This time next year, if everything went to plan, the Bellingford MAT would have grown to about twenty schools, and with the obvious economies of scale they could really start to rack up a profit. Then there would be a clear role for Andrew Harrison, who had been rather irritating in the last six weeks, hassling him rather too frequently about a job. He would also by then probably be able to get rid of Barry Pugh, who would have served his purpose. He could barely cope with looking after five schools and giving him any more would be positively cruel. He made so many mistakes it wouldn't be too difficult to arrange a pretext for dismissal. A disciplinary, perhaps, leading to a settlement and a confidentiality agreement. The idea of a pay-out irked him somewhat when it came to Pugh, but he dismissed that as overly emotional. On any rational analysis it was a price worth paying and it was a tactic that had served him well in the past. And he could probably get it down to a meagre sum, given what he knew about the disciplinary at Barry's last school, the one that, conveniently, never actually went ahead. If he played it right, Pugh would probably want to pay them to avoid the scandal! What was that phrase again? 'Information is power'. Yes, that was it.

He smiled and looked around the tables of the coffee shop, full of the trendy, fully networked and integrated movers and shakers of the digital age, tapping away at tablets, white earbuds dangling. It was the perfect place to meet before a meeting in Central London. It had all the trappings of an independent outlet: roughly-stripped wood, industrial metal, exposed brick walls, sourdough and exotic grains and juices; what few people realised, however, was that it was owned by McDonalds. He surveyed the hipsters again, with a growing sense of satisfaction and of his own value. He almost wanted to hug himself. *Information is power*, he thought, *information is power*.

"You look very pleased with yourself." A woman's voice, playful in its tone, interrupted his thoughts.

Damn, Alastair cursed silently. He hated giving himself away, hated not seeing the other person arrive, hated being on the back foot from the beginning.

"Hi Camilla, how are you?"

He rose from his seat and they exchanged two air kisses.

"I'm good, thank you, Alastair, and you?"

"Yes, very well. Everything is going swimmingly. Anyway, what would you like?"

"Oh, just a soya flat white for me please."

She surveyed him as he went to the counter. Was that an Armani suit he was wearing? And, more importantly, what was this meeting about? What was he trying to get out of her?

He came back with her coffee and sat down.

"So, Camilla, let's cut to the chase. I've got a meeting at the House in an hour."

She looked impressed. "At the House of Commons? Who with?"

"Grovelle, actually. We're working on something. It's part of his Great Reform Bill."

"Really? Well, I never. Give my regards to Marcus, won't you?"

Alastair raised an eyebrow. "Yes. I'd heard you two were close."

"Don't believe all you hear, Alastair. You'd be surprised by some of the things I've heard about you."

"Hmm, yes, fair point. So, Coldewater Academy?"

A look of alarm flashed across Camilla's face. "What about it, Alastair?"

"I need to know just how far they got in their investigations. And I need to talk to you about Fairfield."

*

The lesson flew by. Before he knew it, Miss Hartley was saying, "Okay, everyone, great work today. Could you just have your books ready to be collected and pack away, please? Carlton, can you collect the books for me, please? Thanks."

There was a flurry of activity, as excited chatter bubbled above the sound of scraping chairs and bags being unzipped and zipped. Packing away was given an extra urgency because the lesson was followed by break and conversations turned to debating the relative merits of the sausage roll and the cheese toastie. They piled towards the door. "Are you coming canteen, Karim?" asked Ben, a tall, willowy boy who had sat across from Karim on the table.

"Oh, no. I have to go back to the unit now. We have break and lunch at a different time."

"Will you be in the lesson tomorrow?"

Karim looked at Ahmed.

"Yes, Karim's in English for the next few weeks."

"Great. See you tomorrow, Karim."

"Yes. Goodbye." Karim was thrilled but confused. It had been such a long time since he had felt anything approaching happiness that he was unsure how to express it, so he fell back on his default position of blank deference.

As he was passing the teacher's desk, Miss Hartley stopped him.

"Well done today, Karim, that was excellent. I'm looking forward to you being in the class for the next few weeks."

"Thank you, Miss."

As he passed she lowered her voice and said to Ahmed, "And we'll talk later, Ahmed, okay?"

Later that night at Karim's house, Joan and Eric talked quietly, alone in the front room. They were delighted when Ahmed had told them how well it had all gone. They had pressed Karim for his thoughts, but had learned that it was a waste of time to force it. He had hardly spoken at all for the first couple of months, so any kind of communication was a bonus, but there were signs that he was growing more comfortable with his situation. His English was certainly improving in leaps and bounds.

Eric poured two glasses of sherry. "Time for a little celebration, I think," he said.

They clinked glasses.

"Shakespeare! Who'd have thought it," said Joan.

"You know, I really think he's going to be all right," said Eric. "Let's drink to Karim."

"To Karim."

Just above their heads, Karim lay on his bed. He had the photograph of his family in one hand and the letter from the unit in the other. He was a churn of emotions. He was thrilled with the lesson. He had understood most of it and had said a couple of things. But more than that he had spent an hour with children his own age. They had been nice to him. His eyes stung as he thought of it. And then his delight was swept away by a surge of guilt. How could he feel anything other than grief and sorrow and anger when his family were dead and his sister was missing? What kind of a Muslim was he? If only he could find Evana, then everything could start again.

He picked up the copy of *Macbeth* that Joan and Eric had bought for him and began to read, his finger painstakingly following the lines. It was late when he finally turned off his bedside lamp and went to sleep, his mind full of images of murder and betrayal.

21

"No, George, that's enough. You've been warned, and moved, and your name's on the board. You've wasted far too much of everyone's time in this lesson. I'm sending for SLT to remove you from the lesson."

Charlotte turned back to her computer to send the standard email summoning the person on patrol. It was rare for her to have to resort to this. Her relationship with the students, even in her most difficult classes, usually meant everyone toed the line, but she had tried everything with George and he just was being awkward. He would have to go, and it was quite likely that this would add to the impetus for a further exclusion. He was effectively on a final warning after causing chaos in a series of lessons taken by junior staff. His intimidating behaviour in the corridors and at break and lunchtime was causing concern as well. Under Jane, a final warning had always seemed to be endlessly negotiable. Under Rick, a final warning meant what it said. Two challenging students had already been permanently excluded that term. Everyone knew he wouldn't hesitate to add a third to the list.

"Oi, Miss, that's not fair. I haven't even done anything. You just don't like me. You're always picking on me."

"You know that's ridiculous, George. I've given you every chance to settle down and get on with your work."

"But I've done my work, Miss," George shouted, beginning to lose his temper. The rest of the class looked on with anxious anticipation. Part of them really wanted the theatre and excitement of George losing it in the lesson, while the other part was slightly fearful of what might happen. He stood up suddenly, clattering his chair over and knocking someone's bag off their desk.

"Oi George, mind out, man," protested the bag's owner, standing up.

George turned to him and placed his hand over the boy's face. George's great pudgy hand, with red blotchy sausage fingers, almost covered the other boy's face entirely. He pushed him hard and he crashed backwards into the desks behind him, sending more bags and pens flying across the room.

"Shut your fucking face. Don't you 'mind out man' me, you twat."

A strange silence descended on the room. Normally in this kind of situation there would be pandemonium, with the injured parties fighting back in an epic display of pushing and shoving, with the occasional punch thrown and a baying crowd infected by a collective hysteria. Here, everyone knew instinctively that this was dangerous and George was unpredictable.

He walked towards Charlotte. She stood up, her heart racing.

"George, calm down. Mr Westfield will be here shortly. Don't make things worse."

"Have you sent that fucking email, Miss?"

"Of course I have, George, I told you I was going to. And please don't swear."

"No man, this school is fucking rubbish. Think I'm hanging around for fucking Westfield? You can fucking suck my dick." He moved towards Charlotte's desk, leaned forward and swept everything off it onto the floor. There was a collective gasp as books and papers, pens, board markers crashed to the ground. The keyboard hung, swinging by its lead, over the edge of the desk.

He turned and marched towards the classroom door, kicking over a few chairs on the way. As he left, he slammed the door violently behind him, the bang reverberating around the room, and strode down the corridor.

Inside Charlotte's classroom, several students were systematically picking up the mess that George's outburst had left on the floor, rearranging chairs and tables, and creating neat piles on her desk. Charlotte was checking that Bradley, the boy who had taken the brunt of George's aggression, was all right.

"No, you're sure that you're all right? You don't need to go to the medical room? You know that you'll have to write a statement saying exactly what happened, don't you?"

"No, I'm fine, Miss, honestly. Are you all right, Miss? He really shouldn't have said them things to you, Miss."

"You were very brave, Miss. He's a nutter, is George. One day he's gonna do something bad," said Shafeeza, after she had finished putting all of the pens back in Charlotte's pen holder.

"Yes, I don't think we want to hear about that though, Shafeeza, thank you very much."

She raised her voice and turned to face the whole class, slipping easily back into class teacher mode.

"Okay everyone. Thank you all very much, you handled that nasty incident in a very mature and responsible way. Well done, all of you. Now, let's get back to the poem. Where were we? Oh yes, so let's recap. How exactly do we know that the Duke is a horrible man? It doesn't say that anywhere, does it? But we know it all right, all the same. How does Browning do that exactly?"

Charlotte's legs were still shaking and inside her head, parallel to the lines of the lesson that just came out of her lips from force of habit, was a voice that said to her, *He could have attacked you. He could have hurt one of the other kids.* No-one watching her, not the children in the class, nor any adult passing by, would have known anything untoward had happened. It wasn't until later, in the staffroom at lunchtime, that she began to shake and cry.

*

Karim spent the first lesson in the unit constantly looking up at the clock. He had English next and they were going to be discussing responsibility in *Macbeth*. He had prepared his arguments and his quotes and he was looking forward to crossing swords with Ben. They had had a dry run of the argument at the weekend when he had gone to his flat, in between games of FIFA on Ben's Xbox. Joan and Eric had been a little worried when it was suggested that he go over to Ben's for the afternoon. The Jubilee estate was notorious for its burnt-out cars, street corner drug dealers and its gang turf wars and the bus stop was directly opposite the infamous Trafalgar pub. It was the kind of pub where the excessive consumption of strong drink was less of a health risk than the fights that regularly spilled out onto the pavements outside. Their relief at his safe return had been supplemented by the pleasure of seeing him make friends.

He was a little nervous, though. Ahmed was off sick, so he would be going to the classroom on his own for the first time. Hafsa, one of the EAL teachers in the unit, had asked him several times if he was okay with that and whether he wanted her to take him along to the lesson, but he was adamant he would do it on his own. He was beginning to get rather tired of being treated as an invalid.

He looked up again at the clock. "Miss, can I go English now? It's time."

"Go **to** English, not go English. Just wait for five minutes, Karim, okay? The corridors will still be full. You know where you're going? There's no Ahmed today, remember."

"Yes Miss, I'll be fine."

He fidgeted constantly while he waited for Hafsa to release him. Finally, she said, "Okay, Karim, off you go."

He bolted for the door.

"And leave five minutes early, remember. Come straight back here," she shouted at the fast disappearing figure.

Smiling, she turned to Sharon, the head of the Language Unit. "I wish they were all as keen as that."

126

*

By the time George got to his hideaway he had calmed down somewhat. He ducked out of the building by the far corner of the ground floor corridor and walked around the outside until he reached another entrance. The door led to the bottom of a stairwell that was a little-used fire exit. It led only to a second entrance of a classroom on the first floor. It was one of several eccentric pieces of nineteen seventies design that served little practical purpose beyond furnishing all of the outlaws amongst the students over the last forty years with a handy bolthole, with good vantage points to check for staff on patrol.

He squatted down on the floor beside the ancient radiator, and fumbled in his pocket for a cigarette and his lighter. He needed to calm his nerves and think for a while. Over the years, many students had served the same needs in the same spot, as evidenced by the liberal sprinkling of dog ends on the floor.

He lit the cigarette and inhaled deeply. What the hell had he been thinking of? He knew this was the end. It might have been different with Miss Garner, but Mr Westfield always did what he said he was going to do. Shit. How on earth was he going get any GCSEs now? And what would his dad say? His dad would just batter him, rather than say anything. Just like he had done that morning. Just like he was doing to his mum when he had walked into the kitchen for something to eat. One day, he swore, that bastard would get what he deserved and then he'd be able to look after his mum.

*

The steady click of Rick's shoes on the corridor approached the classroom door. The class heard them get nearer and their suspicions were confirmed when they stopped just outside and the sound was replaced by the crackle of a walkie-talkie outside the door.

They all looked at the door expectantly. It swung open and Rick stood at the entrance.

"I believe you wanted me to pick up George, Miss Green."

"Yeah, thanks, sir. He's run off, I'm afraid. He left about five minutes ago when he knew that I'd called for you."

"Okay," Rick continued, "I'll do a sweep of the corridors. I know where he probably is."

"Oh, Mr Westfield, I er… I just need to fill you in on what happened."

She turned to the class. "Okay, everyone, you need to start answering the questions on the sheet in front of you. I just need to talk to Mr Westfield for a minute. We'll be just here by the door, so you need to get on with it quietly."

They all opened their exercise books and fiddled around finding pens and rulers.

Rick and Charlotte slipped into the corridor and she closed the door.

"Listen Rick, George went absolutely berserk. He'll have to go for this."

"Why? What exactly happened?"

"He was in one of his stupid moods right from the beginning. He was just messing around and disrupting continually. I went through all of the procedures, gave him a final warning and then, when I said I was calling for SLT he went mad. He attacked Bradley, poor lad, and he looked as if he was going to attack me. In the end he settled for chucking everything off my desk on the floor, kicking over a load of tables and storming out. Oh, and he invited me to suck his dick. Charming."

"Are you all right, Charlotte? I can get someone to cover the lesson so you can just have some time to collect yourself, if you want. It's no problem."

"No, no, I'm fine. The rest of the class have been very nice to me. They just need a bit of continuity. I think they were a bit shocked. You can see, they're all getting on with their work nicely."

"Yes, but that's because of you, Charlotte. You're really good with them. I'm sorry you've had to put up with all of this. No-one should have to deal with this kind of nonsense. George has got to go."

He turned to go. "I'll let you know what happens. And don't forget, if you need cover you just have to ask."

*

Out in the open Karim swung left along the side of the school, rather than go in the main entrance. He and Ahmed always did that now. It saved a lot of time, not having to buzz in and show their ID. He felt pretty sure he could remember the way. Running, he pushed open the door on the left, and burst in through the gap. Almost immediately, he crashed into a solid figure standing in the shadows. The figure staggered backwards and Karim tumbled to the ground, his bag scattering its contents on the floor.

"Fucking hell, man, look out," grunted the figure.

Karim, dazed, picked himself up and began gathering his stuff from amongst the crisp packets and cigarette ends. "I'm very sorry. I did not see you."

"Well you should look where you're fucking going, shouldn't you?" For the first time their eyes met.

A look of recognition flashed across George's face.

"Eh, wait a minute. Don't I know you?" He jabbed Karim with his podgy finger in the chest.

Karim's heart sank and then began to race. He instinctively averted his eyes, looking down at his feet, and lowered his voice, using his best English accent.

"No, I don't think so. I'm sorry I knocked into you. Are you all right?"

George ignored him. "Yeah, I know who you are. You're that fucking A-Rab cunt who got me excluded. The fucking Syrian terrorist. I've been looking for you. Still in ISIS are you? Blown anyone up recently?"

He jabbed at Karim's chest and took a step forward with every question. Karim backed off, keeping just out of George's reach. They went through the open door and were in the alleyway by the side of the school. George continued to jab.

129

"You bastards make me sick. We don't want you in this country. We should send you all back and fucking nuke the lot of you. That would sort you out. That's the way to fucking get rid of ISIS."

"Please, I am not ISIS, not Daish. They are responsible. Them and Assad. That is why I am here without my family."

"Family all dead, are they? Fucking good. How many was there? Probably hundreds of the fuckers knowing you lot. Good, stop 'em breeding more fucking terrorists."

By now Karim had backed against a fence and had nowhere left to go. He felt tears welling up in his eyes and his breath coming in short gasps. When he was at school, he deliberately made himself not think of Syria or his family.

George continued relentlessly.

"You got brothers and sisters, or are they all dead too? Mind you," George paused and a leering grin appeared on his face, "probably better to be dead for your sister and your mum." He moved his face closer to Karim until they were just millimetres apart. "You know what they do to the women, don't you? They rape 'em before they fucking kill 'em. By the time they kill 'em, they are begging to be killed. Your mum and sister—"

He was not able to finish the sentence. The fear that had swamped Karim and steadily converted to anger now, uncontrollably, boiled over into rage. All of his feelings, held down for long months in the name of survival, surged to the surface and he drew his head back and headbutted him on the nose. There was a sickening crunch of bone and gristle and a spurt of hot blood. George staggered backwards, crying put in pain. Karim flew at him, punching and scratching and kicking and screaming. George was so surprised he fell backwards onto the ground and Karim pounced on him and continued to hit him, screaming all the while.

George collected himself and using his massive bulk, pushed Karim off. He had the upper hand then. With a couple of hard punches to the stomach and head, Karim collapsed on the floor and George began kicking him. He rolled into a ball to protect his head and ribs as blows rained down upon him. Neither George nor Karim could hear the shouts of staff running towards them.

"No, no, George, stop that, get off him. That's enough."

It took three members of staff to pull George from Karim. George, sweating and breathing hard, stared down wild-eyed over their shoulders at the slight figure on the ground, who lay there, bruised and bloodied and unmoving.

22

Rick paced up and down his study, holding a sheet of A4 in one hand, and gesticulating rhetorically with the other, practising his lines. Occasionally, he turned to the computer and moved on the PowerPoint presentation to the next slide.

"So, this appointment is probably the most important in the history of the school, given the current educational climate. There is no doubt that this has been, and still is, a challenging school, that requires special skills and values to bring success. I believe that I have demonstrated in the last six months that I am the ideal candidate for this school at this time."

Jo, sitting opposite, a large glass of red wine in her hand, interrupted.

"I know what you're trying to do with that line, but do you really think it wise to emphasise the idea that Fairfield is a challenging school? Don't you think that that might come across as making excuses for the kids?"

"Yeah, but it is a challenging school. There's no point pretending it's not, not even in an interview. You know, if they want me, they want me and we're all just going through the motions here."

"Yes, I know, but you've got to be slick and perform well. You don't want people saying it was just a rubber stamp thing."

"What if I'm just fooling myself and they don't want me, they're just humouring me. It'll be humiliating. I have to go in the next day and face the staff regardless of what happens."

"Rick, come on. They'd be mad not to appoint you after what you've done since Jane left. From what Avril was saying the other day the whole staff are rooting for you. I've never heard of that before. Most teachers would rather shoot their Head than praise them."

Rick grunted. "Hmph. Better the devil you know maybe."

"Come on. Let's go through those questions again. And then we need to go to bed. You need a proper sleep before the big day."

She leafed through some sheets of papers lying on the table next to her and then launched in.

"So, Mr Westfield, can you describe for us a particular challenge that you've faced, how you dealt with it and what you learned about yourself in the process?"

*

Avril looked at the clock on her mantelpiece. Midnight. She was a little nervous about the interviews the next day. Two days to whittle down five candidates, first to two and then finally to one. She had been surprised when Alastair had come to see her earlier in the week to ask her to be on one of the interviewing panels. He had never had a conversation with her before. Whenever he came into the school, he met with Rick and the Heads of English, Maths and Science to grill them about exam results, but the most she had ever got had been a clipped "Good morning" as he breezed past in the foyer.

This time, however, he had been smooth charm personified. The Trust wanted, he had explained, to make good use of Avril's wealth of experience. There were several panels planned and the one she was to sit on was on curriculum, alongside Alastair and

Barry Pugh, the Director of Learning. She smiled to herself when she thought of the conversation. She shook her head. They must really think she was born yesterday.

"Make good use of my wealth of experience. Nonsense. They want me involved so they can say the decision involved the old guard as well as them. No, I don't trust them as far as I can throw them," she said aloud. She checked herself. She really must stop talking to herself out loud, it was a bad sign. A very bad sign. She needed to get out more.

She took a final sip of her tea before bed. Why was she being involved though? Lurking at the back of her mind, she had a bad feeling about the whole business. But, no. Surely, they couldn't be that stupid?

*

Rick arrived a little later than normal and joined the other candidates in the meeting room. Tea and coffee were laid on and everyone had an interview pack outlining the schedule for the day. They were due to have a welcome address from Alastair, before plunging into a packed programme that included taking an assembly, doing an in-tray exercise, being interviewed by a panel of students, as well as three other sets of panel interviews. *What a palaver*, he thought, *all of these hoops we have to jump through so that boxes can be ticked.* He had been on the other side of the fence many times and had never been convinced that all of this was the best way to select the best person for the job.

Jo had personally supervised the purchase and preparation of his interview outfit. The crisp white linen collar of his shirt was positively nuclear, against the dark blue of his suit and the silk knitted tie with horizontal stripes. Peeping out from the end of his cuffs were a pair of gold and enamel cufflinks. Surrounding him was a cloud of expensive cologne. He exuded National College of School Leadership style and quality. Unfortunately, so did everyone else. Or nearly everyone. He inserted a finger between his neck and the stiff white collar, and adjusted his tie. It was all just a little too tight.

He looked around the room at the others. Two women sat opposite. One was scribbling handwritten notes on the pack she had been given, occasionally lifting her head to survey the room before adding more scrawl to her pack. The other beamed at anyone who looked at her, her smile revealing a perfect set of impossibly white teeth. They both looked as if they had bought their clothes from an offshoot of *The Apprentice*, possibly online after applying 'hard-nosed executive bastard look' to the available filters.

The same could not be said of the other male candidate, to Rick's left. He looked a little younger than the other and his suit looked as if it had been put on with a shovel. He was carrying at least a couple of stones of excess weight and his face was carrying a slightly unruly hairstyle and a permanently bemused expression, as if he couldn't work out why he had been invited to attend. He couldn't remember applying for the post, it being one of a job lot he had dashed off about six weeks earlier. He spent his time trying to engage the others in conversation and seemed able, in pursuit of this end, to make a 'joke' of anything and everything.

Rick relaxed a little. Avril had told him that the other candidates were, frankly, out of their depth, as if they had been chosen specifically to provide no challenge to Rick. He, for the first time, began to believe that this whole thing had been set up for him and all he was going to have to do was smile and avoid controversy. The coronation would follow tomorrow. This warm feeling lasted for about two minutes.

The door opened and Alastair breezed in. "Good morning everyone, thanks for coming in. We're just waiting for the last candidate. Now, I'll just give out the finalised programme for the day. I'll talk to you all about the Trust's plans for Fairfield High and then there'll be an opportunity for you to ask any questions you might have."

As he was saying this an A4 sheet was being circulated around the table. Rick took a copy and passed on the others to his left. He scanned the sheet to get the names of the other candidates. When he got to the bottom of the list he did a double take. He looked again and then looked up at Alastair, his mouth slightly agape, his heart beating a little faster. There, at the bottom of the sheet, was the name of the missing candidate. At that moment, the door swung open again and the doorway framed a slight, blonde-haired woman in a pencil skirt and immaculately-tailored jacket.

"Good morning, everyone. I'm so sorry I'm late." Her smile was radiant as she came into the room.

"Good morning and welcome," Alastair responded with a smile. "Come in and find a seat. Everyone, this is Camilla Everson."

*

The next two days went by in a blur. He got through to Day Two, but he and everyone else knew he would get no further. When he got the phone call at home, late on the second day, he heard Alastair's honeyed words of commiseration, but didn't listen to them. He put the phone down, numb. Later, when the children were safely in bed and he and Jo were chewing it over for the umpteenth time, he cried a little. He felt so exposed and embarrassed and couldn't think about how he would face the staff the next day. By the time that point had actually arrived, however, his disappointment and sadness had turned to anger. This wasn't over. Not by a long chalk.

23

RICK SAT ON ONE OF AVRIL'S BLACK LEATHER SOFAS AND SHE SAT ON the other, coffee and cake on the table between them. It was late and it had been a long day. They had had several rushed debriefs after the interview but nothing in depth until now, a week later, the daily blur of the school day having left little time for discussion. The staff had been in shock since the announcement of the appointment and Rick had been touched by the number of people who came up to him to let him know how outraged they were. Touched, but after a week, a little embarrassed. He needed to move on.

"Has Goodall been in touch with you? Has he explained?" asked Avril.

"We had a conversation on the phone and he just said that I'd done a great job and that there'd definitely be headship opportunities in the Trust in the future. Thing is, I just don't trust him at all anymore. I don't believe a word he says."

"I just feel so naïve and stupid. I didn't see it coming at all. I was sure they had set it up for you to get the job, particularly when

I read the paperwork on the other candidates. I'm telling you, I was gobsmacked when I saw the piece of paper with Camilla's name on. I went mad. I accused them of stitching you up and being underhand. They almost excluded me from the panel and said I was biased."

"Do you think that that was what they intended at first, but then when Camilla suddenly became available, Goodall changed his mind?

"I dunno, I really don't. I mean they weren't at all interested in my questions. I made it clear I wanted to ask a question about how the candidates would heal the school community and bring it back together and they almost laughed at me, as if the idea of wanting a harmonious school community was the most ridiculous thing they'd ever heard of."

"Yeah, it's a bit nineteen seventies, isn't it?"

Avril laughed. "Yes, I suppose so. God, I'm getting too old for this game. If Camilla is the benchmark, I went past my sell-by date years ago. She is exhausting. That's the thing. No-one could mount a case not to appoint her on the interview alone. She was brilliant, really brilliant. But so were you. And you've done it here. With all the mad kids and parents and everything. I don't think they get the school at all. And I'm worried what she will do to us, particularly with that wanker Pugh in charge of Teaching and Learning."

"So, what happened when you were discussing all of the candidates at the end?"

"I wasn't in on the final one, that was reserved for people higher up the food chain. But in my panel, I argued that it should be you on the basis of the interview and your performance as Acting Head. They didn't want to know."

"Well, thanks for trying anyway."

They both sipped their coffee.

"So, what are you going to do now?" Avril asked.

"Go home and drink a little too much red wine."

"No, you moron, I mean about the job."

"Oh, that. Dunno. I suppose I'll apply for other jobs come September. I just can't see me working for Camilla and I'm not sure I want to hang around for scraps from Goodall's table."

"No, I don't blame you. Still, let's look on the bright side. Just another week and a half until the end of term. And then six glorious weeks off."

"I really wish it was tomorrow. It's so hard coming in every day now. I can't summon up any enthusiasm for it. And there's bound to be some sort of ghastly meeting with Camilla before the end of term. Honestly, I've never thrown a sickie in my life, but I'm tempted to on this occasion."

Avril looked askance at him. "You need to be careful. At least until you get another job – then you can go crazy."

"Yeah, you're probably right. And anyway, I'm straight back into it. I've got that terrible permanent exclusion hearing tomorrow night."

"George Mason? Oh my God, you poor thing. Have you met his dad?"

"Unfortunately, yes, I have had that pleasure. And I know he is going to be awkward about it, despite all the CCTV. He always is. Still, it'll be the full monty tomorrow, so there'll be plenty of backup, what with the authority's representatives and the Chair of Governors."

"There's no chance they'll overturn it, is there?"

"Well, I wouldn't have thought so, but then what do I know? I thought I was going to be the next headteacher."

"What about Karim? He's still not back, is he? Is he all right?"

"He's due back next week, but according to Ahmed, he's taken it very hard. It's really set him back and he's gone back into his silent mode. It's like it's triggered the PTSD again."

"That poor boy, as if he hadn't suffered enough. And he was doing so well."

"Yeah, I know. It certainly puts my troubles in some kind of perspective. But it's all made me even more determined to sort it all out in my last week as Head. I'm going to make it right for Karim, if it's the last thing I do.

*

139

Charlotte looked out across her classroom from her desk at the front. Her Year 10s, in the last lesson of the day, were grappling with a literature exam question, heads bowed in concentration. A couple of boys at the back had their heads bowed, not in concentration but in sleep, having finally succumbed to the sweltering heat that swamped the room. The heatwave had lasted for four days and there was no sign that it was going to break any time soon. Her classroom was on the wrong side of the building for this kind of weather, having soaked up the relentless sun for most of that time. Walking into the room was liking wading through soup, and every class that did so squealed their complaints about the fug of sweaty odour left by the previous inhabitants. All the windows were open to the maximum but not a breath of air disturbed the blinds.

At this time of the year this weather, which would be so welcome, so glorious in a week's time, was positively unhelpful. It simply reminded students and teachers that the holiday was close, but not yet there. Even the top sets found it hard to work and an atmosphere of being in early holiday mode pervaded the building. The kids were like footballers at the end of a long hard season, their team in no danger of relegation or winning anything, content to wallow in mid-table obscurity, going through the motions and waiting for the beach and the pool. Lunchtimes were taken up with preventing water fights breaking out and the sticky heat engendered a prickly irritation. Tempers were short and fights were frequent. Charlotte, ever the resourceful professional, made the link for her class with the Montagues and Capulets in Verona and some of them even understood it, that lightbulb moment illuminating some faces reward enough for the attempt.

She looked again at the two at the back. They weren't snoring yet and no-one had noticed except her. Time to exercise the tactical blind eye and hope that there were no learning walks going on. She smiled in recognition. She too, was waiting for the beach. She checked her watch.

"Okay, everyone," she announced, "can you all stop writing now, please? Make sure your name is on every sheet of paper and have your papers at the side of your desk for me to collect."

She circulated the room to the accompaniment of sighs and stretches as the stillness of the previous hour loosened. Predictably, one student called out, "Miss, when are we gonna watch a DVD? Nobody else is still doing work like this."

"Nice try, Jadene, but I don't believe that for a minute. If you're very good, we might watch a bit of Shakespeare on the last day."

This provoked general, good-natured groaning, as she knew it would, but her timing was precise and the bell prevented it going any further.

"Right, make sure your chairs are up and off you go. See you tomorrow."

There was a limp chorus of goodbyes as the class, flushed, crumpled and slightly glistening, made their way out. The boys were so exhausted by the heat and Shakespeare they couldn't even make a token effort at pushing and shoving or personal abuse, and the classroom cleared, leaving Charlotte surveying the aftermath of another day at school. She began the daily ritual of tidying up, picking up litter, straightening up piles of books and checking her emails.

After five minutes there was a tentative tap at the door and Kwame and Kevin came in.

Charlotte looked up from her screen.

"Hi guys, what's up?"

"Hi Charlotte, good day?" asked Kwame.

"Yeah, pretty good, apart from the weather. I feel like I'm clinging on until the end of term, you know?"

"How are you feeling about tonight?" asked Kevin.

"You mean the exclusion meeting? I've got mixed feelings about it, actually."

"You know the unions have said we'll refuse to teach George over what happened? He shouldn't have been here anyway, he'd done enough to be excluded three times over."

"Oh, I don't know. I'd have him back if he apologised and went for a long time. I get on pretty well with George normally. He was just in a bad place. He's as much a victim in this as anyone else."

141

"You're joking? As much as Karim? After what that lad's been through."

"I know, I know. It was horrible what he did to Karim, really unforgiveable, it's just that I've talked to George, I know what he gets at home every day."

"Come on Charlotte, just because you're a saint doesn't mean everyone else has to be. No member of staff should have to face that level of aggression and intimidation at work. It's just not right. And as for what he did to Karim, if that had been on the street he would have been charged with GBH. They were thinking about it for a while, I heard." Kwame's disbelief at Charlotte's approach came through loud and clear.

"You can't make excuses for George's behaviour, even if he is living with a psychopath," reasoned Kevin.

"They're not excuses, they're explanations. There's a difference."

There was an awkward silence. Charlotte shook her head.

"Listen guys, I appreciate your concern, I really do. And I know that George has got to go because of what happened. I can't imagine what Karim has been through in the last year or so. It's just that I think, what kind of future does that leave George? How is he going to recover and turn himself into a decent human being? This is not doing anything other than pushing him further into the shadows. Honestly, there are no winners here."

*

The atmosphere in the room was calm and business-like. It seemed as if the protocols surrounding the running of permanent exclusion hearings had been designed expressly to suck all of the passion and emotion out of the proceedings, leaving a dry and legalistic husk behind. The rigid turn taking of statements and questions and statutory procedure generated an airless, safe space.

Rick flicked through the fat folders of the submission bundle and surreptitiously surveyed the people around the table, as the Chair of Governors, Adrienne Smith, led the proceedings. Directly opposite him sat George, in his school uniform, the shirt collar straining against his bulging neck. To George's right sat his father. The resemblance was clear. He was an enormous man, once blond like George, now simply bald, the folds of flesh on his skull like the channels left by the sea in wet sand. They glistened with sweat. He was wearing a black suit which he filled to soft stretching point. He too had attempted to button his collar but had failed and instead had hidden the gaping neck with a fat tie knot. What he couldn't hide was a swastika tattoo peeking above the top of the collar on his neck. His hands fiddled with the bundle of papers, flashing two prominent 'Love' and 'Hate' tattoos on his knuckles. There was a faint, but unmistakeable, aroma of heavy drinking surrounding him.

To his right sat a tiny, sparrow-like woman with long, bleached blonde hair, and a permanently fixed smile. She didn't pay much attention to the bundle, preferring instead to alternate between gazing straight ahead with a fixed, thin smile or casting her eyes downwards at her feet. Whenever her husband spoke, she turned to look at him, hanging onto his every word. Between the three of them, the mother and George silent and deferential on either side of the father, there was an almost perceptible crackle of tension.

It was a painstaking business. After about an hour and a half, all of the submissions had been heard, evidence reviewed and questions asked and answered. The Masons and their representative were asked to leave the room and wait outside while the committee considered its judgement. They were waiting for all of fifteen minutes before the clerk of the committee came out to summon them back in.

The Chair of Governors rambled through the approved script, finally arriving at the judgement.

"Having given due consideration to all of the submissions, and after careful review of the evidence, the committee has decided to uphold the permanent exclusion." The pronouncement continued in the same vein while Mr Mason, his brow furrowed with concentration, struggled to understand what was being said. He could contain himself no longer.

143

"Hold on, hold on, let's talk English. Are you saying my boy is being chucked out?" He jabbed his finger at Adrienne as he spoke.

She hesitated, torn between expressing outrage at the proceedings being interrupted and fearful of pouring more petrol on what was evidently a raging fire.

"Er, yes, that's right, Mr Mason."

He exploded with anger. Both George and his mother went into what was clearly a familiar damage limitation strategy. They had obviously seen this kind of temper before. Their eyes were firmly on their shoes.

Adrienne tried to reassert her authority. "Mr Mason, I really must ask you to moderate your language. This is not helping."

"Moderate my language, my arse. My boy is being discriminated against because he's English. You saw the CCTV. You saw that fucking terrorist attack him. He broke his fucking nose for Christ's sake. All he did was defend himself. I'm telling you, this fucking country is going to the dogs. You have to be black or a Muslim to get anything these days. We're fucking overrun with the bastards and they all want to destroy our way of life and fucking get benefits while they're doing it. Did you see that thing on the news about those attacks in France? All of 'em let in supposedly as refugees from Syria. Refu-fucking-gees, my arse. And we are soft enough to let 'em all in. Jesus wept." He shook his head in incomprehension.

Rick had heard enough. "Mr Mason, I'm sorry but these comments are highly offensive. In fact, they're probably illegal. I must ask you to calm down and listen to reason."

"Calm down? Who the fuck are you to talk to me? You lot just look down your nose at ordinary white English people. Offensive and illegal, are they? Well I'll tell you, it's what most ordinary people in this country think. But you lot are completely out of touch. I bet you lot all fucking voted Remain for a start. You've got no fucking idea. You're just like that Labour Party bitch, what's her name? You know, the one that slagged off the White Van Man for flying the flag. Fucking hell, it's no wonder we're going to the dogs if we're ashamed of the flag."

At this point Mr Mason's representative leant behind George and touched his father on the arm, whispering, "Jimmy, this is doing you no good. You need to just listen now."

Mr Mason angrily shook off his arm. "No, Gary, they need to listen, not me."

Rick interjected again. "Mr Mason, I really must insist that you leave now."

Mr Mason stared at him, a mocking smile spreading slowly across his face.

"Oh, you really must insist, must you? Who the fuck are you? You aren't even a proper headteacher, you. You couldn't even get them to give you the job. They saw what a mess you'd made of it since January and they fucking binned you straight away, first chance they got. You're a fucking nobody, that's who you are, mate."

Rick got to his feet, incensed.

Mason's smile spread ever more dangerously.

"Oh yeah, you want some do you? Nah, mate, I don't think so."

Both the Chair of Governors and the authority rep on either side of Rick reached across and lightly touched him, pulling him back down.

"Rick, just sit down, please," Adrienne insisted.

It was enough to break the spell and Rick sat back down, his heart racing.

"Nah, I thought so. Come on, we're going. There's a terrible smell in this room."

He stood up abruptly. scattering his chair behind him. His wife jumped out of her skin and flinched. George got to his feet, ready to follow.

"Jimmy, do you really think…" began his wife.

He didn't even bother replying. He simply grabbed her by the top of her arm, and dragged her out of her seat towards the door. Her feet almost left the ground. He stopped and turned back to Rick, jabbing his finger at him.

"And you, you cunt, you'd just better watch out that's all. I wouldn't be doing any more late nights in school on your own, know what I mean?"

The three of them surged out of the door, with Gary a few steps behind them. The faint breeze their hasty exit produced was fragranced by the sour, sweet tang of old beer and cigarettes. As they made their way down the corridor, Mr Mason's ranting, unhinged voice came through the open door, fading into the distance. George was silent throughout, dying inside.

BOOK TWO

1

RICK LOOKED ACROSS AT THE RADIO CLOCK. TWO THIRTY.
Shit. He'd been awake for hours, tossing and turning, the knot in his
stomach getting tighter and tighter. He shifted position yet again in
the bed, trying to find that sweet spot that would allow him to sink
into oblivion.

He had always dismissed colleagues who had talked of
'that Sunday night feeling' or the growing feeling of dread that
descended as the end of the holidays approached. He had never
been able to understand it. By the time the end of the holiday
arrived he was always desperate to get back to work, whether it
was as a PE teacher, thinking about getting the football team to
the regional finals or latterly, as a Senior Teacher, working out new
strategies to boost achievement. He wasn't a workaholic, in the
sense that he loved the holidays and had a lot of other stuff in his
life to look forward to. He had always considered himself pretty
lucky compared to some of his friends who seemed to hate their
jobs and simply lived for the weekend, Christmas and two weeks

abroad in the summer. He had often wondered what that must be like. Now, he knew.

Not even the outstanding exam results, announced just a couple of weeks ago, could take the edge off this insistent, intravenous drip of anxiety. He felt cheated. He couldn't even enjoy his moment of triumph. Against all the odds their GCSE results were up by about ten percent. Both he and Avril had been in school when they were released and they had to double check the data when the headline figure popped out the other end of the computer. Jean, the data officer, ran the programme three times, before they all embraced the reality of what they had done. They permitted themselves a moment of whooping and high-fiving, before they donned the mask of the sober professionals once more.

Jane had rung him at home that same evening to check the results and to add her congratulations. They had had a nice chat and she had given him some thoughtful advice about how to deal with the Camilla situation, but he hadn't really been listening to it. He had his own ideas about 'the Camilla situation'. The thing that did strike him, however, was the fact that Jane was clearly in a bad place. She didn't say that, but there was something about her voice, that tone of bright, brittle cheeriness, that made him think that she was looking into the void, even while she was talking to him. She was on her own. At the very time she needed her work, her lifetime's passion, to fill the gap and absorb her completely, it had been taken away.

In the darkness he shivered. At least he had Jo and the kids, he thought, looking over again at her. As he did so, he caught sight of the clock again. Two thirty-five. Time to shift onto his other side.

*

Barry surveyed the room from his bed with some satisfaction. In the pale light seeping in at the edges of the blinds, he saw the outline of his new suit, shirt and tie combination that Alison had neatly laid out on his special teak clothes stand. If he strained, he could just about make out the gleam on the toe caps of his

Church's brogues. He was excited about tomorrow, but he never had any trouble sleeping once he had decided to. He often felt it was simply a matter of will, and those who were plagued by insomnia were, in some fundamental way, weak. It might sound harsh, but there it was.

He would just take a last look at his priority list for tomorrow and the rest of the week and then he'd get to sleep. He reached for his clipboard which, as always, was by the side of the bed, and reviewed the targets ticked off for today and those that were coming up for tomorrow. Tomorrow he had a meeting with Alastair at Bellingford about priorities for the year for the Trust as a whole and then Tuesday he was at Fairfield to address the staff on Ofsted. He was really looking forward to that, especially to seeing Westfield eat humble pie in front of Camilla. He deserved to have his nose rubbed in it. How the whole Fairfield crew had got away with it for so long was beyond him. He blamed the local authority. Such old-fashioned, and well, frankly, socialist ideas were discredited long ago but these dinosaurs were determined to cling on to the old ways. It was almost as if they enjoyed being social workers rather than proper teachers. It was so patronising. Part of him felt sorry for Westfield. After all, he'd had a terrible set of leaders to follow in the formative years of his career as a senior leader. Garner and Howarth were positively antediluvian. Was that the right word? He made a note on his checklist to look it up in the morning so he could use it when he explained to them, as he clearly was going to have to do, where they were going wrong. At least they had dealt with Garner. He felt a glow of pride when he thought back to that and to Alastair's fulsome praise for the way he had handled it.

Howarth would be next and it wouldn't be long either. Westfield would follow shortly after, if it had been up to him. Westfield had always had an air of amused superiority about him when he had deigned to speak to him in the past, a sarcasm quite out of keeping with his origins. He really should remember that he was nothing more than a jumped-up PE teacher after all. But strangely, Alastair seemed to think he had something about him. Oh well. Even Alastair could make mistakes.

He was looking forward to telling Alison all about his great triumph at Fairfield. It was sure to be a triumph. He'd be able to use that Ofsted training presentation, if he made a few amendments. Job done. It was a shame she was sleeping so badly at the moment and was occupying her own room. Still, that allowed him to tick the sensitive husband box on his check list and anyway, it wouldn't be for too much longer. A good job with the mess at Fairfield and a pay rise that Alastair had hinted at and he would be able to surprise Alison with that newly-decorated dining room she had been going on about. He made a note on his clipboard, laid it down on the bedside table, slipped his earplugs and face mask on and settled down to sleep.

*

Jane sat alone in her front room, staring at the television with the sound down. The room was in darkness save for the flickering light from the screen. It was midnight. She had already been to bed, at about 7.30, but as usual she had just lain there unable to sleep, until she finally admitted defeat and came back downstairs to the front room. She found that she could stay there on her own for hours at a time, as long as there was something on the screen in front of her. But it was the mindless babble of talking and music she couldn't bear. Silence soothed her.

She read a lot, she always had, and she churned through book after book, remembering nothing of what she read. Sometimes the reading hurt her, a pain behind the eyes, and the book, even the slimmest of paperbacks, seemed just too heavy to lift up. It was then that she turned to the television, knowing that the next day, or sometimes even later the same day, she would be refreshed enough to pick up the book again.

She looked again at the side table by the sofa. There were two piles of pills: one pile was composed of a couple of boxes of Fluoxetine, tablets of 40 milligrams to be taken once a day. The other pile was much higher. Boxes and boxes of paracetamol. Maybe tomorrow she would feel a little better. Maybe tomorrow would be a better day. She would start again tomorrow.

*

"But we've heard nothing from the school, Ahmed, nothing at all. And Mr Westfield assured us personally that he would get in touch to keep us informed. I don't understand it, I really don't."

Joan nodded. "And he's been ever so good, Mr Westfield has, all the way through this. He rang us straight away about the permanent exclusion. And he came round, just before the hearing, to check that Karim was all right, didn't he, Karim?"

Karim was sitting opposite Joan and Eric, next to Ahmed on the sofa in their living room.

"Yes, that is right. He told me that everything would be all right and that I'd be back at the school in September," he said.

Ahmed interjected, "I'm sure Mr Westfield means well, but he has made promises before that he couldn't keep, remember? You shouldn't build up all your hopes."

"But that was the boy's fault, not Mr Westfield's. And now the boy has been excluded, the school will be safe. I want to go back to my English class and see my friends again."

Ahmed reassured him. "Yes, that's what we all want as well, Karim, of course it is. I will email Mr Westfield this afternoon and ask for some clarification. It's probably just because it is the start of the new school year and there is a lot to do. I'm sure if I remind him, he will deal with it and get back to me."

He leaned forward and patted Karim's knee with his hand. "And now, I need to discuss a few things with Joan and Eric, so why don't you go up to your room and get on with that English work?"

Karim looked panic-stricken.

"I don't have to go somewhere else, do I? I want to stay here with you."

"No, no, of course not, Karim, we wouldn't let that happen." Joan's voice trembled. "We just need to talk in more detail with Ahmed, that's all. Nothing to worry about."

"You go up and get on with that English, good lad," said Eric, adding gentle weight to the idea.

"Maybe we can do the garden later? I can help you dig up some of those potatoes."

"Yeah, of course, Karim, let's do that."

Karim got up from the sofa and left the room, closing the door behind him. They heard his footsteps go up the stairs and into his room above.

They lowered their voices. Eric began, "We're very worried about him, Ahmed. He's still very nervous after what happened. It would be very hard for him if he wasn't able to go back to Fairfield."

"Yes, I know. But he has made a good recovery. He is talking again and his English is getting better and better."

"Better than mine," joked Eric, "though that's not saying much."

"You know that he doesn't have a place at Fairfield? He was only taken on at the Language Unit for two terms, like everyone else."

"Yes, that's what we're waiting for. That's what Mr Westfield was going to speak to us about. But he'd said there wouldn't be a problem. We've even bought the uniform."

"Well, as I said, I will contact him to find out what is going on. And I'll also make some enquiries about the college, just in case. He will definitely get a place there if Fairfield doesn't work out."

Upstairs in his room, Karim lay on his bed, a battered copy of *Macbeth* in his hands. He tried reading but the words swam off the page and he put the book down again and sighed. He listened to the murmured conversation through the floorboards, catching the rise and fall of their intonation as, at intervals, Joan let her emotions get the better of her. He was always being talked about by someone, his future being planned for him as if he were a simpleton or something. At least he could go to Ben's in the week to play FIFA again and talk to someone who treated him like a real person. It was always better to talk than to be talked about.

*

Camilla drained her gin and tonic and looked through the window into the darkness. The lights of townscapes and cityscapes below broke through the darkness and the gaps in the cloud. Another twenty minutes and they would have touched down. It had been a wonderful holiday, all six weeks of it, but she had had enough of lying by the pool, eating and drinking and, a little too frequently, dancing. She'd even read a book. No, she was refreshed and ready for what lay ahead at Fairfield. Alastair, in several phone calls and meetings, had made it crystal clear what he expected, on all fronts. She wondered how much his wife knew, but then dismissed that thought from her mind. She could not afford to worry about that. After all, Alastair was holding all the cards. She turned her attention again to Fairfield, which for someone of her skills and experience presented a much more manageable challenge. She smiled to herself. They wouldn't know what had hit them.

2

RICK WAS A LITTLE PUZZLED. HE'D ACCEPTED THE FACT that there hadn't been an SLT meeting in the last week of the holidays as usual, although he still thought it rather odd. He had got in early on Day One to make himself available to Camilla and help orientate her in unfamiliar circumstances, but there had been nothing beyond a brief hello. His office was about three yards away from Camilla's, along the corridor, but her door remained resolutely closed. Eventually, she pinged an email to SLT with a revised agenda for the day attached, including the welcome back staff meeting at nine o'clock. His name was against the main item of exam results. *Nice to be consulted*, he thought, *not the best of starts.* The only other point of interest was the SLT meeting fixed for the afternoon, with no other specific items for discussion.

During the staff meeting she was charm personified. She explained to the staff that as she had had nothing to do with the exam results, she was leaving that to Rick to lead on, but she was effusive in her praise of Rick and to the staff in general. It was a clever move, and made the first impression of her as being someone who was generous rather than petty. Her second master stroke was in proclaiming her intention to come down hard on low-level disruption and to back up the staff in dealing with aggression from students.

When Rick had finished taking the staff through the highlights of the exam performance he sat down, having engendered a positive, feel-good atmosphere. Camilla bounced up onto the stage, a picture of energetic efficiency, and fiddled with her memory stick in the hard drive. When it fired up, her PowerPoint presentation sprang into life, with the title, 'Zero Tolerance' monumental on the screen behind her. On the front row, right at the end furthest away from her, Avril rolled her eyes at Rick and muttered, "Oh, sweet Jesus, not this again. Lord have mercy on all of us sinners." She strained every sinew of her professionalism to mask her utter contempt for the concept, reasoning that Camilla, as a new head, needed the support of her senior colleagues and a fair crack of the whip. It was what natural justice demanded. She bit her tongue throughout the presentation and did not catch Rick's eye after that first profanity.

Camilla opened her address.

"Zero Tolerance, ladies and gentlemen, zero tolerance. A phrase that is often bandied about in educational circles these days, almost a trendy catchphrase. But what exactly does it mean and why is it relevant for us on this first day of a new chapter in Fairfield's history?"

Kevin, in his customary seat on the back row, couldn't help himself. He whispered to Kwame, "Buggered if I know. But I'm pretty sure that you are going to tell us."

"It is always good to start a new year with some good news," she continued, "and you have quite rightly been celebrating your very good exam results. I'd like to add my personal congratulations to the whole staff."

She paused and surveyed the audience, smiling.

"But," she began again.

"Here we go," said Kevin, sitting up in his chair.

"But that was then and this is now. Those results aren't good enough. And next year, we will be celebrating better results. But we'll only be doing that if we are honest enough to admit that for too long this school has accepted second best and has made excuses for underperformance. That all changes from today. Today is Day One of a new regime, Day One of a no-excuses culture, Day One of Zero Tolerance."

The words were like throwing a bucket of cold water over the audience. All of the energy, all of the enthusiasm, all of the collective determination evaporated. They all moved forward in their seats to better hear precisely why they were so bad at their jobs.

"From this moment on, there will be zero tolerance of low-level disruption in class, zero tolerance of students not doing their homework, zero tolerance of defiance and aggression towards staff. In return for this uncompromising support of staff in doing what is a very difficult job, I expect the highest ethical standards of work and demeanour. And, accordingly, there will be zero tolerance of badly-planned lessons, zero tolerance of books not being marked, zero tolerance of staff leaving at 3.30 and getting in at 8.30, zero tolerance of not challenging students, zero tolerance of sloppy uniform, lateness, poor attendance, poor attitudes. And, absolutely zero tolerance of mobile phones."

She was a clever woman, there was no doubt about that. People in the audience had been gradually stirring, thinking to themselves how wonderful it would be to work in a school where they were backed up to this extent and where none of the problems on Camilla's long list existed. And then she finally nailed it by mentioning the bugbear to beat all bugbears, mobile phones. The mounting approval bubbled to the surface and there was a ripple of applause and a few outbursts of approval.

Avril turned to Rick.

"It's all so simple. Why didn't we think of all of this?"

What was left hanging in the air was a vague but unspoken impression that the previous regime, including Rick, had been rather liberal when it came to behaviour. His low simmer of irritation was beginning to gather pace. At one bound Camilla had brilliantly associated Rick and Avril and the rest of SLT with failure, despite the record exam results, and herself with hope and aspiration for something better.

For the rest of the day she was ensconced in her office and Rick, across the corridor with his door open, was aware of a series of middle leaders trooping in throughout the morning for individual meetings. When they left, closing the door behind them, their expressions uniformly serious, they trudged down the corridor with the troubles of the world on their shoulders.

He had plenty of work to be getting on with, but his concentration was disturbed by a brooding sense that she was putting him in his place and making him wait. He was thinking through how and when exactly he was going to confront her, when an email popped into his in-box, elbowing aside the tens of others that swamped it, only to be deleted without being read. The title of this one caught his attention: 'Re: Karim Atbal'. It was from Ahmed.

"Shit," he exclaimed. The second he read the title he realised, without reading the text, that he had messed up. Not in an irretrievable way, he could put it right if he acted straight away, but he would need to pass it in front of Camilla, if only in an information-giving way.

"What's up? You look like someone's died. I've got zero tolerance for whingers you know."

He looked up. Avril, a broad smile on her face, was in the doorway.

"Eh? Oh, come in, come in. And shut the door. You might as well because no-one seems to want to come in and have a conversation."

Avril stepped into the room and closed the door.

"Haven't you had a meeting with her yet then?"

"No, she hasn't favoured me with that honour yet. Though judging from what I've seen, I'm about the only person she hasn't met yet."

"Yeah, that's what I came to talk to you about. I've spoken to a few of them and Camilla has made an instant impression. They're all shell shocked at what she's expecting out of them. No thank you or well done for the great exam results. Just, it's going to be much more professional in the future."

"More professional? What the hell does she mean by that? Doesn't she understand what those results represent in a school like this?"

"Clearly not from her zero tolerance speech. Anyway, it's fairly obvious that it's going to be a rocky ride."

"Have you had a meeting with her?"

"Me? No, don't be silly. I'm way below her horizon. What's that expression they use with the Royal Family? You know, they are 'bypassing a generation'. I'm effectively Prince Charles and she's looking for a few Williams. My days are numbered, Rick. I'm part of the problem, not the solution. Anyway, enough of that, what were you looking at when I came in?"

"Oh God. I've completely messed up Karim's place on roll here. I just got an email from Ahmed asking what the situation is."

"Why, what happened?"

"I dunno. I think I must have been so pissed off when I didn't get the job, I just went into meltdown. I was supposed to offer a place to him at the end of term but I completely forgot."

"You can put that right pretty easily though, can't you? After all, there are plenty of places."

"Well, it's got to go via Camilla now. I'll bring it up at the meeting this afternoon."

"And what about you and the job? Did you talk it over with Jo in the summer?"

"Yeah, we talked it to death. I'm gonna apply for jobs from week one and see what happens."

Avril pondered for a moment. "I have a feeling that you won't be the only one."

*

By the end of the SLT meeting that afternoon, everyone round the table wore a haunted look. Two hours of implied criticism and nit-picking was wearying. Camilla, on the other hand, seemed energised by being in charge so comprehensively. They had got through an enormous amount of business, much more than usual, largely because there was little discussion. A few of them, still getting to grips with the new regime, attempted to put forward alternative viewpoints, or extend the discussion, but Camilla, in the chair, steamrollered through all of that and ploughed on to a decision. She steered their passage through the agenda with a relentless grip on the wheel. By the end the meeting had degenerated into her talking with the occasional piece of answering the question or information-giving from the others. In Camilla's world view, discussion was for wimps.

Rick, like the others, eventually dried up and contented himself with nodding, correcting factual mistakes, and writing notes. As he did this, he gradually, over the course of the two hours, shut down inside. She might as well have been addressing a room full of bollards for all the input they were expected to have. He couldn't look at Avril, who had been rolling her eyes and trying to catch his for the last hour and a half. He sat quietly and decided to raise the Karim issue under Any Other Business.

Camilla gathered together her papers.

"Okay, everyone, let's just quickly reiterate what has been agreed."

Everyone else in the room was limp and sweating, with undone collars, jackets removed, slumped in their chairs. Camilla was still crisply efficient. She radiated an icy self-possession. Still in her tailored jacket, there was not a sign of a bead of sweat, or of any kind of fatigue at all. Rick wondered whether she was taking some kind of amphetamine. Then, his imagination on a roll, he mused that she could well be a replicant, or an alien that had turned over two pages at once in the how-to-appear-like-a-human manual. He shook himself and willed the concentration needed to get to the end.

She rattled through a list of things that had been 'agreed' and then indicated that the meeting was over. Behind the glazed expressions and vacant, slack-jawed slumping, everyone gave thanks to whatever God or force of nature they looked to. Everyone except Rick.

"What about Any Other Business? We haven't done that yet," he pointed out.

At that precise moment, everyone imagined horrible revenge being enacted upon him: torture and grisly methods of murder flashed across their minds. Please no, they thought, not Any Other Business. Haven't we suffered enough?

Camilla looked at first nonplussed and then the faint stirrings of irritation played across her features. She clearly was not used to chairing a metting with other intelligent, autonomous life forms. She collected herself.

"I'm sorry, Rick, you have some other business?" She smiled at him and then favoured the rest of the group with the dying embers of the smile.

"Yes, sorry, it's just a quick thing about our Syrian refugee, Karim Atbal," Rick began.

'Ah yes, I've heard of him. There was something in the paperwork about the permanent exclusion, isn't that right?"

Rick nodded and quickly reprised the story for her benefit.

"So, what exactly is the problem then?" asked Camilla, after he had finished the details.

"Well, it's just that his time in the Language Unit is over. He's done two terms, you see. And we were going to offer him a place on roll in the actual school from the beginning of September. But I forgot to organise it, what with everything that was going on at the end of the summer term." Rick trailed off, embarassed at bringing everyone's attention to bear on his h umiliation at the hands of Camilla back in July.

"So, he hasn't got a place here and he won't be starting on Wednesday then, is that right?"

"Err, yes that's right. But I was just raising it because I assumed you would want me to go ahead and offer him a place and get him in here. We do have plenty of spaces."

"Yes," said Camilla, "we do, don't we? Funny that. But no, Rick, that's the wrong assumption. Don't offer him a place. Things have changed."

There was an icy silence in the air. She may as well have just grabbed his head and forced his nose into a trough of mud on the table. Nervous eyes darted around the room. Before the spell was broken, Camilla gathered her papers again and repeated, "Okay everyone. Thank you very much. See you all tomorrow."

She stood up and held open the door, waiting for them all to stand. The last thing she wanted to do was leave the room first so that they could all breathe a sigh of relief and disbelief before they started slagging her off. They filed out in silence. When Rick got to the door he stopped.

162

"We need to talk. Do you have five minutes now?"

Camilla was on the verge of saying no, but thought better of it and changed her mind.

"Okay, if we must. Let's do it here," she said, closing the door.

The both sat at the same end of the table.

"I'm not sure you understand the full picture with Karim," Rick began.

Camilla raised her immaculately-shaped eyebrows.

"Well, why don't you enlighten me?"

"Karim has been through a terrible time in the last year. His mother, father and brother were all killed in Syria and his younger sister is missing. He travelled with her most of the way and ended up in Calais. He was admitted to the UK last summer and is now with foster parents in Longdon. He was allocated a place at the Language Unit in January and has done exceptionally well. He's a very intelligent young man, exactly the kind we would normally choose to join the school after the placement is over. After what happened to him here in the summer term we owe him a place. Morally. It would be a devastating setback if he had nowhere to go."

"Yes, I understand that one of our pupils was permanently excluded as a result of the incident. And yet the CCTV clearly shows that it was the Syrian boy who attacked our boy."

"There was massive provocation. The committee was right to uphold the exclusion. The staff would have gone mad if it had been overturned."

"Yes, well all of that is going to change now. What the staff think about anything means nothing to me. I run the school, not them. This boy is clearly an accident waiting to happen and what happened to him in Syria, although most unfortunate, is not our responsibility. Our responsibility is to our own students and their results. We absolutely cannot afford to invite into the school problem students. We are not social workers. So, the boy will not be offered a place and furthermore the Language Unit will close down at Christmas. It has already been decided."

Rick was struggling to process what Camilla had just said. He wondered if he had misunderstood.

"So, you're comfortable with just leaving him with nothing?" he said, his brow furrowed.

"He won't have nothing. The local college will be desperate to have him."

"Longdon College? Have you ever been there? It's like the wild west. He needs something better than that."

"It may well be like the wild west, but, again, that is their problem, not ours. And, if there's nothing else, I need to get on."

She rose from her seat and moved towards the door.

"Woah, hold on. There is something else. Is this the way it's going to be then? No discussion about anything? You haven't even called a meeting with me about the headship. I must be one of the few people you haven't seen today. Don't you think we need to talk about the way forward and clear the air?"

She shook her head.

"No, Rick, I don't. It's quite straightforward. I was appointed over you in the summer. I'm not going to hold your hand over that, there are too many things to do here. If you can't deal with that you should think about getting another job. I would support any application you made. If you choose to stay, you might learn something. It's entirely up to you. I hope I've made myself clear. Was that the kind of conversation you wanted to have?"

He chose not to answer that last question. Camilla looked at him for a second or two and then turned to the door.

"I'll see you tomorrow."

As the door closed, Rick was left to ponder all that had just happened. He muttered under his breath, "You've made yourself perfectly clear. Thank you very much."

He gathered up his papers and made his way back to his office. Closing the door, he picked up the phone and rang the number Ahmed had left in his email. He'd ring Joan and Eric as well, just so that they were clear. If Camilla wanted to treat people like dirt she could explain it to them herself.

3

BY 7.30 IN THE MORNING THERE WERE ALREADY FIFTEEN
members of staff on the gate, filtering the early birds through. By
eight o'clock there were twenty-five. At Camilla's insistence, the
slightest uniform infringement was picked up and the student
sent packing back home to sort it out. Some of these were serious
breaches and would always have been dealt with severely. One
student returning with blue hair, for example, or the boy with an
elaborate razored pattern in his shaved head, they were obvious
candidates for the early bath. Many others, however, were genuinely
mystified as to why they were being directed back down the path
with a standard letter in their hand. As far as they were concerned,
this was them making a big effort to comply on the first day of a
new school year.

Behind the vanguard of uniform checkers was a second phalanx
of uniform amenders. They were dealing with a steadily-lengthening
queue of students who had to be supervised while doing up their
top button, fastening their tie to the regulation length, tucking their

shirts in, removing make up, measuring skirts. There was a cloud of shock floating above them that threatened at any moment to change from sullen compliance into anger.

Kevin, out on the gate out of curiosity more than duty, positioned himself at the back and to the side where he was fairly safe from having to challenge students over their outrageous choice of clothing. One problem was that he, like many of the old staff out there, had no clear idea any more what exactly the correct uniform was. He stood next to Charlotte, who was half-heartedly challenging anyone who made it through that far.

In a lull in the proceedings he said to Charlotte, sotto voce, "It's the intellectual challenge that attracted me into teaching. What about you?"

She controlled her impulse to snigger and whispered back, "What a load of old bollocks all this is. She's alienating half of the good, compliant kids in the school. We must be sending about three hundred of them home."

"And on the first day too. So they'll miss all those messages about standards and expectations that we always start with. Brilliant planning. You can see why she got a CBE."

"And this is when the uniform is good. She'll have a breakdown when she sees what it's like in December."

Camilla had clearly decided to stamp her personality and presence on the students from day one and she positioned herself in the vanguard, making it absolutely clear that she was the new headteacher and that she was in complete control. She issued breezy "Good mornings" in between hauling students up for the most minor of uniform infringements. Every now and then she would issue fulsome praise for any student walking past in exemplary uniform, a tactic that was subtly taken up by one or two of the other staff members present who were desperate to subconsciously signal to the new Head that they were made of the right stuff and could be relied upon in the future.

Standing in the knot of staff just behind the vanguard, out of Camilla's eye line, was Rick. The queue of students had thinned by this time and Rick scanned the path leading from the entrance gate.

He checked his watch just as two familiar figures turned into the school through the gate and began to walk down the path. Even from two hundred yards away they stood out from the handful of other students still coming in. The boy on the left, tall and willowy, was dressed in a new school uniform, the bright blue of the blazer almost luminous. It was the kind of uniform that was the norm for new Year 7 students eager to impress, but on someone who looked like a Year 11 boy, it stood out from the crowd. Year 11 students never had new uniforms. Which of Fairfield's parents could afford the expense of a new blazer just for two and a half terms?

As the two figures came down the path, Camilla was almost purring with satisfaction at this vision of perfect compliance. She smiled broadly and said, "Good morning. That uniform is absolutely perfect. Well done, you're a model for all the other students to follow."

The boy looked at her and his face was lit up with a shy, tentative smile.

"Thank you, Miss," he said.

"And what is your name, young man?"

"Er, it's Karim, Miss."

"Karim." Her smile flickered for a moment, as if she half remembered the name. "Well, keep it up Karim, that's an excellent start."

Karim and Ahmed walked past her towards Rick. Ahmed strode towards him, his hand extended.

They shook hands.

"Morning, Ahmed, good to see you. Hello, Karim, how are you?"

"I'm fine, thanks, sir," Karim replied.

He walked with them to the main entrance of the school.

"If you come this way, you can wait in the foyer. I'll speak to her about the situation and she'll see you in a few minutes."

"Are you sure this is going to work?" asked Ahmed, walking through the door Rick had opened for him.

"No, no I'm not, but I think it's worth a try. And Karim has already made a good impression with his uniform."

He showed them to a waiting area, explained who they were to Steph on reception, and went back outside. The bell was about to go and the rush of students had dried to a trickle, with just the usual suspects running down the pathway to try and avoid a late detention on their first day of a new school year. Camilla turned back towards the school, leaving other people to deal with the latecomers. Rick sauntered up to her.

"Camilla, can I have a word please?"

Camilla scowled at him.

"What about?"

"Karim and his support worker, Ahmed, are here to speak to you."

She looked puzzled.

"Karim? The Syrian boy we spoke about?"

"Yes, that's right."

"Why on earth is he here? Did you not understand what I said to you about that? He doesn't have a place and I have no intention of giving him one."

"You've just met him and complimented him on his uniform. I really think you should at least meet with them. You saw what he was like. He'd be a real asset to this school."

Camilla opened her mouth to reply but stopped herself, a furious expression on her face.

"My office, now," she hissed, and strode ahead of him through the entrance doors. Rick scuttled after her, a series of doors closing in his face as she marched to her office. When the door closed behind Rick, she turned on him.

"Don't you ever, ever, do that again. If I tell you to do something you do it without question, or I'll come down on you like a ton of bricks and you'll be facing a disciplinary charge. I never, repeat, never see parents or carers without an appointment, and I never, ever respond favourably to being bounced into something I don't want to do."

She was quivering with rage, but her voice was icily quiet and dangerous.

Rick was taken aback by the naked ferocity of her words. He summoned his resolve.

"Camilla, I don't want to make life difficult for you, not least because I know that you can make life so much more difficult for me. You are the Head after all. But let's be clear, I'm not going to clear up your own mess. It's your decision not to take him. It's a very bad decision, in my view, but that's your job. Normally, I would support you, because that's my job, but not in this instance."

"Oh, don't give me all this rubbish. You're loving not supporting me. You're making a point, that's obvious to everyone. Well, you can forget it. If you think I'm going to back down, you've got another think coming. This is our first confrontation and I'm as sure as you are that the staff will know all about it, probably from you, and they'll be watching to see what happens."

"Not everybody works or thinks like you do. I'm not the slightest bit interested in winning public battles over you. It's quite obvious that I've got no future here. You've won, and I'll be going as soon as I can get another job. So don't take this out on Karim. And don't underestimate Ahmed either. If you don't see them, or you don't offer Karim a place, he'll go straight to the *Advertiser* and probably the national press. They'll love this story. New Super head kicks out brave, tragic Syrian refugee. I'm sure Alastair Goodall would love headlines like that on your first day in post as headteacher of his new school."

Camilla paused, digesting Rick's words. Finally, she said, "Okay Rick, that'll do for now. Be in your office, I'll need you shortly to tour all of the form rooms with me."

"And Karim? What are you going to do?"

"Don't push it. I'll drop by your office shortly."

She turned her back on him and went to sit at her computer. The meeting was clearly over.

By this time all of the offenders had been dealt with and the first day of school started only half an hour later than planned. The phone calls of complaint started from the moment everyone was in form time and senior staff were, on Camilla's instructions, patrolling the corridors relentlessly. Camilla herself refused to take any of the calls, handing them on to her two Deputies, Avril and Rick. When the first of the irate parents, with smirking teenagers in tow, arrived at the school demanding to see the new Head, she followed a similar approach. Steph tentatively poked her head around Camilla's office door. She said, "Camilla, I've got Mrs Andrews in reception with Courtney. She's not very happy. She's demanding to see you."

"She can demand all she likes. I will never see anyone in this school without an appointment. It's a rule. If she's determined to stay, pass her on to Avril or Rick, whoever is free. Don't bother me again about parents, understand?"

Steph had never been spoken to like that by Jane, or by Rick in his brief reign as headteacher. Her eyes reddened and she managed to reply, "Oh, yes, of course. Sorry Camilla," before hurriedly scurrying out of the room.

All this time, Karim and Ahmed sat in reception, watching the comings and goings with interest, wondering when they would be granted an audience with the new Head.

Karim whispered to Ahmed, "It seems a little, um, a little different to last year. There's lots of people shouting and crying. I don't understand what's happening."

Ahmed nodded at him. "I get the feeling that the new Head is a little different to Mr Westfield."

"Is that a good thing, do you think?"

"I don't know. Hopefully, we'll find out soon, if we ever get to see her."

Ahmed went up to the reception desk and asked the question.

"Excuse me, do you know when Ms Everson will be able to see us? Mr Westfield asked us to wait here and it's been nearly an hour already."

Steph smiled from behind her computer.

"I'll just see if she is ready for you." She picked up the phone and dialled an extension.

"Ms Everson? Yes, the Syrian boy and his support worker, Mr Hussain, are still here. Have you got time to see them now?"

There was a pause.

"Okay, yes. I'll bring them through."

She turned to Ahmed.

"Yes, if you'd like to follow me. She's got a short window now for a few minutes."

They followed her down the corridor, Karim behind Ahmed, brushing down his uniform and straightening his tie. Three minutes later they reappeared and spoke briefly to Steph again on reception. They were to wait again in the foyer until the Head of Year 11 came to take Karim to his new form.

Sitting back down, Karim looked across at Ahmed.

"So, what do you think?"

Ahmed grimaced. "I think it's a bad thing."

"What did she mean 'on trial'? Have I done something wrong?"

"Different kind of trial, Karim. It means you're just here for a few weeks until she makes her mind up. I've just got a bad feeling she's looking for a reason not to have you. I might be wrong, but she just wasn't very welcoming."

Karim shuffled in his seat and stared out of the window at the rustling leaves of the oak trees outside.

"I wish Mr Westfield was here. Maybe he could explain it all to her."

Ahmed leaned over and patted Karim on the knee, smiling a brittle smile. "It'll be fine, Karim, you'll see. Let's give it a chance, eh?"

They both turned to stare outside into the green canopy, flecked with splashes of yellow and orange as the first leaves began to turn in anticipation of autumn, and waited in silence.

By the last period of the morning, all of the parents had been fobbed off and the phone calls had begun to dry up, so it was safe for Camilla to venture out. She breezed into Rick's office.

"Rick? I need you for half an hour or so," she said, before turning on her heels to Avril's office, Rick trailing in her wake.

She knocked on the door and without waiting for an answer, opened it and walked in. Avril looked up from where she was sitting, evidently in a meeting with Charlotte, blinking in surprise.

"I'm sorry to interrupt, Avril, but I need you now urgently. Can you come with me and Rick and I'll explain on the way?"

She looked across at Charlotte, who was staring as if in mid-speech, mouth half open.

"It's Ms Green isn't it, Head of English? You should come too. It might be instructive for you."

Both Charlotte and Avril got up and followed her out of the office. They caught Rick's eye when they got outside. Charlotte was intrigued. Avril was incandescent. Rick was silent. Camilla set a cracking pace and sailed out of the foyer into the main corridor. She walked into the first classroom.

"Good morning, everyone," she barked.

The tutor, Tony Smith, turned round from the whiteboard where he had been taking the class through their timetables for the year and looked at Camilla, blind panic on his face. The class, a Year 9 form, did the same.

"I said, good morning everyone," Camilla repeated, her voice taking on a harder edge.

The class were baffled. They had heard her the first time. But then a deeply buried, almost primordial instinct kicked in and they remembered some long-forgotten routine from primary school and some of them rather sheepishly chorused, "Good morning, er, Miss." Tony was so shocked he found himself joining in the chorus, until he remembered himself and stopped, changing his panic-stricken expression into what he imagined was a steely professional glare.

It was an embarrassed mumble rather than a lusty chorus and it died before it had started as they realised they did not know what the new headteacher's name was.

Camilla cut across them. "In this school, from this moment onwards, when a member of staff comes into your classroom you stand and say 'good morning'. Understand?"

Sitting at a table near the front, a large, vaguely unkempt girl, with watery eyes that looked in several directions at once, put up her hand and said, "Miss, what if it's in the afternoon?"

Avril, who by this time had edged her way into the room and stood at Camilla's shoulder, said, smiling at her, "Maisie, you say what's appropriate."

Maisie looked up and seeing Avril, smiled back at her. "What's appropr... approp, what's that word mean, Miss?"

"Well, Maisie, it's—"

"Could you take this girl to sit outside my office, please, Miss Howarth?" Camilla's intervention, cutting across Avril, was an instruction, not a question. Avril realised there was no point in trying to explain that Maisie was on the spectrum and had a suite of rather esoteric complications to deal with. She sensed, somehow, that Camilla didn't do complications. She was, in truth, glad of an excuse to leave this coercive pantomime. She had no appetite to trail around watching Cruella De Ville humiliate random students.

"Could everyone stand please?" Camilla continued after Avril had left. The class all got to their feet, with a cacophony of chair scraping. Camilla walked around the room, scrutinising each student in turn. She stopped in front of a spotty boy with a shock of mousy hair.

"Top button undone. Go and stand outside."

Then it was a girl whose skirt was too short.

"Skirt. Go and stand outside, please."

After she had finished, she turned to the teacher, still frozen, mouth open, at the front.

"Mr Smith, please ensure that next time you have checked everyone's uniform. Tomorrow morning send anyone whose uniform is not up to scratch straight to reception. In this school there is now zero tolerance for sloppy uniform."

With that, she turned on her heels and blazed out of the room and on to the next one. She spent the next hour visiting every form room in the school. By the time she had finished, she had ejected a further hundred students from form time and had organised for their Heads of Year to send them home with a standard letter explaining the uniform policy and the consequences of not following it.

At two o'clock Camilla left the building. She had a meeting, apparently, at Bellingford with Alastair Goodall and Barry Pugh, although no-one knew anything about it until she had gone. When she left, it was as if a dark cloud had lifted and the sun had come out. They could all breathe a sigh of relief. Creeping out of her office, looking both ways and back again, like a diligent primary school child crossing the road, Avril took the opportunity to scuttle along to Rick's office.

His door was closed.

That's funny, thought Avril, *that's not like Rick. I wonder if he's in there.*

She knocked. After a moment there was the sound of rummaging around and then footsteps coming towards the door. The handle turned and the door squeaked open a crack. Through the narrow gap, Avril saw Rick peering through.

"Oh God, it's you. Come in, come in," he sighed in relief, flinging open the door wide.

Once inside, Avril settled herself and launched in.

"What a nightmare! Can you believe it? She's worse than all the stories. Poor little Maisie Fredericks was in floods of tears outside her office. I tried to explain her situation to Camilla but she just interrupted me and went on about getting rid of an excuse culture."

Rick shook his head. "I've already been on the TES jobs website. There's no way I can work with her. She's a monster. She won't even talk to me."

"I wonder what'll happen when the parents start to kick off. And the kids. They won't put up with this for very long."

"I don't think she's bothered about that. After all, look how she's refused to speak to any parent or see them. Half a dozen have been up to the school already."

"I know," said Avril, "I've had to see a couple of them and try to talk them down. It's very difficult when you agree with what they're saying, but even for her, we've got to be supportive publicly and try to bring her to her senses behind closed doors."

"She won't listen to us. I wouldn't waste your breath to be honest."

Avril nodded. "You're probably right. She seems very confident. She must be, if she is out of school on the afternoon of her first day with students in the building. Can you imagine Jane doing that? It's bizarre."

"She's at Bellingford, apparently, having a meeting with the big cheeses. She didn't even tell us, and we're supposed to be in charge now she's not in the building."

"What on earth can be so important that they've called her to a meeting now? What can they be talking about?"

*

The three of them sat at one end of a large, polished oak boardroom table, a luxuriant bouquet of flowers in between them, the scent of lilies overpowering all of the others and hanging heavy in the air. To the side was a cafetière, three bone china cups and a plate of thickly-covered Belgian chocolate biscuits. A smiling young woman, in an elegantly understated blouse and slacks, poured the coffee and then looked up expectantly.

"Thanks Sandra, that's all for now. I'll ring if we need anything else." Alastair Goodall radiated a smile in her direction and she left the room for her office next door, where she sat in a daze, transported to a secret place of her own making, a place where one's deepest desires could come true. The warm trance lasted for several minutes before her phone rang and she was once again thrust back into her ordinary work-a-day world where she was a secretary who lived in Cheam with her parents and who had a poorly-paid job in a nearby school.

"So, Camilla, how have the first couple of days been? You indicated on the phone that all was not well." Alastair's query was delivered like a solicitous doctor to a recovering patient.

Camilla sipped her coffee and thought.

"Well, it's even worse than we thought, but before we get on to that, there's a more pressing problem that arose this morning. I've been badly let down by Westfield, who has landed me with an awkward problem."

Camilla went through the issue of Karim and his place at the school. Alastair listened, making a few notes as Camilla gave him the essentials.

"I'm not quite with you here, Camilla. What exactly is the problem? You've got spare capacity, haven't you? It would be extra money. I'd have thought you'd want every spare place filled."

"It would be easy to fill the spare places with the no-hopers that no-one else wants. The kids that have been expelled from three schools already because of appalling behaviour. Another twenty

175

kids like that and not even I will be able to improve the school. And this boy in particular is just an accident waiting to happen. I've been through his file: severe post-traumatic stress disorder, only just started speaking again, already been involved in a permanent exclusion and a violent incident in school. Is he really the kind of student you want me to accept in Year 11, when we should be throwing everything at the results?"

Barry, following as best he could, chipped in, "No, I think you're right Camilla. You can't afford to carry passengers."

Alastair ignored him and carried on as if he hadn't spoken.

"My understanding was that he was the victim in that incident. And Rick's worries about newspaper headlines are quite justified. The nationals would jump on this if you don't take him. What have you done so far?"

"I've given him a place on a trial basis, with no guarantees. I'm pretty sure he won't be with us in the long term."

"You know you can't do that officially, Camilla, don't you?"

She snorted. "Come on, Alastair, you and I both know we can do just about what we want. That's the point of Academies and Trusts, after all. The point is, I need to know that I have your support, and that that dreadful Language Unit, for the flotsam and jetsam of the world, is going to go. No amount of money is worth the hassle that causes."

Alastair thought for a moment.

"The Language Unit will be closed by Christmas. Now we're no longer a Longdon school, we have no obligation to the local authority, and we don't need the money." He flashed a knowing smile at her. "There are other, easier ways of generating money. Now, what are the other issues?"

"The school is an absolute basket case. The students run riot and no-one seems to think there is a problem. The uniform is shocking – they appear to have four different uniforms according to the descriptions and guidelines they have in various publications. And the parents! My God, they are like a cross between *EastEnders* and *Shameless*. Barrack room lawyers, shouting their mouths off about their rights, using foul language. They're aggressive and have treated my staff with no respect."

Barry shook his head and tutted.

"And," continued Camilla, warming to her theme, "mobile phones."

Alastair raised an eyebrow.

"Mobile phones?" he repeated.

"They are allowed mobiles. The kids are all on their phones. I've never seen anything like it."

"No," breathed Pugh, "that's shocking." He hoped he had successfully communicated how shocked he was.

Alastair put his cup down.

"They are allowed mobile phones in lessons?" he probed.

"No, no," said Camilla. "No, in the corridors at break and lunch."

Pugh shook his head. "That's terrible," he pronounced.

"And yet," Alastair continued, "their results were outstanding. They must be doing something right."

"Yes," said Camilla, "those results haven't helped me. I can't understand how they have done it, apart from it being just a freak accident. A couple of rogue markers in one or two core subjects."

"Yes," agreed Pugh. "That must be it. Exactly, a couple of rogue markers. Exactly."

Alastair looked at him. Sometimes, Barry felt a little uncomfortable when he did this and he did it fairly regularly, but everything must be all right because he never said anything negative at the same time.

Alastair took his time. His hands were together with his fingertips in a Sherlock Holmes-style brown study. It was a technique he liked to use when others in a meeting were waiting for him to make a decision. He had perfected the art of making delay look like deep, serious consideration of a range of tricky options rather than not having a clue about what to do and why they should do anything anyway. Barry, on the other hand, had developed a skill set that was the mirror image of that.

Finally, he pronounced the judgement of Solomon.

"It's time for Plan B. Sooner than I thought, but we obviously need to go for a blitzkrieg approach. A scorched earth policy, if you like."

Barry Pugh nodded, desperately hoping that neither of them would ask him his opinion. He had no idea what Plan B was. He couldn't recall discussing Plan B. Or Plan A for that matter. In his panic, he had forgotten that no-one ever asked him his opinion about anything, so he was safe.

"Yes, good," agreed Camilla. "I was hoping you would say that."

"Yes," nodded Pugh.

"So, to recap. Barry," Alastair began.

Pugh, startled, began hyperventilating. He put his cup of coffee back down on the saucer with a bang, slopping a brown puddle into the crisp white china, and blinked up at Alastair.

"Barry, you will go in on Monday and do your Ofsted presentation as agreed after school. This will be on the back of the news that you have heard from a reliable source that Ofsted is imminent."

"But it won't be. Imminent, I mean," interrupted Barry. "They've only been an Academy since January. Ofsted won't be for another, umm, five terms."

Alastair looked pained. Camilla barely supressed a snort of derision.

"No, Barry, we know that, but do you really think anyone there knows it? This strategy needs the whole school to be on pre-Ofsted lockdown. We need everyone working their socks off and putting in the hours. We need fear, Barry, fear. At the Ofsted training it will be announced that you, Barry, as Director of Learning, will be in the school on, say Thursday and Friday, interviewing the staff and doing a series of learning walks."

"Learning walks, yes, I see," Barry nodded.

"As a result of these visits, Camilla will announce the school is in a crisis of shockingly low standards and that if Ofsted were to come a-calling, the school would inevitably be found inadequate. You, therefore will be assigned to be in Fairfield, say, three days a week, monitoring the situation. We will use this engineered crisis to introduce suitable state of emergency measures and on the back of your lesson observations and performance management we will get rid of whoever we need to get rid of."

"And who is that?" Barry asked.

"Oh, you know, the Old Guard, the union troublemakers, people who question what management do, anyone with loyalty to Jane Garner and the old regime."

Camilla delved into her bag and pulled out a sheet of A4 paper.

"These people, I think," she said, passing the paper over to Goodall.

Barry looked at her and then across to Alastair.

"Umm, do you have another copy for me, Camilla?" he asked.

She smiled. "Sorry Barry, I didn't think I'd need one for you."

Alastair's smile matched hers as his flicked down the list.

"Yes," he agreed, passing the paper over to Pugh, "these people."

Barry Pugh looked at the sheet he had just been handed and his eyes widened. It took a moment for his smile to join the other two.

"Yes, these people," he agreed.

4

"So, how did it go today, Karim? Did you see Mr Westfield? Was everything all right?"

Joan and Eric were full of questions for him when he got back later that afternoon. He knew they were excited for him and he didn't want to worry them, so he gave them a version of events they'd be happy with.

"Yes, it was good. I was put into the same form as Ben, and I met some of his other friends, Raysharne and Alex, who were both very friendly."

"Did you have any lessons, love?" asked Joan.

"Just one in the afternoon, English. We were sorting out rules and things with our form tutor all morning. And we had an assembly. There are a lot of new rules, according to Ben."

"Oh, that's good, dear. Maybe this new woman is going to sort out the school. She must be good if they gave her the job over Mr Westfield."

"Yes, you're probably right."

"And was Ahmed with you all day?"

"Yes. He'll be with me for the first week or so and then I think it will be reduced. There are some other refugees that have been allocated to him, apparently."

"Oh, are they from Syria too?"

"Some, I think. I'm not sure."

He thought back to when Ahmed had told him this. He established that there were no young Syrian girls in the new group of refugees and that there had been no news of any Syrian girls in Calais. That was the only thing he was interested in as far as Syria and Syrians were concerned. He felt guilty about it, but he couldn't concentrate on anything else apart from Evana.

Later that night, as he lay on his bed looking at her photograph, he thought about what had happened at Fairfield that day, what he hadn't told Joan or Eric. Just thinking about it made the knot in his stomach return. The assembly where about fifteen Year 11 students were screamed at and hauled out of the hall to be sent home on an exclusion. The assembly where Ms Everson harangued everyone, shouting that they were letting the school down and that their uniform, their attitude, their behaviour and their grades were all a disgrace. The form time interrupted by Ms Everson bursting in and making everyone stand up and then repeating the same ranting lecture, resulting in a couple more students being removed and sent home. One of them had been Raysharne, Ben's friend, who had first looked stunned when he was told to get out and then shaken, his eyes red and brimming with tears. He had left the room eyes down, shaking his head. Karim hadn't dared speak again, just in case Ms Everson came back.

He had a restless, disturbed sleep. When he did finally stop tossing and turning, he slept fitfully, troubled by a strange dream of being somewhere that was eerily reminiscent of his journey from Syria across Europe, with queues of exhausted people, all being shouted at by soldiers with sub-machine guns and being hauled out of lines and forced into huddles by the butts of the guns. Everyone in the queue, regardless of their age, was wearing a Fairfield school uniform.

He awoke at 5.30, to a tangle of sheets and sweat, gasping for breath, and lay there for another hour, not able to sleep, before finally admitting defeat and hauling himself out of bed and downstairs. He looked out of the kitchen window. It was already warm and the sky was cloudless. It was going to be another scorching hot day.

He survived breakfast, forcing himself to respond politely to Joan and Eric's mixture of concern and enthusiasm, and was relieved when the knock came on the door.

"That's Ahmed. I'll see you later."

He grabbed his school bag and made for the door.

"Bye love, good luck," said Joan. She restrained her tendency to give him a hug and watched him go, powerless.

"Good luck, Karim," Eric added. "Have a good day."

"Yes, goodbye," he mumbled, scrambling through the door to avoid any further conversation.

Joan and Eric exchanged a glance and then a hug, as they watched him walk down the path with Ahmed.

The bus journey was stiflingly hot. Ahmed made a couple of attempts to make conversation, but Karim was miles away, lost in his own thoughts, silently staring out of the window. It was a relief to get out into the open air and to feel the breeze dry the trickles of sweat inside his shirt. They turned into the school path and joined the queue that had already built up as students were being dealt with by the army of senior staff standing outside the school entrance. Just like the day before, kids were removed from the queue and sent home with standard letters to a backdrop of sullen, simmering resentment and, in some cases, outright defiance and hostility. They were met with harshly-raised voices from some of the teaching staff. Camilla was centre stage again, barking and hostile, as if she were dealing with inmates at a prison.

Ahmed and Karim got past this section of surveillance and were expecting to turn left into the top playground before going into the school, but were surprised to be met by an extended wing of staff directing them and all the other students who had passed muster on the uniform front to the right and the top playgrounds and tennis courts.

They followed the stream, aware of a quiet exchange of complaint amongst the students. Up ahead, a familiar voice called back to them.

"Hey, Karim, what do you reckon? Do you think we're all gonna be shot?"

A teacher with a clipboard, a new recruit to Camilla's army of quislings, raised his voice. "That's enough, Ben. We'll have quiet on the way, please."

Ben didn't answer but hung back to allow Karim and Ahmed to catch him up.

"This is a load of old crap, isn't it?" He kept his voice quiet.

"What is going on, Ben? Why does everyone have to come this way?" asked Ahmed.

"It's a new rule, apparently. We all have to start in the playground in fire drill positions to do another uniform and equipment check."

"Every day? Do you have to do this every day?"

"Think so," he replied, "or until they get fed up of doing it I suppose."

Karim maintained his silence, even with Ben. The press of bodies on the way to the playground was making him feel closed in and he could feel his heart racing. He tried to make himself breathe in and out deeply and regularly. When they turned the corner of the building onto the playground there were hundreds of students beginning to coalesce into orderly lines, with operations being directed by form tutors, with Heads of Year supervising. The air was full of bawled instructions and admonishments.

"Straight line please, 9C."

"No talking."

"Single file, eyes to the front."

"Billy! Billy get out of the line, now. Stand over there. Move. NOW!"

"Register order please."

Ahmed left Karim with Ben, and went over to mill around with some of the other unattached staff, to observe the military manoeuvres of about a thousand children from a distance. Their form, 11D, were always placed next to the fence of the tennis courts for fire drills. Ben turned back to Karim to make sure he knew what to do.

"Karim, we've got to stand over here with the form. It's where we always are, okay? You'll be first in the queue because you're first in the register."

Karim's face was blank, pale and sweating. He did not appear to have heard what Ben had said.

"Karim? Are you okay? You look terrible. Karim?"

He reached out and grabbed his shoulder. He jumped as if he'd been slapped around the face and pulled away.

"Uhh? What? What are you doing?"

Ben spoke more gently to him.

"Karim, it's okay. You just need to stand here."

He led him to the front of their line and then went to take up his place halfway down the line.

A silence settled on the straight lines of uniformed figures. Form tutors walked down the lines slowly ticking off who was present. Then they started again, stopping by each student in the line and eyeing them up and down, checking their appearance against a pre-printed list of requirements. At regular intervals, students were hauled out of the line and sent to line up in what came to be called 'Death Row', waiting for someone more important to bellow at them and tell them how they were a disgrace to the school. They would be the second wave of students to be sent home that morning, with the official letter outlining which particular school rule they had violated.

A third sweep of the lines began, with each student being asked to open their bag and show their essential equipment, a procedure that generated another cohort of criminals to be dealt with. The morning shift of scavengers, enormous seagulls and rooks that were perched in the trees and on the top of the tennis court fence, shifted from talon to talon watching the proceedings unfolding beneath them. The birds began to grow impatient as this unusual gathering was preventing them from swooping down and hoovering up the cast away half-eaten sandwiches and crisps that usually littered the playground after the breakfast shift.

As time dragged on, the silence in the rows of the students endured, punctuated by the harsh guttural croaking from the birds and the isolated, haranguing shouts from the teachers. The sun beat down relentlessly. It was going to be a beautiful day, the latest in this unusually late-flowering heatwave. Karim, at the front of the line, was dripping sweat. His skull pounded with a throbbing, tightening headache. The mesh-linked fence of the tennis court was in touching distance and the pattern of the wire grid began to swim before his eyes. He swayed momentarily, unsteady on his feet, before abruptly correcting himself and forcing himself upright with an effort of will. The thousand pupils in silent straight lines pressed upon him, and each echoing shout from the patrolling officers made him jump back from the barbed wire. There was a sudden surge forward and he found himself pressed hard up against the fence with the soldiers screaming at him to get back, hitting him with batons. He looked around, eyes wild and staring, trying to force himself back to where he had last seen her. "Evana! Evana, where are you?" He tried to force himself back through the crowd, but was pushed back against the fence and the soldiers' batons forced him to the floor, trampled and downtrodden by the boots of a thousand people.

When he awoke, he was blinded by the glare of the sun directly in his eyes. Shielding his face with his hands, he squinted through his fingers to see Ben and Ahmed lifting him up.

"Karim. Karim. Are you okay? What's the matter?"

He tried to explain but nothing came from his mouth, except jagged, rattling gasps. His heart was racing. Why did they sound so scared? What had happened? His thoughts were interrupted by a screaming woman's voice.

"Get back into line! This instant! You're behaving like animals. Back into line, now!"

The other senior staff there joined in, shouting and pushing until some semblance of order had been established. Camilla, forcing her way through the crowd of students, appeared in front of Karim, who had just that moment been helped to his feet.

"You! I might have known it. What on earth do you think you are doing, disrupting everything like that? You could have caused a major accident. Mr Westfield, take this boy back inside. I'll deal with him later."

Ahmed went to speak but Rick immediately touched him on the arm.

"Later. Later. We need to help Karim to the medical room."

Ahmed looked at Camilla and shaking his head, turned away to join Rick and Karim slowly making their way out of the playground to the main building. As they went, silence descended on the straight lines of the students, with the frantic, sporadic shouts of the guards gradually fading as they got further and further away.

*

The next day, Ahmed arrived at the school without an appointment. He had timed his arrival to be after the morning checks had been done. He did not want to spend any more time than necessary in the school after the events of the day before. As he came through the main entrance he noticed that the foyer was standing room only as every available seat was taken by parents with sullen-faced students of all ages.

He went up to the reception desk, where a harassed-looking Steph was answering the phones while simultaneously placating the increasingly fractious parents in the waiting area.

"Good morning. I need to see Ms Everson, please."

Steph balanced the phone between her chin and shoulder, remembering to attempt a customer-friendly smile.

"Morning. Do you have an appointment?"

"No, it'll only take a couple of minutes."

"Yes, I'm sure, but you still need to make an appointment. If you'd like to ring us, I'm sure we can fit you in in the next few days."

"No, I'm sorry, that won't do. I need to see her now. Is she in her office?"

Steph's smile wobbled and her eyes flicked around. "Umm, yes she is, but she's in an important meeting. If you'd…"

The end of Steph's sentence floated on the air, unheard by its intended recipient. Ahmed strode down the corridor to the side of reception.

"No, no, wait. You can't go down there, she's…"

Ahmed reached the door in a few strides, knocked and walked straight in.

Camilla was sitting at her table, her feet up on a chair in front of her, drinking coffee and reading that morning's Daily Mail. She spluttered her coffee in shock, sat bolt upright and began to protest.

"What on earth are you doing bursting in here like this? How dare you. Get out, at once, before I call the police."

"Don't worry, Ms Everson, there's no need for that. I'll only be a minute."

"You will be no such thing, you'll leave."

Ahmed cut across her.

"I will leave, the second I've finished this. Just listen, for once in your life. You've won, Ms Everson. Karim will not be coming back to this school. He'll go to Longdon College, where there is some sense that they want him and that he'll be treated properly. You should be ashamed of yourself, the way you treat your students here. Do you have any idea what happened yesterday? Karim had a panic attack, a flashback of his time as a refugee escaping a war zone and a dictatorship, a flashback triggered by your outrageous treatment of your students yesterday. Shouting and yelling in children's faces, public humiliation for the most trivial of things, children in tears, keeping them in silence in the full sun for an hour. This is not a school any more, it's a prison camp, and we will not be part of it."

Camilla had recovered her poise, having established that this wasn't some random madman from the street.

"Well, Mr Hussain, I'll overlook your rudeness, bursting in here without an appointment. I'm sorry if Karim was unwell yesterday. He has had a difficult time and he obviously is not ready for mainstream school."

"He was perfectly ready last summer, and he made great progress, when Mr Westfield was in charge."

"Yes, well, he is no longer in charge. We run a zero tolerance regime here, Mr Hussain, and we will not bend for anyone. As soon as you make an exception the whole regime crumbles and you're back running a chaotic madhouse of a school. That is not going to happen."

"No, Ms Everson. As soon as you bend to accommodate the individual you are showing the strength of the school and its philosophy and you are teaching the children a valuable lesson. You are not preparing them for military service. You are preparing them to live together harmoniously with all kinds of other people."

"That's nonsense."

Ahmed raised the flat of his hand high in the air.

"No, Ms Everson, I do not seek to have a debate with you. I am not trying to convince you. You are certain you are right and will not listen to any view you disagree with. I'm just telling you. And I will be telling the *Advertiser* as well."

He turned on his heels, deaf to her spluttered protestations, and marched out of her office. When he got to reception he smiled at Steph.

"I'm so sorry to cause trouble. I've finished now."

He walked to the exit and at the threshold he turned back to the parents sitting in the waiting area and said, "Oh and by the way, if you're waiting to see Ms Everson, she's in her office on her own drinking coffee and reading the paper, hiding from all of you. Good morning."

By the time he reached the gate at the end of the path, the first parent had stood up and was making her way down the corridor, child in tow.

5

KARIM STRETCHED AND YAWNED, RED AROUND THE EYES. His room was in darkness, save for the silver blue glow from his computer screen. It was late and he had to be ready to go back to Longdon College tomorrow. The first day had been all right, well at least compared to what had happened at Fairfield. He went red whenever he thought about that, embarrassed that he had fainted, but he knew that he couldn't go back, even if they had wanted him to. Ahmed was right, the school had changed without Mr Westfield in charge, and even the thought of all those straight lines and shouting and bullying was too much for him. He got the impression that at Longdon he would be left on his own to get on with his education quietly, without lots of rules to worry about.

He looked up at his computer screen again and began to close down the sites one by one. He spent too much of his time late at night scouring sites to get the latest news about the war and the plight of the endless stream of refugees. He checked the official government-approved sites, shaking his head at their flagrant lies and distortions, as well as the opposition sites and finally those UK-based sites supporting the refugees. He seized upon any references to unaccompanied child refugees, pursuing links down an ever-diminishing trail that inevitably led to chilling details about the fate of the displaced: drownings, people trafficking, rape and forced prostitution, hunger and despair. There were the occasional case studies of the happy endings, Syrians who had made it to countries in western Europe and were now safe and settled.

He supposed that he was now one of those rare success stories, but he certainly didn't feel like one. He felt tired and sad and empty and alone. He felt angry. He felt like a specimen in a zoo. He felt...

Not a moment too soon, his train of thought, swallow diving towards self-pity, was interrupted by the ping of his phone. He glanced down at it, smiled, and opened the Snapchat message. It was Ben.

Yo, Karim, my man. Are you up?

Yeah – Syria surfing.

You okay? You looked bad the other day.

Yeah, I'm fine now thanks.

What was it?

Panic attack, I think. I had a kind of flashback about the journey through Europe.

Has that happened before?

Not really. Sometimes can't sleep very well. Strange nightmares, that kind of thing. Never during the day before though.

Why do you think it happened?

I don't know. It felt sort of the same – straight lines and shouting. Like being a prisoner of war.

You coming back?

No, can't do it. Went to College yesterday.

Longdon?

Yeah.

Is it as bad as everyone says?

Karim stopped to think for a moment. He hesitated, his thumbs poised above the key pad.

Other students very loud and badly behaved. Most teachers ignore them and focus on quiet kids who want to work. A few refugee kids there. Think I'll be okay. What is the phrase? Keep head under?

If you keep your head down, you mean?

Yes, if I keep my head down.

There was a pause. Karim waited, wondering if Ben was still there. Then the text materialised on screen.

Gutted you won't be coming back. Was looking forward to being in the same class!

Me too.

You wanna come over at the weekend for a FIFA tournament? Raysharne and Alex are coming.

When?

Saturday at 2?

There was another pause before Karim replied. In the vacuum, Ben fired off another question.

Scared I'll whup you? Crystal Palace 4, Aleppo FC 0?

You very funny boy, very big imagination.

We'll see on Saturday. Don't be late, if you can handle it.

Ben?

What? Still there?

Thanks.

Karim turned his phone off. He lay back on his bed in the darkness and wiped his eyes, the tears glittering in the ghostly blue halo from his PC.

6

"Why the bloody hell have we been summoned to this meeting anyway? We had two whole days of bloody meetings last week. What more can there possibly be to talk about?" Kwame grumbled.

He had caught the mood of the whole audience, who shuffled in their seats, bubbling with resentment that this hour-long meeting after school had been sprung on them without warning. They were also still in shock after Camilla's uncompromising approach to the beginning of a new school year and were half fearful, half fascinated about how she was going to follow it up in week two.

"I know, I've got so much to do as well," Charlotte replied.

"Maybe she's going to apologise for her performance last week. You know, she realises now that she overreacted and that she needs to be more subtle and thoughtful about the best way to motivate people." Kevin said this with a lopsided smirk on his face.

Kwame snorted. "Of course, because that's what headteachers do, isn't it? Apologise. Show some humility. Reach out and build bridges. Dear Lord. More likely she's going to announce a programme of public floggings."

Charlotte interjected, "Look, here they come. And by the look on their faces, you might not be too far wrong, Kwame."

They looked up towards the entrance door. Rick and Avril came in first and made their way across the front of the audience to sit together on the front row at the far side of the Hall. Their faces were grim and set, with eyes cast down to the floor. They took their seats and put their heads together, whispering. The buzz of chatter died down to be replaced by a strained, expectant silence. Usually, both Avril and Rick were all smiles and would chat to people in the audience as they came in, regardless of the subject of the meeting, but this sombre entrance was like a bucket of cold water.

"Has someone died?" asked Kevin.

"Not yet, but it's only a matter of time," replied Charlotte.

Their conversation was cut short by the door to the Hall swinging open a second time. In walked Camilla, all smiles, chatting to a smaller man behind her. He was wearing an expensive-looking suit and carried a clipboard in his hand. They climbed onto the stage and the man sat at one of the seats to the side of the lectern, while Camilla went to stand behind it.

"Good afternoon, everyone," she began, "and thank you for being here so promptly. Lisa, if you'd like to take an attendance register while we start, please?"

Lisa, who was sitting on the first seat of the front row by the door, almost jumped out of it, a look of pure panic written across her features. "Yes, Miss Everson, of course," she stuttered. She spent the next twenty minutes craning her head from her vantage point to make sure she hadn't missed anyone tucked away on the back row, ticking names on her staff list.

This intervention added a few degrees of frost to the atmosphere, and attitudes began to ice up once again.

Charlotte mouthed to Kwame and Kevin, "An 'attendance register'? 'Miss Everson'? What the…?"

They both looked incredulous, but confined themselves to wide-eyed shrugs of incomprehension, as Camilla had started to speak again.

"As you all know, the Trust has been in the school for the last few days, doing learning walks and getting a feel for the way the school works. I'm sorry to have to tell you that we have been shocked by what we found. There is clearly a culture here of accepting very low, sloppy standards. Standards of behaviour, uniform, teaching, speaking, presentation, safeguarding, everything. This cannot go on. We are expecting Ofsted this term and I have to tell you that if they came tomorrow we would almost certainly fail and be put into a category. That category would be Special Measures, and I don't need to tell you what that would mean for the school and everyone sitting here today. People would lose their jobs and we would have to endure an almost permanent presence of Ofsted in the school. As I said to you all last week, in this school from now on, there will be a zero tolerance culture. I meant what I said."

She paused and gripped the side of the lectern, glaring at the faces in front of her. The faces registered sullen resentment and anxiety, for the most part. Those staff with a more naturally questioning mindset were both angry at the unprecedented criticism of the school after their best ever exam results and baffled by the use of the Ofsted word. As Kwame whispered to Charlotte and Kevin, "But we only just had Ofsted last year. What's all this about?"

She didn't answer as Camilla ploughed on.

"We've put together an emergency programme of measures, and I can assure you that we will be doing everything we can to ensure that standards rise and that no-one is in danger of losing their job as a result of a bad Ofsted report. One part of that programme involves Barry, who is a trained Ofsted inspector, and who will be spending three days a week in Fairfield interviewing people, doing learning walks and getting all key staff 'Ofsted ready'."

"Oven-ready more like," Kevin harrumphed to himself. There was a snort of suppressed laughter, as his comment was caught by several people on the back row.

Camilla glared even more fiercely at the crowd, this time aiming her disapproval at the back row.

"This will start from Wednesday. But just to get the ball rolling, Barry is going to take us through the latest news from Ofsted, directly from his Senior Inspector briefing last week. Ladies and gentlemen, Barry Pugh, Director of Learning at Bellingford Multi-Academy Trust."

Camilla led the applause, that was taken up politely by most of the crowd, as Barry stood up and walked towards the lectern. He looked up from his clipboard and smiled hesitantly. He began, his eyes darting around the hall.

"Good afternoon, everyone. I'll just get my presentation ready and we'll begin."

After thirty seconds of fumbling with his memory stick, with Camilla giving everyone in the audience a Vulcan death stare, he loaded his PowerPoint, looked over his shoulder to check the correct slide was displaying, and began. Like a politician trying to appear relaxed and informal, he removed his jacket and started with a harmless, not very funny joke about modern technology. Neither he, nor anyone else in the audience, knew as he started, that he had already reached the high-water mark of his achievement that afternoon. It would be a long, slow, painful descent into crippling incompetence and mind-numbing tedium.

*

The day before had started so well. He had worked on the presentation for Fairfield for most of the afternoon while Alison had prepared a late Sunday roast. He took a break from his work to eat, conscious of the fact that he would have to get back to it before long. Alison didn't mention it once, she was just immersed in the preparation of the meal and then the clearing away and the stacking of the dishwasher. Even during the meal she was strangely quiet, as if she resented having to do it. Barry thought it would help him gain a few brownie points if he made coffee after the meal, so he clattered around the kitchen, turning a simple job into a performance.

"Here you are, darling," he had said, in a sing-song voice, coming through with the tray. "I've made the coffee."

He waited. There was silence.

"How's the coffee, darling?" he said finally.

"Hmm? Oh, it's fine, thank you."

A tiny worm of irritation gnawed at him. It really wouldn't have taken much for her to have said it spontaneously. After all, she often told him off for not being spontaneous, but it wasn't just him, now, was it?

"I've got that big presentation at Fairfield tomorrow afternoon, if you remember?" he said.

"Oh yes, that's right. Will you be late then?" Alison tried not to let her voice sound too full of hope.

"No, no, I'll be back by six at the latest. It's just that I'll have to spend a lot of time preparing the PowerPoint and the notes this evening. It's very important to the Trust, you see."

"That's nice, darling," she said.

"Barry," she continued, "have you thought any more about decorating the dining room, like we discussed?"

"Not really, darling, I've got a lot on my plate and I think I need to get established at Bellingford before spending all the money."

"But we discussed it Barry, you promised."

Barry's voice took on the tone of a slightly exasperated primary school teacher who has patiently explained something blindingly obvious several times already, but who has the depths of compassion and forbearance to be able to patiently explain it all again.

"Yes, but darling, I've been through the money. Let's leave it until the summer, like we agreed."

We didn't agree that at all, thought Alison, *it's just what you want, as always.*

"As you wish, dear," she said. "You know, I saw an interesting job that I was going to apply for. It's in the accountants down in the village. Really convenient."

Barry shifted in his chair.

"A job, Alison? Why on earth would you need a job, dear?"

"I don't need a job, Barry, I want one. I want to use my skills and be useful and get into the world again. I really think it would help."

He bristled. "Help? What do you mean 'help'? Are you saying I can't provide for you? I don't want people thinking you have to go out to work."

"For goodness sake, it's not 1955, Barry. It's perfectly normal for both husband and wife to work. It's not as if we have children to look after."

Barry's expression hardened. "What are you trying to say, Alison?"

"I'm not trying to say anything, Barry, I just would like to work again. You're too sensitive about all of this."

"No, no dear, I am not too sensitive. Not at all. Look, as I've said, I've got a very important day tomorrow and I'm going to do some work on the presentation now, I'll probably take a few hours to get it right. But perhaps I could make it up to you later? What do you say?"

Alison tried to control her annoyance at his attitude and her exultation that he would be locked away in his study for the rest of the evening, leaving her blissfully free to enjoy her book.

"Actually darling, if you're working, I think I'll sleep in the other room tonight. I don't want to disturb you."

"No, you wouldn't disturb me, honestly."

"But I don't want to be disturbed either. You get on with your work and we'll talk again about it all tomorrow."

Barry looked doubtful. "Well, if you're sure."

"Yes, I am." She smiled at him. "You go up. And good luck tomorrow."

He left, thinking to himself, "You always manage to argue her down in the end, you old dog."

She stayed on the sofa, thinking to herself, "What is wrong with him? Why can't he let me do what I want?"

She felt her anger rise and her eyes began to smart. She reached for *Madame Bovary*, opened it and was immediately soothed.

She woke at about two in the morning with a raging thirst and a headache, and crept downstairs to the kitchen to get a glass of water and some paracetamol. She hesitated on the creaking top step of the staircase so as not to wake him, and tiptoed down the rest, holding her breath, her heart hammering. She was still furious with Barry about his attitude to her idea about the job. Actually, she was furious, she realised, with Barry about just about everything. She swallowed the pills and drained the glass, putting it down on the surface next to Barry's clipboard.

That bloody clipboard. It summed up everything she didn't like about him. She picked it up and glanced down at it, in the dim light cast by the cooker. She had never read it before, never even held it, such was Barry's careful guarding of it. The first few pages were obviously Barry's notes for the presentation at Fairfield the next day. She turned them over until she got to the usual targets pages. She read down the list of targets, most of them ticked off as having been achieved. What a way to view the world, she thought.

She flicked over the page. There was a different sheet of targets there, with more pages underneath. She read through them. There were targets for work. There were targets for money. There were targets for holidays. This was a picture of a perfectly-controlled life that she faintly recognised. It was the nuts and bolts of the life of her husband, the life he spent so much of his waking hours thinking about and planning, but a life in which she played no part at all. She was invisible. She was not named. She was not considered. She was not *there*.

She flicked through the pages again, just to double check. She began to cry, just a few grudging tears, as the realisation washed over her that, to Barry, she was no more significant than the chair she was sitting on at that moment. A useful part of the household, no doubt, but no more than that. Just a few tears, but they were enough. She pulled herself together, controlled her breathing and thought, her eyes half-closed, her chin resting on her fingertips. Yes, that was it, that's what she would do.

She went next door to the dining room, where Barry often hammered away at his laptop, careful not to make a sound. There it was. His laptop gleamed in the shadows, in the middle of the dining table. She turned it on, desperately hoping that it wouldn't make that ridiculous Windows noise and bring him downstairs to investigate. She waited, hardly daring to breathe and then exhaled in relief as it booted up in silence.

She typed in his password and clicked on the USB symbol and opened up the last document, a PowerPoint presentation labelled 'Fairfield. Sept 2017'. It was an official Ofsted file that he had obviously amended. And now, she thought, she was just going to amend it some more. He was getting off lightly. After a few mouse clicks she saved it and then browsed the web for something suitable. Her heart was in her mouth as she pressed print, but then she thought, so what if he hears it? We'll have the row now, rather than later. I just won't get the satisfaction of seeing this through. She picked up the pages from the printer and closed down the laptop again.

Then she went back to the kitchen to that loathsome clipboard. She removed the pages of his own notes, leaving the top copy in place and left the clipboard where she had found it. Finally, she took a glass of water and tiptoed back up the stairs as quietly as she could. She didn't know if it would work. She imagined that Barry, being the kind of man he was, would check through his papers before delivering the session. Oh well, it was worth a go. She settled down under the duvet and imagined him delivering the speech with those notes. Tick that box, matey. She laughed into the pillow to suppress the sound. It was sometime before she finally fell asleep.

*

They all felt as if they had aged prematurely, having experienced entire lifetimes in the previous forty minutes or so. Whole continents could have split from larger land masses, glaciers carved out valley formations, tectonic plates shifted inexorably. Aeons had passed and still Barry Pugh ploughed on, as ashen-faced adults turned to dust in front of him.

He had started fairly well, back in the Jurassic era, with his only fault being a tendency to commit the cardinal sin of reading the text on the PowerPoint slide. That and a monotonous, humourless delivery rendered the start of the proceedings as averagely dull for an after-school training session, but nothing that couldn't be endured. But the mistakes began to stack up. At one point in his session, as rigor mortis was setting in, Barry spoke for about six minutes, referring to a slide of the presentation while behind him the screen was greyed out.

The car crash continued. He clicked his cueing device to move on to the next slide and turned over the top page of the notes on his clipboard. And then he froze. There in front of him was a colour copy of the cover of a publication entitled *Big and Busty*. He looked up from his clipboard and surveyed the audience, blinking and licking his lips. He looked back down at his clipboard, an expression of existential dread on his face. He seemed to be stuck in that sequence of activities as if they were in a never-ending loop.

He clicked again and looked behind him at the screen. A wave of relief broke over him. The slide bore the legend, 'Recent changes to the Inspection schedule'.

"Ah, yes," he managed to croak, "this section is extremely important. As you can see from this next slide, this has huge implications for classroom teachers in advance of an Ofsted visit."

At last, thought the classroom teachers in the audience, something of use. They sat forward in their chairs as Barry clicked to move on to the next slide. On the screen behind him a huge image of two lions copulating flashed into life, with the proof of the lion being the King of the Jungle revealed to the audience in glorious technicolour.

There was a ripple from the audience and then a few isolated bursts of laughter. Barry looked up at them, nonplussed, and then turned to look at the screen.

"Wha…? Oh, I'm terribly sorry, I've no idea how that got there, I'll just move on."

He had started to sweat. He looked down again at his notes, forgetting the awful spectacle of the printed first page of *Big and Busty* that he had laid back down on his clipboard and turned it over, struggling not to reveal it to the front row, his fingers slippery with sweat, fumbling with the pages.

He proceeded with the presentation as great spreading stains of perspiration made their way across his light blue shirt. He ignored his notes and crash tackled his way through the slides, a task made more difficult by the fact that at random intervals, there would be another slide of some exotic species of animal locked together. After the third such picture he abandoned the slideshow and delivered yet another apology. He mumbled and croaked his way until the end of his slot and finished by saying, "Thank you very much everyone."

Camilla, her face like thunder, began the applause, which was joined in by everyone until it was tumultuous. Kevin turned to Kwame and Charlotte. "That was the best after-school presentation we've ever had. Barry Pugh is obviously a stage name."

Barry shuffled from the podium back to his seat, his shirt, light blue at the beginning of his talk, now dark and mottled. As he gathered up his papers with slippy, sweaty hands, *Big and Busty* escaped from the sheaf of notes and fluttered, this way and that, to land face up at Camilla's feet.

7

It had been a public humiliation that would have crushed most people with an ounce of sensitivity or judgement. Barry had neither. His lack of both self-knowledge and self-doubt was staggering. His first comment to Camilla when they reached the sanctuary of her office had been, "Well, I think that went quite well before the, er, difficulties at the end, don't you?"

Camilla looked at him, wondering whether he was being ironic, or at the very least, sarcastic. His beaming, earnest face immediately answered that one. Barry didn't do irony.

"Quite well? You thought it went quite well?" asked Camilla in disbelief. "And what was your view about the pictures of animals rutting? And that vile pornography that escaped from your clipboard? I suppose they were a triumph as well, were they?"

"No, no, no, of course not. But all of that is further proof of how sick this whole place is. That was obviously sabotage from someone wanting to undermine the changes we want to implement."

"Sabotage?" queried Camilla. "Yes, of course, I hadn't thought of that. Do you have anyone in mind? And how could anyone have got access to your USB stick and your clipboard?"

"Well, I'm not sure, but I have my suspicions. The crowd on the back row were very disrespectful. Laughing and talking from the beginning. And I have to say, Camilla, I was not impressed by the reaction of Westfield and Howarth. It was almost as if they were junior members of staff, not Senior Leaders. I wouldn't put it past them to have been involved."

"Hmm." Camilla thought for a moment. "Well, you've got an immediate opportunity on Wednesday to strike back. I'll draw up a programme of learning walks and I'll make sure that the people you've just mentioned will be on the route. I think it would also be, umm, instructive if we organise you to shadow Avril and Rick when they do their break and lunch duties. See what you think of the corridors."

Barry smiled, the penny dropping.

"And perhaps a report of the visit, with copies to the Trust and the Governors, naming and shaming, might be helpful."

Camilla leaned forward and laid a hand on Barry's knee.

"It's so reassuring to find we're all on the same page," she gushed.

Barry went slightly pink and his heart swelled. He could barely breathe.

Fifteen minutes later, he floated out of Camilla's office, down the corridor and out of the front door to the car park. He had been dismissed after spending the latter part of the meeting being allocated tasks, each of which was designed to undermine and catch out the members of staff whose names had been on the list.

He roared the BMW out of the entrance, still surfing on the wave of what he mistakenly considered to be Camilla's fulsome praise, not noticing the random knots of teachers who watched him go, sniggering and gossiping about the debacle he had presided over in the Hall an hour or so earlier. Each throaty roar of the 3 litre engine formed a soundtrack to the music video that played in his head, of Camilla, dressed all in leather, repeating in a chorus, "on the same page, on the same page".

Alastair Goodall surveyed the tables around him. A sea of crisp white linen as far as the eye could see. The debris from a series of expensive meals was immediately removed by a sequence of different, unobtrusive and efficient waiters, so that no-one important enough to be eating in that restaurant had to be inconvenienced by the sight of anything remotely messy or unpleasant. After all, thought Alastair, what was money for if not to protect rich people from the grim realities of life? Not that he was rich, of course. It was just that he enjoyed being able to pretend for a few hours at a time. And where better to pretend than in a restaurant such as this, a stone's throw from the Palace of Westminster, where ministerial expenses took care of the minor details such as the bill.

His mobile vibrated into life, wrenching him from these musings. He picked it up and scrutinised the screen. "Ah," he breathed, a smile flickering across his face. He pressed the green icon and answered.

"Camilla, how are you?" he said. There was a pause.

"Yes, so I understand," he continued. The next pause was longer as Camilla got into her stride. In the middle of the pause, Grovelle came back to the table and helped himself to another glass of wine, and indicated to Alastair that he should continue the call. Alastair raised his eyebrows, nodded at him and did just that.

"He did what?" Alastair's eyes widened and his expression grew incredulous. The next pause was even longer. He suddenly burst out laughing.

"You can't be serious. *Big and Busty*? Oh, my word, that's priceless."

Across the table Grovelle looked up, his attention caught by a familiar title.

"Yes, I know. I told you, he's a prize idiot… What? Yes, I'm just having a late lunch with Marcus. Yes, that's right. Yes, of course Camilla, I will. You all set for the next part of the masterplan? Yes? Good. Okay, darling, speak soon."

He pressed the red button and put the phone back down on the table, a self-satisfied half-smile on his face.

"Well, Camilla. That sounded very intriguing, Alastair," Marcus said, relieved to be speaking again. He was never comfortable with his own silence.

"Yes, she sends her regards by the way, Marcus."

Grovelle's eyes flashed and he licked his lips.

"Yes," he intoned, "I'd be disappointed if she didn't."

Alastair gathered himself.

"So, Marcus, where were we? You've been dying to tell me something since I arrived. Come on, spit it out."

Grovelle leaned over and dropped his voice.

"Confidentially, between you and me, I'm being lined up for Home Secretary, so I've got to deliver on these reforms, otherwise I've got no chance."

"Home Secretary? But you've only been at Education for five minutes. How does anybody in government ever get to grips with their brief?"

Grovelle looked across at him with a mixture of incredulity and pity.

"Don't be silly, old boy. It's completely unnecessary to know what you're doing and how policy works in your department. That's what the civil service is for. Goodness me, it would cause a stir if a minister stayed around long enough to understand the policies associated with their ministry. No, that would be very dangerous."

"So, what's the current Home Secretary done wrong then? Why are they being axed?"

Grovelle smiled and took a sip of his wine.

"I'm afraid Sebastian didn't bear down hard enough on immigration."

"Didn't bear down hard enough? Good God, what do they want? Immigrants being shot in the street?"

"You can scoff, Alastair, but tough decisions have to be made and then delivered. Some people are made of the right stuff and they step up to the plate and do whatever it takes."

"People like you, Marcus?"

"Exactly. Other people, weak people essentially, dither and listen to the opposing arguments. It's Darwinism of the purest kind," he smirked.

Alastair constructed a thin smile. Even he hesitated to ponder the precise process of natural selection that had produce Marcus Grovelle.

"So, to cut to the chase, your initiative is in trouble and you need me, or rather my Trust's schools, to rescue you. That's it, isn't it."

A dark cloud flashed across Grovelle's face.

"No, Alastair, as you well know, that isn't it. There's as much in this for you as there is for me, and don't you forget it. Many schools have been scared off by the unions and are too frit to take up the opportunities afforded by the Great Reform Act, specifically in respect of apprenticeships. You can steal a march on all the others, and make a national name for yourself in the process, by piloting the National Service and National Health apprenticeships for fourteen-year-olds. Give me a commitment, a binding commitment, with a September 2019 start date, that Fairfield, and the Bellingford Trust in general, will host the national pilot."

Alastair took another sip of his double espresso and then slipped in a stiletto question, up to the hilt, neatly between the second and third ribs.

"And what exactly is in this for me, Marcus?"

Grovelle's eyes glittered.

"Oh, I think we can make this worth your while, Alastair," he said.

*

By the time Barry's BMW pulled in to the driveway of his home he was feeling a little less chipper. As the journey progressed, the throaty roar of the engine was less and less in evidence as he replayed the events of the afternoon in his head, and the flourish of his foot on the accelerator, trumpeting his triumph at every traffic light, became a tentative prod. He could not shift the image of two lions copulating from his mind, never mind the *Big and Busty* page floating down to rest at Camilla's high-heeled shoes. Even the memory of her hand resting on his knee was beginning to fade, to be replaced by the sight and sound of the staff sniggering in the audience.

He racked his brains, again. How on earth had his notes and memory stick been tampered with? And who would have been able to do it? There were plenty of candidates who would have wanted to do it. He was used to people's jealousy. But who had the opportunity to do it?

He trudged over the gravel to the house and shut the door behind him. The hallway was full of the most delicious smells of dinner cooking.

"It's only me Alison," he called, hanging his coat up and resting his case on the side table.

Alison appeared at the end of the hallway.

"Hello, darling, how was your day?"

She walked up to him and pecked him on the cheek.

"Umm, fine thanks. What's for dinner? It smells lovely."

"I've done your favourite – pepper steak. But come and sit down and tell me all about your day."

They went through to the living room and sat next to each other on the sofa.

Well, thought Barry, *this is rather nice. Alison is being very affectionate and pepper steak for dinner as well.*

"So," Alison continued, "how did your presentation go? I want to hear all about it. Start from the beginning."

Barry went a little pink, swallowed, and started to run through a fictitious account of the day, a day of triumph and acclamation.

Alison listened carefully, occasionally interjecting to add admiring comments of encouragement.

By the time Barry had reached the point of describing his standing ovations from the audience, she could barely contain herself. She managed to croak, in between a fake coughing fit, "I'll just go to the kitchen to get some water and check the dinner."

She got up and coughed her way to the kitchen, shutting the door behind her. Once there, she grabbed a tea towel and giggled into it, tears streaming down her face. She took a few moments to compose herself and dry her eyes with kitchen roll before going back to rejoin him in the front room.

"Sorry, darling, what were you saying? The bit about the audience's reaction to the pictures in your slide?"

Barry stopped, mouth half open, wondering. Had he mentioned pictures? Why was Alison… He stopped and shook himself.

Stop being paranoid, he thought to himself, *it's nothing*.

"Yes, darling," he continued, "they absolutely loved them."

8

Two days later, Barry was waiting in the foyer at Fairfield. He was early, the first to arrive after Steph had set herself up on reception, and he had his clipboard at the ready, noting down anything he could use as evidence against the people on his hit list. He had convinced himself that the fictitious version of events given to Alison was actually true, and that his performance at the training day earlier in the week had been a model of inspiration and authority. His capacity for self-delusion was prodigious and had served him well in his improbable rise up the greasy pole.

Steph, slightly perturbed by his presence at a time of day when she was used to being the only human being in the building, had overcome her annoyance to offer him coffee, and was strangely conscious of being on view. Every time she did something behind the reception desk, Barry seemed to make a note on his clipboard and her sense of paranoia rose. To her immense relief Avril arrived at about 7.30 am. For Avril, this was the equivalent of the middle of the night, but she had wanted to get herself settled and ready to deal with this hostile presence.

She saw him as she came into the foyer and strode over to him, smiling broadly, while cursing his early presence inside.

"Hello Barry, have you been here long?" She extended her hand to him and they shook.

"Good morning, Avril. I've been here since about seven o'clock."

"Ooh, you're an early bird. Has Steph been looking after you? Have you got coffee?"

"Yes, I'm fine, thanks. It's been very interesting to see how things work here at this time of morning."

"Oh, yes? Everything all right, I presume?"

Barry raised an eyebrow. "More or less. Do you not have identity badges, Avril, for safeguarding purposes?"

"Yes, of course, all staff have to wear their lanyards. We're very strict about that."

"But you're not wearing one, Avril."

Avril burst out laughing.

"I've just got out of my car, Barry. It's in the office and I'm just about to put it on. It's in my office. I would be wearing it by now normally, except I stopped say good morning and offer you coffee. Perhaps I should have just ignored you. Or perhaps you expect me to take it home with me and wear it to bed every night. Hmm?"

Barry's annoyance flickered to the surface. "There is no need to be sarcastic, Avril. Safeguarding is a very serious issue."

She looked at him for a second with calm, steady eyes before speaking.

"Yes, it is. Much more serious than name badges, Barry. Well, I'll leave you there. I think you have a meeting with Camilla first and then we are due to do a learning walk lesson two. I'll see you then."

She turned on her heels and went to her office, exchanging a look with Steph, who had busied herself at her counter to be able to hear all of the bad-tempered spat that had just occurred.

Barry made a note on his clipboard as she went.

Five minutes later Rick came through the main door into reception. He smiled at Barry as he walked over to the desk to sign in.

"Morning Barry, how are you?"

Barry looked him up and down and mentally noted his lack of safeguarding badge.

"Fine thanks, Rick, and you?"

"Yeah, yeah, good." Already Rick was exhausted by the effort of being polite to someone he wanted to slap across the face. He could not carry this polite exchange on for very much longer.

"We're doing a learning walk at break with Avril, as far as I remember. Is that what you've got down?"

"Yes, that's right, we've just spoken."

"Good. Well, I'll see you then."

Without waiting for an answer, he turned and went to his office. As soon as he got inside, having poured a strong filter coffee on the way, he shut the door and rang Avril.

"Avril, it's Rick, I've just met little Bazzer Pugh."

"I hope you were wearing your safeguarding badge."

Rick looked down at his chest in a panic.

"No, no I wasn't. I always keep it in my office. I've got it on now though," he said, frantically scrabbling to put his head through the lanyard.

"Tut-tut, Rick. I don't think you are taking safeguarding seriously enough, you know."

Rick was about to completely lose it and start shouting down the phone when the penny dropped.

"Did he say that to you?"

"He certainly did. I met him approximately thirty-five seconds after I got out of my car. I think we've seriously underestimated his stupidity, you know."

"Well, I think today will leave us in no doubt about that. He's doing a learning walk with us at break. I think he wants to see how Gestapo-like we are with the kids in the corridors."

"Yeah. I've got the pleasure first though. I'm doing a learning walk with him period two. That will be interesting."

"Okay, I've got to go," Rick concluded. "Best of luck and see you at break."

*

It was a long, gruelling day. On the learning walk with Avril, the programme had been designed to take in the classrooms of, amongst others, Charlotte, Kevin and Kwame. In each one, Barry, sour-faced, scribbled furiously on his clipboard. He looked through the exercise books of several children in each room, frowning and tutting as he did so.

At the end of the last lesson they visited, the bell rang for break and the class was dismissed.

Avril turned to Barry and asked, "What do you want to do about break? Aren't you supposed to be shadowing me and Rick?"

"Yes, that's right. You just go about your normal business and I'll tag along."

Avril led him into the corridor that was already full of hordes of kids, shouting, pushing, laughing. There were several competing streams: one trying to get to the canteen to buy food, desperate not to end up at the back of a long queue, one trying to get to the playgrounds to grab their preferred spot or to stake a claim to one of the basketball hoops, and the third trying to find their usual indoor cranny before it was take by an interloping group. All of them were in pursuit of their own particular goal while studying their mobile phones for the latest messages.

Rick was already in the corridor striding towards them, negotiating the various streams of humanity coursing along. He would occasionally stop to have a word with a group or individual who were being a little loud or boisterous, and to exchange a hello, or some casual football banter with smiling students looking up from their heated discussions about last night's Champions League goals. He finally caught up with the other two.

"Hello there. How have the learning walks been?" He directed the question at Barry.

Barry was glowering at all of the students in the corridor, but he turned his attention to Rick.

"Very interesting. Very interesting indeed," he said. "Lots of questions raised."

"Questions?" enquired Rick, puzzled.

"Yes, for example, why are all the children on their mobile phones so openly? I'm shocked."

"It's school policy, Barry," said Avril. "We are very strict on mobiles when they interrupt learning, so if they are seen out in lessons they are confiscated immediately. But in the corridor at break and lunchtime, they are allowed."

"Humph," snorted Barry. "It looks terrible. Don't you think it looks terrible?" he asked of them both.

"No," said Avril. "It's normal life, isn't it? They aren't doing anything wrong."

Barry didn't reply but made a note on his clipboard instead. He looked up.

"Okay," he said. "Take me on a walk around the school."

"Sure," said Rick. "We'll go down this corridor to the end and out into the playgrounds. Then we can walk around and come back in through the canteen so you can see the students in a variety of situations. Follow us, and ask anything you need to know."

They continued on a steady progress down the corridor. At regular intervals both Rick and Avril stopped to intervene with a series of students misbehaving: a ball was confiscated; a loud argument was quashed; students running down the corridor were halted, names taken and they were sent on their way separately; a member of staff on duty, Christina, a young teacher in her first year, was involved in a loud argument with a boy who was twice her size. Avril stood behind him, watching him arguing with Christina and enjoyed watching the boy turn round and realise he was now in big trouble. Shamefaced, he apologised when instructed and went to stand outside Rick's office when instructed.

"Thanks," said Christina, "he's always giving me trouble in the corridor on this duty."

"If he does it again, email me. I'll remind him of our conversation," said Rick, continuing down the corridor.

Christina looked puzzled. "What conversation?"

"The one I'll have with him in about half an hour."

All the while Barry scribbled on his clipboard with a face like thunder.

The procession continued in much the same vein for the next fifteen minutes as they tracked a steady route around the school. Barry, in between apoplectic bursts of note-taking, punctuated the patrol with questions.

"Can they wear any coat they like? You don't have a specific coat as part of the school uniform?"

"What about bags? They can bring any bag they like? Not even the same colour?"

"Have you thought about clip-on ties?"

Rick, beginning to tire of Barry's obsession with the appearance of things, muttered, "We think of little else in Senior Leadership meetings."

"What? What was that?" Barry barked.

At that moment Rick swerved away to intervene in a stolen football dispute before things took a turn for the worse. By the time they got to the end of the playground, Barry's head was spinning. He felt as if he had been trapped inside a pinball machine or a tumble dryer, with non-stop noise and interaction throughout the whole route, watching Avril and Rick make a hundred decisions per minute, imposing a benign moral universe on the chaos that surrounded them all. Barry only saw the chaos. He craved quiet and order, straight lines of pupils walking and square tables of pupils reading and discussing quadratic equations and different systems of political representation.

The bell rang to signal the end of break and students dispersed to the four corners of the school to go to the next lesson. A strange quiet descended on the playgrounds and playing field, all of which were littered by the detritus from break-time refuelling. Crisp packets and sweet wrappers blew like tumbleweed across the rapidly emptying plain, and the discarded remains of burgers and sandwiches scarred the landscape. The quiet did not last for long. As they approached the entrance to the canteen there was a rasping croak from above. On the tree nearest to the canteen door were three thuggish-looking seagulls, dead-eyed, the size of small pit ponies, like bouncers in a line outside a dodgy nightclub. It would not have been a surprise to have seen them there smoking a roll-up each, such was their criminal demeanour. Then came a throaty caw from the gutter of the roof adjacent, and a posse of glossy black ravens, each with glittering eye, stretched their wings and clenched their talons in expectation of the feast to come. There was a tumult of calling and wing fluttering and from the heavens hundreds more of them swooped down, scavenging. The ground was covered in seconds, and for the next few minutes they gorged themselves. Inside, the school site staff watched and waited. They would not go outside to begin their litter duty until after the birds were too stuffed to fly away. As Tony explained to his team, "It's a more ecological approach, lads." The team thought privately to themselves that it was more a case of personal safety.

Barry's litany of complaints continued unabated in the canteen, where instead of small boys serving tables of seated students nibbling avocado and quinoa salad, he saw shirts hanging out, spillage of ketchup on tables and cuffs, raucous good humour and vast slices of pepperoni pizza and mounds of nuggets being demolished in the remaining few minutes before lessons.

The staff on duty were engaged in a continual struggle to get students to eat sitting down and keeping an eye out for those who would try to leave the debris of their meal on the table where they had been sitting. The norms of civilised, considerate social behaviour were tirelessly reinforced day after day, but all Barry saw was chaos. When the students had finally been cleared from the hall and chivvied along to their lessons, Barry surveyed the aftermath of break in the canteen at Fairfield. A few isolated chip containers and ketchup sachets littered the tables that were surrounded by higgledy-piggledy chairs left at crazy, random angles. He felt as if he needed, more than anything else, a shower and a lie-down. He turned to Rick and Avril.

"Have you ever thought about those tables with rows of tip-up chairs? Would look much neater."

Avril sighed. "Have you ever thought that schools would be much better places if there were no children in them? Much neater."

She was on the verge of a rant but thought better of it. With a monumental effort of will she held firm to her professional demeanour.

"Come on," she continued, "let's go to my office. We have a meeting to debrief what you've seen so far, haven't we?"

She turned with Rick at her shoulder and walked away. Barry, making one last note on his clipboard, scurried to keep up with them.

*

The meeting in Avril's office was mercifully brief. Barry delivered his verdict on a series of issues, each of them unequivocally damning. Rick and Avril listened in silence as he pronounced judgement on a series of counts, like a jury foreman finding the accused guilty as charged on multiple counts.

As the charge sheet mounted, Rick and Avril looked at each other and rolled their eyes. When Barry got to the end he said, gathering his papers together in his clipboard, "I'll be writing this up as a report and passing it on to Camilla and the Trust, obviously."

He moved towards the door.

"Woah, wait there a minute," Rick exclaimed, his hand raised in protest. "We might have a few things to say about this, you know."

"You do realise that we know that this is all bollocks, don't you?" Avril joined in.

Barry stopped and turned back into the office.

"What on earth do you mean?" he said.

"Well, you clearly haven't got a clue what you're talking about. All of those people you popped in on today were judged either outstanding or good in our Ofsted last year and you say they're crap."

"Unsatisfactory," said Barry in clipped tones as if the word 'crap' was painful to him.

"Yes, that's what I said, crap. 'Unsatisfactory' is Ofsted-speak for crap. Everyone knows that."

Barry began to grow exasperated being questioned like this. As an Ofsted inspector, he was not used to delivering a judgement and then having it disputed. He raised his voice in frustration. "The kids are not scared of you, at all. You show up in the corridor, laughing and joking with them, but their behaviour doesn't fundamentally change. You need to really get stuck in there and grab those kids by the balls and put the fear of God into them. They need to be petrified of you so that when you appear in the corridor they quake in their boots."

Rick was incensed and his voice showed it. Loudly and with a little tremor, he said, "Just listen to yourself. You are criticising us for Safeguarding because of not wearing ID lanyards and you are using language like that. 'Grab them by the balls'? 'They need to be petrified'? Really? Many of these kids are petrified for too much of their lives at home at home as it is. We are certainly not going to add to that. And you inspect on Child Protection? Honestly, it beggars belief."

Barry had gathered himself and regained his composure. He knew that he didn't have to win the argument. He was holding all the cards.

"What you don't seem to realise is that you are meant to be teachers, not social workers or union reps. You do these kids no favours by treating them as victims."

"Hold on a minute, let me get this right. All you've done on this visit is criticise what the kids look like and the fact that they are quite lively at break and lunchtime. They behave like kids, in short. Everything you've said has been about appearance. What their mobile phones look like. Clip-on ties, for God's sake. The wrong colour bags. Lord help us. We've got absolutely no chance."

"At last, Avril. You've finally said something I agree with. You've got absolutely no chance. Camilla will receive the report in a couple of days."

With that, he turned on his heels and marched out of her office.

Avril was shaking by this stage. She looked across at Rick. "You'd better get another job and quick."

"What about you, Avril?" Rick replied.

"Me?" She thought for a moment. "I'm toast."

9

WHEN STUDENTS ARRIVED AT SCHOOL ON THAT FIRST DAY
of the glorious new dawn, they were greeted as before by about
twenty-five staff, checking uniform and sending students home
for infringements. What had been, under the old flabby regime, a
rather pleasant way of starting the day, saying hello to students as
they arrived, chatting to them about a variety of issues from the
trivial to the criminal and doing a spot of uniform checking, had
turned into a modern manifestation of the police state. Students
were sullen and resentful and chat was kept to a minimum.

It was, they were soon to find out, about to get worse. The students
who made it through Check Point Charlie were not allowed to go
into the building but were funnelled into the fire drill positions on
the top playground and tennis courts. It was an educational version
of kettling, preparing students for life in a totalitarian dictatorship.
There they were directed to the form's fire drill position where they
stood in near silence for twenty minutes as the register was taken and
uniform was checked for the second or third time.

Charlotte and Kevin were both Year 9 tutors and their forms were in adjacent lines. They could hardly dare to look at each other on the first day of this new system as they stood in front of their respective forms ticking off names on the list. When an opportunity presented itself, Kevin sidled over to Charlotte.

"How long do you reckon this malarkey is going to last then?" he asked quietly.

"Not sure. Actually, I'm surprised how well they're doing it," Charlotte commented. "They're all calm and quiet and uniform is much better."

Kevin looked at her askance.

"Charlotte, get a grip. It's a novelty. They're in shock. By Friday they'll be rioting. This is completely unsustainable."

"Give it a chance, Kev, you old dinosaur. We could do with some proper behaviour management."

"Hummph. I'll remind you of that in a couple of weeks' time. And what are they gonna do when it's cold and raining?"

Several students were hauled out of line for violations that were hard to explain afterwards. They were harangued by Camilla in a shrieking diatribe and then banished for the rest of the day in exclusion. It was one step away from solitary confinement. The form tutor of any line that contained criminals of this particular stripe was also treated to a look of withering disdain from Camilla. It was felt by many that the next step would be for the member of staff to be hoicked out of the line themselves and be subjected to a punishment beating. This was highly effective in producing a self-policing system. So eager did staff become to avoid a morning humiliation at the hands of Camilla that they patrolled their own line with a Stakhanovite determination to root out misbehaviour and misdemeanours. Tutors that engaged in spittle-flecked bellowing at individuals in their line received commendations and were spared any public dressing-downs.

The rumblings from the parents had not gone away and this new imposition of the Stalag 13 roll call every morning added fuel to the fire. Supportive as ever, the local rag, the *Longdon Advertiser*, splashed parental anger across the front page and carried several quotes from parents furious at the new draconian regime.

Camilla was unmoved by the reactions to her changes and sailed serenely on, even when parents began to keep their children from the school in protest. Meanwhile, her assault against many of the old guard of teachers at the school picked up momentum. Barry Pugh became a familiar sight in the school corridors, clipboard in hand as he strode in and out of classrooms, flicking through students' books with a permanent frown on his face. After a couple of weeks, this led to a number of staff being placed on competency measures, which entailed a short, sharp programme of intensive observations and targets for improvements. All of the staff singled out in this way had previously unblemished records and were left in a state of shock and anger. Among them were Charlotte, Kevin and Kwame.

The next weapon in this attritional war of undermining morale was the imposition of a two-hour, daily after-school detention. The rigid application of the new, very harsh rules and the culture of zero tolerance for just about everything, began to clog up the systems of punishment and sanction. A two-hour Saturday detention was introduced but rather than clearing the backlog it generated more unresolved cases and added to the already crippling workload for stretched and demoralised staff.

A routine monitoring exercise revealed that the Year 11s were far behind where they should be in terms of their grades and that an examination results disaster of biblical proportions was awaiting them next summer unless something drastic was done. Alastair and Barry imposed a whole series of new POCSE initiatives. Staff were required to teach before- and after-school revision sessions, from 7.30 in the morning. Camilla introduced an early closure every Thursday afternoon during which time all of Year 11 and then Year 13 were forced to sit compulsory examination practice, supervised by the teaching staff, who then had to spend hours marking the papers.

Then, inexplicably, new staff began to appear. Strangers turned up in school randomly, despite the fact that no vacancies existed and no adverts had been placed for jobs. When they were quizzed on their provenance in the staffroom, the new people were strangely reticent and, when pressed, vague in their replies. After a few weeks, they would suddenly be put in charge of some area of the school or other and then became oddly influential, being regularly summoned to Camilla's office for discussions and meetings.

The same was not true of Avril nor of Rick. The usual weekly meetings to discuss policy had never really got going after Camilla's appointment and now they had been abandoned altogether. These meetings had been replaced by weekly meetings with Barry Pugh, individually with other Senior Teachers. The meetings were an opportunity for surveillance and bullying. For about forty minutes or so Barry would catalogue the list of failings of the person he was meeting and then set another set of ridiculous targets to be achieved before the meeting next week.

Avril sat slumped and disconsolate on a leather sofa in her office. Barry bristled on the opposite sofa, going through Avril's latest list of failures on a sheet on his clipboard.

"Avril," he said, slightly raising his voice, "I just don't understand what you've been doing since we last met. Nothing, absolutely nothing, has happened about Teaching and Learning since then."

Avril sighed.

"What exactly do you mean, Barry?" she said wearily.

"You have a list of people who are currently on competency for their poor standards in the classroom and their refusal to follow whole-school policy. What have you done about that? Where are we? Have they improved? Are you nearer to dismissing them?"

"No," she said shortly, "no, I'm not."

Barry looked astonished. "What do you mean? Why not?"

"The people you have bizarrely put on competency procedures are all excellent teachers. I've wasted a lot of time going into their lessons and have always seen, without fail, very good lessons. I have absolutely no faith in your judgement, Barry, and I am absolutely not going to go down the road of sacking someone on your say-so. Developing Teaching and Learning is not about liquidating people. This is not the gulag. Do you really think there is a massive pool of talented teachers out there who are ready to replace the good people we've already got?"

Barry opened his mouth to speak, but nothing came out. He thought for a moment, collected his things and left Avril's office without a word.

8

SHE WAS SHOCKED TO FIND HERSELF SITTING IN THE dark in her classroom. The clocks had gone back last weekend and suddenly it was winter. Now, her days began and ended in darkness. She had always liked this part of the year, with its cosy run-in to Christmas, taking in the ancient strangeness of Halloween and Bonfire Night on the way. Her own children had stoked the fire of her enjoyment of this time, with her childhood memories and associations accreted by Harry Potter costumes, firework displays and stories of magic and mystery.

She shivered. The only thing she felt now was the cold darkness. The magic and mystery seemed to belong to another time. Still, she couldn't just sit around moping all evening, she had to get back home for the kids and to do the dinner. She turned to gather up her marking into her bag when there was a voice from the doorway.

"Charlotte? Is that you? What are you doing sitting in the dark?"

She looked up, flustered.

"Oh, Kevin, sorry I just forgot to turn the lights on." She half turned away and rubbed her face.

"Charlotte, are you all right? Here, let's put a light on."

He switched on the light and looked again, catching the glitter of tears in the neon.

"Have you been crying? What's the matter?"

She blinked in the lights and reached for a tissue, wiping her face.

"No, I'm fine, honestly. Oh, I probably look a right mess now. Sorry, it's nothing, really."

Her mascara was smeared slightly across her cheek and her eyes were red.

Kevin walked over and sat down.

"Charlotte, come on, what's happened? Was it Camilla? Or Pugh? Was this your meeting?"

She sighed a long weary sigh and shook her head. The words, when they came, tumbled out of her.

"They're upping my observations to twice a week. They say I haven't met any of my targets and that I'm failing my competency procedure, and that I have to take it very seriously. They say I'm letting down my classes, particularly the Year 11s. And now they say I have to run the half-term revision classes for four days during half-term and that I'm lucky I've got one of the days off. But I can't, Kevin, I just can't. I don't know what's happened to me, I used to be good, I think, but now I can't do anything and I'm so, so tired Kevin, so tired…"

The last few words were interrupted by great heaving sobs and then the sentence collapsed into incoherence. She covered her face with her hands and with an enormous effort of will forced herself to stop crying. Kevin looked on aghast. He had absolutely no idea what to do. His frequent chats with Charlotte were always based on a shared sense of humour and view of the world. They took the piss out of authority, the Tories, the *Daily Mail*. They occasionally shared stories about going on holiday, or dinner parties, or films. They loved teaching, they liked the school and they cared about the kids. In normal times, all of that was more than enough and formed part of that strange tapestry of alliances and compromises that made working life acceptable, given that a week off was never more than six or seven weeks away.

But the one thing that could be said about working life now with any confidence, was that it was anything but normal. The old certainties had disappeared and without them, the old routines, and well-worn tropes just didn't work anymore. Struggling to find a way in this strange new universe, Kevin tentatively put out his hand to lightly touch Charlotte on the shoulder. As he did so he said, "Come on now, Charlotte, this is not you, it's them. You're a great teacher and a great head of department. You always have been and you always will be. It's them. They've done this to you. Never forget that. They're bastards."

He felt better the moment he started talking. He was almost on the verge of taking the piss again, when he rowed back, knowing it wasn't quite time for that. He took his hand away from Charlotte's shoulder. She looked up at him, her face streaked and blotchy.

"Thanks Kevin. I really needed to hear that. It's only the people still clinging on that are keeping me going, honestly."

He passed her a tissue. "Here. Come on now, dry your eyes and blow your nose and let's sort something out."

"I can do the first two things, but as for sorting it out, well, I don't think we've got much chance there."

"Have you talked to the union, Charlotte? They really can't get away with treating people like this."

She broke off to mop herself down with the tissue, a process culminating in an industrial klaxon of a nose blow. It seemed to bring her back to her senses and the old Charlotte emerged.

She smiled. "They can Kev, they really can. Yes, I've talked to the union, but you were at the meetings last month. You saw how useless they were. They are either too scared or too weak. They are not going to do anything to help anyone here. We're all on our own."

"But surely this is just bullying, plain and simple. How can they justify three observations a week? That's totally out of order."

"As long as they follow the procedure, they'll see the process through to the end. And I'll be gone."

"But what about Avril? Surely, she's not saying your lessons are unsatisfactory, is she? She hasn't gone over to the dark side, has she?"

"No, of course she's not. She's been great, really. She kept giving me good or outstanding for the observations she has done. She's had blazing rows with Pugh over it. That's why they don't involve her anymore. I'm observed by Pugh, as Director of Teaching and Learning, or whatever his ridiculous title is, and he gives me inadequate every time. No matter what I do, he can always find something to justify it, even if what he says contradicts what he said the time before."

"God, Charlotte, you've got to keep fighting. You can't let them win like this."

"Can't I? The truth is, Kevin, they already have won. All they have to do is keep going. I can't carry on like this. I think I'm going to resign, probably after half-term. I've talked to John about it. I can't leave after failing a competency procedure, I'll never get a teaching job again. And they know that. I'll probably say that I'll resign if they drop the surveillance and give me a reference. We were thinking of moving up North to be near my sister in Leeds. Houses are much cheaper up there. We could probably afford for me not to work for a while."

Kevin looked horrified. "Move up North? Dear God, that's a bit extreme, isn't it?"

Charlotte laughed. "Don't be such a cliché, Kevin. It's not the Third World. You can even get a flat white and the *Guardian* in Leeds these days. It's not like when you were a student."

"No, you moron, I didn't mean that. I'm well aware of the charms of the rugged hills of the land of your fathers. It's just that, well, what about your career? You would have been in Senior Management in the next couple of years, nailed on."

"To be frank, I don't give a toss about that now. If Senior Management is all about surveillance and bullying and zero tolerance, as it seems to be increasingly these days, I think I'll give it a miss. I'd like not to expect to cry every day. It's my new performance management target."

"Well, listen, don't do anything hasty, all right? Because, you know it's not just you, don't you? There are about seven or eight members of the awkward squad who are on the same competency treadmill. And at least another eight who have either got new jobs for January or they're on interview this week. I've got no idea what the Trust thinks of it all. They must be just a tiny bit worried at the chaos she's causing."

Charlotte looked embarrassed.

"God, sorry Kevin, I forgot to ask. How did your observation go? Are you going down the same track?"

Kevin smiled grimly. "Oh, don't worry about me. I'm too old to give a fuck about any of this. They'll not force me out, not without a hell of fight anyway. It's easy for me, I could retire tomorrow, so they've got nothing on me, and it's driving them mad. I'm quite enjoying it actually. No, it's the younger ones I feel really sorry for, people like you and Kwame, with over twenty years to go."

Charlotte snorted. "Twenty years? The way I'm feeling I couldn't manage twenty minutes."

*

In another room, tempers were beginning to fray. The usual sullen plod through the agenda items of the Senior Leadership Team meeting was interrupted by several items of Any Other Business that Rick had attempted to be tabled for the beginning of the meeting. In the face of Camilla's implacable opposition to her meeting being side-tracked, Rick changed tactics and made no comments about any of the agenda items. Avril, seeing what was going on, took her lead from Rick and was also silent. Given the fact that they were the only two members of the team who contributed to discussion or challenged Camilla's position, the main items of the agenda were over, much to Camilla's fury, after about half an hour.

Tight-lipped, Camilla said, "Okay, everyone, let's move on to Any Other Business. Let's keep this brief if we can, we're all very busy."

Rick shuffled his papers and sat forward in his seat.

"There are some major items for discussion and frankly I'm amazed that they weren't on the main agenda. First is the news that has just been released about the entrance test in November. Is it true that we're moving to having fifty percent of places allocated to the highest achieving students on the test results?"

"Yes," Camilla smiled, "that's correct."

"But that makes us virtually a selective school. You can't do that without consultation."

"But I have."

"But that's outrageous," spluttered Rick.

"No, Rick, what is outrageous is that you can't see that we need to change the student body here at Fairfield. I've successfully lowered our entry numbers down to one hundred and eighty. We need cleverer students and more middle-class parents. If we have the test very early on a Saturday morning in November, say, eight in the morning, the feckless drunken white trash from the ghastly Trafalgar estate will not be able to get it together to get their equally dreadful children into school on time to sit the test. And then we can legitimately deny them a place. Next item?"

Avril stirred. "No, wait a minute, Camilla, you can't just say those things and think it's all right. This is our community you're talking about."

"Yes, and that is exactly the problem. We are saddled with our community, so the least we can do is to weed out the problems to give ourselves a fighting chance. Now, what was the next item, Rick?"

"About thirty kids in Year 11 have suddenly disappeared from the registers. All the difficult kids, the lowest-achieving, worst-behaved kids in the school. All the ones who were trailing in to be interviewed by you for the last couple of weeks. What has happened to them? And why don't we know anything about it?"

"Yes, I think some form of congratulation is due, don't you think? I've successfully managed, at a stroke, to make teaching for Year 11 teachers much less stressful and made it much easier for them to reach their targets by dealing with the worst kids in the school, something that the old regime had clearly failed to do. I've had many messages of thanks from classroom teachers already, and there'll be many more when everyone realises they have gone."

"But how have you done it? You can't just take difficult kids off roll."

"I've made personal agreements with each parent to fund off-site education, via the Trust, at a combination of local tutoring companies, alternative provisions and colleges, on a half timetable. They come off our roll, so they don't appear in our results, but they can sit their exams here along with everyone else. That will probably increase our results by about ten percent."

Rick shook his head, disbelieving. "By washing your hands of them. They are our students. Our responsibility. And where on earth is the money coming from? Does the Trust know about this?"

Camilla was unmoved. "I have absolutely no intention of carrying the can for your failures over the last ten years. And try arguing with hard-pressed classroom teachers in the staffroom that these characters should come back. See what happens to your popularity then."

Avril was incensed. "How dare you treat our school like this?"

Rick interrupted her. "Avril, just leave it for now."

"Yes," agreed Camilla, "just leave it, Avril, I think you've said enough. Now, moving on. Your next item, Rick?"

Rick paused. This wasn't going at all in the way he had imagined. It seemed impossible to lay a glove on Camilla. Even the most blatantly unethical decisions could be spun as being in the best interests of the school and the teaching staff. She was Teflon Woman, with no discernible sense of shame.

He cleared his throat and began. "There's a job advertised on the Trust website. It appeared on Sunday evening."

"That's right," confirmed Camilla.

"The post is called, 'Executive Headteacher'. It also says interviews will be this Friday."

"An admirably accurate summary, Rick. What is your point?"

"Well, what is it for? Why don't we know about it? How will anyone who is any good see it and be able to apply in that timescale?"

"Alastair and the Trust want to add to our Senior Management capacity. This is a Trust decision, not mine. My hands are tied, it has been foisted upon me. It's a trainee headship post and it's to help us deal with the volume of work we have to do on Teaching and Learning."

"So, presumably, any of us can apply for it?" Rick asked innocently.

Camilla slightly stumbled for the first time anyone of them could recall.

"Er, well, yes, I suppose you could. Well, the Deputy Heads anyway. I think the selection criteria will rule out Assistant Heads."

By the time she had reached the end of her sentence, normal service had been resumed successfully, and she was smoothly in control again.

"And have you had any applications yet?" Avril chipped in.

"Just one, I believe."

"Just one," repeated Rick, with a half-smile on his face. "And do you know who that is?"

"I'm sorry, Rick. As you know, all of that is confidential and part of the selection process. Short-listed candidates will be informed on Wednesday. Now, was there anything else?"

She looked round the table. "No? Good. Now let me just remind everyone that the lesson observations of all of you have finally got under way. I will do all of the observations as part of Performance Management. We started today with Gordon." At the mention of his name, Gordon jerked into consciousness, after having spent the previous forty-five minutes wondering whether he was going to get home in time for the football. He had scraped home in his observation in the morning and had gratefully accepted all of the humiliating 'advice' Camilla was delighted to bestow upon him before promptly forgetting every word of it. He lived a goldfish-like existence as a senior teacher, glad simply to survive from day to day and hour to hour. It was in that spirit he masked his features with a concerned and serious smile. Camilla continued, "And I will have done the rest of you by the end of the week. It will be a very busy week, what with one thing and another, so let's crack on."

She stood up and waited for everyone to gather their stuff and file out past her, as was her usual custom. Rick and Avril headed down the corridor to Avril's office. They would be there, debriefing, for some time yet.

10

Alastair looked at the piles of papers on his normally obsessively tidy desk and sighed. He flicked through the piles randomly, occasionally selecting one at random and reading it over again. He looked up at the screen, and scrolled down the fifteen new emails he had received on the same topic.

The same phrases recurred regularly: 'absolute arrogance', 'treating the children harshly', 'Like being in the Army', 'Sophie has lost all confidence', 'ridiculous queueing up in the morning like squaddies', 'detentions for trivial, minor offences', 'endless after-school sessions'.

A few more also turned up, phrases that sent a shiver down his spine: 'outright lies in a meeting', 'Special Needs children being victimised', 'breaking the school's own code of conduct'.

Then there was the correspondence from staff: 'leaving teaching altogether after this bullying treatment', 'staff disappearing without explanation', 'ridiculous demands being made on staff to do endless after-school and holiday sessions and detentions', 'threats made about references', 'lesson observations and Performance Management used to intimidate and bully staff'.

One of the piles consisted of newspaper clippings from that great organ of record, the *Longdon Advertiser*. It was clear, flicking through a selection of front pages, that Camilla's new regime had been greeted by the circulation-starved *Advertiser* as manna from heaven. The sub-editor had had a field day, daydreaming about working for a famous red top on Fleet Street, while conjuring up hysterical snapshots of life in a dictatorship: 'Expelled for putting hand up!'; 'Days in solitary – life at crisis school Fairfield'; 'Thick and Sick! – Gemma, 14, left in tears by Head's cruel rant'.

He shook his head, collected all of the papers together and neatly tapped them into a green card folder, and set it down on his desk. Had he made a mistake about all of this? Of course, he had known that he would have to ruffle a few feathers. Fairfield had needed shaking up, there was no doubt about that, notwithstanding their unexpected exam results in the summer. And you couldn't make an omelette without breaking a few eggs. Yes, that old saying was very true, but what if you were left with broken eggs all over the kitchen floor and an empty pan? Was Camilla the right person for the job? She had had a remarkable impact at Coldewater, but then she had left under a cloud. That was his insurance policy, the fact that he had something on her. He probably wouldn't need it, but you never knew. He had learned that you always needed an insurance policy. To be more accurate, he had learned that it was a good idea to have two.

What was his second one? He couldn't help but be struck by the fact that so many of the letters, after bitterly criticising Camilla, compared her approach unfavourably to Rick's brief reign last summer. He was good, he knew that. But perhaps he had underestimated the particular conditions at Fairfield, conditions that Rick knew well. He was popular with everyone. And he was effective, even ruthless when he had to be. The other thing he knew, which played on his mind, was that Rick had been shortlisted for a deputy head post at another Longdon school. The interviews were on Friday. If he did nothing, Rick would be appointed to that school, he was fairly confident of that, knowing the field of candidates. He really needed him to stay, and be Plan B, even if only for a while.

Finally, he picked up the phone and dialled. He waited for a few seconds.

"Rick? Hello, it's Alastair here. Alastair Goodall. Listen, Rick do you have a few minutes?"

*

He pounded on, the treadmill chewing up the miles, and lost himself, cocooned by his headphones and the free flow of thoughts that repetitive exercise generated. He didn't like doing the gym at night. The dreadful music was cranked up too loud and seeped into his own soundtrack. He'd thought many times of complaining, particularly when, like this, there were hardly any 'young people' around who might appreciate the mindless beats, but he caught himself just in time. He gave himself a shake, embarrassed to find himself turning slowly but surely into his father. The impression was compounded by the reflection in the darkened window panes directly in front of the machine. During the day this looked out on to the car park and an ever-changing vista of cars arriving and leaving. The diverse range of would-be exercisers hauling themselves, their kit, and very often, their young children in and out of the tightly-parked cars was strangely comforting to him. He liked to feel part of a community. He also liked the randomness of it. He could control the playlist on his iPod, the length of the run, the switch from treadmill to rowing machine and back again, but not the endless flow of characters and situations that the window delivered to him.

At night, he was denied all of this. The harsh strip lighting against the blackened plate glass turned the window into the most dazzling mirror and he could not escape the harsh truth of the sweating, shambling, panting figure in front of him, so at odds with the smooth and easy running machine in his imagination. During the day, shielded from this inconvenient truth, he was able to plunder his own back catalogue of great sporting moments. The magnificent diving header that Saturday on Hackney marshes was a particular favourite. At night, he was left with the unvarnished truth and his thoughts always turned to the here and now.

Bloody Alastair Goodall. The cheeky sod, asking him to withdraw from the Downley Park job. What was it he had said? "I'm not sure, between you and me, that Camilla is up to this and I need to make arrangements just in case." Well, it's a bit late for that. God, after the way he treated me during her appointment. And anyway, what's he actually offering? Yeah, okay, an immediate pay rise. And a pretty hefty one at that. A guarantee of a headship, either at one of the other Trust schools within a year, or at Fairfield. He must think I was born yesterday. Wanker!

He suddenly became aware that the young woman on the treadmill next to him was staring across at him. She was wearing pink and grey skin-tight Lycra, and had been effortlessly sprinting for the last ten minutes, producing nothing more than a damp sheen in contrast to his rivers of sweat and hyperventilation. *Shit!* he thought, *I've been talking out loud.* It was a regular occurrence that, lost in a particularly stirring piece of music, and deep into the rhythm of running, he would forget himself and sing along, only to suddenly realise and, red-faced, immediately stop and try to pretend it was someone else. Talking aloud, however, was a whole other scale of madness. The woman, in the ultimate humiliation of gym etiquette, pressed the pause button on her machine, disembarked and went to another machine on the other side of the room.

He lost himself again in his re-running of his conversation with Alastair earlier. What was it he had said? "I just want you to keep an eye out for what's going on and keep me updated." As if he were some kind of little sneak, or something. No, he wouldn't give him the satisfaction. He had a good feeling about the interview on Friday. And, yes, he knew it was a step sideways in some ways, another deputy headship on less money, but it would just be a temporary stepping stone, to a headship somewhere else in a couple of years or so. He smiled to himself again. Yes, it would be worth it just to go into Camilla's office and tell her he was leaving. His smile got broader, as he threw himself into the final minute's sprint.

236

Across the room, unbeknownst to him, the pink and grey Lycra woman was looking over at him, in conversation with a friend. They both burst out laughing.

*

It was nine by the time he opened the front door. He closed it, masking the click of the lock. Jo had probably just got the kids to bed and he was careful not to wake them. The last thing that was needed was an excited tumble down the stairs for cuddles and kisses, followed by two hours of not being able to get back to sleep.

Putting his sports bag down in the hall, he crept to the front room and opened the door. Jo was sprawled on the sofa, a large glass of red in her hand.

"Hi," he said. "Kids in bed?"

Jo looked up and nodded. Her eyes were red-rimmed and she had a strange look on her face.

"Jo?" Rick asked, his forehead knotted in a frown, "you okay?"

"Yes, I'm fine. Well, not fine exactly, but you know..." she trailed off.

"No, I don't know. Come on, Jo, tell me what's up. Is it the kids?"

"No, no they're both fine. I'm just being stupid and selfish really, it's just that..."

She trailed off again, but this time her sentence dissolved in a flood of tears and gasping sobs.

He dashed over to her, put her glass of wine down, and gave her a cuddle as she sobbed into his chest. He stroked her hair and held her until the tears dried up and her breathing was regular again. Then he held her slightly away from him so he could get a look at her face.

She blinked up at him.

"You're all wet, you know. And a bit sweaty." Her face screwed up in distaste.

"Sorry, darling, didn't have a shower." He kissed her on the forehead and began again.

"You're obviously on the mend, so why don't you tell me exactly what the matter is?"

"Not until you give me my glass of wine back. Honestly, Rick, you're such a brute," she said, smiling.

He did and poured one for himself. "Well?"

"I had a meeting with James today. About the partnership."

Rick's face fell as comprehension dawned.

"Oh no, don't tell me. He hasn't, has he?"

"They're not going to give the partnership to me. Just a matter of timing, he said. The maternity leave had come at the wrong time, I hadn't been involved in the Macmillan contract, and Sebastian had done great work while I was away."

"Sebastian? They're not going to give it to that little shit, are they? Jesus wept, what's wrong with these people?"

"They already have. They promised they'll review it in two years' time, but frankly, I don't believe a word he says anymore."

"I can't believe it. They're supposed to be right-on, lefty chambers. Surely, they must be breaking some kind of equality employment law, mustn't they?"

Jo scoffed. "You'd think so, wouldn't you? But apparently not. Doesn't matter anyway, I've just got to keep my head down. If I start making a fuss, it won't just be a partnership I'll lose."

"Oh, fuck the job. Honestly, is it worth it?"

"Come on, Rick, we can't afford to fuck the job. And the worst thing is, we'll have to put on hold all those plans for moving into a bigger house."

"No, darling, the worst thing is that they made you cry. I'll never forgive them for that."

The rest of the evening dribbled away with the rest of the bottle of red and the telly. First a documentary about life in a tough comprehensive school in Liverpool and then a gritty drama about a criminal barrister and her latest case in South London.

"Christ," exclaimed Rick, "even the telly has got notice to improve. Not only do we have to do all of this stuff at work, we have to come home and watch representations of ourselves doing it for the entertainment of the masses. Whatever happened to escapism?"

238

"Let's talk about that in bed," Jo replied archly. "I'm going up. You coming?"

"I won't be long," Rick replied, "I've just got a bit more work to do first."

As soon as Jo had climbed the stairs and Rick was reasonably confident she would not return, he opened his case and went through the copy of his application form for Downley Park. What on earth was the point of going through with that for the prospect of less money for longer? He couldn't just sit on his backside and inhabit the comfortable moral high ground while Jo earned all of the money. He couldn't be content to let her take all the angst and guilt and responsibility. The more he turned it over in his mind, the more convinced he became. He was just going to have to hold his nose for a while. Most people had to do worse.

Finally, after looking at his mobile contacts list, he decided. The phone rang for a minute. He was just about to hang up, thinking it was too late to be calling, when it was answered.

"Rick, good to hear from you. What can I do for you?"

Rick cleared his throat and said quietly, one eye on the door, "Hello, Alastair. It's about our conversation earlier. Is it too late to talk, or have you got a minute?"

"It's never too late to talk, Rick. Never too late at all."

Fifteen minutes later he hung up. With a sinking feeling in his stomach, he climbed the stairs to bed.

11

CAMILLA WALKED TOWARDS HER CAR WITH A SPRING IN
her step. It had been a remarkably successful term and a remarkably
successful last day. She really was as good as people said.

In the building behind her, in four different venues, at least four
members of staff were finishing the term in tears.

*

It was Friday and the clock on Avril's office wall said three forty-five in
the afternoon. As usual on the last day of a half term, the building had
emptied like a football stadium at the final whistle. Avril sat at her desk,
staring blindly at the computer screen in front of her, tears streaming
down her face. She had managed to hold it all together in Camilla's
office, after getting her feedback from her lesson observation that day.
She had been determined not to give Camilla the satisfaction of seeing
her cry, but once she had got back to the sanctuary of her own office
and shut the door, the tears began to flow and wouldn't stop.

She kept going over and over it in her mind. An inadequate judgement. Poorly planned. No differentiation. Poor behaviour management. Poor checking of learning. Little progress made. There had been no-one else doing the observation with Camilla, so there was no way of challenging the verdict. Avril felt humiliated. She had never, in thirty years, been judged as anything less than good and was usually deemed to be outstanding, so to hear the word 'inadequate' come from Camilla's lips was like a slap around the face to her. How on earth could she face the staff, and make judgements on them as teachers, after receiving such a judgement herself? Not that that seemed to trouble Barry Pugh, who strutted around the corridors of the building with his clipboard and no sense of shame for his own inadequacies.

She had managed to ask Camilla, "So, what are the implications of this? Not that I agree with your judgement, of course."

"Well, the fact that you disagree is, of course, part of the problem. But putting that to one side for now, the implications are that you will be observed again with the same class during the first week back after the holiday, and unless there is significant improvement you will go onto the competency procedure."

"Competency?" Avril blinked back at her in disbelief.

"Yes, that's right, according to our policy."

"No, I think you'll find that the policy requires there to be a period of support and monitoring, actually, Camilla."

Camilla smiled back, serene in her confidence.

"No, Avril, I think that you'll find that there have been some changes to the policy. Now, is there anything that I can help you with, in terms of being ready for the observation and the first week back?"

"Help? It's a bit late for help. I think we both know what's going on here, Camilla, and help has got nothing to do with it."

She stood up and collected her papers.

"I don't know what you mean, I'm sure," blustered Camilla, as Avril walked towards her door.

"Oh, I think you know exactly what I mean. Have a nice holiday, Camilla."

She had enjoyed that, walking out and shutting the door of the office gently while Camilla was still spluttering. But now, sitting alone in her office, where she had sat so many times before at the end of another tough half term, she knew that it was a minor pleasure, a successful minor skirmish in a war she was destined to lose. And lose soon. She stared blankly at the computer screen and the tears began to flow once again.

*

Charlotte read the letter over and over again, as if, somehow, the message it contained might change miraculously. She had won a timeshare. She was being fast tracked onto the Senior Leadership Team. She was getting a hefty tax rebate from the Revenue. She had won first prize in a beauty contest. Collect twenty pounds. No, it was none of these. She had been dealt the 'Go straight to Jail' card. She looked again. "Please attend the final disciplinary hearing on Friday 10th November at 4 pm. Please submit any further papers for consideration at least five working days in advance. You may be accompanied at the hearing by a friend or representative."

The rest of the words blurred before her eyes. She couldn't believe it. She had done everything her union rep had advised and had told them she would resign if they dropped the competency procedure and endless surveillance and threats. But still it went on. It was an almost virtuoso display of cruelty, the knife being twisted with a smile. The letter had appeared in her pigeon hole that afternoon, with no time before the half-term holiday to talk to anyone about it. And now her holiday, her precious time with her family, would be poisoned by the gut-wrenching, ever-present fear this would engender. The tears came thick and fast.

*

John Bond's office was a shrine to examinations. The walls were dotted with certificates and framed photographs recording some of the achievements and honours he had picked up over the previous thirty years. 'Examinations Officer of the year, 2005', 'National finalist, exams administration awards 2012', Regional Chair, Exams Officers Association'. There was a series of grade A awards from the regular, impromptu spot checks that exams officers all over the country were familiar with during the summer season. Pride of place was given to the photograph of him, flanked by his wife and two strapping grown-up sons, at the special long and distinguished service celebration that Longdon had organised last year.

Around the room were immaculately cared for pot plants and stately bookshelves with rows of neatly stowed reference works and books of guidance, alphabetically arranged according to exam board and cross referenced by subject. John sat behind his desk, and surveyed the room. On the back of the door, only visible to him when it was closed and he was working away at something, was an A3 poster that the heads of department had photo-shopped ten years earlier. It was of him in a dinner jacket, surrounded by piles of exam papers in the place of the Bond girls, holding an instantly recognisable Luger pistol. The caption read: 'John 'James' Bond – licensed to invigilate.'

He smiled at the memory. He did have, he must admit, a bit of a reputation for being something of a stickler when it came to exams. No head of department was allowed sight of the exam papers. No teacher was allowed casually in the exam hall to check out whether oxbow lakes had come up again this year. No-one was allowed to even hint at explaining anything to a baffled student with their hand up after the exam had started. He knew everyone joked about it, about how he took the whole thing too seriously and that he was a jobsworth who loved being awkward.

He had thought when Camilla was first appointed that she, with her reputation for ferocious application of standards, would appreciate the job he did. He had liked Jane and Rick, they were nice people, but deep down he always felt that they were a bit sloppy, too inclined to cut corners. You couldn't cut corners with exams. Once you did that, what was there left to depend upon? How could you be confident that a student's C grade in English really was a C grade?

It was a bit like performance-enhancing drugs in sport. Once there was a sniff of that, you could never take that sport and that athlete seriously ever again.

He felt foolish remembering that thought now. And even though she had not given him the time of day since starting as Head in September, he still naïvely thought that when he was called in to a meeting that morning, that it would be the beginning of a kindred spirit recognising his importance and worth to the school.

The broad smile had frozen on his face as she went through her agenda: time for new blood, a more flexible approach to the rubric of examination rules, loyalty to the new regime, if he was not able to support the school in facilitating outcomes then Camilla would bring in her own person who would, a very generous package on offer from the Trust in recognition of his outstanding service.

The smile had frozen on her face as he attempted to argue the moral high ground. She had that politician's ability to speak in such a way that no-one could remember the detail of what had been said and that everything that had been said was infinitely deniable. 'Facilitating outcomes' indeed. The very phrase turned his stomach. He had said to her he would consider her offer over half-term and let her know on the first day back after the holiday, but that was only to get out of her office as quickly as he could. He had walked back to his own office in a daze, and, diving into the staff toilet next door, had been violently sick, with trembling legs and pounding headache. He had wiped his mouth and scuttled back into the security of the room that had been his office since the school had opened back in the Seventies.

He sat in his black leather swivel chair, and scanned the trophies of a modest career pursued diligently over nearly forty years. The first fat teardrop took him by surprise. The rest cascaded down, uncontrollably.

*

Rick had navigated the final day on autopilot. He had taken note of a series of people leaving Camilla's office tight-lipped and red-eyed. A conversation with Lisa, looking over his shoulder with a terrified expression on her face, revealed that there had been one candidate for the Trainee Headteacher post and that the interview had taken place that morning. No-one had been informed, no Governors had been present and no-one had seen the person concerned. The interview had been conducted by Camilla alone, and it had all been wrapped up by eight o'clock that morning. There was no paperwork as far as Lisa could remember, but a quick Google search of what she thought the name was, revealed that Patrick O'Malley had been a colleague of Camilla's at Coldewater.

He could barely look at Avril. Normally that would have been minutely dissected by the two of them in a bitchy debrief in her office, but he knew that she was worrying about her lesson observation. He should really go and seek her out before going home to find out what had happened, but he couldn't bring himself to do it. He remembered the look on her face when they had talked that morning just after arriving in school.

"What are you doing here, Rick? I thought you were at Downley Park for the Deputy Head interview. Is everything all right?"

He had felt himself going slightly pink and he had mumbled unconvincingly, "Er, no I decided to withdraw in the end. I thought I told you."

"No. No, you didn't tell me. Why did you do that? Has something happened? I thought it was a great opportunity for you."

"No, no, nothing's happened. I just need a little bit more time, that's all."

"I see." She paused, her lips a tight straight line in her face. "Well, if you need to talk, you know where I am." She turned and strode away down the corridor.

"Thanks," he said, "and best of luck today."

He called out this last part as her back disappeared away from him. She did not reply.

And now, at the end of what had been the worst half term of his professional life, his head was spinning. He needed to sit quietly somewhere for ten minutes, somewhere he would not be disturbed. There was only one place that would do.

He slipped out of his office and went upstairs to the first floor. There, at the top of the stairs, was a doorway that people passed and ignored tens of times every day. He looked both ways before turning the handle and slipping inside. In the darkness, the distinctive smell of the room seemed even stronger, a heady cocktail of pine disinfectant, sour creamy bars of soap and mould. He fumbled his way to the toilet seat, sat down and reached across to the wall to turn the light on.

It was the only room in the known universe where, when you switched the light on, it got darker. The single unshaded bulb, hanging from a cobwebbed central flex, oozed a thick, mustard-yellow pall of light which just failed to reach into the corners of the room. The original staff toilet, it had doubled up as the cleaners' store cupboard for as long as Rick could remember. Perched on the black municipal toilet seat he surveyed the room. To his left, a galvanised grey metal bucket with medusa-headed mop leaning against the wall and several containers of industrial-strength floor cleaner. To his right, precarious piles of medicated toilet paper that could double as tracing paper if the Art Department ever had a supplies crisis. He had used it once on an early visit to this toilet many years ago and the memory of it still made him wince. They had obviously been made of sterner stuff in the days when the school was first opened.

A lot had changed since then. More had changed since September. He couldn't see this toilet surviving Camilla's Brave New World much longer. Probably most people would see that as progress of a kind. Change was a natural part of life. What worked once wouldn't necessarily always work. Sitting in the quiet gloom, Rick rehearsed these arguments over and over again in his head, but it was no good. He could fool everyone else but he couldn't fool himself, either in this strange cubicle or lying awake at night in bed, alone with his doubts as Jo breathed contentedly next to him.

All those people he had worked with over the years, humiliated and reduced to tears virtually every day. Students treated with such disrespect and contempt, as if they were the enemy. The lies, the cheating, the corruption. Avril would be gone before long, he knew that. Patrick O'Malley, his sources had revealed, made Camilla look like Snow White. And what was he doing about it? The inescapable answer that, in this darkened, quiet confessional, he had to face up to, was simple. He was holding his nose, turning a blind eye and taking the money.

He put his head in his hands and began to cry.

*

Camilla was on the M25 heading for Gatwick by four o'clock. As soon as the crush of children had dissipated she had slipped away, avoiding the usual pre-holiday pleasantries. She had had quite enough of Fairfield, thank you very much, with its whingeing and whining, its excuses and self-deception. She felt a quiet satisfaction. The first half term couldn't have gone much better and today was an excellent way to round it off. Appointing Patrick and engineering the departure of a load more bits of dead wood had cleared the way nicely to start the real work on exam results when they came back. She would just have to finish off the rather unpleasant business with Avril. She hoped she wasn't going to make a fuss and would just go quietly. You could never tell with those old lefties though, they were always full of self-righteousness and woolly hypocrisy, standing up for the so-called underdog. Well, their day was done. The end justified the means in Camilla's book and soon everyone would be able to see that a little collateral damage was a price well worth paying for a better school. And then, in time, she'd finally be able to get out of there, with its ghastly, smelly children and their ghastly, smelly parents. A phone call to Marcus when she got back should do the trick.

Smoothly accelerating in the outside lane, past a row of articulated lorries, camper vans and family-loaded Volvos, she reached a hundred miles an hour and began to giggle.

12

Avril checked the car park before committing to parking her own car. She deliberately didn't use her normal designated slot. The whole thing felt to her like a raid behind enemy lines, flying below the radar. She knew that Camilla was swanning around on some exotic holiday somewhere, but she just wanted to double check. She scanned the car park again and was relieved to see only two cars, neither of which she recognised. It was early, midweek, and even the workaholics slept in a little before giving up their holidays to the cause. The revision sessions were due to start in an hour so she had to get a move on.

She really did not want to bump into Rick. She wouldn't know what to say to him. Even now, when she thought of it, she got a little teary. What was wrong with her? She was tougher than this. She breathed in and out a few times to calm down, got out of the car and took a pile of boxes from the boot. It was a relief when she piled it all into her office and was able to shut the door, without having come across a soul.

With a long sigh, she sat herself down in front of her computer and logged on. She spent half an hour transferring files to a USB stick and then looked at the piles of folders and books in her cupboards. This was going to take longer than she thought. When she had got back home that Friday she had spent a long time trying to formulate a plan. It was obvious to her that Camilla was going to drag her through every disciplinary procedure known to man. She would be made an example of, so other 'rebels' could take note of the cost of disobedience.

Avril was not going to put herself through that. She was not going to spend hours planning the perfect lesson when it was perfectly clear that nothing would be good enough. She refused to be dragged through a competency procedure on trumped-up charges for the entertainment of the staff room. But if not that, what? She could not afford to stop working, the finances just did not stack up. But she definitely could not come back into that toxic environment, not even for one more day.

So she had decided. She would come into school when no-one was there, pack up all of the accumulated detritus of her career and never come back. She would ring in sick, with stress-related depression. That, at the very least, would buy her a bit of time. Then she would contact her union. She fretted long and hard about abandoning her students, but with great reluctance, she decided that over the years she had given enough. Now it was time to take a bit back.

She had been able to sleep for the next two days after coming up with something that resembled a plan. And the relief of not having to come back in to be answerable to that harpy was immense. It felt like she was taking control of the situation, rather than waiting for them to do something to her.

Once she had copied across all of her files she logged on to her emails. About fifty emails loaded up. Some people would have been relieved to wave goodbye to all of that, but Avril loved her work and would miss being someone who people sent urgent emails to, looking for advice and answers. She flicked through them systematically, just in case there was something there of importance.

It was the usual old nonsense. And then, almost at the bottom of the list, was an email that caught her eye. It was labelled 'Teacher Pensions'.

She opened it and read it through. She read it again and then clicked on the link it contained, and read that two or three times. She got up and walked around the room a couple of times before going back to her computer and reading it all again. She was such an idiot. Why hadn't she realised before? She must be the only teacher in the country who had not been counting it down. She laughed out loud.

This changed everything.

*

There was a tentative knock at the door. Ben, breaking off from a sweeping move upfield that resulted in a wild shot over the bar, shouted, "Come in."

The door swung open and Ben's mum came in, carrying a tray.

"I thought you'd like some pizza, boys, and I've brought you a drink and some cake as well."

Karim put his Xbox controller down and jumped up to take the tray from her.

"Oh, thanks dear. Just put it down there, there's a good boy."

"Thanks Mrs Johnson, that's brilliant," said Karim, taking in the loaded plates of pepperoni pizza and chocolate cake.

She looked at Karim with a mixture of affection and concern in her eyes. What a lovely boy he was. So polite and such a nice boy as well. Not like a Syrian at all. Not that she really knew what a Syrian was like, it was just what you read in the paper and saw on the telly. And the things some people on the estate would say while you were waiting at the bus stop. After all he'd been through as well. He didn't talk about it and she had learned not to ask for fear of upsetting him, but Ben knew all about it and would occasionally tell her snippets of his story. Karim was used to her gaze that lingered a little too long for comfort.

"How are you, Karim, dear? You still at Longdon College?"

250

"Yeah, I'm fine thanks, Mrs Johnson. I'm doing all of my GCSEs in the summer and I've already been accepted to do A levels next year."

"Well, aren't you clever? All your GCSEs in one year. Well done you. I'm very pleased for you, love. Maybe you could go back to Fairfield and do your A levels there with Ben next year. That would be nice, wouldn't it?"

Ben opened his mouth to speak and then thought better of it. No good had ever come of having a proper conversation with his mother, particularly when it came to disagreeing with her. He had found the best strategy was simply to nod and to turn the subject back to food.

Karim, sensing that Ben didn't want to open up this particular can of worms, said, "Yes, maybe I will do that."

"Well," she said, "I'll leave you to it. Give me a shout if you need anything else, boys." She left the room and there was silence for a minute as the two boys set about demolishing the plate of pizza with single-minded determination. Eventually, through a mouthful of pepperoni, Ben said, "You know my mum really loves you, don't you? She thinks you're like the Son of God. Sometimes I think she prefers you to me."

"Son of Allah, surely?"

Ben sniggered. "Nah, she thinks that, like, you can't be a proper Muslim because you eat pizza and play football and that. She reckons you're just a bit confused and that actually, you must be English, because you're so nice and normal."

It was Karim's turn to laugh. "And she thinks I'm confused?"

"I know. But it's not her fault. She's old and she reads the *Daily Mail* and watches Jeremy Kyle. It's a miracle she lets you in the flat."

"I like your mum. It's up to us to educate her."

"Well, good luck with that."

They fell to finishing off the pizza and then turned their attention to the cake.

"So, what you were saying about Longdon, is that true then? I thought it was a bit of a nightmare."

"Well it was. Still is really, but I've got some good teachers and if you keep your head down and avoid the gangs and drug dealers and be careful on the way there and back, it's okay."

"Still sounds better than Fairfield. I'm telling you mate, you really dodged a bullet there. The new woman is a psycho. Straight lines in the corridors, silence, no phones, chucked out for the slightest thing. I mean, it needed to improve, but this is madness. Everyone in the Sixth Form is thinking of leaving cos they're all treated like the rest of us, like criminals. You know the latest thing? At the beginning of every lesson we have to put our hand over our heart and recite this fucking stupid thing called 'The Pledge'."

Karim was open-mouthed. "No! What the hell is the pledge?"

"Oh, some bollocks about swearing to be a good learner and uphold British values."

"Well I couldn't possibly come back then. Unless I could swear to be a good learner and uphold Syrian values."

"Don't be a wanker, Karim, you lot haven't got any values. Everybody knows that."

Karim jumped on top of him and wrestled him to the ground, with his hand behind his back.

"Aaah!" Ben screamed. "Surrender, surrender. I was only joking, man."

Karim let go of him and they both tumbled apart on the floor, breathing heavily and laughing.

When he had got his breath back Ben started again. "Hey and you know what, man? Last week I saw Miss Green in her classroom, crying."

"Miss Green? No, really? She was a brilliant teacher."

"I know. But everyone's either in tears these days or they're going around screaming at the kids. Half of 'em have already left and they've shipped in some new ones. The new ones are terrible. I've got no idea where they've got them from. It's like there's a branch of Primark just opened that does cheap, crap teachers, or something."

They fell silent.

Ben hesitated and then took the plunge.

"Have you heard anything more about your sister?"

Karim looked across at him, his face serious.

"I spoke to Ahmed the other day. He is involved in helping volunteers in Calais. He doesn't go himself because he's worried about his visa. He doesn't trust immigration. So we did a flyer with Evana's details on and he managed to get loads of copies made. They're being circulated in Calais next week, I think."

He trailed off. Saying it aloud made it seem even more inadequate. His own sister. Here he was, safe, warm, dry, fed, educated and with friends, while his sister was... well that was it exactly. He had no idea where his sister was and whether she was safe. Or even alive. And all he'd done was make a leaflet. His eyes began to sting.

Ben chucked the Xbox controller over to him. "Come on mate, best of three. I'll be Barcelona this time. You can be Palace."

Karim picked it up. That was another new phrase for him, 'best of three'. He had only the faintest idea what it meant, but he thought he'd better knock the shine off it straight away.

"Okay," he said, "best of three."

13

SHE WAS DUE TO MEET THE UNION GUY AT AROUND eleven o'clock in his club just off Trafalgar Square. She checked her phone again. Mike Patrides, yes, that was his name. She had been in regular contact with him, both by email and on the phone, for the past month, and he had been a calm and reassuring presence throughout. When she first spoke to someone on the other end of the union helpline she was not full of confidence. The woman on the other end of the phone was non-committal and advised Avril not to get her hopes up, but as soon as she gave the precise details of her case her tone changed immediately.

"Oh, I see," she had said, "I think I need to pass you on to one of our regional officials who has experience in this sort of thing."

The regional official turned out to be Mike, an ex-headteacher, who now worked full time for the union. For the umpteenth time Avril went through her story. To her surprise, Mike, on the other end of the phone, burst out laughing.

"They did what? Goodness me, I've heard everything now."

"So you think I've got a strong case, then?"

"I should say so. This is the strongest case I've ever heard and I've been doing this for a good few years now. So, how do you want to proceed?"

"Well, I've done a bit of research and I'd like to take out a formal grievance against the Head, as the first step into suing them for constructive dismissal."

"Woah, woah, slow down. We would never advise clients to go down that route. That is possible according to the letter of the law but, in reality, we find that it becomes very difficult to rebuild relationships when the time comes to going back to work in the school."

There was a pause. On the other end of the line Mike's voice asked, "Avril? Avril, are you still there?"

"Yes, yes I'm still here."

"I'm sorry if that's not what you—"

Avril cut across him.

"I'm sorry Mike, I can't have explained this very well. I'm not going back there. I can't possibly work in that environment again."

"But Avril, I know you're signed off sick now, but there'll come a point where disciplinary procedures kick in. And you'll be in a very vulnerable position if you haven't done everything according to the book. I really would advise you strongly to—"

Once again Avril cut across him.

"Sorry Mike, I don't want to be rude, but I'm definitely not going back. I can take retirement in the second week of January, when I'm sixty. I just need a strategy to get me to that point."

On the other end of the phone, in the crackling silence that filled the airways, the faint but unmistakeable sound of a lightbulb going on could be heard.

"You're sixty in January?"

"Yes, that's right."

"And you're intending to retire?"

"Yes."

"And you've checked out the finances and the income and the lump sum and all of that? Yes, of course you have, what am I saying?"

"Yes, that's right Mike, I've done all of that."

She could hear the smile in his voice.

"That, Avril, changes everything. That puts you in the driving seat. This is the kind of case I love handling because there will be a happy ending."

And now the happy ending was minutes away. She was due to meet with him to sign the settlement agreement and then the whole thing would be done and dusted. She checked the address again on her iPhone, and looked down the street until she saw the entrance of a grand hotel-looking building on the right. She smoothed down her coat and went through the entrance, feeling rather self-conscious. She had never been in someone's 'club' before, and the whole thing was both surreal and intimidating if truth were told. At this time of day in her old life she would have been doing battle with hordes of screaming children in corridors and the canteen. To be in a club off Trafalgar Square was not quite the same thing at all.

She stepped into a plush foyer and sank into a thick pile carpet that dampened the sound and turned all conversation into a murmur. Feeling something of a fraud she gazed around, looking for anything that might be a reception area. Immediately, a be-suited flunky in a top hat oozed up to her.

"Good morning, madam. How can I help you?" he breathed.

"Hello. I'm here for a meeting with Mike Patrides."

"Ah yes, Mr Patrides. Quite so. If you'd like to follow me, madam."

He glided away and Avril scuttled after him. Or she would have done if the carpet had allowed it. Instead, she too glided behind Mr Top Hat and found herself deposited at the entrance of a huge high-ceilinged room, dotted with leather chesterfield sofas, and work station islands. It appeared that several meetings were going on in this room, and that in between them there were a handful of individuals tapping away at laptops.

Before she knew it, Mr Top Hat had left her standing there and a small wiry man in a beautifully-cut suit and George Clooney-like silver grey hair was striding towards her with his hand outstretched.

"Avril, it's a pleasure to meet you. I'm Mike Patrides. Come this way and let's get started."

He led the way to a corner table flanked by two chesterfields and indicated that Avril should sit.

"This is an amazing place, Mike. I've never been in a private club before."

"Oh, it's not really a proper private club. You know, it's not Bertie Wooster or anything, it's just a way of having a base in central London. I deal with cases like yours for teachers all over the home counties. It's just more convenient to be able to meet in central London."

"So, you do this kind of thing a lot, then?" she asked.

"Never been busier, unfortunately. Academies, and Multi-Academy Trusts in particular, think they're above the law. Senior Leaders in school should have endangered species status, in my opinion."

He smiled at her. "But enough of all that. You're not here to listen to my views on modern approaches to school leadership."

He rustled in his briefcase and pulled out a file and several sheets of paper.

"I've got your agreement here. I'm required to take you through it and once you're satisfied, get you to sign two copies. I've spoken at length to Chris, and, as we discussed on the phone, I managed to get her to agree, on behalf of the Trust, the higher figure we spoke about."

Avril looked puzzled. "Chris? Who's that?" she asked.

"Chris Frampton, the head of HR at Bellingford Trust."

"Oh, God, Frampton. Why didn't you say so? I had no idea you were on first name terms with her."

Mike smiled wryly. "I've worked with Chris on these kind of agreements many times. Bellingford in particular have got a lot of form when it comes to bullying staff out. Whenever they take over a school they budget for the costs of getting rid of staff."

Avril shook her head. "It's outrageous. I'm almost tempted to take them on and go to a tribunal or something."

"No, don't do that. It's a very stressful process. You've made the right decision, believe me. But, you're right, there is a price to pay."

"What do you mean?"

"They will only agree to a settlement if you agree to do a Harvey."

"Sorry you've lost me. 'Do a Harvey'?"

"Apologies, lawyer jargon. You have to sign a confidentiality agreement. You only get the money on the understanding that you don't talk about the agreement or what has happened at Fairfield. You can't slag them off to anyone. You can't even acknowledge that the agreement exists. If they get wind of you badmouthing the Trust or anyone in it, you'll have to pay the settlement lump sum back."

Mike then spent the next twenty minutes taking Avril through every clause of the agreement. Finally, he passed his chunky fountain pen to her. She held the pen poised above the first copy of the document and hesitated for a second or two. Liberation beckoned and fought a final struggle with Justice. Liberation won. She signed.

Mike walked her to the entrance of the club. She turned and shook his hand.

"Thank you very much for all you've done, Mike. You made a terribly stressful situation manageable."

"No problem, Avril, it was my pleasure. It was one of the most straightforward cases I've ever done, actually. They virtually bit my hand off. They knew they were in the wrong, you see. But what's important for you now is to take your time, rest and relax. Don't underestimate what you've been through. Particularly after all the years you gave to state education. Enjoy the next phase of your life."

She walked off through the door and into the streets of the West End. It was a sunny, early December day. A right turn would take her to Charing Cross. A left turn to Trafalgar Square. She thought, *perhaps I'll pop in to the National Gallery before I get the train home.* She turned left.

*

Back at Fairfield, Kevin was in his familiar position in front of his computer, scanning the Norwegian meteorological site for news of

258

snow. There was a sense of desperation now about his daily trawl through the site. A snow day used to be a harmless indulgence, a little fantasy that staff joked about. Now, under the current regime, it became an obsession. People stopped and asked him about it continually and began to blame him when he couldn't tell them that snow was on the way. A snow day would be sweet release from the hell they now all had to endure.

Eventually, he closed the site down. Isobars weren't going to transform themselves simply through wishing. It was time for his latest WhatsApp bulletin to 'Los desaparecidos'.

He typed the subject line 'News from North Korea' and then the following message:

> 'Kim Jong Ev out of school today. No-one knows where, but rumour has it she is attending a conference planning how to liquidate the enemies of the state. The list of the disappeared and missing grows daily. Joining Charlotte, Kwame, Avril and Jane on the roster of staff we are not allowed to contact are Gordon, Muhammad and Andrew. Fears are also growing about the whereabouts of James Bond, who has not been seen for a couple of weeks. Rumours abound that he actually was a sleeper agent and that his cover was blown when he refused to release exam papers to Patrick O'Malley, the mad new Catholic Deputy Head, or to give him his accurate title, Torquemada.
>
> Current running total of staff gone since September is twenty-one. New staff (many without interview or under equally mysterious circumstances) twenty-three. New staff instantly recognisable. Young (under thirty-five), male, good-looking, wearing three-piece, tight-fitting suits and with a messianic devotion to the regime and the revolution. Small brains, little imagination and less compassion an advantage.
>
> The show trials continue and many staff off with stress-related conditions. Little Bazzer Pugh in rude health. Must be all that walking the corridors in leather trench coat. He is due to release new fitness video, 'Upping your steps the

259

easy way. Free clipboard with every copy'. He is currently in the first bloom of bromance with O'Malley, having bonded over shared interest in ritual humiliation DVDs. They are everywhere together. They now walk the corridors holding hands.

Several staff, who have as yet avoided punishment beatings and disciplinary action, are digging a tunnel for escape purposes, i.e. are permanently out on interview. Rumours reach us that there are still schools out there where people are treated with dignity and respect, but many think this is just propaganda put out by the Resistance to keep our spirits up.

More later. Delete this message!'

*

In the café of the National Gallery, Avril closed the message down, smiling. She felt almost guilty at not being there, but that feeling lasted only a second or two before it was replaced by the euphoria she had been experiencing ever since signing the agreement. She sipped her coffee and began to compose a message.

'Hi Jane. Mission accomplished. Agreement just signed and I am free. Currently looking at Great Art, something I plan to do a lot more of. I enjoyed Kevin's latest bulletin. Have you read it yet? I'm so pleased we are out of there. Shall we meet for lunch later in the week? We could do a matinee at the National Theatre. Let me know. Avril xx.'

14

"Barry, you did promise, remember. And now its spring and the weather's picking up, it's the ideal time to do it." Alison laid her hand on Barry's knee and smiled at him.

He smiled back. "Of course, darling, I think we should go ahead with it. As you say, it's the perfect time. And I think we should reward ourselves for all the work I've been doing with the Trust. The increased salary has started to make a real difference now we're used to it."

"Wonderful. I'll start looking for people tomorrow."

"Be careful who you get, though. There are a lot of cowboys out there, you know. Why don't you go on one of those sites, you know, 'Check-a-builder' or whatever they're called?"

"That's marvellous, darling. I'll start looking tomorrow."

"And who knows? We might want to think about a new kitchen, or even an extension, later in the year."

The next day, when Barry was at work, she began to search online. She felt a bit guilty about being so negative about him.

He wasn't so bad really. Perhaps she had to try harder. He was working all hours after all, and he was doing it for the family. It would all be so much easier if he would just let her try for that job. She was bored out of her mind at home all day. Why couldn't he see that? At least sorting out this decorating was a bit of a project to get involved in.

She posted the details of the job on one of the sites and was amazed to see replies flooding in almost immediately. After a couple of hours she had a shortlist of five builder/decorators and waited for them to contact her directly. A couple rang within the hour and the other three sent emails. One of the phone calls was able to call round that afternoon to have a look at the job and do an estimate.

"Goodness," she thought to herself, "this is so easy and quick." She hesitated for a moment. "I hope they are all legitimate. As Barry said, there are a lot of cowboys around." She looked again at the details of the person coming round that afternoon. "David Jones, Horizon Building Projects. National Federation of Master Builders. Ten years' experience. No job too small. Sustainable projects a speciality." She clicked on the reviews tab, which showed an average rating of 4.8 out of 5 stars. The reviews were glowing: 'Highly recommended. David was polite and efficient', 'A marvellous job. I'll definitely use them again', 'Such a pleasure to have in the house. Polite, charming and reliable.'

She was reassured and began to research colour schemes. After about ten minutes, however, she realised she had not the slightest interest in the relative merits of Teal versus Amaretti cream, nor could she summon up the will to delve into the myriad websites dealing with artisan tiles. She began to browse idly and found herself, inexorably, back on the website of the accountancy firm in the village. She sank into a vivid fantasy of her sailing into a plush, well-appointed office, elegantly dressed as an understated executive, with secretaries bustling around her servicing her every whim, while she effortlessly dealt with the complex and intractable problems of the business world. The fantasy was about to take her to a business lunch in the fashionable restaurant in the clouds at Canary Wharf that she had read about, when her eye was caught by an item in the news section of the site. It was that job again. They obviously hadn't appointed anyone and were trying again.

Her heart began to race and with a sideways glance she clicked on the application pack to download. Well, she reasoned, it wouldn't do any harm to have a quick look, would it?

A couple of hours later she was sitting at the dining room table with papers and notes spread out in front of her. The doorbell made her jump, and she hastily gathered together the papers, smoothed down her skirt and hurried to the front door. She opened it, smiling. Her gaze was met by a tall man who looked somewhere in his early thirties. He had short dark hair, and the remnants of a suntan that set off his startling green eyes. He was wearing a sky-blue linen shirt, outside a pair of stone coloured shorts, and Adidas trainers.

"Mrs Pugh? Sorry I'm a bit late, the traffic is bad today. I'm David Jones." He extended his hand in greeting.

Alison stared at him, nonplussed. "David Jones? Sorry, I er…"

He smiled broadly at her. "David Jones, yes. We spoke on the phone earlier? The builder?" He gestured behind him to his van parked by the kerb. The van bore the legend, 'Horizon Building Projects'.

The penny finally dropped.

"Oh yes, of course. I'm so sorry, I was just in the middle of something." She finally took his hand and shook it. It was cool to the touch, slightly calloused, with long delicate fingers. "Come in, please."

She opened the door wider and stepped back to let him in. As he passed her, a breeze of cologne, with an undertone of sawdust and paint, followed him. It was strangely pleasant.

"Come through. I'll show you the dining room, it's just this way."

She led him into the room and he took out a notebook and a pen and his phone.

"Do you mind if I take some photos? It's just easier when I come to do the estimate later."

"No, no, not at all. Go ahead."

She explained the project to him while he scribbled notes in his book and asked questions.

"I'll just take a few photographs then, if that's all right?"

"Yes, fine," she replied, "I'll be in the front room when you're ready."

"And can I go outside to check the access?"

"Yeah, no problem. Just use the French windows there."

She sat on the sofa in the front room and flicked through some of the *Beautiful Home* magazines she had accumulated.

Well, she thought, *he is charming. Polite and considerate. Not like a builder at all. And terribly good-looking. I'm not surprised he's had five-star reviews. Let's hope his decorating looks as good as he does.*

Five minutes later a call came from the dining room. "Hello! All done in here."

Alison got up and went to the door of the front room. David Jones was in the corridor, notebook in hand.

"Have you finished then? What do you think?" she asked.

"Pretty straightforward job actually," he replied.

"When could you start? And how long do you think it would take you?"

"Well, I could probably fit you in in about two weeks' time. I had someone cancel a job unexpectedly. Husband has just lost his job so they can't afford it now. It would probably take a week and a half. Would normally be quicker than that, but I'm on my own at the moment. I had to let my lad go."

"Oh, why was that?" she asked.

"He was rude to the customers. Had a bit of an attitude. Turned up late a lot, as well. I tried to help him out but some young people just won't be helped, you know."

"Dear me, that's a shame." There was an awkward pause. "Er, so how do we proceed from here?"

"Well, I suppose you've got other decorators coming along. If you want to use me just give me a bell. I'll email you the quote this evening. I wouldn't let you down, I'm very good, you know."

Alison smiled at him. "Yes. Good. Okay, well thanks for coming round. Send me the estimate and I'll be in touch." She showed him to the front door and shook his hand again.

"Bye Mr Jones. Thanks again."

He flashed a green-eyed smile at her. "David, please. And I'll be in touch. Check your email tonight."

He left, the gentle cloud of perfumed air following him. She watched him go, his long, lean, brown legs striding towards his van. He had the build and gait of an Olympic swimmer. "I certainly will, David. I certainly will."

15

HE SAT BY THE WINDOW, LISTENING TO MUSIC AND watching the familiar cityscape of South London slide by. Mock Tudor suburbia soon gave way to graffiti-covered urban wasteland, which in turn was replaced by the chrome and glass fantasies of London Bridge and the Shard and finally, the more reassuring Monopoly territory of Charing Cross. He checked his watch and then looked up the location on his phone.

Five minutes later he walked into the café at the National Portrait Gallery and looked around the sparsely-populated tables. Alastair had already seen him and was looking up at him, beckoning him over. *Typical*, thought Rick, *he's in charge from minute one of the meeting.*

He forced a smile and went over to his table.

"Hi Alastair. How are you?" he said, extending his hand.

"Very well thanks, Rick. Have a seat." He looked at his watch. "Bang on time as well," he said, with a mixture of approval and disbelief.

"I'll just get a coffee first. Can I get you anything?"

"No, no, I'm fine, thanks. You go ahead."

He came back a few minutes later and sat opposite Alastair, careful to place his cup on the table without spilling anything. Alastair didn't need any excuses to think of him as sloppy.

"Interesting place to meet, Alastair. Any particular reason for it?"

"I thought we should always meet away from the schools. I'm sure you don't want any of your colleagues asking awkward questions about the precise nature of your relationship with the Trust. And, it's convenient. I'm meeting Marcus Grovelle in an hour."

"Grovelle! Goodness me, you do move in exalted circles, Alastair, don't you?"

"We're at quite an advanced stage in the negotiations for Bellingford to help him out with his Great Reform Bill. Quite exciting, actually."

"Forgive me, Alastair, if I'm not excited. You don't believe in all of that bollocks, do you?"

Alastair smiled. "Of course I don't, Rick, I'm not an idiot. But our political masters must be obeyed, no matter how deranged their schemes are. That's the glory of liberal democracy. Someone must put into practice their masterplans and profit handsomely from it."

It was Rick's turn to smile. He thought, *of course you don't believe in it. You don't believe in anything, except yourself. You and Grovelle are a match made in heaven.*

Alastair interrupted his thoughts. "But enough of that. What news from Fairfield? What can you tell me?"

"I'd have thought you would know all the news from Fairfield. Haven't you just had a meeting with Camilla, Pugh and O'Malley?"

"Yes, obviously I've had their version of events. I just want to check it against yours."

Rick spent the next twenty minutes telling him the latest horror stories while Alastair made the occasional note in his Moleskine. He probed Rick's contributions with follow-up questions.

"So, you think the Sixth Form is going to collapse as students leave?"

"There are classes of sixty in science because they can't replace the staff?"

"They have just been banned from the Managed Admissions Forum?"

Rick confirmed all of his queries and then went on, "The real issues are the rumours that are flying around about the corruption. All of the new people appointed, including O'Malley, have some connection to Camilla, either personally, or she used to work with them. There have been no proper interviews done and procedures haven't been followed. There are wild rumours about finance and Camilla's posh new car. She turned up in the staff car park in a Porsche the other day. Loads of Year 11 students, the bad ones obviously, have mysteriously disappeared off the roll and no-one knows why or how. There's also a lot of disquiet about the new exam secretary, who is also a friend of Camilla's apparently. The old one, John Bond, was just got rid of, without any warning. He'd been there for over thirty years."

"Good. This is very helpful, Rick. Very helpful indeed. And you haven't been asked to do anything that you would be uncomfortable with?"

"Yes, loads of things, but nothing actually illegal or unethical. She keeps me out of the loop. We hardly ever meet. Isn't she asking questions about why I'm still there?"

"I like to keep everyone on their toes, and Camilla knows that as well as the next person. I've made it very clear that I want you there and that I'm grooming you for another headship in the Trust. She knows she can't lay a finger on you."

"Yes, I'm glad you've brought that subject up. When exactly are you thinking of?"

"Patience, Rick, patience. Virtue will have its reward, you'll see. And now, unless there is anything else, I need to get to my meeting at The House."

He got up. The meeting was clearly over, so Rick followed and they left the café together. Alastair strode off in the direction of

Westminster. Rick watched him go, feeling slightly unclean. *At least,* he thought, *I'm not kowtowing to him like everyone else does. And I might be able to help bring her down.*

He walked off towards Charing Cross, slightly comforted about the ethics of his position. Each step of the walk to the station succeeded only in knocking the shine off his carefully contrived justification for what he was doing. By the time he boarded the train, *Evening Standard* in hand, his sense of shame was as strong as ever.

Back in the National Portrait Gallery café, hidden at a corner table ringed by stately pot plants, Jane and Avril clutched each other, hardly daring to breathe.

"What on earth was all that about, do you think?" asked Jane.

Avril had her phone out on the table and was scrolling through the photos she had taken in the previous half an hour.

"I'm not sure," she said, "but they were as thick as thieves. These photos might come in very handy in the future."

"Oh, Avril, I love retirement. It's such fun. Who would have thought it?"

16

BARRY WAS OUT AT A LATE MEETING AND SHE HAD THE house to herself all evening. She settled down on the sofa and switched between the job application form she had hidden away on the bookshelf and her book. She knew Barry would never find it there. He had little time for reading apart from those dreadful educational reports he had to plough through, so the forms were safe slipped in between *Madam Bovary* and *Great Expectations*. She couldn't actually recall ever seeing him read a proper book.

Both books were behind a framed photograph of her wedding day. As she slipped the form between the books she looked again at the photograph in her left hand. They looked so happy then and so young. Glowing, both of them, with the look of love. She smiled at the memory, even though she found it increasingly difficult to bring back to mind the details of the day. And then her smile changed uncertainly to a broken frown. What had happened to them, those people in the picture? How could Barry have changed so much? She loved him once, she was sure of that, but somehow he had changed. He was not the man she had first met.

But no, she knew, deep down, that that was not true. It was the sort of thing that she might read in one of her books that Barry despised so much. He hadn't changed at all in reality. He was always a mean-spirited misery. It was she that had changed. She had been a timid little thing back then, pathetically grateful that anyone would take any notice of her, never mind an older, more experienced man who seemed to know what to do, like Barry. She bit her lip and put the photo back. No, she could not be that timid little thing any longer, the application was proof of that. Barry would just have to get used to it, or... she let the sentence hang in the air, and turned back to her book.

She was currently immersed in a paperback thriller about a Girl on Bus. Or was it a train? Or was that the last one she had read? They all seemed to have something to do with a girl doing something pretty ordinary that turned out to be quite extraordinary in a clever kind of way. They raced by and you thought you knew what was going on when, right at the end, everything was turned on its head somehow. She much preferred reading to watching films or series on the telly. When she read, she was always The Girl on the whatever, in a way she just couldn't manage in a film. The actors and sets were all too glamorous and she couldn't will herself into being that person in that life.

She was just settling down into hiding in the cupboard in her fabulous, wooden clapperboard house in the woods, holding her breath so that her newly revealed psychopath husband wouldn't find her, when her concentration was broken by the ping of her phone. Irritably, she put down her book and reached for her phone. It was a text message, just a number, no name.

She opened it up and read, 'Dear Mrs Pugh. Just texting you re the invoice, just in case. I've emailed it to you. Please have a look and get back to me. No rush. I hope it is all okay. Regards, David Jones.'

Her irritation evaporated. In a rush of excitement, she opened up her emails on the tablet and looked at the attachment. It all looked all right, though she wasn't sure. Barry was bound to ask her about the other quotes and mansplain the whole thing to death. No, she was decided. She'd reply and go for Mr Jones. David Jones. David. She'd have to wait a little, though. It would look a bit too desperate if she responded immediately, as if she was a pushover as far as accepting the first quote she got.

She turned back to her book and read on. The breathless, racy read, that had so gripped her, now swam in and out of focus, and she found herself reading the same paragraph over and over. Eventually she could bear it no longer. She checked her watch. She'd waited twenty-five minutes. That would do, surely.

She opened up the email again and replied. 'Mr Jones, thanks for your speedy reply. We've looked at a few quotes and have decided to go with yours. When can you start and how much deposit do you need? Kind regards, Alison Pugh.'

She read it back to herself. Yes, that sounded just right. Friendly, but not desperate. A clear hint that we've had lots of other people quoting and a subtle 'we' to make sure he doesn't get the wrong idea. She clicked on 'send' and it whooshed out of the mailbox into cyber space. With a smile, she picked up her book and hunkered down again in the dusty cupboard as the mad husband approached.

*

Barry opened the front door as gently as he could. He'd been relieved to see, as he clambered out of the car, that the lights in the front room were off. He had said to Alison that he was probably going to be back very late and that he had an early start in the morning so he had expected her to go up to bed early without waiting for him.

He really couldn't have faced a conversation with her after the day he'd had. He just wanted to get in, have a bit of quiet time, and get down to a little more work before bed. Alison would just witter on about the decorating or a new kitchen or some such nonsense. She didn't seem to realise that all of these things needed to be paid for and that the job with the Trust couldn't be guaranteed, particularly given the fact that Alastair was in charge. And Camilla.

Still, at least he seemed to have put to bed Alison's ridiculous ideas about working. She hadn't mentioned that for a while. He would have to careful though. Any suggestion that his job was at risk or that they had to be careful with money would just open up that whole debate again about her 'helping out' financially. The cheek of it. He certainly did not need his wife to work. Over his dead body. He didn't care if it was old-fashioned or sexist. He had been brought up with proper values.

He closed the front door silently and crept to the kitchen. He poured himself a Scotch and took it into the dining room where he set up his laptop, tiptoeing nervously across the wooden floor that was prone to irregular creaks and groans. While he waited for it to boot up, he thought back over the events of the day. Alastair had gone absolutely mad at the meeting at Bellingford earlier. He had never seen him so angry.

It all seemed so unfair to Barry. Yes, of course those predicted grades were disastrous, but he had done his bit. It wasn't his fault if there was still dead wood around. If they had taken his advice and got rid of Westfield and Howarth earlier. And that woman Green. And bloody Westfield was still there, neither use nor ornament. And all that stuff about the complaints from the community and the local rag. He was disappointed in Alastair, he really was. He had thought that Alastair would have expected all of this and been brave enough to ride out the storm, but apparently not.

And then Camilla. She always managed to twist things so that they turned out to be his fault. Particularly now she had installed her favourite, O'Malley. He liked O'Malley, he was made of the right stuff and didn't stand for any liberal nonsense. It was probably his Catholic background. All those bloody lefties were usually atheists and commies, with not a shred of patriotism in their bones.

In his opinion, everything had started to go wrong in the sixties and seventies and it had been getting steadily worse. He remembered when he had started teaching, when Tory views had to be kept hidden in the staffroom and all of the common-sense approaches to teaching had been abandoned in favour of multiculturalism and discovery learning. Thank God all of that nonsense was over and done with. Rote learning, direct instruction, harsh discipline had been the bedrock for education for years and it had been trendy madness to ditch them. Grovelle was the man for the job, there was no doubt about that. What was that phrase he used? Children being the victim of the pet theories of the liberal elite and the educational establishment. Exactly.

And now, when those ideas were the coming thing again, he had been exhilarated to find himself on the side of the angels again. Goodall, Everson, O'Malley – these were all people who shared his vision and wanted the same things he wanted. He just couldn't understand why they didn't seem to like him or to trust him to deliver. Well, he wouldn't be the victim this time, not again. He would do whatever it took to get those results. They had to show that their methods were the right ones, at all costs.

He logged on to his account and started typing. It was going to be a long night.

17

THE EXAM SEASON WAS ALMOST UPON THEM. THE FIRST
exam was due to start in at the end of the week and the atmosphere
in school was at fever pitch, with increasingly frenzied efforts to
cram that last, vital piece of information into weary fifteen-year-old
brains. The wheels of the POCSE machine whirred on, churning
out initiative after initiative that Camilla, O'Malley and Pugh
foisted upon heads of department and classroom teachers. Opting
out of such schemes was not a possibility. They existed, therefore
they must be adopted, even in the face of threadbare evidence that
they had any impact on results or learning. Sullen-faced teachers
and students filed in and out of additional lessons, before and after
school, at weekends and during the holidays.

Normally, Rick, as the Senior Leader responsible for exam
results, would have taken a full part in these activities, but although
he was involved in his normal exam prep, he was excluded from a
series of new initiatives that came under the aegis of O'Malley and
Pugh. He first noticed this when his Year 11 class did not show up

to his PE lesson one day. After a few minutes, he wandered into the corridor and popped his head around the classroom next door. There was no class in there either.

He said to the teacher who was surfing the internet at her desk, "Your class gone missing too, Sarah? What's going on?"

She looked up, horrified at not noticing the approach of another adult. These days you never knew who was friend and who was foe. When she saw it was Rick, she relaxed.

"Year 11 are all in a special session in the Hall with Camilla, O'Malley and Pugh. I'd have thought you'd be involved in that, Rick."

He stumbled over his words. "Oh yeah, of course. I just didn't realise your class were involved as well. I'm just on my way now."

He backed out of the door waving and smiling at her, feeling like an idiot. He had no idea what was going on. He walked purposefully down the corridor to the Hall, trying to look casual. When he got there, there were two beefy security guards on the door with walkie-talkies. As he walked up to them they moved to block the entrance.

"Morning," Rick said briskly, "could I just get past, please?"

"I'm sorry, sir," the bigger of the two said, "I'm afraid there's no admittance for unauthorised personnel."

"Unauthorised personnel? What on earth does that mean? I'm the Deputy Head."

The smaller man looked down at his list.

"Are you Mr Westfield?"

"Yes, that's right and now will you please let me into the Hall?"

"I'm sorry, sir, as I said, there is no unauthorised entrance. Strictly on the orders of Miss Everson."

Rick was appalled.

"What is going on in there, anyway?" he managed to get out.

"It's special exam practice, I believe, sir. It's going to go on for the next couple of hours."

"Two hours! I don't believe this, this is ridiculous."

"Yes, sir, of course. Now if you'd like to move away from the door. Perhaps you can take it up with Miss Everson later."

He sulked the next two hours away in his office until it was time for his break duty. He knew there was no point raising it with Camilla. She would either lie or stonewall his questions. He wandered out into the playground, miles away in his thoughts. These days it wasn't quite so important to be alert during break duty. A new contract, imposed just after Christmas, meant that everyone had to be out and about at break, imposing the new single file, quiet play, break time order. It was a surprise to him then when he looked up out of his sombre mood and saw, sitting on the bench under the shady branches of an oak tree, three members of his Year 11 PE class. They must have just been released from the Hall. He sidled over to them and casually asked, "All right lads? What were you lot doing in the Hall this morning that was more important than my PE lesson?"

All three of them looked as if he had just accused them of downloading pornography on a school computer. They glanced nervously at each other.

"Well?" he repeated.

Eventually, one of them cracked. A plump boy with an explosion of acne ventured a hesitant reply.

"Er, we were just doing some extra revision, you know, one of them walking talking mock exams we all have to do."

Immediately after offering this response, his eyes began to scan the floor in front of the bench and the others, grateful for a reasonable-sounding explanation, all joined in.

"Yeah sir, you know, they kind of take you through an old paper question by question and sort of commentate on what you are supposed to do."

"Yeah," chipped in one of his mates, increasing in confidence, "really boring, sir."

Rick's eyes narrowed.

"Why was Ms Everson in there then and all the other bigwigs if it was just that? Jason?"

He leaned forward and bored a laser gaze at the overweight boy who stuttered and stumbled.

"Er, I dunno, sir. I couldn't say, honest."

He was rescued by one of his smarter friends.

"Couldn't have been that important, sir, if you weren't in there, could it?"

Rick stood upright again.

"Hmm. Okay boys, that'll do for now. But if any of you need to come and see me to continue this conversation, you know where my office is. Total discretion guaranteed."

The boys were enveloped in a thick cloud of confusion.

"Total what, sir?" asked Jason.

Rick shook his head and said, "Never mind, boys, never mind." He turned to walk away.

Suddenly, relieved the ordeal was all over and eager to resume normal relations with Mr Westfield, a teacher they had a little time for because of his knowledge of the Champions League, brands of trainers and his infamous, withering sarcasm, Jason shouted after him, "Eh, sir, you going Prom this year?"

Rick stopped and half turned.

"Going *to* the Prom, Jason, *to* the Prom."

"Yes, sir, that's what I said. You going Prom then? Should be wicked."

"When is it then, Jason? Middle of June?"

"Yes, sir, after the exams are over, innit? We wanna see you do some moves on the dance floor."

"Yes, gents, I usually make an appearance," he said, smiling.

"There probably ain't gonna be a Prom this year anyway, fam," interjected Duane, one of the other boys. "Miss has banned about twenty people already."

"Course there is, you waste man. You just need to make sure you don't get a detention between now and the end."

The others burst out into peals of laughter.

"He aint got no chance, man. These days you get a detention for asking a question in class."

A vigorous debate ensued and Rick was forgotten. He turned on his heels and left them to it, brooding on the discussion they had just had. They were hiding something, something that they were more than a little nervous of. And to discover from the students a decision like that about the Prom, well that summed up the whole dysfunctional organisation. Where on earth did her reputation for laser-sharp efficiency come from? It was a myth as far as Rick could see. She seemed to lurch from one kneejerk crisis move to another without any discussion or consultation. He wouldn't be at all surprised if the Prom was cancelled eventually. And he was sure that if it did go ahead, Camilla wouldn't be within ten miles of it.

18

ALISON POKED HER HEAD AROUND THE DOOR THAT HAD been left slightly ajar, her nose wrinkling at the strong chemical smell of the paint in the air. On the other side of the room, oblivious to her presence, David was up a ladder painting the coving. She watched him paint for a few seconds, the sure and steady brush strokes hypnotic in their repetition.

"Would you like a cup of tea, David?" she called to him eventually.

He turned, breaking free of the spell of concentration.

"Hmm? Oh, yes, yes please. If it's not too much trouble."

She surveyed the room.

"You've made good progress, David. I love the colour."

He too scanned what he had done, as if to check.

"Yeah. Once you've finished the preparation, it's actually quite quick to do."

"Why don't you come through to the kitchen? The tea'll be ready in a minute. How do you take it?"

"Milk, no sugar, please."

Alison went back to the kitchen and busied herself with the kettle and teapot. She rummaged in a cupboard for some biscuits and rejected the digestives for the Belgian chocolate ones, smiling to herself as she did so. She was very pleased with the painting so far, it was clearly going to look wonderful when it was finished. And David was so polite and charming. It was nice to have someone in the house during the day to talk to. She wondered with a frown how much longer it was going to take him.

Barry had been quite good about it to be fair. He had not questioned her decision to go for Horizon Building Projects to do the work once she had reassured him it was the best of the quotes. Well, strictly speaking that was true because it was the only quote, but so what? Who was it harming to tell a little white lie? David was clearly very good at his job, the reviews and ratings confirmed that and she really couldn't be bothered to go through the hassle of seeing three or four others. She knew that Barry thought she just swanned around all day drinking coffee and reading books, but the house took a lot of running. Really it did.

Her thoughts were interrupted by David sticking his head around the open door of the kitchen.

"Is it ready?" he asked. "Shall I come in?"

"Yes, come through. It's ready to pour."

He padded into the room in his socks. He'd taken off his overall and was in shorts and a t-shirt. Alison looked up at him, her mouth slightly open in surprise. David, seeing her reaction, was a little embarrassed.

"Oh, sorry, I just thought I'd better take off the overall. You can't be too careful with paint. It gets everywhere. I ruined more than one carpet when I first started doing this job. I can have my tea in the dining room if you prefer."

She smiled and poured the tea. "No, of course not. I was just surprised, that's all. Come and have a seat. It was thoughtful of you to think about not getting paint everywhere."

He came in and perched on the edge of a seat at the end of the table, as if he were about to rush out again.

"So, when did you start painting and decorating? Have you always done that?"

"Yeah, pretty much. I did a sort of apprenticeship when I left school. Wasn't a proper one, it was through a mate of my dad's. I didn't do very well at school, you see. I messed about and was a bit of a joker. And, exactly as all of the teachers predicted, I left school with rubbish results. They weren't that interested in you if you weren't academic. Anyway, I learned decorating and a bit of building and I did a proper apprenticeship. Then I took my exams at college, part-time, and ended up doing A level Art and Design."

"Goodness me, well done you! You proved them all wrong, then."

David gave a wry smile. "I suppose so. I went on to do a business degree and set up my own company. When my dad died he left me a bit of money. I was the only one, you see. And it's steadily grown since then."

"A degree? Did you go back to tell all your teachers that they didn't know what they were talking about?"

"No, not really. They weren't really wrong anyway, I was a pain in the arse in those days. I wouldn't have liked to have to teach me back then."

There was a lull and they sipped their tea quietly. David was the first to break the silence.

"So, what about you, Alison? Do you work? I bet you were a star at school."

"No, not me. I did go to university to do economics and I started training to do accountancy, but I've never really worked. My husband is quite traditional in that way."

"Have you never wanted to, though? After all that study, it seems a bit of a waste."

A flicker of annoyance passed across Alison's face. "No, I haven't. I'm perfectly happy as I am, thank you."

David looked mortified. "No, of course. Sorry, it's really none of my business."

He drained his cup and stood up.

"Well, I'd better get on with it. I reckon I can do another hour now. Thanks for the tea."

He smiled quickly and went back to the dining room.

Alison, still sitting at the kitchen table, could have kicked herself. *What's wrong with you?* she thought. *He was only being polite. Barry's right, you always go and ruin things.*

*

An hour and a half later David had packed up the last of his kit and moved it to the hall.

"Mrs Pugh," he called, "I'm finished for the day. I'll see you tomorrow, okay?"

Alison, deep into her thriller in the front room, called in reply, "Oh, okay David, I'll come and show you out."

She scrambled to her feet and hurried to the hall. She had spent the last ninety minutes brooding on her rudeness to him earlier and she was determined not to let him leave without some signal that she regretted it.

"Thanks David," she smiled at him, "same time tomorrow?"

"Yeah, a bit earlier maybe, if that's all right. I reckon probably two long days will do it. You won't want me hanging around longer than I need to."

"You take as long as you need, David, it's a pleasure having you here, it really is."

She died inside when she heard herself say that. *What am I talking about? He's a decorator for God's sake. Try to get him out of the front door without making more of a fool of yourself.*

She passed him in the hall and opened the front door, just as Barry was getting out of his car, piles of folders in his arms. He crunched down the gravel path towards the open door.

"Oh, hello darling," she said, "you're early today. The decorator is just leaving."

"Yes, meeting finished early for once." He smiled at her and then the smile froze on his face as he looked beyond her to see

David Jones coming out of his house carrying his dust cloths. There was a shock of recognition on his face.

"Pube!" he spluttered. "Er, I mean, Mr Pugh. Hello sir, what are you doing here?"

The frozen smile had turned to a thunderous expression.

"I could ask you the same thing, Jones. What on earth are you doing in my house?"

Alison looked from one to the other, open-mouthed.

"Do you two know each other?" she stammered. "I don't understand. Barry, this is David, the decorator I told you about."

Comprehension dawned on David's face.

"Ah, I see, Mr Pugh," he said, pointing at Barry. He turned and pointed at Alison. "And Alison Pugh? Of course. I should have known."

"Quick as ever, Jones, I see."

"Will someone please explain what exactly is going on?" said Alison, raising her voice.

David looked a little sheepish. "Pu... er, Mr Pugh used to be my teacher at secondary school. Bit of a coincidence really."

"So, Jones, you're decorating now, are you?" asked Barry. His voice dripped with sarcasm, as if it were the latest in a long line of failed jobs he had pursued since leaving school.

"Yes, that's right. It's my company actually. It's going quite well."

The disappointment flickered across Barry's face.

"I see. Well, I can't stay chatting here all day. I've had a long day at work. I'm pleased things have worked out for you, and now, if you'll excuse me."

He moved towards David, who had to step aside to let him through the door. Barry marched past him, slightly brushing against him as he passed, and disappeared down the hall. David raised his eyebrows at Alison.

"I'll just take this to the van and come back for the rest," he said as he passed her. The air was thick with embarrassment and it was with some relief that he loaded the last lot of his stuff. He climbed in the van, wound the window down and called through to Alison, his eyes averted, "See you tomorrow."

He revved the throttle brutally and roared the van down the road.

Alison stood watching it go, all exhaust fumes and brake lights, as it sped into the distance. What on earth had all that been about?

She was soon to find out. Barry was pacing up and down in the kitchen when she went back in, his mouth a thin line.

"Why on earth is he doing our decorating?" he demanded.

"What do you mean, Barry? His company did the best quote."

"I don't care about the quote, I will not have that boy in my house." His voice trembled as he spoke.

"Barry, for goodness sake, what is the matter with you? You're completely overreacting."

"Oh, am I? And you would know, would you?"

"Barry, he's done a great job up till now. He's polite, he's on time and he works quickly. What on earth is the problem? Obviously, he wasn't your favourite pupil, but that was years ago. What did he do that was so terrible?"

Barry's knuckles went white as he gripped the edge of the work surface on the kitchen island.

"He was a little shit who made my life hell as a young teacher. He was a waster then and I'm sure he's a waster now. Just because he's got a bloody white van with his name on and he's supposed to be in charge of some kind of respectable company, well that doesn't mean a damn thing. People don't change, Alison, not really."

She was shocked. She had never seen him like this before. She was sure he was wrong about David. He had been so thoughtful and sensitive. And he had clearly changed. He'd said himself that he had been trouble at school and he didn't have to tell her that. And getting those qualifications and setting up in business, a successful business at that, well, that took some doing. She suddenly felt guilty. Even finding herself calling him David in her own mind made her feel terribly disloyal.

She softened her tone and walked over to him.

"It'll be okay, Barry. He'll be finished in a couple of days and you don't have to see him again."

She laid her hand on his arm and began to stroke it. He flinched and pulled away.

"I'm going to do some work. I've got a lot to do at Fairfield tomorrow, the exams are in full flow. Someone has got to pay for the decorating, you know. Dinner at seven, please."

He marched out of the room, tightly wound like a coiled spring.

Alison watched him go, seething. Her guilt had evaporated. She was tempted to burn the dinner while she continued her thriller. She was in the home straight now and The Girl Had Realised. One day, she thought, she would write her own, about real life. The Girl Burns the Dinner she would call it. That was the trouble with real life. Compared to books, it was so boring.

19

GEORGE DRAINED HIS PINT AND THEATRICALLY LET FLY A spectacular, resonant belch. His drinking buddies around the table whooped and roared in appreciation and he dramatically wiped his enormous hand across his mouth.

"Sorry ladies, no offence," he pronounced.

This provoked another gale of laughter. Behind the bar, the landlord, a tired, pale-looking man, looked over and raised an eyebrow. He was used to the antics of George and his crew. They were regular punters and spent a lot of money in his pub, so he tolerated their raucous behaviour. It didn't usually go too far, and the other locals had learned to stay out of their way. He also turned a blind eye to the fact that there were fringe members of the group who were clearly underage. George himself had started drinking there when he was sixteen, and it was widely accepted that this was part of the cultural apprenticeship of the community.

George slammed his empty glass down in front of the boy sitting next to him.

"Come on, Adam, man. It's your round."

Adam sprang up at once.

"Same again?"

"No, I'll have a nice cup of tea. Course we want the fucking same again, fam. Come on, chop chop. We're dying of thirst here."

Adam returned a couple of minutes later with a tray of lager. They all took their glasses.

"Cheers Adam, nice one," said a lanky youth opposite. He made a show of taking a long draught from the glass, and smacked his lips appreciatively. "Ah, beautiful," he pronounced. "Come on then, Adam, what's going on at that poxy shithole school of yours? How come you ain't been chucked out yet?"

"I've been keeping me head down, innit? My mum would fucking murder me if I got chucked out now."

George was scornful. "Yer mum! What a wanker. Is she still tucking you up at night, Adam? I tell you what though, lads, I wouldn't mind tucking her up at night, I'm telling you."

The rest of the lads around the table thought this the wittiest remark they had ever heard. Adam forced a thin smile and gripped his pint glass silently.

George looked over at him and slapped him on the back.

"Nah, sorry Adam mate, that was out of order. Only joking, yeah?"

Adam nodded. "No problem, man."

"So, come on then, tell us about F-F-F-Fucking Fairfield then. What's going on?"

Adam was relieved to be on firmer ground.

"Ah, it's a nightmare, man. That woman is a right bitch, I'm telling you. It's like being in the fucking army. She's got rid of loads of Year Eleven kids. And the ones she hasn't got rid of are nearly always in detention or in the unit or whatever. You know what she's done? She's banned loads of kids from going Prom. I've been banned because I was in detention last week."

The others were incredulous.

"Nah. She can't do that. You gotta go Prom, man, it's tradition."

"I didn't fucking go," said George bitterly. "I was banned last year."

"You were proper excluded, man. What did you expect?"

"I didn't expect to go, you wanker. That don't make it right. That bastard Syrian ruined every fucking thing."

There were sympathetic nods and murmurs of agreement as George stared morosely into his pint. After a respectful gap Adam started up again.

"I'm tellin' you, at this rate there'll only be about forty kids there. I heard that the kids who've been chucked out or banned are gonna go up there with a load of drink and stuff and just pile in."

George smiled broadly. "Yeah? Wicked."

"Yeah, Rizla pinged me the other day. It's revenge time, fam."

"Revenge?" A light went on above George's head. "When is it?"

"Two weeks on Friday, after the exams."

"Exams! Fuck me, you still doing them? You should be at home revising, Adam, old son."

It was Adam's turn to smile broadly.

"Nah, revision's taken care of, fam. It's the one thing the old witch has got right."

"What do you mean, man?"

Adam looked around the pub and leant forward, lowering his voice.

"Well, it's like this," he began.

*

Karim leaned backwards and stretched his arms high into the air behind him, yawning. He'd just do a little bit more on the Second World War, and then he'd go downstairs and have a break. He rubbed his eyes and refocused on his computer screen. Just a couple more exams to go and then it was over. They had gone quite well so far, he thought, but it was hard to be sure. He had put a lot of hours into revision and was still writing until a couple of minutes to go in all of his exams so far, which he thought was a good sign.

He had been shocked to see, surreptitiously looking around the exam hall, the number of people who finished early, or who did not even start and spent the entire exam with their head down on their arms, asleep. He couldn't understand the point of doing that. Why bother turning up in the first place? Still, that was their problem, not his. His problem, right at that moment, was World War Two.

After about half an hour, Joan called from downstairs, "Karim? Karim love, do you want a cup of coffee and something to eat? Time for a break."

"Ok, Joan, thanks. I'm just coming," he shouted in reply.

When he came down to the front room, there was a cup and plate of biscuits set on the side table next to his usual seat. Eric and Joan sat side by side on the sofa.

"Thanks Joan, that's lovely," he said.

"How's it going then, Karim? Are you on top of everything for your last few exams?" Eric asked.

"Yes, I think so," he replied. "I have my revision planned and I think I've got everything covered."

Joan beamed at him. "You've worked really hard, Karim. You deserve to do well, you really do."

Karim put his cup down and looked at them earnestly.

"I could not have done it without you." He blinked and his voice began to tremble. "I owe you everything."

"Now, now Karim," said Eric, noting with alarm that Joan's eyes had started to fill with tears. "None of that. We don't know how well you've done yet. Let's not get ahead of ourselves, eh?"

Karim laughed. He was grateful to Eric's uncanny English ability to lighten the mood with a silly joke, something he had had to do several times in the last year.

"Have you thought any more about what you're going to do when you've finished?" Eric was determined to keep the conversation going and to steer it away from anything that might trigger Joan's tears afresh. He knew that she was full of anxiety about what would happen when it came for Karim to leave them.

"Yeah, I think I'll probably try and get a part-time job, so I can pay you back some money and maybe volunteer at the Syrian Refugee Project in Longdon."

"Well, don't worry about paying us, Karim," said Joan. "What about a holiday? Have you thought about that?"

"Yeah, Ben and I thought we could maybe go camping in Cornwall and maybe go to a festival. July, I think he said. There's a group of us who are thinking about it."

"Ooh, that would be nice. Cornwall is lovely in the summer, isn't it, Eric? We had our honeymoon there."

Eric nodded. "Yes, you'll have a marvellous time there." He looked at the clock and said, "It's ten, shall we watch the news?"

It was a nightly ritual for them to watch the news together. Karim was fascinated by the trappings of the British political democratic settlement and was constantly asking questions about Parliament, the courts, the press and free speech. Eric didn't wait for the answer and switched on the TV straight away. They sat for the next fifteen minutes silently gripped by a major breaking news story.

There had been another terrorist outrage in central London. A minibus of five men had ploughed into crowds in Oxford Street before blowing themselves up. There were, according to the report, twenty people dead and hundreds injured. ISIS had already claimed responsibility.

Joan sat with her hand over her mouth as if in shock. Eric held her other hand tightly. Karim muttered under his breath in Syrian, an expression of pain mixed with fury on his face.

After about fifteen minutes, the coverage descended into experts speculating on the basis of no new information, and the usual tone of bewildered horror. There was nothing of value to say and the news broadcasters were determined to go on saying it.

Eric turned the television off.

"There's no point watching any more, they don't know anything. How much longer is this terrible violence going to go on for? I can't bear it, I really can't. And all in the name of religion. It's madness."

"It will go on until the end of the world," said Karim grimly. "It will never stop. And people will always hate." His words had a chilling, apocalyptic tone.

"Be careful, Karim. You know what this means for people who look like Muslims, don't you?" Joan had seamlessly slipped back into protective mode. "Remember what happened after that Manchester thing. Don't be out late. At least not until this has all blown over. There are a lot of angry, stupid people out there."

"Yes," he agreed, "a lot of angry stupid people. A lot of frightened people as well."

He smiled. "There's nothing we can do about it. The only thing I can do about it is to revise. So that is what I am going to do. Good night."

He stood up and took his plate and cup into the kitchen.

"Good night love," Joan called after him. "Don't work for too long. You need your sleep."

Karim ran up the stairs to the sanctuary of his room. He logged on to his computer, opened Instagram and checked his messages. There were a few from Ben. He clicked on the latest, delivered five minutes ago.

> *Yo Karim, my man. Whassup?*
> *Hi Ben. Did you see the news just now?*
> *Yeah Man. Serious shit. You okay?*

He paused and thought for a moment, then began typing again.

> *Yeah. Gonna get a lot of hassle in college.*
> *Nah man. College is full of your lot. You'll get hassle to and from college. When is your next exam?*
> *Tomorrow morning. History.*
> *You'll smash it man. And then what?*
> *Last exam on Friday. Science.*
> *You wanna come over Friday?*
> *Maybe. I'll let you know. Gonna do more revision now.*
> *All right. Good luck.*

He picked up his history notes and started to read them, pen in hand. It was no good, he couldn't concentrate. Instead he switched to the internet, logged on to the BBC news site and started to trawl through the details of the incident in Oxford Street. One fringe politician had started to suggest that the attackers were recent arrivals and had been admitted under European Union arrangements for

Syrian refugees. There were a lot of responses to this, including more thoughtful questions about 'evidence' and 'dangerous and inflammatory statements'. Well, that was encouraging, at least. But it was the general public that you had to worry about. Hardly daring to, he clicked on the comments tab under that strand of the story, half expecting what would be there. He was not mistaken. There were already hundreds of responses, written in the most graphic of terms, about the madness of letting terrorists into this country.

He couldn't read any more hatred and closed it down. He reached into his bedside drawer and pulled out the battered photo of Evana and his family. Nothing had come of the leaflet that he and Ahmed had spent ages making and delivering to the site at Calais. Ahmed had said that maybe Evana was still en route from Syria, but it had been two years now. And the stories you heard about what could happen to young girls, well, he couldn't bear to think about it. He put the photo back. When the exams were over he would go to the Syrian refugee charity and ask there. They would know what to do, surely? And he would do something. He had to.

20

S HE OPENED THE DOOR, HAVING SPENT THE SECONDS after seeing his van pull up outside arranging her features in what she hoped was a welcoming, warm smile.

"Morning, David," she beamed at him. "Come in. Cup of tea?"

"Morning. Yes, please. Tea would be great, thanks."

There was an awkward hiatus as he brought all of his stuff through. Alison retreated to the kitchen, not quite knowing what to say next. He moved to the dining room and began setting up. As she busied herself with the kettle and cups, she felt foolish. She really wanted to make this better, to go back to their easy conversation from before Barry's unhinged reaction of yesterday, but she couldn't seem able to easily engineer that.

"Here you are then," she announced brightly as she swept back into the dining room. She couldn't bear the tension so she immediately followed that up with, "Okay then. Just give me a shout if you need anything else," before scuttling out of the room.

It had been a wretched morning. Barry was up and gone by the time she had got up, without a word. Clearly, he was still angry and was punishing her for, well, for what exactly? She supposed that she was expected to agree with him instantly that David was the devil incarnate and needed to be banished from their house for ever. But why should she? He wasn't anything like that now, even if he had been all those years ago.

It hadn't improved. Her imagined easy resumption of cordial relations, perhaps after a few well-chosen words to clear the air, hadn't happened and she was left to brood as the morning ticked by. She spent the time cleaning the bathroom, furiously wielding the scourer like a weapon. Then she moved on to her hidden application form, still secreted away between *Madam Bovary* and *Great Expectations*. She gazed at the job description and selection criteria, but found herself reading the same section several times over. Eventually the words swam in front of her eyes and she gave up and admitted defeat. She couldn't concentrate on it with David next door, methodically and serenely smoothing paint over the imperfections of a grubby wall. Next, she tried her thriller, and became for five minutes The Girl who Wittily Charmed the Decorator, as she gratefully escaped into a life that was not hers.

No, this just would not do, she thought. She laid the book down and mooched around the room listlessly, picking up books from the shelves, straightening picture frames, staring out of the window at a straggly Philadelphus that needed pruning. She had to be bold and straightforward. If he was still frosty, well that would be that and she would have lost nothing. He'd be finished in a day or two and the problem would evaporate on its own. She would casually announce that she had made lunch, just something simple, and then she would just come right out and apologise and ask him about school.

This plan, when it coalesced in her mind, fully and perfectly formed, seemed to lift a weight from her, and she was able to resume the thriller with something like concentration. Refreshed after this latest plunge into a world where characters spoke to each other about meaningful things, she was emboldened. She looked at her watch. She had better set things in motion, before he had stopped for his own sandwich.

When she pushed the door of the dining room gently ajar, and peered round into the room, David was in the far corner, crouching down attending to the skirting board.

"David," she called across to him.

He turned absent-mindedly.

"Hmm?" he said, sounding as if he had surfaced from an enveloping dream.

"Sorry to disturb you, I just thought it would be nice to have some lunch. Nothing special, you know. I just feel we need to talk. I'm a bit embarrassed about what happened yesterday."

His face bloomed.

"That would be lovely," he said, "I'd like that."

Her breath caught in her throat. His smile was devastating and she was covered in confusion, out of her depth. She had to get back to firmer ground in the form of practical details, or she would be lost.

"About fifteen minutes?" she asked.

"Okay, perfect," he said and he turned back to his soothing painting rhythm.

She backed out of the door, desperate to reach the safety of the kitchen before she said or did anything foolish. Once there, she perched on the edge of a chair at the table. A little hesitant smile played across her face and she felt a comforting sense of relief wash over her. After a minute or so, she shook herself as if from a dream and began to bustle around, making salad and finding some cold cuts from the fridge. She set two places around the corner of the table, and waited, silently rehearsing her part of the conversation that she hoped would follow.

A few minutes later David came through to the kitchen, his shorts, T-shirt and socks less of a shock this time. He caught sight of the spread on the table.

"This looks great, Alison. You shouldn't have gone to all this trouble, really."

"It's no trouble, honestly. Anyway, it's done now. Sit down and help yourself, please."

There was an awkward silence, broken only by the musical pattering of cutlery and plates and serving bowls. A louder clash of stainless steel on porcelain, as they both went for the Greek salad at the same time, provoked nervous laughter and kick-started some conversation.

"This is great, Alison, really. I'm used to just grabbing a sandwich from the garage or something."

"Oh, you poor thing. I'd have thought your wife would have sent you off in the morning with a decent packed lunch."

He smiled wistfully.

"Not married actually, so I fend for myself."

Alison looked mortified. "I'm so sorry, David, I didn't mean to pry."

"No, it's fine. I was married, but well, you know. Got divorced finally a couple of years ago. We were together for about four years."

"Do you have any children?"

"No. I don't know whether that's a good thing or a bad thing. It was one of the reasons we split up actually."

"Didn't you want kids then? Was that it?"

He looked surprised.

"Oh no, it was the other way round. She didn't. She had a career and wanted to be out and about. Nothing wrong with that. I think she found me a bit boring actually. Or something. At any rate, it clearly wasn't working, so we split. It was quite amicable. I used to see her every now and again, but then she got involved with someone else and then they married and had kids, so I don't really see her at all these days."

"She had kids? Goodness, that must have been hard to take, after what had happened with you."

"It was at first, but life's too short to be angry with people."

She had been waiting all through the conversation for his tone to change. She had expected some spark of anger or bitterness, or blame, to emerge but there was not a shred of that.

He was sensitive, understanding, measured, kind and warm. Not like a man at all, in her experience. He also, she couldn't help noticing, had sparkling green eyes, and a few flecks of emulsion on his forehead. She fought down a flutter of warmth towards him.

He noticed that she had stopped talking and was staring vacantly at him. He thought that he had better stop going on about himself and ask her something.

"Any way, what about you? I'm a bit surprised that you don't have children. You're younger than Pube, er, Mr Pugh, aren't you?"

A cloud passed across her face.

"Yes, yes I am. But no, we can't. We've tried, but it's not going to happen. Barry doesn't want to go for IVF, it erm…"

She trailed off and filled the gap with a vacant smile.

"Sorry, Alison, I shouldn't have asked. It was a bit thoughtless of me to get so personal."

The tinkling of cutlery suddenly grew louder in the silence.

"Well, this is very nice," said David, shifting uncomfortably in his chair.

"Oh, it's no trouble. And I felt that we needed to talk, to clear the air. I'm really sorry for the way that Barry spoke to you yesterday, there was really no call for it. I don't know what got into him."

"Well, we didn't get along at school. He was, well, a bit harsh and I was a handful."

"Even so, it was a long time ago, there's no reason for him to hold a grudge for this long. What exactly happened?"

David hesitated. "Well, I don't know if I should be talking about this?"

"No, go on, I want to know."

"He was very strict, but he was unfair. He had his favourites, and if you weren't one of them, he would humiliate you. Nobody liked him, not even his favourites. His lessons were terrible, honestly the worst in the school. You had to sit in silence and copy from the board. Well, we just started to rebel and, in the end, there were riots in his class every day. And he was a bully, with the littler kids, the ones he could intimidate. The truth is, Alison, he was a nasty piece of work back then, I'm sorry to say."

He had started slowly, but as he got into his stride the condemnation poured out of him, as if he had been waiting for an opportunity in the last fifteen years to get it all out. When he had finished, he looked up at Alison, nervous of her reaction, as if he himself had only just heard what he had said.

Her face was frozen, horror-struck.

Instinctively he started again, trying to repair the damage he had obviously done.

"But, I'm sure he's a changed man these days, Alison. You know we all make mistakes when we're young. I know I..."

He didn't finish his sentence. Her eyes were red and stinging. They filled with tears which spilled down her cheeks.

"He hasn't changed though, that's the thing, he hasn't."

Her sentence dissolved into heaving, uncontrollable sobs. David got up immediately and crouched down beside her, putting his arm around her shoulders.

"There, there," he whispered in her ear, "don't cry. I'm sorry I said all of that."

She leant on his chest and put her head on his neck, her whole body still heaving with raw, unleashed emotion that she had kept buried for so long.

"I'm sorry I've upset you. You just need a good cry."

She looked up at him at that moment and pulled him into a kiss. Before they knew it, the salad bowl had scattered across the kitchen floor and they were locked in a passionate embrace. David, after a minute, pulled away, put his hand to her cheek, his piercing green eyes looking straight at her.

"I don't know if this is what you want."

She touched her finger to his lips, stood up and led him out of the kitchen.

*

A couple of hours later they were in bed in the spare room, limbs entangled. Alison sat up on her elbow, and tentatively touched his face.

"You know you've got paint on your face, don't you?"

David grinned. "Occupational hazard, madam."

"I suppose falling into bed with the woman of the house could be classed as that as well."

The grin faded. "I've never done anything like this before, you know. This is not just a quick shag."

"No?" asked Alison. "What is it, then?"

"I'm not sure, except it's very nice. You're very nice. You're gorgeous, in fact."

She smiled. "So are you. Quite wonderful." She giggled. "We're not being very cool, are we?"

"Being cool is overrated in my opinion."

Her smiled disappeared and she looked troubled.

"It was very, very nice. But you'll finish the dining room in a couple of days at the most and then you'll go. I can't bear it."

"We'll think of something, trust me."

She lay back on the bed and sighed. She was racking her brains.

Finally, she sat up again to face him, her hand on his chest.

"Do you do new kitchens?" she asked.

21

News From North Korea

Greetings to Los Desaparecidos!

Exams now over, so secret meetings involving Year 11 in the locked Hall, supervised by the Politburo have finished.

Year 11 is forty students down on numbers recorded in September. Funny that – where are they?

POCSE nonsense already started with Year 10. Time released for Year 11 teachers to be used for 'interventions'. Apparently, planning for next year and training to improve teachers' skills is for lefty wimps.

Number of students banned from Prom now exceeds number of tickets sold.

Rumours abound that Fairfield will pilot the new NHS and Social Care apprenticeships for no-hopers in Year 10. Part of new curriculum offer that has got rid of art, drama and music. Too 'communist', according to new research by the POCSE Institute for Lies and Misrepresentations.

New contract to be introduced in September requires all teachers to supervise pupils until 5 pm and for two days every holiday. Marking? Do that in your own time folks.

Kim Jong-Ev achieves new record for number of days out of school for member of Senior Team.

Senior Team to be repackaged as Blondie, with Kim Jong-Ev as Debbie Harry and the endless ranks of young, fit, handsome men appointed in dubious circumstances to SLT and wearing three-piece suits, as backing band. A new album and world tour scheduled for September. Working title: 'Heart of Glass'.

Rumours just reaching us that disaffected, banned students will storm the Prom and take their revenge on Kim Jong-Ev. Don't waste your time guys – she won't be there!

A record twenty-five teachers have managed to dig a tunnel and they will have escaped by the end of term. So desperate are they to leave North Korea that some are leaving teaching altogether and are taking up careers as varied as driving buses, selling insurance, stacking shelves in Tesco and, the ultimate insult to the regime, teaching in the private sector.

Queueing up every morning in the playground in silence so successful that it is being extended to the summer holidays. "Research shows that a lot of learning time is lost in the six-week holiday," says Big Bad Boy Bazzer.

22

RICK LOOKED AT HIS WATCH AGAIN. IT WAS SEVEN THIRTY, the official start time, and still there was no sign of any guests approaching. There were a few knots of teachers standing outside, all in their finest party outfits, apart from those, like Rick, who had had to go there straight from school. Kevin had, as usual, been assigned official photographer status, and his tuxedo and dicky bow combination was completed by a camera with a huge zoom lens. It was a serious bit of kit and Kevin spent his time in between chatting to some of the other teachers, fiddling with knobs and dials. He also took the opportunity, every year, to limber up by taking photos of the staff, singly and in groups, wearing their glad rags in front of the shabbily impressive Longdon Park, an eighteenth century mansion in acres of countryside that had been used as the venue for the Prom for as long as anyone could remember.

Rick paced to the bend in the drive, his shoes crunching pleasingly on the gravel, so that he could get an extended view of the long sweep to the main road. Nothing. He turned and retraced his steps, checking his watch again as he went. It was a beautiful early July evening, warm and sultry, with the scent of honeysuckle heavy on the air. Everything was set for a fitting send-off for the Year 11 students, but the nervous shifting from foot to foot, the glances down the drive, and the stilted conversations spoke of anxiety. This was not like any of the other Prom celebrations any of them had ever attended.

In the previous week the school had been alive with rumours: Camilla had cancelled it. Only forty tickets had been sold. Social media was facilitating a planned storming of the Bastille by the disaffected and dispossessed. In Camilla's new Fairfield there were many members of both groups. There was even a rumour that had surfaced only the day before, that those students who had bought tickets were planning on boycotting at the last moment and had hired a club in town, where alcohol and other stimulants could be ingested.

Rick had considered that the boycott was a realistic proposition and that it had been avoided by the final rumour that had sprung up on Thursday, that Camilla, breaking over thirty years of tradition, was not going to attend. As he himself knew, that rumour was firmly rooted in the truth, and he had made a good job of ensuring the news got around the students.

He thought back to Monday of that week and his surprise at being summoned to Camilla's office. Was she finally going to spring a trumped-up disciplinary on him? Alastair's protection could only last so long. He steeled himself, knocked on her door and went in.

"You wanted to see me?" he began. She was sitting at her desk, hand on mouse, and he just caught a glimpse of the familiar orange of the EasyJet site before she minimised it.

She looked up. "Ah yes, Rick. Come in."

Rick hovered just inside the door. She rarely invited him to sit down.

"I won't keep you long."

That was the phrase she used when she meant 'don't sit down'.

He stood in front of her desk, like a naughty student about to be told off.

"I assume that you are going to the Prom on Friday?"

"Yes," he replied, "I always do."

"Good, I thought so. I just wanted to make sure that you know I'm expecting you to stay for the duration and make sure that everyone has left the site."

"So, you won't be there, I take it?" Rick asked the question in his most innocent voice.

Her eyes flicked left and right. "No, I have another meeting that night."

Bollocks you have, thought Rick, *a meeting with a bottle of red in an expensive restaurant more like.*

He smiled at her. "I suppose you've heard the rumours that there is going to be trouble? Students you excluded and banned coming en masse to gate-crash?"

She bristled. "Oh, I'm sure that's all just talk. But just in case, I need you to be there for the whole event please. You have a, er, good relationship with the students, even the feral ones, and it's about time it actually came in useful."

"Will O'Malley be there?"

"Patrick? Yes, Patrick will be there. Well, at least at the beginning."

Yes, thought Rick, *someone else who is wetting himself at the prospect of meeting a group of kids he's bullied and brutalised all year.*

He contented himself with a thin smile. "Fine. So, was there anything else?"

She thought for a moment and then finally took the plunge.

"Have you heard anything about this, Rick? What do you think are the chances of there being trouble? We must avoid any bad press in the *Advertiser.* Alastair is still exercised about the last front page."

He considered the question. He knew the answer, he just wanted to make her sweat a little.

"I think it's highly likely. There are a lot of students, past and present, who hate your guts. Lot of staff, too, but at least you can be fairly confident that they won't burn the building down. Well, most of them. Just saying."

A look of pure hatred tinged with fury took possession of her face.

"How dare you? Don't you think I deserve some support from my deputy?"

"Calm down, Camilla. I'm not saying that's what I think, I'm simply reporting what other people think."

"And what do you think?"

"Oh," he said, making for the door, "I couldn't possibly comment on that. I'll be there Friday."

He closed the door behind him and walked down the corridors to his office with a spring in his step. He had rather enjoyed that.

And so here he was, spending a precious Friday night on duty, expecting trouble. He sidled over to Kevin, who had taken as many photographs as he could of the staff and was now standing in the shade so he could flick through the thumbnails to check them out.

"So, Kev, do you think anyone's coming tonight?" he asked.

Kevin looked up from his camera. "Yeah, I do actually."

"How come you're so confident? They're leaving it a bit late, aren't they?"

"Look," he said, jerking his head in the direction of the road.

Rick turned around. There, sweeping round the bend, was the first stretch limo of the evening. Kevin got himself into position with the camera and the car crunched to a halt outside the entrance. The doors opened and eight young people, four girls and four boys, self-consciously unfolded themselves from the limo. They were in strict regulation Prom outfits. The girls tottered on high heels, in tight satiny dresses that showcased cleavages of all sizes. They had extraordinary bouffant hairstyles, that had to be slightly repaired or adjusted after removing themselves from the car and encountering the slight summer breeze that drifted across the gardens. There were a variety of shades of spray tan on display, and as they negotiated the treacherous gravel in their heels, they left a trail of glitter behind them.

The boys seemed to have all got their Prom suit from the same shop and this year's look was the ever-popular, very shiny, skin-tight suit, winkle pickers, gold bling jewellery and an assortment of silk ties and waistcoats. The more daring young men had taken a chance on either a floral shirt or a dicky bow.

Their procession into the venue followed a set of unchanging rules that, although not written down anywhere, seemed to be known by all. There was a spontaneous round of applause from the gathered staff, followed by five minutes of photographs, and squeals from the female staff, approving every dress and accessory. The male staff confined themselves to comments about football and mercilessly took the piss out of the rather awkward-looking boys, in an oddly affectionate and good-natured manner.

Then, after a few minutes of this small talk, they made their way into the main building. Their slightly unsteady progress was down to more than the combination of stilettos and gravel. Like all fifteen-year-old Prom-goers all over the country, they had dealt with the alcohol ban that was always strictly enforced, by getting drunk at home or in the pub, beforehand.

After this first arrival there was a steady stream of students in a variety of modes of transport. Some long-suffering parents had drawn the short straw and had driven groups there. There were several more limos, a couple of horse-drawn carriages and one girl, resplendent in leather and Doc Martens, who roared along the gravel and round the turning circle, riding pillion on her dad's Harley Davidson. She was shortly followed by her soul mate, similarly attired, on the back of her father's moped. They embraced, had their photograph taken and disappeared into the bowels of the Palladian mansion.

In the middle of all this, one of the cars that drove in didn't stop in front of the house but carried on around the side to the car park. Rick peered against the sun that was getting quite low in the sky, and made out the figure of Patrick O'Malley, a set line of a mouth and a furrowed brow, behind the wheel. He did not look as if this was where he wanted to be spending his Friday night.

"Oh great," he muttered to Kevin, "Torquemada's here."

"I'll leave him to you, Mr Westfield," Kevin smirked. "I'll go in and you can do small talk. That is way above my pay grade." And then he sloped off, whistling.

A minute later O'Malley came round the corner, remembering at the last minute to fix a smile on his face. He seemed to have been practising it on the way from the car park. Rick was the only person left out front now, bar the burly, taciturn security guard. Everyone had gone into the venue and the disco had started.

"Rick," he said, drawing up next to him.

"Patrick," he replied.

This is going to be a good conversation, he thought. *I'm not going to make it easy for him. He needs me more than I need him.*

O'Malley's smile was beginning to fray at the edges.

"So, are there many here?"

"Not bad. About fifty or sixty. They're all inside. You should go in. I don't think there'll be any more arriving now."

"What do you make of the rumours that some of the banned kids are going to try and get in later?"

He said this with a smile and in a light, airy tone as if he were idly speculating about something unlikely, like an extra-terrestrial invasion, but Rick could see he was petrified and was probably already calculating a respectable time of departure.

"Well, it's possible, I suppose. It's happened before, but we've got security on the gate at the main road and on the door here, so I don't think there'll be a real problem."

O'Malley glanced down at his watch.

"You'll be able to go soon, Patrick, don't worry. But you do have to make an appearance inside before you can leave. Come on, I'll hold your hand."

He led the way to the entrance and the security guard stepped aside grudgingly to let them in. Rick was loving this. For the first time for months, he had O'Malley exactly where he wanted him. On his territory.

*

George was loving it as well. On his territory. He surveyed the scene in The Trafalgar, pint of lager in one hand, unlit cigarette in the other. Friday night in the pub was his favourite time. He could lose himself in the noise and bustle, surrounded by associates and friends. Here he had a place. He was known. People treated him with something close to respect, or was it fear? His jokes elicited laughter and back-slapping. His loud pronouncements on current affairs marked him out as more than a back page man, even if he merely parroted the standard lines he had heard his father spouting every day. They were the views that oiled the wheels of the domestic machine of Mr Mason, a machine of ignorance, intimidation and brutality.

His opinions were treated as if they mattered and they provoked head nodding and mutterings of agreement. George didn't even know if he really believed them, but it was important to have something to say for yourself in this world, he thought, and it was even more important to have someone to blame.

He was in the middle of one of his familiar rants, lubricated by several pints of lager.

"Have you seen what they're saying about those bombs in Oxford Street? Syrians, that's who it was. They found Syrian ID cards on what was left of the bodies. I fucking knew it. As soon as we let the bastards in, this was bound to happen. I tell you, I'd like to get hold of one of them, I'd fucking show him asylum. Bastards."

This elicited a general buzz of agreement, and some of the others joined in, each wanting to outdo the outrage of the previous speaker. It was a bigger than average turnout that night. They had commandeered one side of the main bar and had been drinking since about six. Their usual crew had been swelled by the disaffected of Fairfield school, celebrating the end of the exams, all the while knowing they had nothing to celebrate and they had comprehensively made a mess of their exams and their lives. It was what you did, though. It was expected. You got drunk. You shouted abuse. You had a laugh. To do or be anything else was to be weird, and of all the things one had to avoid, it was being weird. Better even to be foreign.

He thought about the weird kids at school. The Goths and the Emos. Sometimes he thought he hated them even more than the fucking immigrants, with their piercings and black outfits and funny hair and terrible music. They had it all and they fucking chose that. He took a long swig from his lager and shook his head. At least they didn't come in here. The Trafalgar was a haven for the Proper British Lad. With the occasional Proper British Girl thrown in, preferably after many vodkas had been drunk, he thought, grinning lasciviously.

His thoughts were interrupted by a crash. One of the younger members of the group, stuck in the corner of the table and desperate to get to the toilet, had been blocked time and again by those around him, who thought it would be funny to see exactly how desperate he got. Feeling imminent disaster, he could take it no more and climbed up onto the table to escape those blocking his path. He knocked over a couple of drinks and stood in a packet of crisps. At the last moment, just as he was about to leap down and scramble to the loo, someone at the table stuck out a hand and tripped him. He fell backwards into the table, scattering glasses, drinks, crisps and phones everywhere.

There was a slight pause as this sank in. Then there was a roar of laughter combined with the outrage of those who had lost their drink. The table and surrounding floor space was swimming in lager and those closest to the epicentre sprang out of their seats, covered in lager and debris.

The weaselly landlord, who had been looking on from behind the bar for some time, his unease steadily growing, had had enough. He could tolerate this bunch of hooligans as long as they were spending lots of money, but several groups of older drinkers had already moved away and complained to him. It was time for action.

He shouted from behind the bar, "Right you lot, that's enough. You've had your fun, now let the grown-ups take over again, eh?"

He came out from behind the bar and walked over to their table to make the point. Nobody moved.

"Come on, let's be having you. You've all had enough to drink for one night. Off you go."

George stood up, incensed that his night out in The Trafalgar might be ruined.

"No, man. We ain't moving. It was an accident bruv, just chill."

He dwarfed the landlord, who stared at him. This was a battle he had to win.

"I've told you, get out. Now. If you go quietly now, then I might let you back in tomorrow, but don't push it."

"Nah, Sid. We ain't going anywhere."

George sat back down, picked up his drink and took a refined sip of his lager.

The landlord looked at George and then the rest of the table, who were still sitting in stunned silence. He smiled and then walked away without another word. As he went the table erupted into laughter and cheering.

"That told him, George, eh? The old cunt."

Their raucous celebration of a great victory, destined in their heads to be retold and celebrated for years to come, gradually quietened as they became aware, one by one, of two men, in their forties by the look of them, standing behind George, unsmiling. As the silence settled on the pub, George looked behind him. The smile disappeared from his face as he saw them and he blanched.

The one nearest to him put his hand on George's shoulder. He had a scar over his left eye, extending down to his cheek.

"George, me old cock. Does your dad know you're in here, disturbing the peace?"

"Hello Tony," George stammered.

"Don't Tony me, you bag of dirt. It's Mr Collins, to you."

George's voice fell to a whisper. He averted his eyes.

"Sorry, Mr Collins," he said.

Tony raised his voice. "What was that? Speak up, I can't hear yer. No-one can hear yer."

George cleared his throat, miserably, and said it again, louder.

"I'm sorry, Mr Collins."

"There. Now that's better, a lot better. Listen, George," he paused and surveyed the rest of the table, each of whom felt a chill down their spine when Tony's eyes rested upon them.

"And listen, George's friends. Me and the terminator here," he nodded to his right, indicating his silent companion, "we're meeting George's father later on a matter of business. And we would like to be able to say to Mr Mason, who as you all know is an upstanding member of the local community, that George and his friends all behaved themselves in the pub and left at about…"

He looked down at his watch. "…at about nine fifteen. Know what I mean, children?"

There was a sheepish chorus of acknowledgement from the chastened group. George stood up, finished his drink, and said, "Time to go boys."

Tony cackled. "Your lord and master has spoken, children. Off you fuck."

The group picked their way through the debris and out of the pub.

Tony looked across to the landlord, who had resumed his place behind the bar. He winked theatrically at him and Sid returned the wink with a thumbs-up. The rest of the pub went back to their drinking and conversation. The cabaret was over.

*

The disco was in full swing and under the strobe lights, Rick could just about make out the identities of the gyrating bodies. Occasionally, the pursuit of teenage kicks led to Rick and some of the other senior members of staff in attendance having to remind a few people that snogging should be restrained and controlled. The air inside was thick with pheromones, Lynx and Babe Power. It was at moments like these that Rick was most glad that there was a no alcohol policy. Add that to the mix and there would have been carnage.

The familiar and comforting tropes of the Year 11 Prom were being replayed in front of him. He had been asked several times to 'show us some moves' and had dutifully provided appropriate dad dancing to keep the students amused. He had chatted to staff about their summer holidays. He had taken a thousand photos and had photobombed a thousand selfies. Ties and jackets had long been removed, to be replaced by sweat stains and flapping shirts. Expensive gelled and sprayed hairstyles had started to wilt, mascara to run, and regular missions to the toilets were undertaken for running repairs.

Even better, O'Malley was about to go. Rick had had the delicious experience of walking in to the main dance area with him, to be met with a subtle but unmistakeable outbreak of hissing. To his credit though, O'Malley had stuck it out, even though he was snubbed by both staff and students alike, so that he ended up drinking orange juice on the door with the security guard. Eventually, after braving several laps of the venue, hissed at wherever he went, he finally came up to Rick and said, straining to be heard above the music, "I think I'll make a move now."

"Okay," Rick replied. "See you on Monday."

He watched as O'Malley picked his way through knots of people chatting and taking photos, inching his way to the exit. He was about to go and have a sit down in the quiet room when Jason came over to him and shouted, "Eh sir, come on, it's the conga."

He hauled himself to his feet. "All right Jase, if I absolutely have to," he said, and followed him back into the dance room.

*

On the main road by the entrance, a red double decker bus stopped and about fifteen raucous youths got off, George in the vanguard of the battalion. Twenty minutes earlier they had mooched around in the street outside The Trafalgar, George still smarting at his humiliation in the pub and the ruination of his Friday night.

"This is fucking rubbish, man," George had pronounced. "What are we gonna do now?"

"There's always the Prom," ventured one of the others. "Why don't we go up there and try and get in? It'd be a laugh."

"Come on, George man, they shouldn't've banned me in the first place, and you never went last year. They'd shit themselves if we all turned up there mob-handed. They'd have to let us in."

"Yeah come on," George agreed, "let's go shop and buy some more cans and then get on the 165. We'll be there in fifteen."

Their spirits rose with the advent of this new plan and by the time they boarded the bus they were loud, aggressive and objectionable in equal measures. It was an uncomfortable journey for those passengers who had made the innocent mistake of getting that particular bus at that particular time.

The driver was relieved to see the back of them as they all piled off at the stop. Although it was only fifteen minutes away from The Trafalgar they found themselves on a lushly-wooded fast road with detached houses set back behind long, mature gardens. It was golf course territory. They stared at the houses and breathed in the fragrance of money.

"Fucking hell, look at those houses, fam. Why do they have the Prom here? Talk about fucking rubbing our noses in it."

They all stared, each of them lost in a vision of their own. Some were consumed with jealousy, some anger, some inferiority, some acceptance, of a world that existed and that they couldn't change. Eventually they roused themselves. They started off down the road towards the entrance to the mansion when George, out in front, stopped dead.

"Shit. There's security. We'll never get past him without a bit of trouble."

Illuminated by a solitary street light up ahead was the unmistakeable figure of a bouncer. Shaven-headed, with sunglasses and a walkie-talkie. They all ducked tightly into the trees by the side of the road and began talking quietly.

"Listen," said George, "I ain't going back after all this. If we go over the fence here, we can get in that way, go through the woods and end up on the driveway that leads to the big house."

After a prodigious session in The Trafalgar, topped up on the bus with a few cans, this seemed to them the most reasonable plan ever devised. Without any hesitation, the rabble began to shin up the fence and over. Two minutes later, with a few barked shins and bruised arms and legs, they were all over the top and in the woods. Clutching their carrier bags full of lager, they tracked the path while staying in the woods until it turned a bend, so that they would be invisible from the road.

Under the canopy of the trees, the warm night air was soupy with pollen and earthy scents and there was a strange quiet, with only the distant hum of the traffic leaking into the undergrowth. They were an unlikely crew, with baseball caps, trainers and carrier bags, crashing through brambles and whiplash sappy branches. Occasionally, they stopped to get their bearings and they listened to the eerie sounds of snuffling, scurrying wildlife yards away from them.

"Fucking hell, man, what was that?" exclaimed one of them after a particularly piteous set of cries came from a thick clump of rhododendron bushes up ahead. Something was meeting a brutal end in this lush Surrey woodland. They all pulled up and looked around, peering through the swirling blackness. Suddenly, The Trafalgar, with its comforting brash lights and noise, seemed many miles away.

"I hate the fucking countryside," George pronounced. "Come on, let's get on the path."

They didn't need telling twice. They spotted a light in the distance, winking intermittently through the branches, and they set their sights on that, pushing aside branches and thorns that whipped back in their faces when released by the person immediately in front. When they emerged from the trees onto tarmac they presented a sorry sight: faces and arms scratched, out of breath and sweating, they resembled the apocryphal lost soldiers emerging from far eastern jungles unaware the war was over. They were thirsty, tired, disorientated and in dire need of something resembling entertainment to make this great trek worthwhile. Recriminations were beginning to bubble to the surface.

George leaned forward, his hands on his knees, wheezing, red-faced, slicked with sweat. This was the furthest he had walked since he was seven years old, and his head was spinning.

"Jesus," he gasped, "whose fucking idea was this? This better be worth it fam, or there'll be trouble, I'm telling you."

As they filled their lungs with the night air and wiped the sweat from their eyes, they surveyed their surroundings. They were a little confused to see, not the imposing splendour of eighteenth century architecture, but a car park, and a few outbuildings.

"Shit," said Adam, "we've come the wrong way. This ain't it."

"Fuck, that's all we need. I've had enough of this, man. This fucking sucks."

There was a general murmuring of agreement when George said, "Hey, look over there. Who's that geezer?"

The car park was flooded with lighting and they squinted their eyes to adjust. It was Adam who said, "I don't believe it. It's that cunt O'Malley. He was the fucker that had me excluded and banned."

They all looked at each other, each of them thinking the same thing, but waiting for permission to act. George, still bubbling with resentment from earlier slights, gave it to them.

"Come on, let's get the fucker."

23

SHE WENT THROUGH IT AGAIN. BEN LISTENED, BUT HIS mind was elsewhere. He was just trying to make her feel better so she could leave and have a nice time. She didn't get to go out very often.

"So, it's just the four of you, isn't it? I don't want loads of people suddenly turning up. I've read terrible things about news of parties spreading on social media and then before you know it there's a hundred gate crashers wrecking the place and taking drugs and all sorts."

"Mum, relax, it's just not going to happen. Those kind of people are not hanging around waiting for four lads in a flat watching a movie and eating pizza. You can't believe everything you read in the papers."

She frowned at him. "It's all very well being sarcastic about it but I worry about you. When you see some of those lads hanging around outside the shops down there, well, you just need to be careful, that's all."

She put her coat on and turned to look at her face in the mirror.

"You look very nice, Mum. Now go out and have a nice time."

"Just remind me who's coming again."

Ben sighed. "Karim, Alex, and Raysharne. I've told you a hundred times."

"And you won't drink too much, will you?"

"Mum, Karim doesn't drink and the rest of us have just got a few cans of beer, that's all. I've ordered the Domino's and we're just gonna watch *Star Wars* and maybe do a FIFA tournament. We are officially the most boring teenagers in Longdon, you know that."

She smiled and came over to him, wrapping her arms around him and giving him a kiss on the cheek.

He recoiled and wriggled his way out of the embrace. Being nice to your mum had its limits.

"You're the best teenager in Longdon. I'm very proud of you, Ben."

"Mum, get off me. I'm not six years old, you know."

She untangled herself and stepped back looking at him, her eyes sparkling.

"No, but you'll always be my little boy."

"When do you think you'll be back?" he said, trying to get back onto less emotional ground.

"About half eleven, midnight maybe."

"Okay, well have a nice time then." Ben walked her towards the door and finally saw her out, shutting it behind her with a sigh of relief.

"At last," he said out loud. "Now, let's get this party started."

*

Karim was looking forward to this. He had told Joan and Eric where he was going and that he was likely to be back after midnight and not to worry, he had his phone with him 'in case of emergencies'. 'In case of emergencies' was a phrase that Joan and Eric had virtually made their own and it covered a multitude of unspoken horrors from missing the bus to Act of God.

His last exam had been that morning, and as he had packed away his pens and equipment into his pencil case and watched the invigilator scoop up his neatly-stacked papers, he had felt a lifting of a weight. Study had allowed him to block out a lot of difficult emotions and had enabled him to get through life on a day to day basis without confronting the things that he knew he must. Now it was all over, he could start planning.

He went to Friday prayers at the mosque and after emptying his mind of all concerns, had emerged refreshed and determined. He saw Ahmed afterwards, with a group of the mosque Elders and he hung around behind them in Ahmed's eyeline so that they could chat when he had a minute.

Finally the group broke away with much back slapping and hand shaking. Ahmed, smiling broadly, approached Karim.

"Karim. As-salam alaykum."

"Wa alykum as-slam."

They shook hands.

"How are you, Karim? Have you finished your exams?"

"Yes, the last one was today."

"And how was it? Did everything go well?"

"Yes, I think so, inshallah."

"So, what are you going to do with yourself now all of your work is over?"

"I think maybe a holiday with friends from college and then I'm going to try to find a job for the summer."

"And the Syrian Refugee Project? We could use some help there, you know."

"Yes, yes I know. I'd like to come and help out a few days a week if that's all right."

"Of course, Karim. Come along on Monday and we can talk about how we can use you."

Karim hesitated, his eyes downcast. "I was also thinking of going to Calais."

Ahmed's tone sharpened. "Karim, we have discussed that before. You know you can't do that. The last thing you want to do at this moment is leave the country."

"I know that, Ahmed, but I must do something to help Evana. There has been no news at all?"

"No, I'm sorry. But that just means that she is not in Calais, so there is even less reason to go there."

"Ahmed, I can't just sit around doing nothing. She's my sister."

"And I am your friend. And I'm telling you, you must. Everything that everyone has done for you, you want to throw it in their face and trample it on the ground? Joan and Eric, you want to treat them like this? You must be patient."

Karim had left it at that, knowing that Ahmed was implacable in this matter. He'd go along with it for the time being. But not for much longer.

*

O'Malley looked up at the sound of running and a shout. On the far side of the car park was a group of about twenty youths, all with hoodies up and bandanas on, charging towards him, shouting. He froze.

"What the—" he exclaimed, but before he could do anything they had surrounded him, shouting and taunting him.

He was petrified. There was nothing he could do, so thinking as quickly as his terrified brain could, he played for time. Surely, someone else would come to the car park soon. He wondered whether the security guard would hear him if he took a chance and started to scream, and he concluded that no, they probably wouldn't above the insistent thumping of the disco. His only option was to talk.

He held his hands up, outstretched in supplication. "Lads, let's not do anything silly, now. Let's just calm down, and talk this through."

George, his voice muffled by his bandana, walked towards him, imitating his voice, as if it were that of a little girl. "Oooh, lads, let's not do anything silly now. Let's just calm down because I am shitting myself here."

The circle of his accomplices laughed and joined in. George took a few steps towards him and began poking him in the chest.

"I hear that you banned some of my mates from the Prom, is that right?"

"Look, you need to think about what you're doing. You're on CCTV and the house is full of people who can identify you. I think you should just turn around and let me go before you do something you'll regret."

O'Malley had mustered as much calm gravitas as he could. He hoped that they couldn't see he was panic-stricken. He was mistaken.

"Nice try, but for once, it's the kids who are gonna tell you what to do, bruv."

The circle tightened around him and his cries were muffled by the press of bodies. A few minutes later he had been bound and gagged with some of the bandanas and locked in his own car.

"That'll do for now," said George through the open window. "We'll be back, so don't go away. Oh, sorry, I forgot, you can't."

This provoked a chorus of laughter and jeering. George wound the window back up and locked the car.

"Come on," he announced to the triumphant group, "it's round two."

They followed him, hoodies and bandanas still in place, carrier bags stuffed with cans swinging in their hands, as he skirted the car park in the direction of the thumping bass of the sound system. They rounded a corner and saw the mansion. In the light that spilled from the open doorway, a second bouncer was clearly visible.

"Shit," cursed Adam, "another one. Now what?"

They huddled together hard up against the wall of the building, out of his eye line, waiting for inspiration to strike. Just as they were beginning to lose hope, they saw the familiar flare of a match, followed by the glowing tip of a cigarette. The bouncer, taking a drag from the cigarette, stretched and began to walk away from the entrance, away from them and around the corner.

George looked in, a smile spreading across his face. "Yes! He's on a fag break. Come on lads, we're in."

He sprinted to the door, keeping as close to the wall as he could, weaving in and out of the bushes, in case the bouncer returned early.

The others followed and they all piled through the entrance into the warm yellow light of the foyer. One or two students, taking refuge from the dance floor, or en route to the toilets, looked up in alarm as the rag tag army burst in, euphoric after their successful kidnapping of O'Malley, and the ease with which they had gained entry. It seemed to them that there was nothing they could not achieve.

And then, reality dawned on them. They looked at each other with their carriers of lager, hoodies and trainers, and then at the Promgoers, who gaped at them open-mouthed, in their shiny suits and tight dresses.

"Look at the state of us, man," whined Adam. "We stand out like a sore thumb. What are we gonna do now?"

George considered for a moment and then pronounced his judgement.

"We're gonna blend in, bruv, blend in. And, we're gonna have a little drink, and a little dance, and a bit of a laugh, for as long as we can get away with it."

Adam's face registered disappointment and the rest of the crew looked sheepish.

George felt like a lion leading donkeys.

"Or, you can bottle it and all just fuck off home. You're on your own."

He took a can from his carrier, cracked it open and, and took a long, deep draught. Then he placed the bag behind the reception desk, the open can in his pocket, and he sauntered towards the dance hall. The others watched him go. When he had disappeared into the flashing lights and pulsing shadows, the others looked around at each other, leaderless and unsure.

It was Adam that was the first to crack.

"Oh, fuck it," he said, "might as well."

He went through the same series of actions as George, and followed his route towards the promised land. One by one the others all followed.

The two Promgoers, who had observed the whole scene with a growing sense of fascination from the corner, watched them go. They turned to each other.

"We've got to see this, come on."

"First things first," said the other, reaching for his phone.

He opened Instagram and, in a blur of texter's fingers and thumbs, he messaged, "Prom just been invaded by George M and his gang!"

The news spread like wildfire.

*

Rick checked his watch again, and took a drag from his cigarette. He had slipped out of the house, weary of the thumping bass and flashing lights, and had made his way to the terrace at the back of the mansion. It was strictly out of bounds for the students as part of the licensing agreement, but it was understood that staff could use it for temporary respite throughout the evening.

He sat at a table on the terrace in the darkness, looking out onto manicured lawns, grateful for the cool quiet out there. Kevin had been there when he arrived, enjoying a solitary cigarette on his break, so he took the opportunity to ponce a cigarette from him, a treat all the more delicious for its rarity.

"Jo would kill me if she saw me with this," he confided to Kevin, savouring the grey-blue smoke wisping away into the night sky.

"Well, your secret's safe with me, Rick," he replied.

"Another half an hour and that's our lot, I think," said Rick. "Music off, lights on and the wait for the parents to pick 'em all up."

"Yeah," agreed Kevin. "All over for another year, eh?"

"It's gone pretty well, actually. Better than I expected."

"Yeah, it could have been much worse in the circumstances. At one point I thought we'd only have twenty kids here. Nothing like it used to be, in our heyday."

"No. There've been a lot of changes."

Kevin hesitated for a moment and then plunged in.

"I'm surprised you've stuck around, actually, Rick. I thought you would have got a headship somewhere else. It must be soul destroying, working under this regime."

It was Rick's turn to hesitate. He was normally very discreet when it came to talking about the leadership of the school, and had an instinctive professional loyalty, regardless of his own opinion. He had resisted the temptation to spend the last year slagging off Camilla and Pugh to anyone who would listen, and he would have had an eager and receptive audience, but it hadn't seemed right to him to turn into that kind of Senior Leader.

But now, his resolve weakened by a long year of humiliations, and lulled into conspiratorial mood by the shared cigarette in the darkness, he cracked.

"Yeah, it is, Kevin. It has been. And who knows? I might jump ship early next year if things don't change. I've just tried to do my best and head off some of the madder innovations she wanted to introduce, but looking back, I've failed dismally at that. I might as well have gone, to be honest."

He kept quiet about his pact with the devil that was Alastair Goodall, but he was feeling increasingly tainted by it, and for what? There was no sign he was going to get any benefit from it, apart from his enhanced salary for the last year. It sat uncomfortably with him anyway. Maybe he should knock that on the head as well. The whirl of conflicting thoughts left him unable to say more.

He stood up, looking at his watch once again.

"Come on, no point moping around here. It's time to wind this down, while we're still ahead."

"Yep, we'll get no thanks for worrying about it. Let's go, I think we've all done enough for one night."

They walked back in. As they turned the corner, there, framed in the light spilling from the entrance, was one of the teachers, peering into the dimly-lit terrace.

"Rick? Rick, is that you?"

"Yeah, who's that? Mary, is that you? What's up?"

He screwed his eyes up at the figure obscured by the light behind her. He had correctly identified Mary, the Head of Art.

"I think you'd better get in here, quick. We've been invaded."

She disappeared back into the building. Rick and Kevin looked at each other, baffled.

"Invaded?" said Kevin. "What on earth does she mean?"

When they got back in the building the first thing that told them something might be amiss was the unmistakeable smell of marijuana.

Kevin wrinkled his nose.

"Is that what I think it is?" he asked.

"Who the hell is stupid enough to come to the Prom and smoke weed?"

Then one of the Promgoers burst from the disco room and ran towards them.

It was Jason.

"It's George, sir, George Mason. He's gone mad."

They ran to the doorway and looked in. There in front of them, in the middle of the dance floor amidst a crowd of teenagers, was George, can of lager in one hand and enormous spliff in the other, swaying and dancing to the music.

"What the bloody hell…"

Kevin grabbed Rick's elbow.

"It's not just George, look," he said.

Around the room, the rest of George's crew were similarly engaged, smoking, drinking and dancing. Their dancing was not quite as hypnotic and dreamy as George's. Instead, they were taking great pleasure in bumping into each other and anyone else who came within range. As Kevin and Rick watched in horror, this transformed itself into synchronised barging of other innocent dancers, who were sent flying across the dance floor, crashing into other. At the far side of the dance floor, the DJ, who ten minutes earlier had been looking forward to winding it down with couple of slow numbers, looked on, at first bemused and then increasingly concerned. A series of teachers who had been supervising the dance floor had tried to intervene with the interlopers. They were ignored and then threatened by their former pupils, who were emboldened by their success so far.

Rick had seen enough.

"You stay here on the door, Kevin, I'll only be a minute."

He dashed out of the room and spoke first to the security man on the main entrance, who had returned from his fag break and was blissfully unaware that anything was amiss.

"Hey, where the hell have you been? We've been invaded and you didn't see a thing."

"What? What do you mean, 'invaded'? No-one has got past me without a ticket."

"Never mind," said Rick, "radio your mate on the front gate and get him up here, pronto, and then both of you get yourselves to the dance floor. We need you to earn your money."

"What about the police? Shall we ring for them?"

Rick thought for a moment.

"No, not yet. We don't need them yet. Go on, man, hurry."

Back on the dance floor the carnage continued. Then, like a bucket of cold water thrown over rutting dogs, the mood was broken. The music stopped immediately at the same time that the flashing strobe lights were replaced by the harsh overhead neon strips. The dancers stumbled and stood still, blinking in the unforgiving glare of the illumination.

A strange silence filled the room and the dancers and teachers looked round at the newly exposed hooligans, left like flopping fish gasping for breath out of the water. It was filled by a commanding voice from the doorway. All eyes were drawn in that direction.

"All right everyone, listen up. The party's over, I'm afraid. A little bit early, but I'm sure you'll understand why. All students here with Prom tickets, you need to head next door with all of your stuff and get yourself ready. Parents and cars will be arriving in the next five minutes. Let's make sure we don't give them anything to worry about, especially on a night like this."

There was an outbreak of grumbling about the turn the evening had taken.

Rick held up his hands and started again.

"Yes, yes, we all know you're disappointed, but we were nearly at the end anyway. There might even be a few keen parents already here waiting outside. So, let's start to make our way through, please. And if I could ask a couple of members of staff to go through as well, just to make sure all is well?"

Three or four of the staff stepped forward and began to usher students out of the room. As they went, the invaders, looking round at each other, began to put up their hoodies and fiddle with their bandanas.

"Oi, you lot. There's no point hiding your faces, we've all seen you and we all know who you are."

They stopped, embarrassed.

"Now listen. You've made a big mistake coming here tonight. You really shouldn't have done it."

One boy was bold enough to air his simmering sense of grievance.

"We should have been here anyway, sir. That old cow shouldn't have banned us, she's mental, you know she is, sir."

"Eh, that's enough of that. Whether you think you should have been banned or not, you were, and that's all that matters."

Two or three others joined in, adding their voices to the argument.

"It's not fair, we get the blame for everything. Fucking teachers always think they're right. We've had enough."

Rick hesitated. He had counted them. There were fifteen of them and about eight members of staff. They were drunk and stoned and very angry. He knew that it wouldn't take much for this to turn ugly. Soon the two security guards would arrive, and they, as a rule, did not do subtlety or negotiation. He knew that he would have to arrive at an agreed resolution in the next couple of minutes or risk disaster. He started again, hoping that his anxiety about the gravity of the situation did not bleed into his voice.

"No, no. no, that's not going to get you anywhere. You need to start thinking sensibly about this, so that you don't get yourself into any more trouble. The police are on their way. The security guards will be along in a moment. If I were you, I'd want to be leaving here as quickly as I could, without drawing attention to yourself."

A familiar voice broke in, interrupting him. It was George.

"What's the point of doing that, 'cos you'll just give all of our names to the police anyway? You've already said you know who we are. You must think we're fucking stupid."

This intervention stirred the pot again, and there was more rumbling from the mob.

"Language, George, please. And, no, I don't think you're stupid and I never have done. For a start, I have no idea why you're here anyway. This is not even your year group and not even your Prom. But let's not go into that now. The point is this. I give you my word that if you all leave quietly now, taking all of your stuff with you, and there is no trouble with the parents or on your way home, then we'll say no more about it."

"See," snorted George, looking round at the others, "he obviously does think we're stupid. Don't fall for this lads, he's obviously gonna grass us up."

"George, as far as I know, all you've done so far is gate crash a party and smoke a bit of weed and drink too much lager. You shouldn't have done any of those things, but they're not hanging offences. Or are you worried about something you're not telling me?"

"No, course not," George snapped back.

He turned his frustration on his colleagues. "See what he's doing? Typical bloody teacher, he's twisting everything. He'll dob us in it all right, you see if he don't."

It hung on a knife edge. One voice from the mob piped up, "Nah, I don't think so, George. Mr Westfield ain't like that, he ain't like the others. He always does what he says."

There was silence as they considered this idea and in that silence it was over. The first of them walked towards the door, followed by a couple more. Then, the rest of them followed. As they passed him to get through the doorway Rick said, "You could probably get a lift home with some of your mates, if you ask nicely."

Finally, only George remained, standing in the middle of the dance floor. Rick said to the last few members of staff, "Do you guys want to go and help outside, while George and I have a chat?"

They slipped quietly out of the open door through to the hubbub beyond.

George clutched his lager and stared with a set face at Rick.

"So, George," Rick began. "Are you going to go along with this and leave quietly? I meant what I said about not taking it any further."

"Nah man," George sneered, "don't come it with the concerned, caring chat routine. Why should I listen to you? You're the one that got me excluded. You and that Syrian cunt."

"No, George, you got yourself excluded, you know that as well as anyone."

"You got an answer for everything, ain't you? If my dad were here, he'd batter you for what you did."

"Yes George, you're right, he would. And he'd do a pretty good job of it as well. He's good at battering people. But who would he go on to batter after he'd finished with me, George, eh? And then what would happen? Because there comes a point where using your fists just isn't enough. But you already know that, don't you?"

George's grip on his can of lager had been steadily increasing as he had listened to Rick, his knuckles whitening as he squeezed in rising anger. Without warning, hurled the half-empty can with all his strength at Rick's head with a roar of rage. Rick ducked and the can thudded into the wall behind him, spray spuming everywhere with an angry fizzing. George started forward and grabbed Rick by the lapels.

One of the qualities that had served Rick well as a teacher in a tough urban school was his unflappability. He had ice running through his veins and the capacity to exude calm when all around him were panicking. He knew that George was a very big, powerful lad who didn't need the amount of alcohol he had consumed to make him dangerous and unpredictable. But Rick himself was tall and well-built. Years of sport and the gym had left him with a confidence that he could look after himself.

He put his arms through George's and laid his hands on his chest, firmly exerting pressure on him.

"George, man, calm down. Don't make things any worse than they are."

George, still incensed, tried to wrench Rick towards him by the lapels, but found that Rick was too strong for him.

Rick's voice was quiet and even and he looked George directly in the eyes.

"George, come on. You're your own worst enemy. Give yourself a break. Let go and calm down."

There was one final attempt to overpower him. When that failed, with Rick looking steadily at him throughout, he gave up and with a howl of frustration and despair he pushed Rick to one side and stormed out of the room, barging past students and teachers alike, some sent flying like skittles as he turned the air blue with an extended volley of industrial language. He snatched up his carrier bag of lager from behind the desk and charged through the ground floor until he found the doorway to the terrace. He crashed past the two security guards who were skulking around, desperately trying to avoid being called into action, and disappeared into the cool darkness of the gardens.

24

Karim leaped up and punched the air, sending his controller flying.

"Yes!" he screamed and began singing, "Campeones, Campeones, ole, ole, ole!" while doing a little dance of celebration. His team, Aleppo FC, had just won the World Club Championship, after a nail-biting series of games.

There was a mixture of groans and congratulations from the others, who lounged around on the floor, surrounded by pizza boxes and empty bottles of beer.

"You were lucky, man," moaned Raysharne. "On another day I would have thrashed you, I'm telling you."

The others shouted him down.

"All right, all right," he conceded. "You won, Karim, I get it. Next time though, yeah?"

"Whenever you're ready for me, man," he retorted, "whenever you're ready."

Ben checked his phone as the celebration died down.

"Shit man," he exclaimed, "it's half eleven. My mum'll be back any minute. Look at the state of the place. She'll kill me."

"Come on, calm down," said Alex. "We'll just clear up fam. It's not like we've had a wild party, is it? Just get a bin liner and that'll be that."

They scoured the room, filling one large bin liner with boxes, the last bits of pizza crust, lager bottles and Karim's coke bottles.

Raysharne picked up a large empty bottle of coke and looked closely at it.

"It's so weird being with someone who doesn't drink beer, you know what I mean? Is it because you're Muslim, is it banned for all of you lot?"

Karim laughed.

"You lot are so ignorant. No, it's not banned, plenty of Muslims drink. I just don't like it, that's all."

"That's why my mum loves Karim, he's such a good influence," said Ben, grinning. "I really need you to do something bad, Karim, to give me a break."

There was a pause. It had been a good night, but it was time to go.

Alex, Raysharne and Karim gathered up their stuff and said their goodbyes.

"All right, see you then, Ben. Thanks yeah. It was a good night."

"See you, boys. I'll message you in the week about Cornwall, all right?"

After the ritual of fist bumping they left, bouncing down the stairs three at a time. It was nice to be in the fresh air and to be walking along after three or four hours of DVDs and Xbox.

"That was good, wasn't it? That *Star Wars* film was savage, man."

"You gonna go Cornwall then, Raysharne? What do you think?"

Raysharne looked dubious. "It's camping, innit? Can you do Xbox in a tent?"

The other two burst out laughing.

"Nah man, you might have to read a book instead," said Karim. Raysharne looked horrified.

"A book? I couldn't do that, bruv, it's not natural."

They got to the corner and stopped. It was a little cooler now, with a gentle breeze making the clouds overhead scud along. It was quiet. The traffic had thinned out and there were few people in the street.

"You getting the bus, Karim?" Alex asked.

"Yeah, mine goes from over there," he replied, pointing.

"We're going this way man. All right, see you next week, fam."

"Yeah, see you."

More fist bumps followed and Alex and Raysharne crossed the road and shoulder crashed each other down the street. Karim watched them go, smiling to himself. They turned the corner and disappeared from sight. He headed in the opposite direction, towards the bus stop in front of The Trafalgar. He fiddled in his pocket as he walked, found his headphones and started listening to his iPod. It had been a good night and a great way to mark the end of his exams. He was pleased that he'd spent it with just a few people. He didn't really like crowds.

He thought again about his plans for the summer. He'd said yes to the Cornwall idea, but the truth was that the idea of camping was difficult for him. He had bad memories of tents. It reminded him of some of the dark days he endured on his way from Syria to the UK. He couldn't see being in a tent as anything other than misery. And then there was Calais. He was determined to go. He rummaged in his wallet and found his precious photo of Evana. One way or another he would find her so that she could have the things he had found in England. So that she could be safe and happy, like him.

He hadn't dared say it to himself before. It had always felt like a betrayal to be happy, when so many weren't. And if he was, he wanted that for her. It was the least she deserved.

*

George could just make out the driveway and main car park from his vantage point under a canopy of trees. He watched as a succession of cars driven by dutiful parents came to ferry the punters back home. He saw Mr Westfield pacing along the drive and around the car park, occasionally scanning the horizon, before having a conversation with the security guards.

He drained his last can of lager and extricated his last cigarette from the packet. He wiped his eyes and put his head in his hands as he squatted on a fallen tree trunk. Why did this always happen to him? Why was he here on his own, watching other people with friends and family who gave a toss about them? Even if he had been allowed to go to the Prom last year, you could bet your life that no-one would have turned up to give him a lift back. And there wouldn't have been a queue of people offering him a lift either way.

How many more things could go wrong for him, he wondered. Humiliated in his own fucking pub. He couldn't even escape his dad in the boozer. Humiliated in front of everyone at the Prom. Even those cunts who were supposed to be his friends fucking baled out. They'd all be laughing about him now, proper pissing themselves. "Did you hear about George? Silly cunt got told by Mr Westfield. What a wanker!" Fucking Westfield. Him and that Syrian twat, the fucking terrorist. He'd give anything to fuck them over.

This went round and round in his mind and with each repetition he became more and more bitter, more and more angry, more and more sorry for himself. A movement on the horizon and a noise snapped him out of his downward cycle of despair. Looking towards the house he saw the two security guards get into a car and drive down towards the main road. They must be going, he thought.

He listened. He could hear nothing coming from the house, only the wind in the trees around him. He must be the last one there. He stood up cautiously, stretched and then lit his last cigarette, strangely comforted by the cloud of blue grey smoke he exhaled that hung in the branches around him.

It was time to make a move. He came out from the trees and half ran, half walked to the side of the mansion, which was all in darkness save for a couple of dim security lights. It was only when he reached the terrace that he remembered that he had left his jacket inside, behind the reception desk.

"Shit," he exclaimed. His keys and wallet were in his jacket. If it was all locked up, he was snookered. He'd have to walk home. *How much worse could this night get*, he thought. He went up to the door leading to the terrace and tried the handle. He couldn't believe it, it worked.

"Yes, you fucking beauty, at last something has gone right," he muttered under his breath. "Useless fucking security guards. I could do a better job than them."

It was dark inside, but occasional security lights, studded along corridors, gave off a faint light that allowed him to pick his way through the rooms and corridors to the main entrance. He inched his way to reception, bent down and felt behind the desk and with a shout of triumph pulled out his jacket.

"Yes! Things are looking up. Unless," he paused and began to rifle through the pockets, "unless some fucker has robbed me."

Wrestling with something bulky inside the pocket he finally pulled out two items and laid them down in front of him. In the dim glow of the security light he could make out his wallet and a set of car keys. Baffled, he looked at the keys. He picked them up and turned them over in his hand. What the hell were these?

Comprehension dawned on his face and he burst out laughing, unrestrained, throaty laughter that echoed through the darkened and dusty corridors of this stately pile, disturbing the ghosts of the past.

Taking a final drag from his cigarette, he flicked the butt into the corner, and ran helter-skelter back towards the terrace door. He didn't even bother closing it and it flapped in the night breeze.

*

He gripped the steering wheel for all he was worth, and bowled along the country lane. It had taken him a minute or two in the car park to get the hang of it, but all of his lessons kicked in and it all came back to him. The car was bigger than he was used to and he had to work out where the indicators and lights were, but once he'd got that sorted, he was flying. Nice car though. How could he afford this? Maybe teaching is not for mugs after all.

He couldn't work out how to change the radio and he was driving along to some geezer just talking. There was no music. What kind of radio station was this? Is this what O'Malley listened to all the time? No wonder he was a cunt. He risked a glance down at the screen. Radio Four, it said, whatever that was.

The road had changed now into a proper Longdon road, with shops and kebab houses. That meant police cars, so he told himself again to concentrate. Drink had dulled his reactions and the lights blurred before his eyes. Come on, concentrate. He had decided he'd go to The Trafalgar and park there and abandon the car. Then he'd walk home. It would be too obvious to leave the car near his house. He wasn't stupid. Once it all came out with O'Malley, he'd have to face the music, but fuck it, he'd cross that bridge when he came to it. At least he'd had a bit of a laugh. That was as much as he could expect in this shit life, to be honest.

The geezer on the radio was still droning on. Talking about the tragedy of Syria, for fuck's sake. The fucking tragedy of Syria was that they were all here, pretending to be refugees and blowing us all up in the name of fucking Isis. Just like they did in Oxford Street. Just listen to the twat. You can tell by his poncey accent that he don't have to go anywhere near the fucking tragedy of Syria. He probably lives in one of them big houses up by Longdon Park. The only fucking Syrian he sees is the one that does his garden on the cheap.

George couldn't bear to listen to it any more. He jabbed at a succession of buttons on the dash until finally the radio died and there was silence, apart from the rumble of the tyres on the road and the hiss as others cars flashed past. Nearly there now. He pulled in to the road where The Trafalgar was and swung round so that he could park slightly set back from the main road, just by the pub's car park. He left the keys on the driver's seat, shut the door behind him and looked before starting to cross the road.

That was when he saw him, a slight figure standing alone at the bus stop. He stopped in his tracks and caught his breath. It was like an offering.

"Oi," George shouted, "I've been looking for you, you fucker."

Karim didn't hear him until the last minute. He was listening to his iPod, lost in a world of his own. He turned round and saw George, almost on top of him. He turned to flee, but George was on him before he knew it and brought him down into the gutter.

*

"So, did you have a nice time, Ben love?"

"Yeah, it was fine, Mum. You must have just missed everyone, they've only just left. What about you? How's Auntie Grace?"

Before she could answer, there was a loud ping from a phone. They both looked around.

"Is that yours, Mum?" he asked.

"No, mine's here, love," she replied, showing her own phone to him.

He looked across the room and there on the sofa, half hidden by a cushion, was a phone with the screen alight. He went over to have a look.

"Karim's left his phone. Idiot." He looked more closely at the screen and saw the message. It was from Joan and Eric. "Everything all right? You're a bit late. Message us to let us know what's going on."

"Listen, Mum, I'll just run down to the bus stop, just in case he's still there. Joan and Eric'll start to panic if he doesn't answer."

His mother looked doubtful.

"All right then love, but be quick, won't you? Come straight back. And be careful."

He grabbed a jacket and his keys and sprinted down the stairs, phone in hand. When he got out into the street he jogged, thinking that Karim would just be standing at the bus stop by then. *He probably hasn't even realised his phone isn't there*, he thought. He turned the corner, half expecting to see Karim at the stop in front of The Trafalgar but there was no-one there. He pulled up, breathing hard.

Damn, he thought, *the bus must have come already.*

He turned to go back home, when his eye was caught by a commotion beyond the bus stop, on the other side of the road. There was some kind of a fight going on. A well-built young man was standing over a crumpled heap in the road, repeatedly kicking and screaming abuse. Ben stared, with a growing sense of unease that turned to horror as he caught a glimpse of a brightly-coloured purple hoodie.

"Karim?" he whispered, hardly daring to acknowledge what he was witnessing. He was not a brave boy. This was the kind of scene that kept him awake at night, living in a neighbourhood like this. He'd rather run a mile than get involved in any violence on the streets. Young people, young men especially, regularly got stabbed around this area. But then a switch clicked in his brain.

"Karim! Karim!" he shouted for all he was worth, and he began to run full pelt towards the incident.

The other boy looked up from his exertions and was astonished to see a figure sprinting towards him, screaming. He launched himself into George and sent him flying, and then half turned his head to see Karim lying on the floor, motionless. In his hand he clutched a crumpled photograph. His face, caught in the beam of the street lamp above was swollen, bloodied and bruised, his eye already closed up. He was strangely still and silent.

He crawled over to him and began hysterically calling, "Karim! Karim, man, come on."

He reached over to cradle his head in his arms, and try and get him on his feet, when he was grabbed from behind by an enraged George, who had picked himself up from the ground and charged at this intruder who had interrupted his business. Screaming obscenities at him he dragged him from Karim's prone body and punched him in the solar plexus. Winded, Ben went down like a sack of potatoes and George launched a fresh assault, kicking him when he was down. Ben curled into a ball. He felt the first few kicks before he heard a distant sound of a siren, a pulse of blue lights and a screech of brakes. Then darkness swamped him.

A few yards away, in the gutter, Karim's phone, spilled from Ben's hand after the first assault, suddenly lit up the darkness and a ping announced a message arriving. The screen read, "Are you okay? We're starting to get worried. Message us. Joanxx"

*

The two fleets of emergency service vehicles crossed at speed in opposite directions on Longdon Road, the insistent blare of sirens and piercing blue light show barely causing those still on the street to raise an eyebrow or look up from their business. It was business as usual on Friday night in the early hours in Longdon. If there hadn't been sirens and squealing traffic, people would have noticed the difference and concluded that something was seriously wrong. As it was, few people saw the fire engines heading west and the ambulance heading east.

Three fire engines careered round the tight entrance bend into the driveway of Longdon Park. The dusty glow that had begun to illuminate the tops of trees as they had got closer to the mansion was transformed into an angry, flaring conflagration, with roaring flames leaping thirty feet into the night sky above the chimneys and rooftops of the house.

The driver took a sharp breath.

"Bloody hell, look at that. That is a big fire, man. We're going to need serious back up. Radio for more units, quick."

His partner flicked on the radio system and began to speak across the crackling airways.

The driver continued down the driveway and swung into the side car park to locate the water hydrants. He screeched to a halt, making his partner sway violently in the passenger seat.

"Woah! Careful man, what are you doing?"

"Get back on the radio. We're gonna need the police and an ambulance. Look over there."

He followed the direction indicated. There, jumping up and down in front of a bench, was a man in some distress. He was bound hand and foot and totally naked. They looked at each other, baffled.

"What the…?"

25

THE NEXT MONTH PASSED IN A BLUR FOR RICK. IT FELT AS if he had blinked and then it was the end of the school year again. Last year, when he went into the six-week holiday after the body blow of missing out on the headship at Fairfield, he had thought that there would never be such a miserable end of summer term for him again. Looking back on it now, that reaction seemed selfish and pathetic and he felt ashamed of it. He knew now that there were things that were much more important than one's career. He really should have known it back then as well, without having to learn it the hard way.

Ben, thankfully, had fully recovered, at least physically. He had suffered a couple of broken ribs and a broken nose, but was now on the mend. George had been picked up the same night and was charged with grievous bodily harm. The national media had picked up the story, which had led to some uncomfortable door stepping of school staff by journalists. Camilla was both petrified and furious about the coverage. She had only just recovered from the *Longdon*

Advertiser's front page coverage of the Prom: 'Drugs, Alcohol and Arson: The Fairfield School Prom'.

Her instinct had been, as ever, to blame someone else for this calamity. She wanted to blame Rick, but was constrained by Alastair Goodall's support for him. Goodall had been flooded with testimony from parents, students and staff about Rick's extraordinarily calm management of the events at the Prom, events that everyone who had been there agreed could have been so much worse.

She tried to blame O'Malley for being careless enough to allow himself to be set upon by a gang of stoned, drunken teenagers. She managed to maintain that position until he finally returned to school three weeks after the incident. He never talked about what had happened to him, and on the surface, he seemed to have made a full physical recovery, but he was never really the same again after this. He avoided situations where he might be called upon to supervise large groups of students by himself and whenever he was in that situation with other staff, Rick saw a glimmer of fear in his eyes.

Rick, on the other hand, did not spare himself blame. He went over the events of that night again and again, wondering whether, if he had acted differently, then George would not have been around to do what he did. Maybe Karim would still be walking around, enjoying the end of his exams like everyone else.

Karim. He thought of Karim every day, lying in intensive care, his body wired up to a plethora of devices and monitors, unconscious still, even four weeks after the attack. He thought of his foster carers, Joan and Eric, who kept a vigil by his bedside and of Ahmed, his support worker, who had worked tirelessly for Karim and untold others in the same situation. Rick visited every week and sat at the end of the bed with Joan and Eric. Sometimes Ahmed was there and occasionally there were some of the elders from the mosque. He didn't say much, just sat and watched and brooded. It was important to him somehow to show that people cared about Karim that were not his immediate family. It was important to show solidarity with Joan and Eric, with the Syrian community and with the Muslim community as a whole, at a time when everything seemed to be conspiring to drive a wedge between them.

He would stay for half an hour, make polite conversation and then leave. Joan and Eric, in between bouts of despair about Karim's future, would talk about his recovery and the stages they would need to go through. Part of Rick's silence was also an unwillingness to extinguish their hope. Whenever he let his guard down, and allowed himself to think about the future, he was beset afresh with gloom and guilt. He didn't think Karim was ever going to pull through and so the only way he could deal with that prospect was to resolutely not think about it, to hide it away in a dusty corner of his mind.

Camilla had not made a visit to the hospital. She had delivered the requisite form of words to the media in the immediate aftermath and had conjured an appropriate sad and serious face while doing so, but no genuine emotion troubled her consciousness, save a mild irritation that the incident had generated collateral damage to her and the project. She was grateful, if anything, that she had made the decision not to offer him a place. At least that meant that the focus was mainly on Longdon College rather than on Fairfield and her.

On the very first day of the holidays, Rick's alarm went off at 4 am. Like a well-oiled machine, he and Jo got the kids up, dressed and breakfasted them and then loaded them into the car that had been packed to the gunnels the night before with luggage, snorkels, tennis rackets and beach equipment. Double checking the note for the cat sitter/plant waterer, then the timer for the security lights, they finally locked the front door and drove off at 4.45 am, heading for the Channel Tunnel.

With every mile of road the car travelled, Rick could feel the pressure slipping from his shoulders. A month in an exclusive campsite on the Costa Brava was Jo's answer to the anxiety that Fairfield had produced. She looked across at him as he drove. His face was drawn and tired and the touch of grey around the temples she had teased him about had spread. They had a lot to talk about in that four weeks and there were big decisions to be made.

They were well into northern France, singing along to Rick's specially made nineties mix tape, by the time Camilla arrived at a deserted Bellingfield for her meeting with Alastair. She had been irritated by the summons because it would delay her normal departure for sunnier climes, and she, more than anyone else, she felt, deserved a holiday. She checked her make up in the car mirror before swivelling her legs out of the front seat, collecting her bag and slamming the door.

I really hope he's not going to suggest another weekend conference, she thought, as she made her way through the car park. *He is rather dishy for his age, but I can't abide being on tap, not for anyone.*

Her heels clicked insistently on the way down the path. It was an unfamiliar experience for her to be in school on the first day of the summer holidays and she was struck by the strange air of calm that clung to the building. It was a warm, sunny day and as she went through the main entrance the shady foyer seemed tranquil and welcoming. The reception desk was abandoned. She was just considering what to do when Alastair strode round the corner. Camilla expected a peck on the cheek and a continental embrace, and was surprised to find herself disappointed by his extended hand and thin-lipped, set-mouthed greeting.

"Camilla. How are you? Come this way, we're ready to start."

He turned to go back the way he had come, striding ahead, leaving Camilla to ponder the meaning of this frosty greeting. Asking the question but not waiting for the answer. A face that looked as if he'd been sucking a lemon. And what did he mean by 'we'? We are expecting you, that's what he had said.

He stood to one side and proffered the open door to her. She walked in and then struggled to mask her surprise at seeing the person already in the room. She recovered herself and, smiling, said smoothly, "Marcus, what a nice surprise. What are you doing here?"

Grovelle sprang from his chair, his usual oily smile fixed on his face.

"Camilla, how lovely to see you. You're looking radiant, my dear, radiant."

Goodall's face achieved the impossible while witnessing this and became even stonier. His lips pursed until they were almost inside out. Grovelle, who was not the most sensitive of men in terms of social nuance, received the signals and hastily reconfigured his planned double air kiss and cheeky squeeze, into a brusque handshake.

"Sit down, Camilla, please," Goodall continued. "We've got a few things to discuss."

She frowned. "What exactly is going on, Alastair? Why have I been summoned out of the blue? And why is Marcus here? I would have thought that he was far too important to attend a meeting in a school." She turned to Grovelle and continued, "This must be the first time you've been in a state school without television cameras, Marcus."

Grovelle's oily smile wavered, but Camilla did not wait for a reply. She turned back to Goodall.

"Well, what is it? If I didn't know better, I'd think that you were going to sack me, Alastair."

Goodall reached for a folder and opened it.

"There are a lot of people who think you should be sacked, Camilla, so please don't rule it out so quickly."

Camilla's smooth self-possessed exterior slipped.

"What? You can't be serious. I've completely transformed that school, you must be aware of that, surely?"

Goodall leafed through the wad of paper inside the folder, perusing each sheet.

"Ah yes, of course. Yes, 'transformed', yes, quite. Let's have a look. A senior member of staff attacked at the school prom. A listed building burned to the ground by your school's pupils while high on drink and drugs. A Syrian refugee, a model citizen, lying on a life-support system in Longdon hospital, beaten to a pulp by one of your pupils. A Syrian refugee, who you, with all the compassion of Mrs Thatcher after a bottle of single malt, more or less kicked out of the school."

He looked up over the sheet of paper. Camilla shuffled in her chair.

"Shall I go on? Let's see. Forty percent of the staff have left after your first year in the job, some with no jobs to go to. I have another file, twice as thick as this one, full of letters and emails from parents, complaining about your high-handed and unreasonable behaviour in the way you treat students and staff. There are allegations detailed here of mismanagement of school budgets, of biased appointment procedures, of questionable practices in respect of public examinations."

"Hold on, this is ridiculous. You know what a state the school was in. You know that it's standard practice to take drastic action in the first year, if you're going to have any chance of making an impact and changing the culture. So please, don't waste my time and insult my intelligence with these half-baked accusations from embittered staff with an axe to grind."

"Would you be confident if we announced an investigation into all of this?" asked Goodall, watching her reaction closely.

There was a pause.

"Of course I would be confident, but there is no need for any of this."

She looked across at Grovelle with an appealing smile. "And what is Marcus doing here anyway? What has any of this got to do with him?"

Goodall looked at him and raised an eye brow. "Marcus?"

Grovelle cleared his throat. "Of course, Camilla, we think you've done a fantastic job. But I have a bigger challenge getting my Great Reform Act from the statute book into reality. We had planned to pilot some of the less popular measures at Fairfield. Your unfortunate publicity of the last couple of months makes that rather stickier than it should be."

Goodall interrupted. "Let's cut to the chase, Camilla. Marcus is more polite than I am. I don't think you've done a marvellous job at Fairfield. And all of the catastrophic blunders means that everything is resting upon your exam results. If they are disappointing, then we will not be able to carry on with the current arrangements. It'll be the last straw. Great exam results will be the latest news and people have very short memories in this game. You're only as good as your last headline."

Camilla had stopped listening to him and felt a huge wave of relief wash over her. She tried hard not to show it and maintained a serious sad face.

"Alastair, I appreciate your openness with me. I think I can reassure you that everything will be all right. Of course, there are no guarantees as far as results are concerned, but our last soundings were predicting very good results indeed."

She leaned forward and laid her hand on top of Grovelle's hand on the table.

"And Marcus, I don't think you need worry about your new initiatives. Fairfield will be the very place to help you make a mark on posterity."

Goodall scowled. "Hmm, well I suppose only time will tell. It'll be a long summer waiting, that's for sure."

Grovelle blinked and beamed at her. His lips and his eyes glittered. "I'm sure it will be worth the wait, Camilla, I really am."

*

He knew that they had pulled it off the minute he walked through the door. There were a handful of staff there, as always on the day before the official release of exam results, to process the massive download of data from the exam boards and to ensure the computer churned out the numbers on their key performance indicators. All the work that had gone in throughout the year came down in the end to a few numbers that popped out of the other end of a computer programme. The numbers could make or break careers, they could trigger Ofsted inspections, emergency local authority interventions, votes of no confidence in governing bodies. Across the country the night before, headteachers and other senior leaders of schools would have endured a sleepless, stomach-churning night, before trudging in to learn their fate.

The two members of staff that Rick first saw in the foyer, the exams secretary and the data manager, had broad smiles and spoke in an animated, warm fashion when they greeted him. They were both new appointments in the last year, both of them parachuted in as ex-colleagues of Camilla, and normally they treated Rick with cold disdain. Their warmth could be partly explained by the half-empty champagne glasses in their hands.

Jean, the data manager, said, "I think you'd better go in and see Camilla. She's in her office with Barry Pugh and a bottle of champagne."

His heart sank. Little Bazzer Pugh, that was all he needed. Oh well, he would just have to be brave and get it over with. He took a deep breath and knocked on her office door just at the same moment that a peal of laughter erupted from behind it. He went in and there were Camilla and Pugh, champagne flutes in hand, grinning broadly.

"Well," Camilla broke off, "look who it is. We were just talking about you, Rick."

"Oh, were you," he replied, slightly disconcerted. "I thought you would have been talking about the results."

"Oh, we've done that already, Rick. We've been here quite a while. Now, how was your holiday?"

A frown passed over his face. Personal small talk was not Camilla's usual style.

"Fine, thanks, but the results? What did we get?"

Camilla looked across at Barry, and then back to Rick, smiling. She told him.

He did a double take. The figures Camilla had just revealed were astonishing. Rick repeated them back to her.

"Are you sure about that, Camilla? That seems unreasonably high to me."

"We are the best-performing school in the Trust and the only schools above us in Longdon are the private schools."

"But, how…?" Rick trailed off.

"You don't seem very pleased, Rick. Perhaps you wanted the school to do badly. It does rather outshine your performance last year. The record has been comprehensively broken." Barry Pugh was almost purring as he said this.

"No, no," he stammered, "it's just that…"

He was finding it hard to complete his sentences, such was his disbelief at the numbers.

"And now, if you'll excuse us, we have a lot of work to do to publicise this magnificent achievement," said Camilla. Her tone of voice was standing up and ushering him to the door.

He left the office in a daze. The door closed behind him and he stood in the corridor in a daze. A fresh peal of laughter rocked Camilla's office. Rick realised he had not been offered champagne.

He came back the next day to see the children collect their results. He could barely face Camilla glorying in the reaction of the staff to the outstanding results, but he wanted to congratulate his Year 11s and share in their success. There were also a few people he had to talk to before he finally made his mind up about what he was going to do.

The morning passed in a blur of high fives, whoops and cheers, selfies and pictures of students with teachers, all smiling and brandishing their results sheets aloft. Rick, standing to one side in the dining room just behind the tables bearing orderly piles of results envelopes, checked his watch. Where were they? He couldn't wait much longer, he had another, more important, job to do that day.

Just as he was thinking about cutting his losses and leaving, he saw, over the heads of the crowds of excited students and the few proud parents, a familiar group come in, their faces tense with anticipation. He watched them collect the envelopes, open them, and one by one go through the cycle of joy, relief, disbelief and comparing with each other. Rick sidled closer while he was observing this and timed his run to perfection. Just as it looked as if they were going to join the crowds outside, he made his move.

"All right, Jason? How did you get on?"

The boy looked up.

"All right, sir. I'm amazed, I did brilliant. Seven grade 6s and three grade 5s. Got a grade 6 in English. I can't believe it."

"Well done, Jason, that's brilliant. You really deserve it. What about the others?"

Rick knew, before he got the answer, that they would have performed above their wildest dreams as well. After the customary

347

congratulations he leaned towards Jason, and in a lower voice said, "Actually Jason, I need to talk to you about something. You and the other two. Come along to my office and let's have a chat. It'll be, um, quieter there."

Jason looked across at his two friends. They both nodded and followed Rick out of the dining room and along the corridor to his room.

Twenty minutes later they left. At the threshold Rick said to them quietly, looking around before he spoke, "Okay, thanks lads. Your names won't be used, I promise. And don't you go talking to anyone about this either, all right? I'll be in touch."

Rick watched them troop out and then he locked his office door and headed back to the car park. He had another visit to pay and he wasn't looking forward to it. It would be the hardest thing he did that day, that was for sure.

*

"Okay, thanks Kevin, thanks very much. Yes, yes, I know, it stinks, but then what can we do? Okay, take care, I'll be in touch."

Jane replaced the receiver and looked across at Avril. She repeated the results Kevin had given her. Avril's face fell, dumbstruck. She opened her mouth a couple of times to speak, but nothing came out, like a goldfish out of the tank gasping for air. Finally, the words came.

"But… but, that can't be right, surely? That's better than last year. I don't understand."

"I know, I know. I actually feel bad that I'm not happy for the kids," Jane agreed. She thought for a moment. "You don't think we've got this all wrong, Avril, do you? What if she's a genius? What if zero tolerance actually works and they are much better than we were? What if we were actually holding the kids back all those years?"

Avril snorted. "Bollocks to that. You know as well as I do, that this is all smoke and mirrors. Mark my words, there's a scandal waiting to come out here, across the country."

"I can't bear all the gloating that woman will do. All the 'I told you so's' and the smugness."

"Me neither," agreed Avril, "and it'll get worse. This will embolden them. They'll get rid of even more so-called 'challenging' kids this year. Who the hell gives a damn about the kids that are harder to teach? It makes my blood boil, it really does."

"I feel we need to do something, but what can we do?"

They both sat in silence for a moment in Jane's kitchen, staring at a plate of Avril's cupcakes. She reached out and took a bite from one.

"I think we need to talk to Rick. It's time to ask him about those photos."

*

The silence in the room was punctuated by the steady bleep from the life-support machine, its wires and tubes encircling Karim's prone body like tendrils from a parasite plant. The vase on his bedside table contained fresh flowers, a splash of vivid, vibrant, colourful life that stood out in a sterile environment.

Rick, sitting in a chair at the foot of the bed, was reading a sheet of paper that Eric had handed to him. He looked up.

"Six grade 9s. He got six grade 9s."

"Yes," smiled Joan, "that's right. But it's all changed these days. I'm not quite sure what that means exactly."

"A nine is the same as an A*. That's the highest you can get. He got that in every exam he took. It's…"

Rick paused and looked down at the paper again. "Well, it's extraordinary, really, in the circumstances."

Joan beamed. "Six A* grades. Well, we thought so, but we weren't sure. We're very proud of him. It means he could make a real success when he starts his A levels in September."

Eric looked down, a flash of pain across his face. He looked back at Joan.

"Joan, love, I'm not sure he'll be going to college."

"No, well, he'll probably go to a proper Sixth Form, with results like that."

"No, Joan, I mean that…"

She snapped at him. "I know what you mean, Eric. He will be all right. He will do his A levels, I know he will." Her tone was fierce and not to be argued with. Her eyes had begun to glitter with tears

Eric glanced across at Rick.

"It was good of you to come in and visit, Mr Westfield. We do appreciate it. People seem to have lost interest somehow."

"I'm sorry to hear that, Eric. Do you not get many people visiting then? I could come a bit more often. That is, if you don't mind."

"No, no, there's no need for that. Ahmed comes along and there's often someone from the mosque."

Joan perked up. "And Ben and Raysharne and Alex come along when they can. Lovely boys."

She wiped her eyes, leaned over Karim's still body and, carefully negotiating the festoon of wires around his head, used a flannel to clean his face.

Rick stood up and shook hands with Eric.

"Okay, goodbye Eric. I'm very pleased about Karim's results."

"Thanks for coming in, Mr Westfield."

When Rick got to the door he turned back.

"Bye then, Joan. Nice to see you."

Joan did not look up from tending to Karim.

"Yes, thanks Rick. See you next week."

Eric went over to her and put his arms around her. She began to sob, quietly at first, but then with great heaving gasps.

He left them, closing the door on their world of private despair, his eyes stinging as he made his way through the corridors and out into the car park. He barely noticed a car or a traffic light on his drive home and was surprised when he found himself pulling into his road. Looking around, he had no memory of the journey there, having been lost in thought about what he was going to do next.

The phone call that evening from Jane finally made up his mind.

26

HE STRODE OUT INTO THE MIDDLE OF THE CORRIDOR, where it widened out to accommodate traffic from four tributaries, and checked his watch, walkie-talkie in one hand and a letter in the other. The silence was broken by the shrill tones of the bell, and the doors opposite him and further down the corridor opened, spilling students of all shapes, ages and sizes into the thoroughfare. Soon, it was a raging torrent, a white water surge of kids and he stood in the middle of the corridor where he had a sight of all four corridors that led into this larger space. He was like a huge rock in the middle of spring meltwater. At six foot four, he towered above the rapids careering past him, kids on their way to their next lesson.

"Oi, don't do that you chief…"

*

"Where's English this year?"
"We're out in the huts, I think."

"Ah man, it'll be freezing out there come December…"

*

"Kelly! Kelly! Wait up…"

*

"Eh, did you see *Eastenders* last night?"
"It's lame, man…"

*

"You done your science homework, Deepak?"
"It's not for today, is it?"
"Yeah, man."
"Oh, nah. I thought he said Friday."

*

"Is your mum all right then?"
"She's gotta go hospital today, so I dunno. I'm waitin' for a message."

*

"Love those Vans, man. Seriously. Has no-one seen you wearing 'em yet?"

*

"It's Messi, obviously bruv."
"Messi? Don't be weird. He can't head the ball, man. Ronaldo is the king…"

*

"You goin' rehearsal after school?"

"Nah, forgot my cello, innit."

"Sir'll let you lend his, betcha."

"Borrow. It's borrow."

"Uh?"

＊

"I jus' don't get why Trump was voted in. Pussy grabber."

"Terrible hair, as well. It's like a flap or something."

"I swear it's like a wig, you know."

＊

"Have you read it? It's brilliant. Like *Harry Potter*, but cooler."

"You got it then?"

"Yeah, I'll lend it you if you like."

"Will ya? Brilliant. Bring it tomorrow, yeah?"

＊

"Remember, Miss said she was gonna blow something up in the lesson today."

"Oh, yeah. Come on then..."

＊

"I reckon Miss is havin' a baby y' know."

"Nah, she's just got a bit fat."

"I'm tellin' you. She's pregnant. I reckon it was Mr Brooks, as well..."

＊

"Come on, Darlene, our group is goin' first. We gotta get the scripts and everything..."

"Yeah, man, whatever."

"Darlene, come on, it's important."

*

Far above the tide of humanity that swept past him, he bellowed his usual litany of instructions, exhortations and threats, and took his part in the regular conversations that the children attempted, always returning to the key message: Get to your lesson quickly.

And then, almost as quickly as it had sprung up, the surge died down to a trickle and then eventually the riverbed was dry, with just the odd straggler to chivvy along. At this time of year, it tended to be small, bewildered Year 7 kids, bent double under their new school bags that seemed bigger than them, blinking around, desperately trying to locate room B26 without looking like a loser or in any way drawing attention to themselves. Satisfied that the changeover had been successfully managed, he turned to the letter in his hand and read it again. He had read it so many times he would have been able to recite it if asked. The message it contained was not improving with repetition.

Dear Parent, Carer or Guardian,

I am writing to you to inform you of a change to our behaviour policy that will come into effect from next Monday, September 10th.

Building on the remarkable success of last year, when the new leadership of the school transformed the behaviour of students in lessons, we are now planning to turn our attention to behaviour in the corridors. Last year a lot of learning time was lost by students arriving late for lessons or, when they did arrive, causing disruption by their unruly, noisy and boisterous behaviour. To prevent this loss of focus during lesson changeover, we are introducing a new system where students will be required to walk in single file on the right-hand side of the corridor in silence. This will ensure that they arrive at their next lesson on time and in the correct frame of mind to begin learning at once.

To make sure that this new policy works from the beginning, all staff have been instructed to be in the corridors between lessons. Any student who breaks this new rule, either by talking, running or by not being in single file, will be given a same-day detention of one hour. Students committing the same offence again will be placed in the internal inclusion room for two days in the first instance. Further infringements will result in Saturday detentions and exclusions.

I am sure I can count on your support as we continue to transform Fairfield High School into the best school in the area, a school of real excellence. In parallel with this development I would also like to announce a change to lunchtime arrangements. Lunch will now be taken in the dining hall in Form groups, supervised by Form Tutors. Form Tutors will lead their form through structured discussion of topical issues taken from the day's newspapers. This practice, common in many private schools, will teach Fairfield students how to interact in a calm and quiet manner at mealtimes and will also train them to take part in civilised debate about current issues.

Both of these measures have been implemented in several schools across London, run by the most inspirational and impressive young headteachers who are prepared to think out of the box and challenge the way things have always been done. These early pioneers have been very successful, and some of the most challenging schools in London have been transformed, attracting the attention of ambitious and forward-thinking educationalists across the world. In following a similar path, Fairfield High is blazing a trail and challenging the sloppy approaches to education that have held us back for far too long. One day, all schools will be adopting these methods, and they will be trying to catch up with us, not the other way round.

Remember, the next stage of our transformation starts on Monday September 10th.

Yours sincerely
Camilla Everson
Headteacher

He looked around the empty echoing corridor and thought of the energy and vitality and community of just a few moments before. All human life had been there, good and bad, and now it was to be crushed. Stamped on. Excised. He shook his head and, screwing up the letter in his hand into a tight ball, set off for his office. With every step, he recalled the incandescent fury he had unleashed at the Senior Leadership meeting the day before. His policy of withdrawing from comment, of keeping his head down and just getting on with the job, had disappeared the minute he had sat through the first of the assemblies that Camilla had called to introduce the new policy.

By the time Rick had walked into the Senior Leadership meeting at the end of the afternoon, he was a coiled spring of outrage. He had spent the day stoking the fires of his opposition, heaping fuel on the fire by seeking out like-minded people to chew it over with. If only Avril had still been there. There was no way she would have taken this lying down.

He took his seat and a second later Camilla arrived.

"Well, good afternoon, everyone, if we can get straight down to business. I've got another meeting to go to after this, so we need to be quick. Item one on the agenda is—"

She wasn't able to tell everyone what exactly item one was. Rick interrupted her. There were horrified glances around the table and the sound of hell freezing over.

"No, Camilla, we can't get straight down to business, actually."

She stared at him, an eyebrow raised.

"What on earth do you mean, Rick?" she said, a tone of menace in her voice.

"You can't seriously expect us to just sit here and discuss paperclips when you've just announced an utterly monstrous change to our behaviour policy without any consultation whatsoever."

"I can and, what's more, I do, actually," she replied. "What you describe as a monstrous change is seen by the silent majority as common sense. What's wrong with being the adults in the room and imposing silence on unruly kids? What's so marvellous about allowing pupils to run amok in the corridors, so that they burst into lessons late, loud and disruptive?"

"Run amok? My God, Camilla, what's wrong with you? Why on earth did you become a teacher in the first place if you hate children so much? You can't stand them being human beings and talking to each other, can you? Or the staff either, come to think of it. Yes, it's messy and a bit ragged at the edges, and you are not in complete control of it, but that's life. You can't control everything."

"Oh, you're such a cliché, Rick. A bleeding heart Guardian-reading liberal. 'The poor children, how can we be so mean to them?' Get a grip, for goodness sake, it's embarrassing listening to you. This will deliver better results for the children because they'll learn more. That's what they need, tough love. It's a hard world out there, and they need to be ready for it. We have to prepare them."

"Prepare them? What sort of world do you think this is preparing them for, exactly? Which profession or employer wants its workers to move around the building in silence? Not the prison service. Not the Army. Are we training everyone to take Holy Orders with the Trappist monks? Have you heard of the Human Rights Act? Or is that being a big wuss as well? Did you read George Orwell at school? Did you ever stop to—"

"Enough!" Camilla screamed at him, her face contorted in reddening fury. "That's enough. How dare you question my decisions in such an offensive manner?"

She banged the table with such force that their cups rattled. All the other members of the team looked down with set faces at their paperwork, and fiddled nervously with their pens.

Camilla, liberated by her unusual loss of control, carried on.

"When I took over this school, it was a madhouse. The children were rude, ill-disciplined and scruffy. The staff weren't much better. And now, after a lot of hard work, in the teeth of opposition from dinosaurs like yourself, someone who's more like a union rep than a deputy head, the school is a place of order and calm."

"The school is a place of fear, and repression and bullying. And all you've done is got rid of the kids with the most challenging needs."

"Be quiet. Nobody has the right to disrupt the learning of others."

"No-one except you, apparently," Rick snapped back.

"I make absolutely no apologies for insisting on a scholastic atmosphere in this school."

She carried on in the same vein but Rick switched off at the 'no apologies' line. In his experience, any authority figure, a school leader or a politician, who used the phrase, "I make no apologies for…" were inevitably going to justify some appallingly draconian change. He imagined that petty dictators throughout history had done the same. "I make no apologies for…" – insert the example of historic abuse of human rights of your choice, Hitler, Pol Pot, Stalin – any of them would have appealed to the common sense of their victims and the commentariat in the same way.

He had managed to remain in the meeting, simmering, until they were finally released, but he had made up his mind long before the end. And now, a day later, having reached his office with the letter in a crumpled ball in his hand, he decided to act. Camilla was out yet again on some meeting of national importance, and Rick sat in his office, using his freedom from tyranny to surf the internet. He looked at the headship jobs in the *Times Educational Supplement* online. There were loads of them, many re-advertisements, the schools having been unable to recruit at the first time of asking. There were a couple in Longdon and one just over the border in the next borough.

Just as he was about to click the button to download the application pack, his phone rang.

"Hello," he answered, "Rick Westfield."

"Good afternoon, Rick Westfield, it's Alastair here." Alastair clearly did not feel the need to identify himself with a surname as well.

They went through the polite formalities before Alastair got down to business.

"So, Rick, I'm sure you know it's the September meeting of the Partnership next week."

"Yeah," he replied, "I've had the agenda. Looks quite interesting."

He wasn't completely lying. As always, there were some useful ideas to be discussed. For all its faults, POCSE wasn't only the domain of the deranged or the ruthless careerist. But, if truth were told, he was not looking forward to this particular meeting. It would be even more nauseatingly sycophantic than usual, and Camilla would be treated as a cross between royalty and deity. And it would be the first one he had attended without the corrective cynicism and humour of Avril. Her special talent for puncturing pomposity came into its own at this meeting. The agenda had a slot on it for a presentation from Camilla about her "Journey to Excellence via Zero Tolerance Street". Avril would have hugely enjoyed that, he thought.

"So, you'll have seen that Camilla is due to speak about the transformation of Fairfield High."

Rick bristled. "Yes," he said in clipped tones, "yes, I did notice that."

"I want you to prepare a PowerPoint presentation, going though how you've achieved this success."

"Me? Why on earth do you want me to do that? Isn't that what Camilla is going to do?"

"Yes, that's right. But I want you to do one as well. You will have at least a partial role in the presentation. Don't worry, I'll send you the headings for the presentation and the facts and figures. You're a very good public speaker, you'll make a great job of it."

Rick hesitated.

"What exactly is going on, Alastair? Is Camilla going to fall under a bus? Is there something you know that I don't?"

Alastair laughed at the other end of the phone.

"The answer to that question is always yes. Look, there's nothing for you to worry about. I'm trying to engineer an opening for you at Carlton High School in the Trust. I need you to make sure everyone knows the part you played in Fairfield's success."

"What do you mean, 'an opening'?"

"The Headship, obviously. It's important you don't say a word about to this to anyone. And I mean anyone. Either about Carlton High, or about the presentation I've asked you to produce."

"But—" began Rick.

Alastair interrupted him.

"You're going to have to trust me on this, Rick. After the conference next week, everything will be clear. Okay?"

"Yes, but…"

"I've just sent you what you need for the presentation. Check your email. Send me a copy when you're finished. And ring me if anything else occurs to you. Bye."

The phone went dead, leaving Rick holding the receiver in his hand, baffled. What the hell had all that been about?

*

As agreed, the white van dropped her off around the corner from Wimpole, McKenzie and Grant, the accountancy firm in the village. It wouldn't do to attract any gossip at this stage. They had been so careful. She leant over to the driver's seat and kissed him.

"Best of luck," said David. "You look fantastic. They'd be mad not to give you the job."

"I'm the one that's mad for going for it. For all of this."

"No, you're not. This is your time now. We agreed. Go and do it and see what happens."

She got out of the car and looked back in.

"I'll text you. Will you be around?"

"Of course. I'll come and get you, okay?"

She leaned over the passenger seat and gave him a passionate kiss.

"What was that for?" he asked, with a grin.

"You're beautiful, you know that, don't you? I don't regret this, none of it."

He clasped her hand. "You're the best thing that's ever happened to me. Now go, go and get a job."

She extricated herself from the car and, after looking furtively around the car park, she set off for the High Street, smoothing down her suit as she went.

He watched her go. When she was out of sight, he looked all around the car and all around the car park. He held out his hands in front of him and looked at them as well, front and back, his face a picture of wonder. He had never been as happy as this before and wanted to look at everything and remember it all. Just in case something went wrong.

*

"And you're sure? Absolutely positive?"

Alastair cradled a tumbler of single malt, swirling the golden liquid so that it caught the light from his anglepoise. He listened to the voice on the other end of the phone.

"Because there's a lot riding on this. I can't afford to get this wrong."

There was another pause and Alastair's concentration was total.

"So, let's just be clear. You're telling me that the allegations from Coldewater have resurfaced and that there is at least one ex-member of staff who is prepared to blow the whistle? Yes, I see. What do you mean, it's worse than that? How much worse could it get?"

When he had finished listening he put the receiver down and drained the whisky in one gulp. Then he poured himself another two fingers. He reached for a set of keys lying on the desk top and after fiddling to find the right one, unlocked the top drawer of his desk and pulled out a sheaf of letters bound with an elastic band. Leafing through them, each one bore a slash of red ink: 'Final Demand', 'Notification of Action', 'Your account has been passed on to the Bailiffs'.

The whole plan depended on the expansion of the Trust next year and the year after. The additional schools would generate a huge amount of extra revenue, and with good results no-one would question a hefty salary increase, not to mention the possibilities of the creative recycling of funds. The lack of accountability for the Trusts and the lack of financial transparency was deliberate and very helpful, but suddenly the plan seemed to be teetering on the edge. Scandal would tip it over.

He looked around his study, which was on the top floor of a Victorian three-storey detached house in Wimbledon. It was covered in photos of his children growing up, with many family photos of them all smiling and happy on a series of glorious Mediterranean holidays.

Everything he looked at stared back at him accusingly: his top of the range Apple Mac, the black leather Barcelona chair, the Bang and Olufsen hi-fi. He opened the sash window, lit a cigarette and leaning through the open window, sent a stream of grey blue smoke into the cool night air. The street was full of detached houses with gravel drives, and enormous people carriers, fringed by exotic and luxuriant foliage. It had taken him a long time to get here and he wasn't going to let it go without a fight. There would be casualties from this, but he was damned sure he wasn't going to be one of them.

Grinding out the stub of his cigarette on the brickwork below the window, he flicked it out into the darkness. When he left for work the next morning, there it was, lodged in one of the pair of perfectly-manicured globes of box bushes either side of the front door.

27

THE DAYS UNTIL THE POCSE CONFERENCE DRAGGED. THE agonising wait was made worse by the extension of the police state of zero tolerance within the school. The dull ache of this regime, like a rotting tooth, with its stupidity, its bullying, and its pettiness, was given added piquancy by a timely reminder of the further horrors that were to come.

On the second day of term, a day that was, as usual, given over to training events, Barry Pugh was scheduled on the agenda as giving a presentation on the new initiatives that were starting at Fairfield that term. There was a buzz amongst the old staff, who still fondly remembered his Ofsted talk of the previous year. Alas, there were no similar fireworks of incompetence. Pugh was greeted at first with sullen faces and the merest hint of a hiss. When his talk was over, forty-five minutes later, the staff had been so bored into submission that they could not even raise a hiss. They were left with sullen faces and a stony silence, which seemed to render his shuffling of papers and walk back to his seat on the front row into a never-ending crawl to the gallows.

Although events had numbed them to any further outrages, there was still a sense of disquiet as Pugh announced the launch of the Grovelle initiative. So it was true. 'Non-academic' students were being spared the torture of wholly inappropriate GCSE exams and were going to serve apprenticeships in the NHS and social care institutions instead. The second outrage was that 'academic' Sixth Formers, if there were any of them left in the building, were going to do a new teaching initiative that had them earning money for operating as 'Apprentice Teachers' lower down the school.

So, two different kinds of student were going to be exploited, one group wiping aged bottoms, the other babysitting bored classes for a pittance. It wasn't that long ago that either of these mad schemes would have been met with derision and strike action, but now, people who were battered by austerity and punch drunk with institutionalised bullying, merely shrugged and got on with the task of keeping their nostrils just above the rising tide of excrement.

The details served to sharpen Rick's vitriol as he burned the midnight oil writing the presentation Alastair had demanded of him. He had actually put together two separate presentations, charting the glittering success of Fairfield High School and the Bellingford Trust. One of them was a convenient fantasy of hyperbole, distortion and lies, the other told the truth. It made him feel as if he had some kind of a choice.

On the evening before the conference he was interrupted twice by phone calls. The first, from Alastair, was a stiffener, designed to bind him in to the cause. Alastair confirmed that it was more than likely that Rick would give the speech, not Camilla, and that he should be prepared for what would be a huge opportunity. Half an hour later, Jane rang, and spent ten minutes reminding him of his values and what was at stake.

With the good angel and the bad angel perched on each shoulder, he pressed on, covering all bases. At about eleven, Jo popped her head around the door.

"Are you still working on this? You need to get some sleep, darling."

He looked up, bleary-eyed.

"Nearly done. I won't be long."

"Have you decided then? Do you need to talk about it anymore?"

He shook his head. "No, no thanks. I think I know what I'm going to do."

She came over and laid her hand on his shoulder.

"You know, whatever you decide will be the right decision. I'll support whatever you go with in the end."

He took her hand from his shoulder in his and kissed it.

"Thanks, that means a lot to me, you know that, don't you?"

"Listen, don't be up much longer. You need to sleep."

"No, I won't be. Just a few things to add."

Jo kissed the top of his head and went up to bed. Rick turned back to the computer screen and began typing again.

It was nearly midnight when he closed down the presentation. He yawned and stretched and was just about to switch the light out when his mobile rang.

"Shit. What now?"

He went back to the desk where he had left his phone and picked it up. The illuminated screen told him who was calling.

"God, are they still hassling me? Why on earth is she calling me at this hour? There's nothing else they can say."

He thought for a moment about letting it ring, but he cracked and pressed the green phone symbol.

A voice at the other end said, "Rick? Is that you?"

"Hi Avril," he said, trying to mask his weariness. "You don't really need to ring again, you know. I've spoken to Jane this evening already."

"I know, she told me. You obviously haven't heard the news."

"News? What news? I've been working all night. I haven't seen any news."

There was a pause.

"Avril? Are you still there? What's going on?"

"It's Karim."

He listened, barely able to take in what was being said. When Avril hung up, he went back to his computer, booted it up, opened his presentation again and started typing. It was two in the morning when he finally crawled into bed.

*

When he walked into the conference venue, just off Parliament Square, he knew that something was afoot. It was nine thirty and the foyer was full of familiar faces milling around, swapping anecdotes about their results, and jockeying for position. Rick joined a queue to sign in and scanned the room. At the far side he could just make out, through a scrum of suits, Barry Pugh, holding a cup of coffee and looking up at Alastair Goodall, smiling and hanging on to his every word. He couldn't see any sign of Camilla yet, and still had no idea whether he was going to be called upon to perform or not.

When he got to the front of the queue he gave his name, signed the sheet and was handed an ID card. The young woman began taking him through some arcane point of administration but Rick had already stopped listening, the knot in his stomach clenching tighter as nervous adrenaline flooded his body. He became aware that the woman was touching his hand and slightly raising her voice.

"Mr Westfield? Mr Westfield, did you hear me?"

Rick blinked at her, confused.

"What? Sorry, I was miles away. What were you saying?"

"I was just explaining about the television cameras. You'll see them when you go in. That's just for Mr Grovelle's speech, they'll be gone after that."

"Oh, yes. Yes, of course. Thanks."

He moved away from the desk with his shoulder bag and papers and found a space, so that he could stand, uninterrupted, and discreetly check his pockets. He rummaged in each one, just to check. In the left one was a silver memory stick. In the right, a black memory stick. Good. With a deep breath, he made his way to the entrance of the auditorium and slipped in.

It was an imposing space and this year's conference showed the growing influence of POCSE. There were no group tables, but instead row upon row of seats, theatre style. There must be about five hundred people expected, Rick thought. That prospect was not helping the knot in his stomach. He slipped into a row near the back, with a handful of people around him so that he did not stand out, and watched and waited. No doubt Alastair would seek him out before long.

Safely hidden in his seat, Rick surveyed the front of the hall. There, right at the front, was Marcus Grovelle, who smiled and beamed and sipped his coffee and looked around with the air of a celebrity that was used to being watched. To one side, Alastair was deep in conversation with Camilla, with Barry Pugh looking on, an expression of growing alarm on his face.

Rick was too far away to hear their conversation but every now and then Camilla turned around and the expression on her face was one of incandescent fury. Alastair maintained his career diplomat bland smile and spoke in a low voice, occasionally laying a hand on Camilla's arm, when her voice began to rise. He was obviously keen to prevent any embarrassing outbursts, particularly as they were only five yards away from the Secretary of State for Education. Barry, looking on, paralysed with fear and incapacity, looked as if he desperately needed the toilet.

Eventually, the conversation ran its course, and Camilla moved away and sat at the end of the front row. Barry scuttled along to join her and sat in the adjacent seat, but was rewarded for his loyalty only by the cold shoulder. Camilla half turned her back on him and began scribbling notes on a pad she had pulled from her bag. Rick half smiled to himself as he watched Barry's efforts to ingratiate himself failing dismally, and then noticed Alastair striding down the side of the hall coming directly towards him. He looked up and Alastair turned on the full beam of his smile as he approached. He beckoned Rick out of his seat and greeted him in the aisle with an outstretched hand.

"Hi Rick, you all set?"

"Morning Alastair. Yes, I'm ready, I just wasn't sure whether I'm doing the whole thing or not."

"What? Oh, yes, of course you are. Camilla knows all about it. She's got to deal with something else."

"She didn't look very happy about it, to be honest. What's going on?"

Alastair took Rick by the elbow and gently pulled him close. He lowered his voice.

"There's nothing for you to worry about, Rick. It's just that there's other stuff going on in the background. Just remember what we spoke about?"

Rick looked puzzled. "What do you mean? What did we speak about?"

"Carlton High. Remember?"

"Oh, Carlton High. The headship?"

There was another tug on his elbow, sharper this time, and a hiss from Alastair.

"Keep your voice down, Rick. We don't want everyone knowing about it. Particularly as the current Head is here today, eh?"

"Oh, no. No, of course not."

"You just need to be ready for when you are on stage. It's me first, then Marcus and then you."

"You've done very well to get Grovelle here again, Alastair. Have you got something on him?"

A look of alarm flashed across Goodall's face.

"No, of course not. What on earth do you mean?"

A broad smile covered Rick's face.

"Calm down, Alastair. I was only joking."

The mask reappeared.

"Yes, of course. Okay, Rick, I'm looking forward to your speech. Remember, you need to make it easy for me to get you that headship."

He tapped his nose and moved on to his next piece of string pulling.

Rick watched him go. He was strangely beginning to feel as if he were in control. He had never seen Goodall so jumpy. Something was going on, but what exactly?

His thoughts were interrupted by the ping of his phone. Looking down, he saw a WhatsApp message from Avril:

"Good luck today. Remember to do the right thing. Jane and I are in the front row, to your right. For moral support. Avrilx"

He looked up and there, right in front of the stage, were Jane and Avril, who had stood up and were waving at him, with great smiles on their faces. He returned the wave, a little more discreetly, and smiled back. He sat back down, hoping that no-one else had seen.

How on earth had they got in? Their names wouldn't have been on the list. My God! Goodall, Everson and Pugh would spontaneously combust when they saw those two on the front row. Banquo's ghost, doubled. *Ne'er shake thy gory locks at me.*

His phone pinged again. Another WhatsApp, but this time it was an unknown number. He opened it, and felt his mouth hang agape as he read it.

"Hi Rick. Here to give you moral support. Let them have both barrels. Regards, Charlotte Green."

His mind was reeling. Charlotte? Here? He looked up again, and there in the middle of the crowd, he saw three figures standing, looking back towards him. Charlotte, Kwame and Kevin grinned at him.

Before he had a chance to collect his thoughts, his phone pinged again. This time it was John ('James') Bond. "Heard about the conference. I'm here to see justice prevail."

He looked up. Yes, there just in front of him to the side, a dapper-looking John Bond was there, in a white linen suit, like our man in Havana, giving him the thumbs-up. Rick mirrored the gesture, his mind reeling. What on earth was going on? Who else was going to show up? He didn't have long to contemplate the question. His phone once again poked him in the ribs, this time making him jump. Another unknown number. "All right, sir, we're here for Karim." He looked around the room in what was turning into a routine. There, a few rows ahead of him, in the middle of the row, were Ben, Raysharne and Alex. They turned to acknowledge him, but not for them enthusiastic waving and gesticulation. Their faces were set and serious and they nodded at him in recognition. Surely, thought Rick, they should be in school.

He reached into his pockets and pulled out both memory sticks. As he played with them, switching them from hand to hand, the atmosphere in the hall changed and a hush descended. Rick looked up to see Alastair taking to the stage and striding to the lectern. After the first few words of Alastair's introductory address, Rick's concentration tuned out and heard no more. He was snapped out of his own troubled thoughts at the very end of the speech, by the tumultuous applause that always greeted Alastair at these events.

The atmosphere ratcheted up yet again as Marcus Grovelle came to the lectern. At this point the lighting also changed subtly as the camera crews rolled into action. Grovelle was a good speaker, there was no doubt about that, but not even Martin Luther King would have kept Rick's attention.

Grovelle parroted the buzz words of the professional politician: 'Let me be clear', 'Fit for Purpose', 'Moral Mission', 'Standards', 'Traditional values', 'Trendy Liberals', 'Moral Relativism', 'The Liberal Elite', 'Gold Standard', 'PISA League Tables'.

These meaningless, empty signifiers regularly punctuated the agonising debate going on in his own head, but none of them wrested his attention away from his own thoughts towards Grovelle's portentous rhetoric. And then one word did. "Camilla". He sat up and pricked up his ears. Grovelle had entered the closing stages of his speech that he had saved as a eulogy for Camilla Everson, casting her as a latter-day Jean D'Arc, fighting the forces of trendy liberalism on the side of the forgotten lumpen proles. As he did this a spotlight picked out Camilla on the end of the front row and a camera pointed at her. She smiled as his tribute gathered pace. He segued from this into a self-promoting passage about the piloting of the radical new initiatives of his Great Reform Act at Camilla's school, Fairfield High.

She was still framed, dazzlingly, in the spotlight, when a commotion at the back of the hall interrupted Grovelle's carefully choreographed crescendo to his speech. He looked up, blinking into the television arc lights, and pressed on, but more and more people in the audience began to turn to the back of the hall to see what the growing hubbub was about. He stopped, mouth agape, having finally made out what was the source of the distraction. There, at the entrance to the auditorium, were three uniformed policemen, and a senior officer in a dark suit. Like a surreal tennis match, the heads in the crowd turned to stare at them and then swivelled their attention as one of the conference organisers pointed to the front row. All heads turned in unison and all eyes tracked the pointing finger until they rested on one face, a face still in close-up on the television screens around the room. A face frozen in disbelief and mounting fear. Camilla Everson.

28

CAMILLA GULPED AND HER EYES DARTED AROUND THE room as if looking for an escape. Every last detail, every nervous twitch, every bead of sweat was cruelly magnified by the pitiless stare of the television camera and presented to the crowd. The tennis match continued as heads swivelled this way and then that, eagerly following this new drama, trying to make sense of what was unfolding before them.

There appeared to be a rather heated exchange between the man in the suit and the master of ceremonies who was in charge of all of the organisational aspects of the venue. Eventually, the forces of law and order appeared to prevail over the forces of jobsworthdom, and he reluctantly, muttering all the while under his breath, glided down the aisle to the front of the hall where he bent down to Camilla and spoke to her, pointing to the back of the hall at the police party.

Camilla's face was contorted in rage and embarrassment. Jobsworth wrung his hands and bowed and scraped until Alastair

Goodall decided to wield the knife. He later convinced himself he was doing it out of compassion and there were times later in life, when he looked back on this episode of his career, that he really believed that. He joined in, bending down to Camilla. He said one sentence and Camilla gathered her stuff, got up and made the long, slow walk to the back of the hall, acutely aware that by now, every pair of eyes were looking at her. Even Grovelle had stopped speaking by this stage and the camera crew had turned their cameras to track Camilla's walk of shame. When she got to the end, one of the policemen put an arm around her back and ushered her out of the hall and the building. It was only one step away from being led away in handcuffs.

As soon as the door closed behind her, there was an audible gasp from the crowd and then a buzz of chatter. Grovelle was marooned at the lectern, his speech unfinished. The POCSE lieutenants, scattered around the hall, imposed some semblance of order by standing up and staring at those who were still talking. With eyes on the stage, they listened half-heartedly to the last thirty seconds of Grovelle's speech. At the end of it, Grovelle looked around expectantly at the crowd, but no applause was forthcoming. He slunk from the stage, at first in silence and then accompanied by a rising babble of incredulous gossip.

The noise of the gossip screened the conversation between Grovelle and Goodall at the side of the stage from prying ears. The keen observer, however, would have noted some small signs of tension between them. Grovelle, furious that his planned media coup for the six o'clock news had been ruined by these shenanigans, stood right up against Goodall to make his point, eyeball to eyeball. Or as close as he could, given the fact that Goodall was a good foot taller than him. It was like watching a pair of footballers arguing, each deciding whether to risk the head butt. Grovelle walked past Goodall, making sure that there was the slightest, deniable, contact between their shoulders, and stomped off down the aisle and out of the venue, the cameras watching him all the way. Goodall smiled placidly, fully aware that he was being filmed.

He walked down the aisle in the same direction as Grovelle, aware that he only had a few moments to manage this situation. He got to Rick and sat down beside him.

"It's down to you now, Rick. Everything is down to you to rescue us all from this mess. You ready?"

Rick nodded. Alastair patted him on the leg.

"Good man. Come on."

They both walked down to the front of the stage, and gradually an expectant quiet fell upon the room. Alastair walked to the microphone and began to speak.

"Colleagues, I really must apologise for the events of the last few minutes. I think that it's only fair for us not to speculate about what has happened and for us to wait until the full facts are known. Luckily, we are able to turn to Rick Westfield, Deputy Head at Fairfield High, to lead on the next item on the agenda. Please give your usual welcome to Rick Westfield."

He stretched his arm out, inviting Rick to replace him at the podium and he walked up to a thunderous round of applause. He gripped the lectern and stared out at the audience, blinded by the arc light still flooding the centre of the stage. He began to speak and found his throat dry and hoarse and no words would come. He coughed, a machine gun rattle, and reached for a glass of water. Drinking deeply, he then shuffled his papers and started again.

"Ladies and gentlemen, it falls to me to speak to you this morning about the recent journey Fairfield High School has been on. A transformation, I think I was asked to call it."

He looked up again and was disconcerted not to be able to see individuals in the audience.

"Excuse me for a moment, will you? I do like to be able to see who I'm talking to."

He stepped away from the lectern and took a step towards the edge of the stage out of the direct light. Surveying all of the audience he saw Jane and Avril on the front row to his left, smiling up at him. Then in the middle were Charlotte, Kwame, and Kevin and to their right, John Bond, white suit luminous in the crowd. He scanned the rows at the back and picked up Ben, Raysharne and Alex. They were all waiting for him to make his move.

Rick smiled at the audience. "Yes, everyone is here. Apart from the police, obviously."

This provoked an outburst of laughter, some genuine, some nervous. As the laughter died down, there was movement at the back of the hall. Coming in at the back, Rick was shaken to see three people come in together. It was Eric, Joan and Ahmed. They picked their way through and found three seats together on the back row. Rick walked back to the lectern.

"If you'll just indulge me a little further, I've just got to find my memory stick. I've got to make sure I get the right one, or the police may come back."

There was more laughter and Rick used the minute of space it gave him to rummage in his pockets. He brought out two memory sticks, and inserted the silver one. The list of files was displayed on the screen for all to see. He double clicked on a file called, 'Fairfield's journey. The Truth'. The presentation blossomed into life behind him, a title slide with the legend, 'Fairfield High School: A Journey to Excellence via Zero Tolerance street.'

"So, that's the title of the presentation. I'm sorry about that, it was the title I was given."

He brandished his black USB stick high above his head.

"I've got another presentation on this memory stick. This is the presentation they wanted me to give. It's got the same title, but it's full of lies, misrepresentations and false claims. It's the presentation that Camilla was going to give. It's bollocks, all of it."

There was a gasp from the crowd. Goodall sat, stony-faced, his head in his hands. Barry Pugh clutched his clipboard, like a comfort blanket. Everything he believed in was crashing round his ears.

"Two years, almost to the day, I sat where you're sitting now and listened to Camilla Everson talk about the transformation of Coldewater High School through using a zero tolerance approach. What a wonderful picture she painted! How simple a vision! If only we would just see sense and drop all of the trendy liberal crap and treat kids like cogs in a machine, they would learn Latin and quadratic equations and working-class kids would be equipped to storm the barricades of power and privilege. It's an appealing vision. Real social mobility, at last, after years of trying and failing. It would be being cruel to be kind. They would thank us for it later.

"I'm sorry colleagues, it's all nonsense. Simple, back to basics solutions nearly always are. Life and learning, and social relationships are much more complicated than that. Where is Coldewater today? Struggling, that's where. Twenty percent drop in outcomes. And before anybody says that's because Camilla is not there, what kind of system depends upon one person? How can it be deemed a success, when it's not sustainable and it's not repeatable? It's doomed to failure. It's a giant con trick.

"I've talked to many people from Coldewater. The whole thing is smoke and mirrors. A combination of cheating, manipulating figures, gaming the system and getting rid of key people. But you all knew that, didn't you? Or you suspected it. You didn't say anything, like me, because you want to believe it. You want to think that we can do better than we do for working-class kids and you want to get behind anything that seems to deliver it.

"But, hold on a minute, I'm getting ahead of myself. I'm supposed to be talking to you about the miracle of Fairfield High, not Coldewater. And I will, I promise you, I will. But first, I have to talk to you about something more important. Something that illustrates the absolute bankruptcy of zero tolerance."

He paused. The audience was hanging on to his every word, the silence and the concentration almost painful. He clicked his cueing device and the slide moved on. On the screen was a gigantic picture of Karim Atbal, in his Fairfield High School uniform. There was a cry from the back of the hall and everyone turned to look. In the back row they saw an older white man put his arm round an older white woman, while an Arab-looking man next to them looked on in concern.

"I want to talk to you about Karim Atbal."

The faces all turned to the front again.

"You may have heard about Karim. He was the young Syrian boy who was savagely beaten by some other young people in

Longdon a few months ago. It was clearly a hate crime, a racially motivated attack."

He paused again and surveyed the crowd and let them ingest the seriousness of the topic.

"He was a Fairfield student for a while. He was seventeen years old and had been through more in the last few years of his life than we will ever experience in a lifetime. That's a lifetime of threescore years and ten, not a lifetime of seventeen years. His father, mother and brother were killed in Aleppo in a bombing raid. He escaped with his younger sister and endured the most terrible hardship as they made the journey from Aleppo to Calais, via Turkey. He spoke English because his father had been a professor of English at Aleppo University. He was a highly intelligent young man.

"He was kept in Calais, in the Jungle, waiting in squalid conditions until this country was shamed into doing something about unaccompanied child refugees. This was the time of the 'hostile environment' for immigrants at the Home Office, when all refugees were not welcome here. His sister went missing before he got to Calais. He has not seen her since and at the time of his death, he did not know whether she was dead or alive. He feared, reasonably, that she had been forced into child prostitution by people traffickers. He had planned to go back to Calais if he could to try and find her, or at least get word to Calais that she existed and that the authorities should look out for her.

"When he first arrived at the Jungle he was suffering from post-traumatic shock syndrome and was mute for six months. But then suddenly, he got lucky. For the first time in years. He was placed with two foster carers in Longdon who gave him a safe and secure home and who loved him and cared for him as if he were their own. He had a Syrian support worker, Ahmed, a man who works tirelessly to help refugees, mainly Syrian, in this country. All three of them are here today, to see that Karim is properly recognised. Joan and Eric and Ahmed, we will try not to let you down again."

He gestured as he said this to the back of the hall. Everyone turned round, straining their necks to see who they were.

"He came to Fairfield, via Longdon's Language Unit, and made an immediate impression on all of us who met him. He was kind, polite, determined, highly intelligent. Above all, he was forgiving and grateful and tried to see the best in people. He did very well and we were all looking forward to working with him to get him through his exams. He made one catastrophic mistake, though. He made the terrible mistake of coming to Fairfield High at the same time that Camilla Everson implemented a zero tolerance regime there. She effectively denied him a place in the school, arguing that we had to look after our own and that he would bring down our results and eat up our resources.

"We turned our back on him, a young person in the most desperate of circumstances. We should hang our heads in shame that this is our response. We shouldn't be asking the question, 'what can I get out of this young person?' We should be saying 'what can I do for this young person? How can I help?' That is what we would have done in a woolly-headed, liberal, caring, tolerance-max environment. The kind of school, in short, that Fairfield used to be, but which is now somehow, suddenly denigrated and despised by people like Mr Grovelle.

"And the ultimate irony is, of course, that last week, Joan and Eric and Ahmed found out that Karim had achieved six grade 9s. He took six exams after a year, and got the highest possible grade in every one."

Rick took another sip of water and fiddled with his papers on the lectern.

"This could have been a very different speech. For weeks since the attack Karim has been lying in intensive care, wired up to every life-support system known to man. All of the amazing resources of the NHS, the incredibly skilled staff, the high tech equipment, the dedication, the love, all placed without question or hesitation at the service of Karim, regardless of who he is or where he is from. Regardless of his religion, his ethnicity, his sexuality, his politics. Simply content to serve the people, whoever they are. That's what a national education service should have provided for Karim – unquestioning care and support. You remember that, don't you?

Before we had to deal with all of this nonsense about league tables and private sector management expertise."

Rick paused again and slowly swept the audience with a penetrating look, leaving each one of them to consider their own complicity in what had gone before. After what seemed an age, he released them from their torment.

"We're actually very lucky. We have been given a second chance to get this right for Karim, having failed him and thousands of other kids so badly. Last night, Karim regained consciousness for the first time since the attack. I'm delighted to tell you all that the doctors now think he will go on to make a full recovery."

The audience, who had been transfixed into moist-eyed, breath-holding, silent concentration, erupted into a paroxysm of whooping and cheering. A spontaneous outburst of applause broke out and people got to their feet, their ingrained professional decorum shot down and utterly destroyed by the emotional roller coaster they had been on for the last few minutes. After a minute or two, Rick held up his hands to them and signalled that they should sit back down, a smile indicating he understood their emotion and was part of it as well.

"So, I am standing here today saying to you all, please don't make the mistake of thinking that a zero tolerance regime begins and ends at the school gate. It seeps into the world and into our communities and it feeds into and feeds off the appalling racist attitudes that seem to have become more acceptable these days. We are all told to listen to the 'genuine concerns' of the people. These concerns are legitimate, the right wing populist pundits tell us. No, they're not. These pundits, these politicians, they have no interest in what is right and good. They are concerned only with protecting their own seats from racist voters who now don't feel quite so guilty about being racist. What happened to leadership? To showing people that there is a better way to be in the twenty-first century?

"There will be some people sitting here today, good people in the main, who are thinking, but this is a different kind of zero tolerance. In school, it's about not letting pupils break little rules so that they respect authority and will abide by the big rules as well. Again, I say to you that actually, it's about much more than that. We should be teaching pupils the much harder lesson that in the world, social relationships need to be negotiated and compromises have to be made and that people have to work hard at getting along. That's the real world, not one where you are held in solitary confinement for making a mistake. That just breeds resentment of authority wielded without judgement."

As his speech progressed, there were increasing numbers of people nodding their heads in agreement. Rick looked out into the crowd and realised he would have to bring it to an end soon, otherwise he would lose them.

"I don't want to take up any more of your time lecturing you about the right approach in schools. I've sat through far too many presentations, some of them in this hall with all of you, given by people who claim to have all the answers. Personally, I'm fed up with so-called Superheads, honoured for their outstanding work before being exposed as charlatans a few years later. Leading schools is a terribly difficult job. There are no easy answers. The 'rapid improvement' Ofsted and governing bodies are always demanding is actually a euphemism for cheating. Real improvement, sustainable improvement, is slow and incremental and unspectacular.

"So, I'm going to leave you, presumably to listen to a few more presentations telling you how to do things properly, in a few minutes, right after I've explained how Fairfield High achieved its unprecedented, spectacular results. I've got a slide for each part of the strategy, you'll all be delighted to hear."

He clicked his cueing device and a new slide appeared. It said, quite simply, in huge letters, unadorned with graphics or animations, 'WE CHEATED'. Again, there was an audible gasp from the audience, followed by a few ripples of nervous laughter.

"Apologies for the crap PowerPoint, but I wrote this in the early hours of this morning. Yes, folks, we cheated. Our exams officer of the last thirty years, John Bond, a man of unimpeachable integrity, was sacked by Camilla and one of her cronies was installed in his place. John's here today. Give everyone a twirl, John, let them see that you are a real person."

Slightly embarrassed, Bond, resplendent in his white linen suit, stood up and gave a sheepish wave.

"The new exams officer did exactly what was expected of him and released all of the exam papers early. Camilla and various other members of the Senior Team, people that she had appointed, I hasten to add, took the school hall full of Year 11 students through each paper a couple of days before the exam. I have several students willing to give evidence to that effect."

He went on, with a separate slide for each crime and misdemeanour. He covered getting rid of thirty badly-behaved Year 11 students, sacking people unfairly, misusing the competency procedures, forcing staff to sign gagging clauses, using lesson observations as a surveillance tool.

He finally came to an end.

"There's a lot more, believe me, and I have documentary proof of all of it. I won't bore you any more with the details. I just want to finish by saying, this cannot go on any longer. We have to say, enough is enough. We must be strong enough to reject the latest trend for macho leaders who try to ape the private sector without any understanding of what leading Teaching and Learning is actually about. We have to be brave enough to stand up to the tyranny of the league tables and the distortion of best practice it has encouraged. We have to understand that staff and students need to be nurtured and encouraged, not bullied and brutalised. We have to be brave enough to fail and to let others fail on our watch. It won't be easy, but if we don't change, there'll be nothing but a wasteland left to defend."

He clicked his cuer for the final time to leave the picture of Karim on the screen.

"Thanks for listening and let's not forget the reason why we need to treat people properly and to teach the children by example, so that they learn to treat people properly. We need to remember Karim and all the other Karims we look after every day."

He began to fiddle with his computer and after leaving the picture up on screen as long as he could, he closed it down, so that he could retrieve his memory stick and leave. He really didn't want to hang around now, he felt exhausted and vaguely sick. He needed to get home and surprise his kids when they got back from school.

He clicked the various buttons to a deafening silence. The audience were dumbstruck and were struggling to process everything they had just listened to. Barry Pugh would have assumed the foetal position if he had been able to move. Instead he rocked on his chair, clinging to his clipboard.

Then, when the silence began to hum, Jane and Avril at the front of the hall got to their feet and began to clap. Then Kwame and Kevin and Charlotte joined in, and John Bond. The applause spread like a wildfire. Rick looked up, puzzled. Everyone was on their feet, clapping wildly and whooping for more.

Leading the applause from the side of the hall was Alastair Goodall, with the zeal of the new convert. The Queen is dead. Long live the King.

29

He was on his third glass of red, explaining the day's events to Jo, when he got the call. He was sprawled on the sofa in the front room, and his mobile interrupted. Picking it up, he sat bolt upright.

"Shit," he exclaimed, "it's Alastair Goodall. What shall I do?"

"Take the call. Let's see what he's got to say for himself."

He answered.

"Hello, Alastair. What can I do for you?"

The voice at the other end said, "Is this a good time to talk?"

"Yeah, it's fine, just go ahead."

"Well, Rick, I have to congratulate you. That was a fine performance this morning."

"It wasn't a performance, Alastair. I said what I thought."

"Funny that you haven't said it before now. Some people might think you should have done something about it earlier if you felt that strongly about it."

"And they'd be right, I should have. I was a coward."

"Well, I think you've been very clever, actually."

"Clever? How do you mean?"

"Well, it was an inspired idea to make sure all those people were in the audience, pulling the heartstrings and orchestrating the applause. Brilliant, actually. I think I've underestimated you."

"Sorry to disappoint, but that wasn't me. I've no idea how that happened."

There was a pause as Goodall was recalibrating at the other end of the line.

"So, you just lucked out then?"

"Yeah, that's one way of putting it."

"Don't get me wrong, it's a brilliant quality to have. Successful people have to be brilliant and lucky, and I am very appreciative of successful people. Even those who have just stabbed me in the back."

Rick sighed. "Can we get to the point, Alastair? It's been a very long day."

"I propose we shelve the Carlton High plan. It's more important to go straight to plan B."

"Plan B?" he said wearily.

"I need you to step into Camilla's shoes. She is obviously going to be, er, out of the picture for a while. You'll take over as Head and you'll implement your own vision of school improvement. You know, all that love and community. All that stuff that had people self-lubricating this morning."

"What about Zero Tolerance?"

Goodall scoffed at the other end of the phone.

"Zero Tolerance? That is so last year, Rick. Immersive Love is the coming thing, and you're the man for the job."

"Immersive Love? Dear God, Alastair, don't you believe in anything?"

"Don't be silly, Rick, of course not. Well, only me. I believe in me."

In that instant, Rick had a picture of a post-nuclear apocalyptic scene. From underneath the charred and smoking piles of rubble, emerge entire colonies of cockroaches, unscathed, the only survivors, ready to adapt and prosper in the new wastelands. Then, following the cockroaches, dusting down his Armani suit and scrambling over the dead bodies, would be Alastair Goodall, looking around at the devastation before pulling out his mobile to make a call.

"No, sorry Alastair."

"No? What do you mean, no? If you're holding out for the Carlton job, well that would be a mistake, believe me."

"No, I'm not holding out for the Carlton job. I mean just no. I don't want anything from you. Don't call again."

He ended the call, turned his phone off and went back to his glass of red.

*

Barry Pugh pulled into his driveway, the troubles of the world on his shoulders. He was still struggling to make sense of what had happened. First Camilla, then Marcus Grovelle showing his darker side and then that extraordinary performance by Westfield. It was pure exploitation of that young Syrian boy's situation. Yes, of course it was a tragedy, but to lay the blame somehow at Camilla's door, well that really summed up Westfield.

But the thing that was really troubling him, nagging away like a toothache, were all those allegations on Westfield's presentation about cheating. He felt sick just thinking about it. Particularly given the fact that there were whistle blowers already lined up. There would be an investigation, there was bound to be, and then he'd really be in trouble. And Alastair? What the hell had he been playing at, leading the applause like some groupie?

He'd tried to ring Alastair and Camilla, but no-one was answering his calls, so he'd worked late at the office, gone for a drink to mull things over before finally coming home. He switched off the engine and sat for a moment in the quiet darkness. He was in no hurry to go in. Frankly, Alison wasn't much of a support these days. He didn't know what the matter was with her. She was distant and hardly said a thing. He wondered if she was still sulking about him putting his foot down about that job. And she had behaved very strangely over that decorator, that ghastly Jones. What a nasty

385

shock that had been. She could be so selfish, despite all the sacrifices he had made for her.

He roused himself from this brooding and collected up his papers and his coat and closed the car door. The gravel crunched underfoot as he walked to the front door. He noticed that the house was in darkness and when he opened the front door, the usual smell of cooking was not there to welcome him home.

"Alison," he called, "Alison, I'm home. Everything all right?"

The calls echoed in the corridor but no answer came. Switching on the lights he made his way to the kitchen, which was also deserted. On the kitchen table lay his clipboard.

"That's funny," he thought, "I was sure I had that with me."

He stopped, dead still.

"Well of course I did, I had it at the conference this morning. I don't get it. Whose is that?"

He walked over to the table and picked up the clipboard, which was indeed an exact replica of his. There was only one sheet of paper attached to it. It was a set of targets, ticked if achieved:

Get new job	√
Get new partner	√
Get pregnant	√
Leave husband	√
See solicitor re divorce	√

Underneath she had written:

I tried Barry, I tried so hard, I really did. I'm sorry.
Alison x

30

T<small>HE ONLY SOUND IN THE ROOM WAS THE HUM OF HIS</small>
computer, the angry buzzing of the strip lighting, the regular,
even ticking of the wall clock, and as an undertone, the occasional
splutter from Andrew's light, rhythmic snoring. It was early still,
about ten in the morning, but he had been in the office since seven,
and after checking his emails, reorganising his digital filing system
and checking the post, his work for the day was over by eight. It
was a regular pattern by now, and he often passed the second half
of the morning sprawled on the huge leather couch that dominated
one half of his office. There had been a time when the sofa had
been a signifier of his importance and status. Now, it was simply
a convenient place to nap, to fill up a few of the hours he was still
compelled to spend at work.

At first, he had felt a little guilty about it and worried that he might
be discovered, but, as the months passed by, it became increasingly
obvious that no-one would be visiting his office and therefore he
could sleep on, confident that he would not be disturbed. He was in

the middle of a delicious dream, where he was standing at the summit of an imposing hill, addressing hordes of followers in the valley below. They were hanging on to his every word, adoration on their upturned beatific faces. The dream followed its usual course, figures from Andrew's past one by one turned up to listen to his words of wisdom, and enthusiastically joined the throng. He braced himself for the ending, when he would realise that he was in fact entirely naked, and that everyone in the crowd below would suddenly realise and start laughing at him. The faces below began to change their expressions, from adoration, through disbelief to horror and finally scorn. The denouement of the dream was shattered by the harsh ringing of the telephone on his desk.

He woke with a start and fell from the sofa onto the floor with a thud. Dazed, he looked around him, trying to make sense of the noise. It sounded like – the phone. Of course, the phone. He scrambled to his feet, and made a grab for the phone before it stopped ringing. It had been a long time since anyone had called him. The days when he had a secretary to screen his calls and prepare him were long gone. It was one of the many indignities he had had to suffer in the last few months as budget cuts and a disappearing service took their toll.

"Hello," he said, as if he wasn't quite sure how he was supposed to answer. "Er, Andrew Harrison here."

He listened as the caller went through what was obviously a detailed and complex set of proposals. He occasionally interjected with questions, a look of growing incredulity on his face.

"And when would this be from?" he asked.

"I see. And this was all decided yesterday?"

He listened again. He wasn't quite sure how to properly phrase his next question.

"Umm, and this is all, umm, genuine, is it?"

He half expected one of the guys from Planning or Children's Services to shout out, revealing they were the authors of this hilarious practical joke, but no such revelation was forthcoming.

"No, no, that's excellent. Tomorrow. Yes, we'll talk tomorrow. Look forward to seeing you then."

He put the phone down, and looked around his office, hardly daring to believe what had just happened. The walls of his office were bare, marked only with the outlines of the photos he had taken down several months ago, when he couldn't bear to look at them anymore. They reminded him of the days when he and his department mattered, and for a long time now, they had been a painful reminder of his irrelevance. On a whim, he pulled open the bottom drawer of his desk. Yes, there they were still. He pulled them out and laid them on top of the desk. Prince Charles, Tony Blair, that American woman, all with him, smiling.

He dusted them down and, walking around the office, he replaced them one by one on the walls in their old positions. He started to hum as he did it and he ended up at his window, still with the impressive panoramic view of the skyscrapers of Longdon. He drank in the view, breathed in deeply, exhaling a long slow breath of contentment. A small smirk appeared on his face as he murmured to himself, "The Empire Strikes Back."

*

Kevin popped his head around Rick's office door.

"Stop pretending you're working, Rick, and get back onto the *TES* website looking for jobs."

"Hmm?"

Rick looked up from the excel spreadsheet he had been poring over for the last hour, as Kevin came in, closed the door behind him, and wandered over to have a look at what exactly was on Rick's screen.

"Oh, you really are working. Sorry, I take it all back. Listen, leave that for a moment and go on the BBC website. Have you seen it this morning?"

"What? No, I've been too busy. What's going on?"

"Have a look yourself," Kevin replied.

Rick clicked on the site from his favourites tab and began reading.

'Government in crisis as minister is removed.'

"What the hell?" said Rick, incredulous. "Grovelle's gone?"

"Yeah," smirked Kevin, "and it gets better. Grovelle has been moved to Northern Ireland."

"Northern Ireland? That's like Siberia in the eyes of our Government. What on earth has he done? Has he been caught with his trousers down?"

"Keep going," said Kevin. "The story below."

Rick read aloud, "Camilla Everson, awarded a CBE in last year's honours list, was arrested on Monday on suspicion of embezzling public funds. Everson, who was nominated by the former Education Secretary, Marcus Grovelle, for the honour, was also implicated in allegations of exam cheating at her current and previous secondary schools, both in South London. The Department for Education would not comment when asked about these developments last night."

"My God," gasped Rick, "I bet they wouldn't."

He paused for a moment, piecing together the bits of the jigsaw.

"So, what's gonna happen here?" he asked. "What will the Trust do?"

"Well, it'll be you, they'll ask you to act up, at least in the first instance, surely?"

Rick snorted.

"I don't think so, Kev. Alastair Goodall is not going to give me the time of day now after my brainstorm on Monday. I've committed professional suicide."

"Professional suicide? You're joking. Have you not seen Twitter? You are trending massively. The camera crew kept filming you. It's all over social media. You've even got your own hashtag: #Wecheated."

"I've got no idea what any of that means. How come you know all about this stuff and I don't and you're an old git and I'm young and dynamic?"

"I read all about it in Saga magazine last month," Kevin replied. "Look, I haven't got time to explain it all to you now. Ask Jo when you get home. She lives in the real world. All you need to know for now, is that the numbers are with you. You're this year's Jeremy Corbyn."

*

Andrew had spent the rest of the day making phone calls of his own, trying to reassemble his old team, occasionally stopping to pinch himself to make sure that all of this was really happening. By about three in the afternoon he was exhausted, his adrenaline surge having finally subsided, and he stopped for a break. Five minutes after he got off the phone, it rang. He snatched it up, excited about who it might be.

The voice at the other end said simply, "Andrew. Is that you?"

"Yes," he said warily, "this is Andrew Harrison here. Who's calling, please?"

"It's Alastair. Alastair Goodall. I've been trying to get through to you for ages."

Andrew burst out laughing.

"Well, you haven't been trying very hard, Alastair. I've been expecting your call for the last eighteen months. I seem to recall that you said you'd be in touch. Something about a job with the Bellingford Trust. What happened?"

"Ah, yes, sorry about that. I've been dealing with an awful lot of issues. Anyway, they're all resolved now, so here I am, as promised, offering you a job."

"A job, Alastair? With the Trust?"

"Yes, that's right. Director of Learning across the whole Trust. Really prestigious post. Very impressive salary, actually."

"I thought Barry Pugh was Director of Learning. Across the whole Trust. On a very impressive salary. Or have I got that wrong?"

"Er, no, no that's right . But to be honest with you, Barry is really not up to scratch. He hasn't come to terms with the new realities. He is still wedded to a Zero Tolerance culture and I'm looking for someone more forward looking. Someone with authority and gravitas."

"And Barry knows all about this, I assume?"

Alastair hesitated.

"Well, er, well no, not as yet. But we can't be squeamish about these things. We have to act quickly. I need you to help me give the Trust more weight, to help us get through some of these unfortunate misunderstandings."

Again, Andrew laughed.

"No, Alastair, what you really mean is that you need someone to come in and front up an organisation that has been accused of cheating and probably worse. Because if that doesn't happen, there is a real chance that the Trust will go under."

"Oh, come now Andrew, don't exaggerate. That is never going to happen."

"I'm afraid it already has, Alastair old boy. You're too late. I'm not going to take up your very generous offer of a job, because I've already got a new job. I was offered it this morning and I accepted. Well, actually, to be strictly accurate, it's not a new job, it's my old job."

"What do you mean?"

"Hmm, how can I put this to you gently? I know. All of the Trust schools are being taken out of your control. The Trust is being wound up and the schools are all coming back into local authority control, under my leadership. Haven't they told you yet? They're probably trying to get through to you on the phone. You're fucked, matey, and it couldn't have happened to a nicer person. Byee."

"Andrew, wait, wait, listen…"

Andrew placed the receiver back on the cradle. He poured himself a scotch, turned off the smoke alarms and lit the rather nice Havana cigar he'd been saving for his last day. With a bit of luck, he'd have plenty of opportunities to buy another one, before his last day actually came around.

BOOK THREE

1

IT WAS ONE OF THOSE PERFECT MID-JUNE DAYS IN England, when even the crowded, dusty streets of Longdon can seem to hold out the promise of beauty and possibility. The sun was high in a blue, cloud-flecked sky and a faint breeze rustled the canopies of the ancient oaks that ringed the playing fields and entrance of Fairfield High. They were gnarled and statuesque, taken for granted by those that worked there, but occasionally, on picture-perfect days such as this, they gave a clue as to the origins of the school's name.

This was once a fair field, cleared from the Great North Wood centuries before. It had seen many gatherings of people down the years, and now the swaying trees bore witness to another. The front of the school was thronged with dignitaries and invited guests and the speeches were being delivered over the rustle of the leaves above and the clink of champagne flutes.

Avril was there, dressed in her finest wedding frock. She had tried to persuade Jane to come along, but she had refused. "I can't go back, Avril," she had said, tears in her eyes. "It's still all too raw for me, what happened there that day. All of it is ruined. I'm pleased for Rick and all of the others, but I need to move on. One day maybe, I'll go back, but not yet." Charlotte, balancing her canapés and champagne glass, while whispering a commentary on the proceedings to Kevin and Kwame, was at the back of the crowd, delighted to have been invited. She glanced round the crowd as if looking for someone.

"So, what happened to little Bazzer Pugh then? Is he not here?" she asked.

"Pugh? Good God, no. He left before there was an investigation. He'd been involved in all of the exam cheating, you see. Harrison, the guy on stage, agreed not to pursue it if he went quietly. Rick was bit pissed off, but there was nothing he could do."

"So, where is he now? Some kind of advisory job with the Department for Education? The last refuge of the scoundrel."

Kevin laughed. "Charlotte, you're so cynical. No, the last I heard, he was Head of Careers in some tiny private school in deepest Surrey."

"How the mighty are fallen, eh?" said Kwame. "There's a lesson there for all of us."

They turned their attention back to the speeches. Just behind them in the crowd was John Bond, resplendent in the bright sunshine in his white linen suit. He had stood in as exams officer that year to help out the school. Camilla's placeman had been dismissed after the investigation by Ofqual, the examination watchdog, and the school had needed someone with experience to get them through the exam season. He had also agreed to train up the new appointment, who was starting in a few weeks now all of the exams were over. He'd be happy with that as his final professional act, to ensure the ethical standards of the school's next exams officer. Once that was done, he could slip back to his life of retirement, perfecting his garden and perhaps finishing the *Times* crossword every now and again.

The latest in the series of speakers was drawing to a close. Andrew Harrison was a picture of easy contentment, the restoration of his empire, or at least a scale model of it, having breathed life into the shell it had become. His plump, newly-scrubbed skin, pink and fragrant, strained out of the top of his collar and against his red braces as he pointed his suit at the crowd and beamed at them.

"And so, it only remains for me to thank Rick Westfield for this day. It has been a real pleasure to come here and perform this ceremony for such a good cause. It's a reminder of why we were all so delighted about the change of heart of the government over the role of local authorities in education. It's just such a shame that it took a crisis for them to realise the truth of what many of us involved in education had been saying for years. And," he continued, looking across at Rick, with a smile on his face, "we shouldn't forget that if it were not for the courage of Rick in speaking out, then none of us would be here for this splendid occasion. So, without further ado, I'm going to hand you over to Rick, for a few words before I cut the ribbon and declare this magnificent building open."

He stood to one side and beckoned Rick to take his place centre stage. There was warm and generous applause from those gathered there and Rick took a moment or two to survey the crowd. He made eye contact with a number of particular individuals that he was delighted to see and mouthed a few words of greeting or thanks to them in turn. Before he started, he made sure that he had got the position of Karim, Eric, Joan and Ahmed in the crowd, so that he could invite them up onto the stage at the right moment.

His speech went through the formalities and conventions demanded by such an occasion and before long he had smoothed his way through the gears and had arrived at the final section.

"So, once again, on behalf of the school and the local community, I must thank Andrew Harrison and Longdon Education Authority for providing the funds to establish the Language and Refugee Centre as a permanent part of Fairfield High School, in this splendid new building you see before you."

Andrew smiled with what he hoped was the right amount of modesty and humility and the crowd rewarded him with a fresh burst of polite applause.

Rick continued.

"It's with great pleasure that I invite Karim, Joan, Eric and Ahmed up onto the stage to perform the opening ceremony and the cutting of the ribbon on the Karim Atbal Language and Learning Centre."

He gestured to them to come up on stage and they made their way to the front and then up the steps, Karim needing Ahmed's arm and a crutch for support. As they came up, Rick introduced them.

"You all know Karim, of course. As I am sure you also know, Joan and Eric are Karim's foster parents and Ahmed his support worker from the Syria Refugee Project. I'm delighted to be able to tell you that Ahmed has accepted a position at the new Language and Learning Centre, as Director of Refugee Support Services. I see this as representative of our commitment to always treating refugees with love, compassion and support rather than with suspicion."

There was a thunderous outburst of applause for this sentiment and Rick passed on the scissors to Joan. She, with a nod from Eric, passed them on to Karim.

Karim leant on his crutch and looked out into the crowd.

"Good afternoon, everyone. I can't tell you how pleased I am to be able to be here with you to make this speech. There were many times over the last nine months that I thought that I would never be able to walk again, or go out, or do the most basic things. But if there is one thing that I have learned from my experiences of the last few years, it is that the impossible can be achieved if you have good people around you helping you along the way. And that is one of the reasons that I was so determined to be here today for the opening of this wonderful building. It allows me to say thank you to the many people who have helped me and to the school, Fairfield High School, for their support. It has got me through some very dark times.

"My father would have been particularly proud to see a school building named after his son. He was a professor of English in Aleppo and he taught me from a very early age that Britain was a tolerant and civilised place. That it had a long history of welcoming people from all over the world who had faced persecution or war in their own country. It has even more meaning, given my father's beliefs, that the building is dedicated

398

to the education of refugees." His voice began to tremble and he paused for a moment.

"I want to thank in particular Ahmed, who is standing with me here, as he has done since I arrived in the country with nothing. My wonderful foster parents, Joan and Eric, who I believe were the English people my father was thinking about when he told me, all those years ago, that Britain had a proud history of welcoming refugees and helping them rebuild their lives."

At this, Eric beamed at his shoes and wiped away a stray tear. Joan wept with abandon. Ahmed, a broad grin on his face, put his arm around her shoulders.

"I'd also like to thank the whole school community. Mr Westfield, who came to visit me in hospital and never lost his faith in me. All of my friends, and especially Ben, who saved my life."

He gestured to the main body of the crowd where Ben was standing. His mother, bursting with pride next to him, leaned over and said to him, flicking some dust from his shoulders, "Such a lovely boy, that Karim." Ben wriggled uncomfortably, but allowed himself a smile at his mother's fussing.

Karim gathered himself for his final words.

"I have been very lucky and very blessed. The one thing that would make my luck complete, would be for me to see my sister Evana again. I would give anything for her to be here, to meet all of you wonderful people and to be one of the first students in this new building. I…"

He stopped, overcome by the idea of Evana and where she might be. It had been years now, and every day made it less and less likely she would ever be found. With one last push, he forced the final sentence from his mouth, tears on his cheeks, his voice faltering.

"I declare this magnificent building, the Karim Atbal Language and Learning Centre, duly open."

He leaned forward, snipped the ribbon with the scissors, and with the applause ringing in his ears, embraced Joan and Eric on the stage.

*

Later in Rick's office, Andrew Harrison sipped coffee from the school's best china.

"Well, it's been an excellent day, Rick, an excellent day. I really think we can do great things together here."

Rick gave a wry smile. "Alastair Goodall said something very similar to me once."

"And to me," Andrew replied, "but then, he would say anything to anyone to get what he wanted, and look where that got him."

"Where did it get him? Do you know what he's doing now?"

"Yes, haven't you heard? He's taken a lease out on some old premises just off the High Street in Longdon and he's opened a private school. They offer places for kids who are at risk of being excluded permanently from schools. They take them, for a hefty fee of course, and do various programmes with them and enter them for their GCSEs."

"He certainly knows how to spot a gap in the market."

"Trouble is, what do you think these kids are like, who end up going to his school?"

"Pretty challenging, I'd imagine."

"'Challenging' is your educational professional euphemism for it. And you can't be seen to be criticising the kids. I'm under no such compunction, especially not in this room just with you. They're borderline criminal. Psychotic. Feral. Deranged. Medicated. You get the picture?"

"And what's your point exactly?"

"Well, if you can't get these kids to settle down and achieve, with your highly trained, dedicated, compassionate and patient teachers, how do you think Goodall's institution is going to do it, with their ragtag army of barely-qualified chancers, moonlighting from their day job?"

"Good point. So how do they do it?"

"They cheat. They let them play on computers all day. They deal drugs outside the centre. But because this keeps these mad kids out

400

of the hair of hard-pressed headteachers in mainstream schools, no-one is going to complain."

"Good to know that Alastair's found his own level, doing something he loves. What's the name of this august academy of learning?"

"'Last Chance Saloon', believe it or not. I had no idea he had such a sense of humour. Anyway Rick, I need to be making a move. It was a fantastic occasion today. The centre is going to make a real difference."

"I hope so. Thanks for coming along and for the support with everything. I'll be in touch."

He closed the door behind him on the way out.

Rick enjoyed the sudden quiet that descended when he closed the office door on the outside world. The sun was lower in the sky now and cast dappled light through his venetian blinds onto the rug in front of him. He would just take five minutes. He stretched his arms out and rotated his neck back and forth, working the stiffness and stress through his muscles and out. Then he stood up and paced around the room a few times to clear his head. He parted two slats of the blinds and looked out. The new building stared back at him, framed by the ancient oaks, a reminder of what had been said in front of it earlier that day.

He went back to his desk, cracked his knuckles and started typing. There was a lot to do.

2

SHE SLEPT WITH HER RUCKSACK ON HER BACK AND HER hand on the knife that was in a sheath strapped around her waist. It was uncomfortable, but she'd got used to it over the last couple of years. Several times people had attempted to snatch it, but it was too valuable to lose, so she never took it off. Because of that she never took a shower and she stank. When she thought of it, she went hot with shame. Back in Aleppo, she had loved bathing and covering herself in perfumes and lotions that her mother bought for her. Her father would pick her up, wrapped in her bath robe and breathe in deeply, his face buried in the crook of her neck. "My beautiful flower," he would call her. "You smell like a rose bush."

But now she loved her stink. It kept people away from her and distance was what she craved more than anything. So she didn't think of Aleppo and the baths and her parents. At least, not very often. Sometimes, no matter how hard she tried to prevent it, those memories crawled back into her brain, and after the momentary, intense pleasure they brought her, they pushed her over the edge of despair and torment again, with hot tears. So she tried to keep them away.

She thought instead about food and water and sleep and Calais. She spent hours thinking of these things: planning, speculating, fantasising. She also spent a lot of her time thinking about men. Not in the way that other fourteen-year-olds might think of them. Fourteen-year-olds that were safe and secure and cared for. Fourteen-year-olds that were selfish, and obsessive and ungrateful. Fourteen-year-olds that surfed the internet and didn't do their homework and were depressed by social media but kept that to themselves.

She thought only one thing about men. Where they were in relation to her. She spent hours locating them and then making sure she was as far from them as possible, surrounded by other girls or women. She knew what they could do. What they did do. What they had done. She wondered if Saleh and Karim were like that and the thought made her cry in a way that all of the horrors she had endured in the last couple of years didn't. Saleh wasn't anything now. He was dead, like her mother and father. She could barely remember what he looked like and could no longer call up an image of him.

She lay on the rucksack, on a makeshift camp bed, in a tent occupied by three other women. It was time to sleep but before she closed her eyes she would check where the entrance was in relation to her bed, check her knife was in place, and pull the battered photo from her pocket for the final time. Karim was still there, his smiling face calling to her from the hot and dusty streets of Aleppo in front of their house. The street where Saleh and his friends were killed, while playing football, by a carpet bomb. She stared at it, touching his face with her finger, blocking his beaming, infectious smile, then put it away, deep in her pocket, and with one hand on the handle of the knife she closed her eyes.

Sleep came to her almost immediately, and, as she knew it would, it was accompanied by vivid images of her journey. They had been luckier than many of the others. Their father had withdrawn a large amount of money from his bank account, knowing that they might have to make arrangements to leave Aleppo at any moment. It was getting more and more clear that they had to get out. There was enough money to buy their passage with the people smugglers and they divided the rest between them and sewed it into their clothes.

A perilous sea crossing at dead of night, herded in lorries, walking for hours, queueing at borders, slumped in coaches and trains, it was a gruelling ordeal of exhaustion, fear and hope. Strangely, she thought of this as a magical time now, because she was with Karim and they were headed towards England and freedom. Her father had told her many times that Britain was a democracy that the world envied and a country that had always been on the side of the oppressed. She had idolised her father, who, it seemed to her eleven-year-old self, knew the answers to everything.

It was at a train station when it happened. She couldn't remember now whether it was Serbia or Hungary. A terrible crush of people, tens of thousands of them at a border, with fences and barbed wire. Policemen with machine guns shouting and pushing. Another group of people, handing out water and food and blankets. Women, mainly. There was a surge and people fell down screaming. Her hand slipped out of Karim's and then she was on the floor under the relentless crush of boots and shoes before someone grabbed her and pulled her out. She couldn't see Karim anywhere. She had never seen him since that time. She strained her head to see over the heads of the crowd and began screaming his name desperately. "Karim! Karim, where are you?" until the man who had her by the hand, pulled her back towards him, slapped her across the face and dragged her away.

In the chaos, no-one saw. Or no-one wanted to see. And that began two years of torment that she could not describe, even to herself. Every night, men doing things to her, unthinkable things that she had not known about, that her father, who knew everything, had not told her of. They would pay to use her, along with the other girls they kept locked up in an apartment block in a town somewhere. And then there were the beatings and the casual cruelty. She still had cigarette burns on her arm. A scar on her forehead. A slightly loose tooth.

She tried several times to run away but was always caught and dragged back, each beating worse than the one before. But she was never beaten too badly. She had a beautiful face and as the gap-toothed man with only four fingers on his right hand told her, "Your face pays the rent and keeps you alive, baby." She wondered if he had children.

And then, one day when she was taking the rubbish out, she overhead a furious argument between one of her captors and a man who had called round claiming they owed him money because the girl he had been with a few days earlier had given him an infection. He burst in, passed the man who had answered the door and flew up the stairs, two steps at a time, with a knife in his hand. The other man shouted the alarm and galloped after him. Evana furtively looked out from the door to the yard and saw that they had left the front door open. While furniture and bodies were crashing around upstairs, and with the screams and the threats echoing in her ears, she slipped out of the front door and ran for her life, not daring to look round.

Luckily for her, there were still endless streams of refugees picking their way across Europe. It wasn't long before she attached herself to such a convoy, gratefully submerging herself in the anonymity of the herd. From that point on, her every movement was westwards, her every thought was of Calais and of Karim.

The next day, the other women in the tent told her to go with them and they queued for breakfast. They did the same at lunchtime. They took her to a series of larger tents in between the meals where there were a lot of smiling European people who got them to paint or tried to give them English lessons. She found it difficult to get used to the idea that these people wanted nothing from them, they just wanted to help.

It was a strain. There were many Syrian voices all around her. And there were many Syrian young men, around Karim's age. She was continually jumping up, looking around, seeing someone who looked vaguely like Karim. Once, she was sure that she had seen Karim walk past the entrance to the tent. She sprang up and sprinted out and after him, shouting his name hysterically. She caught up with him and grabbed his shoulder, spinning him around. He stared at her in disbelief, muttering curses under his breath, shook her arm from his shoulder and carried on walking. She stared after him, open-mouthed, and slunk back to her tent, defeated.

On the fourth day the women took her down to the administrative centre, which in reality was simply a larger tent with compartments. They told her she had to register and that that was the safest way of finding Karim. They left her there, twelfth in the queue. When she finally got to the desk the official said, "Passport?"

She handed it over and the man scrutinised it, looking from the passport to her face and back again.

"Your name, please?"

"Evana Atbal."

"Age?"

"I'm fourteen. Nearly fifteen."

"Your English accent is very good."

"My Father was a professor of English at university. He taught me English."

He looked down at the passport again.

"You say you will be fifteen soon. When exactly is your birthday?"

"June 14th."

The man smiled at her. "You do know that that's today? Today is June 14th. Happy birthday."

She looked a little confused, as if he were making a joke. She looked around, unsure, and then said, understanding dawning on her face, "June 14th, today? Yes, today is my birthday."

She looked at him and saw his smile break out again. Her face crumpled and tears began rolling down her cheeks. She strangled the huge sobs that were gathering pace and strength, and battled for composure, scrubbing the tears from her face.

The official was thrown by her reaction. His boss had been right. The only way to deal with this was to be absolutely straight. It was a mistake to let yourself get swept up in people's stories.

He spoke again in a firm and even tone.

"Are you here on your own?"

"What?" she replied, baffled by the question. She had been on her own for so long, it seemed a ridiculous question to ask.

He tried again, a little more gently this time.

"Is your family with you?"

"My family? No, they are dead. All of them. Except Karim. I think he might be in England. That was where he was heading. And his English is much better than mine."

She took him gradually through her story. He made notes, filled in sections on a form, looked at her closely and thought. Finally, after careful consideration, (because, as his boss often said, you don't want to be giving people false hope), he said, "I think, Miss Atbal, that you may be eligible for asylum in the United Kingdom. Could you just wait there, please?"

He disappeared into another room in the tent, behind his desk. He took the form he had been filling in and her passport, with him. Five minutes later he was back.

"Could you follow me, Miss Atbal, please?" he said. She got up and went through to the rear section of the tent. There were two officials there sitting at a desk with a single chair in front of it. There was one row of chairs set back from that and a series of tables down the side of the tent loaded with piles of leaflets and advice sheets.

The two officials, a man and a woman, introduced themselves as Graham and Margaret and took her through a long set of precise and detailed questions that were clearly designed to ascertain her identity and to test every aspect of the story she had given them. Whenever Evana tried to interject or ask them about Karim they pressed on with their own questions. Eventually, they seemed to be satisfied. They put down their pens and papers and smiled at each other.

"Well, it's good news, I'm pleased to say, Ms Atbal. We are going to recommend that you are placed on the unaccompanied minors scheme and be offered asylum in the United Kingdom. There will be a coachload of people in a similar position to yourself on Friday. You will be transferred today to an official holding unit where you will be able to shower, clean your clothes and sleep securely in a single room. Now, if you'd like to follow me, please."

She stood up, unsure of what had just happened. Was she going to England? She could hardly dare to hope that that was what was happening. She was going to see Karim, she was sure of it.

"And Karim?" she asked, rising excitement in her voice, as she followed the woman.

Margaret stopped and turned back to her, smiling. She loved it when they could actually help someone and give them their lives back.

"Karim?" she replied, eyebrows raised. "What about him?"

Evana, excited though she was, was losing a little patience now. Had they not been listening to her?

"Karim, my brother," she explained. "He…"

She trailed off. Her eye had caught sight of one of the piles of leaflets on the table. It was a little older, a little more battered than the others. It was…

She snatched it up.

'Have you seen this girl?' it said in bold large print. 'Evana Atbal, from Syria, is missing.' The text continued, finishing with 'Please contact Karim Atbal via the Syrian Refugee Project, Longdon, London.'

"Look," she shouted, brandishing the leaflet in the woman's face, "it's me. Me, Evana. It says 'Contact Karim Atbal'. He's there, he's there, he must be there."

She collapsed to the ground, sobbing.

Margaret looked in alarm from Evana to her colleague, to the leaflet and back to Evana. She knelt down and gently got Evana to her feet.

"Evana, you need to come with us dear. Come through into this other room. There's something we have to go through with you."

The two officials looked at each other over Evana's head as they helped her into the other room. They were both suddenly weary and their boss's advice didn't seem quite so helpful as it had done five minutes before. All three disappeared behind the tent doorway.

*

The air inside the tent was hot and heavy. By mid-afternoon the sun had been beating down on the stretched canvas, unprotected by any shade, for hours. The atmosphere was oppressive, despite the unrelenting cheeriness of the purple-shirted volunteers who buzzed around the rows of tables with pens, paper, and bottles of water. Even they had begun to wilt in the face of the heat and the growing fug of sweat. Any enthusiasm for English language lessons had long since shrivelled up and both students and volunteers had fallen back on politeness and colouring in work sheets to get them through the last half hour of the session.

Karim stretched and yawned, rubbing his eyes, before taking the sheet from his student, a middle-aged Syrian man, whose demeanour during the lesson had wavered between the twin poles of gushing gratitude and bored fury at the indignity of it for a proud man such as he. Karim was a model of patience, both encouraging and deferring to the older man's status, something that not all of the English volunteers, well-meaning though they were, understood or could manage.

They could begin to wind down soon, he thought to himself. There would be food in the volunteers' tent and then Ahmed had said that there would be music later that night. They had agreed to do the morning session the next day before clambering back into the transit van with the others. A good run through the Channel Tunnel and they'd be back in Longdon by late afternoon. He'd probably be able to get in a final walk around the whole Jungle again to check out the new arrivals before they had to leave. In the next row, Ahmed was taking his student through the mysteries of the British supermarket.

Karim, shamed by Ahmed's continuing efforts, looked down at the sheet in front of him.

"Good. Well done, Mr Farzad. Now, how would you ask for directions to the library in English?"

He thought about Ben when he had described some of the lessons to him.

"They won't need to worry about directions to the library," he had said. "There won't be any libraries left by the time they get here. Teach them the word for food bank. That would be more useful."

He smiled at the memory. Ben had threatened to come along to the Jungle to see it for himself, but had not yet gone beyond the promise. "Maybe next week," was as far as he ever got.

"Maybe next week," he mused aloud.

"What? I'm sorry, what did you say? Did I get it wrong?"

Karim snapped out of his daydream to see the puzzled and anxious face of Mr Farzad, a man who had been an architect in Syria, trying to make sense of this baffling answer to his query about the library. He permitted himself the indulgence of replying in Arabic, and then forced himself to concentrate on the last bit of the session.

Just another fifteen minutes, he thought, *and then we're done.*

"So, Mr Farzad," he said, an encouraging smile on his face, "let's go through that again."

*

"What do you mean, he might be here? I thought you said he'd been attacked." Evana's voice rose in panic as she struggled to remember all of her English.

"No dear, he was attacked, but that was nearly a year ago now. He's fine now."

"But if he got to England, why would he be here? It doesn't make any sense."

"We think that he might be one of the volunteers that come to Calais to help the people stranded here. You know, with food and lessons, that kind of thing. You've probably been to some of the sessions yourself."

Evana's face suddenly fell.

"You mean the groups of people doing with paints and English?"

Her command of the language had begun to fall apart under the pressure.

"Yes, that's right, Evana."

"But he wasn't there. I asked and no-one knew anything about him."

She grabbed at the forearm of the woman, Margaret, who had been explaining the whole thing to her for the previous half an hour. Her voice rose and her grip tightened.

"Why don't you know if he's here or not? You are in charge, you must know. Why are you saying these things, why are you…"

Evana's sentence tailed off into incoherent sobbing and her shoulders shook and heaved. To be given some hope after all of this time and then to have it snatched away was more than she could bear. Margaret gently pulled her by the arm, and with her free arm encouraged her to rest her head on her chest. As she sobbed, Margaret stroked her back and spoke to her soothingly.

"Evana, listen to me. Ssh now, everything is all right. We don't know who is here exactly because they are volunteers, there is no register and they come and go. They are not part of the Immigration Service, they don't work for us or the government. Do you understand?"

Evana looked up into her face, her thick black lashes webbed with tears. She nodded and sniffed loudly.

"Here, take this and dry your eyes. What we will do is go along there now, to where the lessons usually take place, just to check. Okay? And if he is not there we can ask, can't we? We have a photograph. So, up you get, follow me."

As they both left, Margaret's supervisor popped her head around the end of the tent.

"Everything all right?"

"Yes, I'm just taking her to the volunteers' section."

The supervisor frowned and looked at her watch, tucking her clipboard under her arm as she did so.

"I'm not sure that's really appropriate, Margaret."

"Five minutes, that's all. It'll save more work in the long run, trust me."

She didn't wait for permission to be granted, but hurried Evana out of the tent. As she went she thought, *Damn. Why did she have to turn up just at that moment? Not exactly generating a hostile environment for immigrants, was I? There goes my promotion.*

411

Karim had battled through the fatigue induced by the sticky heat of the tent and had done a respectable job of listening to his student ask and then give directions to the fictitious library. He watched over his shoulder as Mr Farzad consolidated the vocabulary by following the written cues to write out a script of the conversations they had practised. This would take them comfortably to the end of the session and allow him to tune out a little behind the mask of concentration that his face presented to the world.

As his mind slipped away, he was transported by memory to the back room of their house in Aleppo, cooler in the punishing heat of the afternoon because of its east-facing aspect and the shade of the orange trees that grew in the courtyard. Every now and then the breeze disturbed the bead blinds, giving him, Evana and Saleh welcome relief as they pored over their English books. Most of the time his mother and father made the lessons fun, with board games and role plays and colouring, but as his father said, "Learning needs hard work and application, children. The English language is the hallmark of the International Citizen. The person that can speak Arabic and English is the King of the World."

"Or the Queen, Daddy," Evana had retorted, as quick as a flash.

"Indeed, my Princess, or the Queen."

Karim smiled at the memory. It seemed so real to him, as if it were yesterday. He could hear Evana complaining about him messing around and deliberately speaking nonsense words.

"Karim," she would irritably tick him off, wagging her finger at him, "Karim, stop that. Karim…"

"Karim?"

He stopped short, rudely pulled from his reminiscence. What was that? It was almost as if she were there, the memory was so real.

"Karim, is that really you?"

But no, it couldn't be. His mind was playing tricks on him. He shook himself, suddenly aware that all other conversations in the crowded, stuffy classroom had stopped. He looked up, and found to his surprise that everyone was looking at him. He stared around the room, covered in confusion.

"What's the matter? Why are you all looking…"

His eye finally travelled to the back of the room and there, right at the back, in the aisle between the two banks of desks, was a young woman with one of the officials from Immigration with her. She was vaguely familiar, as if she were someone he used to know a long time ago. He stared and his heart began to pound against his chest. His breath came in short gasps.

"Karim, it's me," the familiar face said simply.

Finally, he spoke or tried to, but no words emerged, Arabic or English. And then, with a supreme effort, he managed to say, in between the heaving sobs that had descended on him without warning, "Evana? No, it can't be. Evana?"

Mr Farzad, next to him, a great smile on his craggy face, touched his arm and said, "Of course it is her, you silly boy. Of course it is her."

Karim looked at him blankly. Mr Farzad had never said that number of English words unprompted before.

"Well go to her then, my dear boy. Go to her."

He took Karim's elbow in his arm and gently lifted him up and into motion from his chair. And then, in a blur he was off, scattering the chair into the aisle, running towards her, arms outstretched. Evana ran to meet him, shaking off Margaret from her arm, and tumbling and stumbling down the aisle she lost her footing and fell to her knees in front of him and skidded the final few feet. He dropped down to his knees and they slammed into each other's arms, crying and shouting and hugging in a whirlwind of feelings that they could not control.

All around them, refugees, immigration officials, and volunteers alike, all stood up as one and there was a surging, rushing thunder of applause and cheering, English and Arabic shouting melting into a hybrid language of love and joy.

Watching from the front row, at the back of the scene, Ahmed bent down to Mr Farzad, who had sat back down, contenting himself with a broad smile and a nod of the head.

"Well done, Mr Farzad. That was very good English, you know."

Mr Farzad turned to him. "Yes, I was very pleased with that. But then," he said, looking to the front with unalloyed pleasure at Karim stroking Evana's hair, "I have had a very good teacher."